WHAT'S YOUR HERO'S NAME?

WHAT'S YOUR HERO'S NAME?

A NOVEL BY

STEPHEN TRAHAN

IQI PUBLISHERS
ST. ALBANS, VERMONT

What's Your Hero's Name?
First Edition, October 2020

Edited by Donald Lefebvre
Cover and interior design by Winslow Colwell/Wren Song Design

The text of this publication was set in Adobe Minion.

Published in the United States by IQI Publishers, St. Albans, Vermont

ISBN: 978-1-7347947-0-0

Printed in the United States of America

This book is dedicated to all the characters in my life, present and past, who influenced me in some way, many of whom are in this book. Without you all I wouldn't be the character I am. Most importantly, all the hard work that went into this book is dedicated to my wife Lise. How she ever put up with my 'character' for five decades is truly a miracle of love.

IT WAS SNOWING LIKE A BAD DOG. MARC WAS WATCHING IT come down from the picture window of his winter vacation home. He usually loved watching it snow because he and his wife Leonie were snowmobilers. They had bought their 100-year-old cabin in Saint Alexis-des-Monts because it was in the heart of Quebec's snowmobile country. From here one could ride a snowmobile to anywhere in Canada if you had the gumption. But tiny St. Alexis is also at the very edge of civilization, where paved roads and power lines come to an end. As Marc's father used to say, "Even God doesn't know where this place is."

Tonight, though, U.S. Vice President Marc Z. Grégoire wasn't too pleased with the heavy snowfall, the product of the season's third nor'easter. Anxiously he walked to the spare bedroom window to check his snow gauge. "Twenty-six inches of new snow!" he said to his wife.

Gently wringing her hands, she replied, "It has been snowing hard all day."

Marc said, "Yeah. And where the hell are the snowplows? They're usually out after 13 snowflakes."

While being snowed in was usually a cause for joy for snowmobilers, tonight was very different. Just over an hour ago, Marc learned that the North Koreans had launched a missile toward Tokyo. The missile's rocket engine failed causing it to drop into shallow waters just east of Noto Island. A Japanese Defense helicopter searching the area detected nuclear radiation, and an evacuation of the lightly populated island was underway.

But the panic in Tokyo was unprecedented.

"Would you call Yvon and ask him where the damn snowplows are?" Marc asked his wife.

"Well, I won't use that kind of language, and why don't you call him?"

"Because my French sucks, and you're a native. It'll be much quicker if you call." With a lowered chin he added, "Please."

The call was quickly concluded. "What do you mean they're on eff-ing strike?" Marc's eyes were wide open in disbelief. "We need to get out of here."

Reluctantly Leonie replied, "Yvon said the provincial plows were called but they can't come until tomorrow afternoon, if they come at all."

Marc went back to stomping back and forth from his wood stove in the living room to the kitchen side window where he could check the roads. He had already given his Secret Service detail orders to be prepared to head south as soon as the plows came, but that didn't ease his anxiety of being stuck 162 miles north of the U.S. border during a crisis, even if he wasn't needed.

There was little he could do. Local snowplow drivers weren't willing to bust the strike, and it would be dangerous for a helicopter to try to maneuver through the mountains in this storm. It was no use going to bed as he'd just lie awake thinking. What he'd really like was two fingers of Cognac, but if someone did call he wanted a clear head so he decided the only thing to do was try to sit and watch the fire, usually his favorite form of meditation.

At 8:05 Marc heard the ringing of the sleigh bells attached to his porch door. 'Who would be coming in at this hour?' he thought. It was Secret Service Agent Jim Martin. Marc asked, "What are you doing out there Jim, you'll freeze." Without a word, Martin kicked the snow off his boots and came in from the porch. The VP stood there with the door wide open and a fixed look at his lead Secret Service agent. Martin's face was grave, and there was a long hesitation before he finally said, "Mr. President, I have a message from Washington. President Morris is dead."

SHOCK PASSED THROUGH MARC'S ENTIRE BODY. HE QUICKLY SAT in a kitchen chair and pulled one out for Martin. Martin waived off the chair and began to speak, slowly and solemnly. "Sir, members of the Cabinet were assembled in the White House Situation Room with President Morris. While talking with General Chaffee, Morris excused himself and went toward the men's room. A few minutes later a woman's scream was heard. Mrs. Morris found her husband on the floor. Medics arrived immediately and began CPR, but they couldn't get a pulse. He was rushed to the ER where more resuscitation was attempted … without success." Lowering his head, Martin added, "There is no apparent cause of death." After a solemn moment or two Martin asked, "Sir, the Chief of Staff wants you to call. I know your secure line is down, do you want to use mine?"

Many anxious thoughts flashed through the VP's mind. Chief among them was that he was now the President of the United States – and entirely unprepared. He wished he had been more insistent about participating in Morris' meetings, but Morris rarely allowed it. Now wasn't the time for regrets.

The VP quickly pulled on a pair of boots and a snowmobile coat and followed Martin's trail through the snow to the little chalet next door being used as a base for his Secret Service detail. Martin placed the secure call and handed the phone to the Vice President, saying, "Sir, it's Tim Houseman."

As the VP took the phone, Jean LaBarge – usually referred to as Sûreté

John – a Sûreté du Quebec police officer, quietly asked Martin if he should leave the room. Martin shook his head and whispered back, "You are about to be protecting the President of the United States." Sûreté John's eyes opened wide as he slowly rose from his chair and stood erect.

"Tim, Marc Grégoire here. Tell me it isn't true."

"Sir, I truly regret to say ... President Morris has passed. His body is being closely examined, and an autopsy will be conducted as soon as the medical examiners arrive. At this point, there is no apparent cause of death, no signs of foul play, no bruises, contusions, nothing. He had his physical 11 days ago and was found completely fit. I wish I had more to tell you, Sir, but I believe Agent Martin told you everything we know so far."

The VP responded, "Yes, but I was hoping you would have more."

"The Secret Service and the FBI are seizing all the food and liquids the President had access to, and they're questioning everyone in the building. They aren't letting anyone leave until they're interviewed."

Marc cautioned, "Well it's obvious what they're thinking. Don't interfere. Let them do their job."

Tim said, "Yes, Sir. And Fox News has already reported that the President was rushed to the hospital. Other networks are demanding answers. What are your thoughts about an announcement?"

"Well, the staff knows about it, knows that Morris passed?"

Tim replied, "Yes, Sir. Everyone in the White House knows."

"So the news is already out. Tell Paul to prepare a brief statement, and although seconds count, he needs to ask the Secret Service and the FBI what he can say and what he can't say. And no matter what, he must not link the North Koreans to Morris' death, not yet. Paul will be asked over and over again, but all he should say is there are no indications of an assassination. The media will be all over it – assuming the worst; we have to keep that hosed down. It'll be a challenge but Paul will have to handle it as best he can. Now I need to talk with General Chaffee, and while I'm talking to him, get the Chief Justice's phone number and ask him to stand by for a call from me."

"Yes Sir, but when will you be arriving here at the White House? We, ah – we need you in charge."

"Yeah, well ... it will be hours. We're in a hell of a predicament here, as I'm sure Martin has already explained." The VP glanced at Martin who nodded yes. "Tell Paul when the media ask where the Vice President is, all he can say is that I'm on the way to Washington. But for security reasons, my location cannot be given. Now General Chaffee, please."

"Yes, Sir."

The call was quickly transferred, and the next voice heard was that of the Chairman of the Joint Chiefs of Staff. "Milton Chaffee, Sir."

"Hello, Milt."

"Good evening, Mister Vice President."

"The North Koreans finally stepped over the line?"

Marc heard a deep breath at the other end of the phone, then, "We've confirmed that the missile off Noto Island is armed with a nuclear device. It didn't go off, for reasons unknown."

"Could it still go off?" the VP asked.

"Possible, but unlikely."

"Was it heading for Tokyo? Do we know what the intended target was?"

Concern crept into the General's reply because he didn't like saying no. "Not at this time, Sir. When the missile is recovered we'll know how much fuel was aboard, and if the electronics are recovered intact we should know where it was programmed to go."

"So it could have been one of our West Coast cities?" the VP asked.

Confidence returned to the General's voice, "That's correct, Sir. But it would have never reached the U.S. mainland, we would've taken it down over the ocean." Marc knew this to be true; he was aware that the U.S. was well prepared to take out an ICBM, especially from a proletarian like North Korea.

General Chaffee asked, "Sir, at the Japanese Prime Minister's request, President Morris authorized the Seventh Fleet to send in a team to examine the device and make it safe. They've been dispatched. May I presume they have your authorization to continue?"

"Will it be safe for them? What if it's on a time delay or something?" the VP asked.

The General replied, "Very unlikely. It is more probable the detonation sequence was improperly programmed."

Marc ordered, "The team may proceed, but make sure the area is totally evacuated before they touch anything."

"We've been assured the area is completely evacuated, Mister Vice President. Indeed many of the Japanese are trying to leave the country. All the airports are packed."

"They're worried about a second attack?" asked the VP.

"Yes, Sir."

The VP paused a moment, then asked, "Can we get Gabe on the line with us?"

A couple phone clicks later, the deep, authoritative voice of the Secretary of Defense came on. "Marc? Gabe. You on your way back?"

"No, but I'll be on the way soon. It's going to take a while, though. What's the alert status of our forces in Asia?"

Gabe Arnold replied, "The equivalent of Threatcon Delta. Europe's in Charlie."

Marc said, "Okay. I'm going to rely on you two to establish the appropriate alert level. Be sure to confer with Secretary Rikes, but Gabe – you make the final call."

Now the VP pressed the burning question: "Gentlemen, what are the possibilities the North Koreans will take a second shot?"

"That's a concern," Gabe replied.

"Yeah, but technically, do they have missiles and warheads ready?"

Gabe looked at the General with raised eyebrows. The General took the cue and carefully replied, "We didn't think they were prepared for this attack. As it turned out, it looks like they weren't."

The VP said, "But we do know they have more missiles; apparently what we don't know is if they have another nuclear warhead ready to go. Gabe?"

Gabe responded, "They certainly have all the mechanical components, it's the weapon's grade uranium…" After a moment of thought, he turned his head toward the General and said over the phone, "I think, Sir, for planning purposes, we must presume they have everything, for at least one more launch." The General raised his right hand over his chest and fixed his stare on Gabe; he knew Gabe was right.

There was silence at both ends of the line.

After a moment the VP said, "Alright; Gabe, I'm putting you in charge at the White House until I have better communications. If you need a decision from me, you'll have instructions on how to reach me but it probably won't be secure. Now I have to ask, if North Korea sets up another missile for launch, can we take it out before it gets airborne?"

"Yes, Sir, if so ordered."

"Then so ordered. If the North Koreans set up another missile for launch, test or otherwise, you are directed to destroy that missile on the ground. But that's all, just take out the missile and do as little collateral damage as possible."

Gabe replied, "Yes Sir. But they use trucks to launch their missiles; if they park their launch truck under an overpass, we may have to take out a bridge."

Marc replied, "Understood. Now make sure the Secretary of State immediately warns North Korea and China that if there is any further movement of any type of missiles in North Korea, the missile will be destroyed. She should use diplomatic channels of course, but I also want the world to know I have issued this order. So have Paul pass it to the media as soon as Jane makes her notifications. Any questions?"

"No Sir," Gabe replied.

"We won't miss, right?" asked the VP.

Gabe replied, "No, Sir. Once they stand up the missile, it takes them at least an hour to arm and program it. They have to input GPS coordinates, altimeter settings, and enter a host of other instructions – and that's valuable time for us to get a lock on it."

There was a pregnant pause before Marc asked, "What about nuclear fallout – if we hit the missile in place?"

Gabe answered, "We can hit it – the missile – without causing the nuke to go off. Once it falls to the ground it will be radioactive debris." Gabe waited a few seconds to add, "On *their* ground. They'll have their hands full, but it shouldn't go off."

The VP wasn't comforted by the last remark. "The ramifications of a nuke going off – anywhere – would be disastrous, especially if we cause it. It could start World War Three … with no winners." After a deep breath Marc added, "We can only hope that the Koreans will heed our warning. Ask Jane to use the strongest language possible with North Korea. As Secretary of State she must make it clear to them what will happen if they ignore us."

"I'll tell her, Sir."

"And tell her why."

"Yes, Sir."

The VP said, "Okay, let's get Tim back on."

"Sir, Tim Houseman here."

The VP asked, "Are you in the Situation Room? Is everyone there?"

"Yes, Sir."

Indeed the members of the Cabinet were all around the Situation Room conference table – on the very edge of their seats. Marc was silent for a few moments of thought; after a few seconds he said, "Put me on speaker."

With a push of a button the Chief of Staff announced … "Ladies and Gentlemen, the Vice President of The United States."

The official announcement sent a shiver through Marc's arms and chest causing him to pause for another moment, but he somberly began, "Good evening, Ladies and Gentlemen. Our nation is in a state of emergency. In a few minutes, when the news about President Morris is publicly announced, the eyes of the entire world will be on us, Japan and North Korea." Trying to relax his voice a bit, he continued, "Unfortunately it will be some time before I can get to Washington. I know the delay and the secrecy about my current location will cause more concern, but my travel must remain covert because I have only a small, protective detail. Rest assured that as soon as possible, I will speak to the public and put the inevitable rumors to rest.

"What is very important for you – and indeed the entire world – to know is that we will neutralize North Korea's nuclear arsenal without resorting to nuclear weapons ourselves. We are – not – on the verge of nuclear war."

He was thinking of repeating that last part but remembered who his audience was. He took a moment for a deep breath, then added, "For the next few hours it will be possible to contact me, but difficult. The Secret Service will have instructions, but we may not have immediate access to secure communications. If an order needs to be given though, it can – and will be – done.

"Until I can resume regular communications, I'm counting on you all to do your jobs and make the decisions that need to be made. Look around the table there. Who you see are the finest minds in the world. Working together I know that collectively we'll get through this emergency successfully.

"I have asked Secretary Gabe Arnold to take charge there in the White House, mostly because our immediate concern is Defense related. He knows how to reach me if needed. He has my orders to destroy North Korean missiles on the ground should it appear that they are preparing another launch. I know I can count on each of you to support him."

Not sure what else he should add, he just asked, "Do any of you have any pressing questions?"

Secretary of State Jane Rikes immediately asked, "Sir, can you tell us where you are?"

The VP answered, "Director Gibble has my permission to inform the Cabinet about my location and to keep you apprised of my progress during the trip back to Washington. But it's not to leave the room by any means."

Secretary Rikes had one more question: "When will you take the oath of office, Sir?"

"My next call will be to the Chief Justice for some guidance, and depending on his advice I may be taking the oath in the next few minutes. You will all be immediately informed when I assume the office. Now I need to get underway, so I'm going to ask Tim to take me off the speaker."

The VP was back on the line with Gabe and Gabe alone. "Gabe, I know there's a legal procedure which can be used to declare me as incapacitated to execute the Office of the President. If enough people back it, the Speaker of the House could be brought up to act as President. Now soon, some very heavy decisions will need to be made, and I don't want anyone else to" – his voice faltered before he finished – "bear the burden of making the decisions that I've been elected to make. So if you need to abort an 'internal coup' for lack of a better term, then call the Sûreté. We'll stop and I'll call you. Keep in mind, you've been up here, there are no cell towers between here and Louiseville, and satellite phones don't connect well in heavy weather. But the Sûreté's communication system is working well, it's just not secure."

Gabe picked up what the VP was putting down, so it was with reluctance he pointed out, "Sir, in your present situation, you don't have access to the nuclear codes."

"And we're not going to goddam need them," the VP shot back. "If nukes start flying we can all kiss our collective asses good-bye."

"Yes, Sir," Gabe replied, then added, "I was just pointing out if..." but he decided the sentence needn't be completed. The Vice President returned to the original issue: "The Speaker is a Democrat, I know. And this is a golden opportunity for them to install their man in the presidency – the President is dead, and no one knows where the Vice President is."

Gabe reminded Marc, "But the Cabinet has to approve it, and that won't happen. The Democrats could try to take it to court, but the Chief Justice himself will have spoken with you, and he certainly won't rule on anything on the spur of the moment – not in six hours and not in the middle of the night."

Marc took a breath, then with fire in his voice ordered, "All the same, get one of the White House lawyers working on it, maybe Katz. Have him study all the contingencies and how we would thwart any moves the Democrats try to make. He knows as well as you and I that if the D's want to do it, they'll stop at nothing – nothing. So we got to be goddam ready."

Gabe responded, "Yes, Sir. It'll all be a non-issue once the press finds you, *which*" – there was a purposeful delay in his voice – "is what we can resort to if necessary."

Chief Justice Alan Birdsong was next on the line. Houseman announced, "Mr. Chief Justice, the Vice President."

"Good evening, Justice Birdsong."

"Good evening, Mr. Vice President. Uh, I hope this call doesn't have anything to do with President Morris being rushed to the hospital."

"I'm very sorry to say that President Morris has passed away. Furthermore, the cause of death is not apparent. I know this news is shocking, but we have to do what needs to be done. So I have some questions about taking the oath of office." After giving Birdsong a few moments to express his dismay, the Vice President pressed on.

"I know that the oath can be given by anyone authorized to administer oaths, such as a Justice of the Peace. My son, who is with me, is an elected Justice of the Peace. Is he authorized to administer the oath in a foreign country, because we are not in the U.S?"

Naturally Justice Birdsong asked, "Where are you?"

The VP explained for personal security he could not say. Birdsong acknowledged the VP's concerns and gravely continued, "The writers of the Constitution never anticipate that a U.S. President would take the oath of office outside the U.S., and therefore there is no specific constitutional advice. Your son would not be authorized to administer an oath outside of the state whose voters elected him Justice of the Peace. If there is a U.S. judge or similar authority available where you are, they would be the appropriate person to administer the oath. If there is not, my advice is to wait until you are back in the U.S. to take the oath."

The VP said, "That could be too late. I may need to use presidential authority before I get back to the U.S."

Birdsong replied, "I understand. Well, you could ask a local authority to administer the oath now. Whatever you decide, Mr. President, the oath should be witnessed and well recorded. As soon as you are on U.S. soil, I recommend you retake the oath."

At the end of the call, the VP concluded that because the emergency involved nuclear weapons, he should indeed take the oath immediately. After a few moments of thought, he told Martin, LaBarge and Bertrand LaPlante, the second Sûreté officer, to come with him back to his cabin. He instructed Secret Service Agent Mathew Akins to stay near the secure phone. The trio of officers trudged through the deepening snow behind the Vice President back to his cabin. When he opened the door, there was Leonie staring at the glowing wood stove. Slowly and intently she turned her head toward her husband and demanded, "What's going on?"

THE VICE PRESIDENT WHISPERED IN HIS WIFE'S EAR, "WELL … you're about to become the First Lady of the United States."

Her reaction was silent, but the realization and ramifications of what her husband just said were instantly processed. A chilling wave traveled from the top of her head down through her body until it numbed her feet. Marc helped her to a chair. When she regained her ability to speak, all she managed to say was, "What happened?"

Marc explained what had happened, what was happening, and what was about to happen. He gave her a few moments to let it all sink in, and when he felt she was composed enough he asked her a favor. "Would you call Yvon again, and ask him to come here – right now."

"How's he supposed to get here?" she asked.

"On his sled. He has a Ski-Doo Summit, he'll get through this stuff easy. Tell him it is very, very important."

The call was placed, and Yvon said he'd be right over. The Vice President explained to his wife and son what Birdsong told him, and based on that advice he planned to ask Yvon, a 'Notaire,' to administer the oath of office.

"But he can't even speak English!" Brian argued.

His father replied, "He doesn't have to. All he has to do is read the oath in segments, which I'll mark, and I will repeat after him. Mom will explain to him what he's doing, and he can refuse if he so chooses. Once we get back in the states I'll ask you to swear me in again." This quieted his son. Brian was then asked to get out his camera and set it up on video.

Soon Marc saw a lone headlight coming through the heavy snowfall right up the middle of Rue Notre Dame. The distinctive sound of a two-cycle Ski-Doo was heard, and Marc watched as the bright light turned into the Grégoire driveway. Once again the sleigh bells on the door rang out as Yvon came in, helmet under his arm. He was immediately greeted by his friend Marc, and in his bastardized French, Marc told Yvon he needed a favor. After Leonie explained, Yvon's reaction was yes, of course, he would administer the oath, but he thought such an honor should be given to a judge or a government minister. Marc assured him he was the man for the job, and after it was done he'd have another big favor to ask.

"When do we do this?" Yvon asked in French.

Marc replied, "Toute suite." He showed Yvon where to stand and instructed Brian to get the video ready. Then he went into the spare bedroom and came out with a plain sheet of paper with the oath of office. With Leonie's help it was explained to Yvon that he should raise his right hand, read from the sheet of paper, stop at all the yellow marks, and allow Marc to repeat the words before going to the next phrase. Yvon expressed his doubts about reading English but said he would do his best.

Everyone got in their place. The VP picked up a booklet on the U.S. Constitution and solemnly placed it over his heart. Slowly, almost hesitatingly, he raised his open right hand to ear level, then straightened his fingers and tightened them together. Yvon followed by raising his shaking right hand.

If there were a fly on the wall with a camera, the picture frame would show Marc and Yvon in front of the glowing wood stove, staring at each other with all the seriousness in the world. Leonie, legs still tingling with weakness, standing close beside her husband. Brian, with his praying hands covering his nose and lips, head lowered, would be at his mother's side. On the threshold to the next room were three men standing at attention in perfect formation: Secret Service Agent James Martin and Sûreté du Quebec police officers Jean LaBarge and Bertrand LaPlante.

Barely able to pronounce the words, Yvon Matteau began the oath. The President repeated every phrase in perfect English:

"I, Marc Zephyr Grégoire, do solemnly swear that I will faithfully execute the office of the President of the United States

And will do to my best ability, preserve, protect, and defend the constitution of the United States of America."

Yvon knew very well he had murdered the pronunciation, but at the end he asked, "Fini?"

The President said, "Fini. Good job, Yvon," and turned to his wife for a kiss.

She whispered, "Congratulations, Mr. President." Brian shook his father's hand and repeated, "Congratulations, Mr. President." Handshakes went all around, each accompanied by a somber congratulations. He thanked everyone in turn.

The new President had only this to say: "I wish," pausing as he looked toward the ceiling and beyond, "that this was under different circumstances." Turning toward his wife, he saw tears coming down both cheeks. She was afraid, very afraid. He took her in his arms and whispered something to her, then he just held her. The room went dead quiet.

Brian broke the stillness by quietly going over to his camera to make sure it was all recorded. It was. He thought to himself that he now possessed one of the most important videos of the 21st century. How was he going to protect it?

The President took the paper from Yvon's hand and went to the table. Flipping the paper over, he got out his pen and wrote:

> Yvon, Tonight you and I made history for the United States and Canada. Thank You for your great assistance. The people of the United States and I are grateful for your service.
>
> Your Friend,
>
> Marc Z. Grégoire
> President of the USA

After handing the document back to Yvon to keep, the new President said, "Now I got a real favor to ask you."

THE NEWLY MINTED PRESIDENT ASKED HIS WIFE TO EXPLAIN TO Yvon that he wanted him to lead them on his snowmobile to Louiseville. Shocked, Leonie refused and wanted to say 'Are you out of your mind?' Brian overheard his father's request and got right into the conversation. "You can't get through this deep snow. You'd get stuck or lost, and probably die of a heart attack trying to get back – all in total darkness." Agent Martin was in full agreement and pointed out, "Sir, the trail markers must be buried in deep snow. We wouldn't be able to find our way."

The President hesitated for a second before pointing out, "With all humility, I have to say that our country needs a President, one they can hear and see, and make decisions. Whether I like it or not, I'm it. I need to get to Washington, and right now the only way out of here is sitting in our garage." His finger was now at eye level and pointing out the back window.

"All I need is one or two experienced sledders to come with me. Yvon has a sled that is made for deep snow, and he certainly knows how to ride it. Sûreté John here has the same sled, and he's an expert with it. They'll bust the trail. I'll follow on my VK Professional which is built to plow through deep snow. After me," turning to Brian, "if you're willing, you'll follow on your Mountain Max. We can use your strong back if one of us gets stuck. But you don't have to come."

Brian, Leonie, and Martin all wanted to interject, but the President wasn't done. Looking at Martin he said, "Of course we won't try to follow the trails. We're going right down the road," and turning toward Brian, "just like your grandfather would do if he were here today." Turning back toward Yvon he added, "Yvon will have his GPS and I'll have my Tom Tom. It'll show the roads, streets, intersections, and the river, so we'll know exactly where we are at all times."

Yvon had heard his name mentioned several times but didn't understand much other than "sleds" and "GPS." So before anyone could say another word, he begged Leonie, "Qu'est que c'est?" The President nodded toward Yvon and said to Leonie, "Ask him." She reluctantly translated it all, adding her own strongly worded opinion that she didn't like the idea one bit.

All eyes were on Yvon. He bobbed his head up and down once and said, "Bien sure."

The President smiled for the first time this evening. He asked Yvon what he thought. Yvon said, "Pas problem!" He liked the idea of going right down the road, and he especially liked the GPS idea to help guide him even though he knew the road to Louiseville like the back of his hand. The President turned to Sûreté John for his thoughts. Sûreté John, proficient in both languages, caught everything that had been said. While he hated to disagree with the First Lady, he said, "Let's do it."

"Cool," exclaimed the President. "Now it is 24 miles to Louiseville. We should be able to average at least 10, maybe 15 miles per hour. So it shouldn't take more than three hours – tops."

Agent Martin, whose job was to protect the President from all perils, still greatly opposed the entire plan and was desperately looking for a way to stop it. "Twenty-something miles is a long way in a blizzard, and in the dark. We'll be hitting snowdrifts we won't see until we're in 'em."

The President told him, "And when that happens, keep your hand on the throttle."

Agent Martin took one more shot to stop the expedition: "What do we do when we get to Louiseville? We'll be leaving your hardened car here. We'll have no way to continue south."

The President said, "We'll go straight to the Sûreté du Quebec Police Station and get a car from them." He turned to Sûreté John who quickly agreed and was sure they could have two cars all gassed up and ready to go.

The President proclaimed, "That's that. Let's get geared up."

Martin acquiesced, "Mr. President, if you're going – I'm going with you. I have to."

"No you don't," the President replied. He looked Martin straight in the face, "You don't have to, this is considered above and beyond."

"But I am, Mr. President. It's my job."

The President nodded his approval.

Leonie looked at her husband and pronounced, "If you're doing this, then I'm going with you."

"On your snowmobile? It's not made for deep snow."

"I'm riding on the back with you, Mister President." Her terse tone was well noted. The President could only nod, "Okay."

Within moments everybody insisted they were going.

The President was impressed. "Okay then, here's how we'll line up: Yvon, Sûreté John, me – and Leonie, Brian, Jim, Akins, then LaPlante. You all have ten minutes to pack a small bag. Brian, can you get my sled started and ready to go? And bring snowshoes, just in case. Jim, let's go make a couple of calls."

Agent Martin and the President made their way next door. In seconds Marc was on the phone with Houseman. "Tim, 10 minutes ago I took the oath of office. It was administered by a local notary authorized to administer oaths. He's Canadian. You can announce that I have taken the oath of office, but you still can't say where yet."

"Congratulations Mr. President." With distinct anxiousness, Houseman asked, "When do you think you'll be back here in the U.S.?"

"I plan to be at my home in Vermont in six hours. That may be a little hopeful but that's the plan. I'll retake the oath of office at my residence, and yes, the press can be there. Now, any update on the cause of death?"

"No Sir, but the autopsy has started."

"Okay. I want to be informed as soon as possible, but it might be a challenge to communicate – at least until we get to Louiseville."

"Yes Sir, Mr. President."

Next, Martin called the Secret Service command post. "Please contact the Sûreté du Quebec office in Louiseville, and notify them that the President and his team are on the way, on snowmobiles. Ask them to have vehicles ready to transport the Presidential party to the border crossing at Highgate Springs, Vermont."

"Did you say 'on snowmobiles,' or did I hear you wrong?"

Martin replied, "You heard right. If all goes well, we expect to be in Louiseville in three hours or less."

"How are you going to stay in touch?"

"We're not. Radio silence is a must. But if there is an emergency – a dire emergency – the Sûreté will be able to radio us."

Another voice took the phone at the Washington end. "No goddam way! You are not moving the President of the United States on a snowmobile. Who approved this crazy-ass idea?"

BACK AT THE WINTER RESIDENCE, PRESIDENT GRÉGOIRE FLEW up the stairs to put a few items together, but Leonie had already done that for him. She was all but suited up. Marc pulled everything on in less than a minute. He grabbed his helmet and gloves and headed down the stairs with Leonie closely behind. Before she lowered her helmet on, the President gave her a kiss. She said to him, "You know, you should have a Cognac before we leave." Marc stepped back into the kitchen and pulled a small glass out of the cupboard, filled it halfway with Courvoisier V.S. He then solemnly raised the glass arm's length toward his father's racing picture and said, "Here's to you, Dad – you'd never believe what I got myself into now." Then it was down the hatch. As he was reaching toward the cupboard to return the bottle, he thought out loud, "Why not?" and slid the flask-sized bottle into an inside pocket.

Once again the sleigh bells on the porch door jingled as the President and First Lady left the building. The team was all lined up in the driveway. Yvon was sitting on his idling sled dusting the snow off his glowing GPS. As Leonie went by she patted Yvon's gloved hand. He gave her a thumbs up and a wink of encouragement. As Leonie climbed on the VK, the President leaned over to switch on the rear hand warmers and plugged in her helmet warmer wire. Her helmet also housed a two-way communications system that allowed her and Marc to talk to each other. In a few moments everyone was on their sleds, except Brian who was standing next to his and revving up the two-stroke engine. The President stood up on the running boards of his idling snowmobile, turned toward the rear sled and gestured for a 'thumbs up – I'm ready' sign from each rider. Each gave the requested 'thumbs up' all the way to Yvon. Then, like a NASCAR flag-man, the President dropped his chin to his chest and thrust his left hand forward with the index finger pointing ahead like a pistol. As he sat down and put his thumb on the throttle, Yvon's sled pulled out onto Rue Notre Dame heading south.

Pierre Laflame and his yapping poodle were in the window next door watching the sleds pull out onto the street. Amazed, he thought, 'This is a hell of a time to go out for a night ride.' It only took a moment for him to realize the group was staying on the road and not heading to the snow-mobile trail as usual. He found it all very curious and very unlike Marc, who was a stickler for going by the rules, especially on snowmobiles. He watched as the seven taillights went out of sight, then looked down at the floor in thought. After a few moments of consideration he hobbled on his crutches toward the phone.

Yvon gunned his Ski Doo up the first hill, everyone following suit. Then they passed the Nouvelle France microbrewery, past the Petro T gas station, all closed up, and onward toward the first bridge over the Rivière du Loup. There Yvon hit his first big snowdrift caused by the wind blowing across the open span of the bridge. His sled dove nose first into the drift, but his wide skis floated the sled back to the top of the snow. The blasted snow completely blanked out his headlight and blew up and off both sides of the cowling. He gave it more gas and rode it through.

Sûreté John saw the explosion of snow and the dancing light rays off Yvon's headlight and knew precisely what happened. He too leaned on the throttle and went right up and through the drift blasting more snow and dazzling light into the night sky! The President was sure the two sleds ahead of him had cut an ample path through the drift, so as not to alarm the First Lady all he did was push his throttle gently. More snow flew up and to the sides, his heavy sled bounced a bit, and seconds later the President was again behind Sûreté John. He watched in his mirror as Brian and the others easily passed through the drift. "Are you still back there, Sweetie?"

Leonie replied, "Yup, yup." She could see Brian's headlight catching up, and other headlights flashing up into the sky, but didn't know how many were there. They were all there.

★ ★ ★

"You're shittin' me, right? Please tell me you're goddam shittin' me!" Ronald Gibble, Director of the Secret Service, was at the White House and was just told the new President and his detail were riding snowmobiles through a raging blizzard. He was screaming mad. "Fuck me to tears, who gave permission to do that?" He quickly learned the new President gave the order himself. "Jesus H. Christ, is this how this guy is going to be to deal with?"

Secretary Arnold heard these outbursts and approached Gibble. "Easy cowboy." Then putting his long pointing finger gently on Gibble's chest, he rebuked, "*This guy* is now your President. I expect you to show the appropriate respect."

Gibble sneered as he turned away. "Yeah that's right. And I'm the one responsible for his safety." He went to a keyboard, brought up Google Maps on a large wall monitor, and pounded in 'St. Alexis des Monts to Louiseville, Quebec.' "Looks like the most direct route back to civilization is through this little village of St. Angele de Premont, but that doesn't look like a main road. The main road is Route 349. Does anybody goddam know which road they're on?"

The painful answer was – no. The cowering supervisor said, "Martin didn't say which way they were going, he just said they were going to Louiseville."

Gibble placed a secure call to the Sûreté headquarters in Quebec City, where he was lucky enough to reach a nearly bilingual officer who said, "I'm sorry Monsieur, but unfortunately all I can tell you is what your man told us."

Gibble was beside himself. "Can you tell us where they are?"

The officer replied, "The Sûreté officers with the President 'ave police radios, mais we don't expect to hear from dem unless dere is a problem. Dey s'pose to keep quiet with the radios."

★ ★ ★

Down in Cocoa Beach, Florida, a festive banquet was being held for the Brevard County Special Olympics which were held earlier that day. Dr. Amélie Grégoire, Major, USAF, was one of the organizers of the event and was sitting at the head table. Nearby sat Special Agent Christine White, Air Force Office of Special Investigations, or OSI. She was the one-person 'team' protecting Dr. Grégoire.

The emcee of the event suddenly approached the microphone and announced: "I have some horrible news, President Morris has died...."

Dr. Grégoire was shocked. It took only a nano second to realize what this meant. 'It can't be,' she thought. But from the corners of her eyes she noticed two men in suits coming to block the banquet hall doors. At the same time Agent White moved toward her and said, "Ma'am, we need to move you to a more secure location."

The Major protested, "But I'm supposed to present the awards for the sailing competition." Agent White grimaced and shook her head.

While Amélie did want to stay, she seriously wanted to talk to her father so she didn't resist the ordered departure. As Dr. Grégoire reached for her purse she whispered to the emcee, "I have to go."

Dr. Grégoire and Agent White moved to a side door which opened directly to the street, and there was a large, black Ford Expedition with two OSI agents in the front seat. Agent White motioned the Major into the back seat, then slid in beside her. The SUV pulled away quickly with a closely following sedan.

"Is my father okay?" the Major asked.

"Yes Ma'am, he's on his way back to the U.S. Arrangements are being made to bring him to Washington immediately."

Amélie asked, "Where are we going, home?"

"No Ma'am, we need you to stay on the base tonight, and Secretary Arnold would like you to call him at the White House."

A few minutes later, the black Ford pulled up to the main gate of Patrick Air Force Base. An OSI agent standing with a Security Police gate guard vouched for the two incoming vehicles. After motioning the vehicles through, the guard asked, "Who's in the black bus?" The agent replied, "The President's daughter. Gotta catch up to them, thanks for the help."

As Dr. Amélie disembarked, four agents immediately surrounded her and accompanied her inside. Waiting for her was the local OSI Commander, Joel Barry, who politely greeted her. "Good evening, Dr. Grégoire. I'm sorry we had to take you away from the banquet. The threat level has been raised on all Secret Service clients." He lowered his chin to add, "I don't know if you've been informed, but your father has taken the oath of office as President of the United States. This makes you a category one client."

A chill passed through her. She took the seat that was offered her and swallowed deeply. "Where is he, my father?"

"Your parents and your brother are attempting to get back to the U.S., but their route of travel has not been released to anyone. I'm sure you have more questions, and Secretary Arnold, whom I believe you're familiar with, would like you to call on a secure phone. You can use my office."

During this conversation, whispering was going on between Agent White and Colonel Woody Joseph, the Base Commander. Seconds later the Colonel intercepted Dr. Grégoire and quietly said, "Hello Doctor, I know this must be quite a night for you. I understand the OSI would like you to stay on base this evening, which I certainly agree with. My wife and I would be happy to have you stay with us. I have a secure phone which would be at your disposal."

"Well that is very kind of you Sir, but I have a dog."

"Agent White tells me Ruthie is very friendly. Please bring her along."

"Thank you again, Sir. Very kind of you both."

Dr. Grégoire sat at Barry's desk while he placed the call. He then handed her the phone and said, "Secretary Arnold." As Barry was shutting the door behind him, he heard "Hello, Gabe?" At the other end of the phone came a warm but concerned voice, "Hi Amélie, how are you doing?"

"Okay, I guess. Can you tell me where my father is?"

"He and your mother and brother, and their protection detail are on snowmobiles trying to get to Louiseville, Quebec. We're concerned about them because there's quite a blizzard going on up there."

"Well, they'll make it. No question about that," she said.

"Yeah, I know. But I have to admit there's more snow coming down there than even your grandfather ever saw. In Montreal it's all freezing rain." Not wanting to worry Amélie any further, he quickly added, "But you're absolutely right, they'll make it. When they get to Louiseville, the Sûreté du Quebec has an SUV and chase car ready for them to go directly to Vermont."

Amélie replied, "That explains why my brother is not answering my texts."

"Yeah, they don't want anyone triangulating on phone calls, disclosing their location. So you won't hear directly from them for a while. We're sending Air Force One up to Burlington to transport them to Washington. We're all, ah, anxious for him to get here."

"Do you know what happened to President Morris?"

"No. It's a mystery. We should know something in a few hours though." To further reassure her he added, "There are no signs of foul play. I'm guessing it was a medical condition. I promise to call you when your father gets to Louiseville. Also, Ron Gibble is here, the director of the Secret Service. He'd like to ask a couple of questions. Is that okay?"

"Sure."

Next on the phone was Gibble. After the required polite hello, he said, "I have a question you might be able to answer, Dr. Grégoire. Your father is traveling from St. Alexis des Monts on snowmobiles. Have you been up there, Doctor?"

"Yes, I've been up there many times."

"Good, good. Well, I've never been on a snowmobile, can't imagine what they're like, sounds awful cold to me. So they're following the road, and we're trying to determine which road they took to Louiseville. Would you know which road your father uses? I'd like to make their trip a little shorter, and of course get them into an enclosed vehicle."

"With all due respect, Sir, you're the director of the Secret Service and you don't know where the President of the United States is?"

What Gibble wanted to say is 'the bastard didn't stay on the phone long enough to get any questions in!' But he remembered whom he was talking to, and Arnold was still sitting right next to him. So instead he said, "Well, when our agent called to let us know they were leaving, we didn't realize there were two options."

There was a little pause before Amélie replied, "Well, when my father is in his car, he doesn't like to go the short way through St-Angele because there are a lot of open fields and snowdrifts. So for the same reason, I'd say they'll go through St-Paulin on their snowmobiles. Listen, Mr. Gibble, I'd just wait for him in Louiseville. It's pretty small, he'll find you. What you may want to do is make sure Highway 40 is cleared from Louiseville to Montreal, and my two uncles, Bruno and Sylvain Archambault, have the contract to plow the roads in that area. The Sûreté will have their number."

"Well, thank you very much, Doctor. And I'm sorry we had to disrupt your evening but I hope you understand."

"Thank you, Mr. Gibble, and really, please take care of my dad." With that, a small tear came to the corner of her eye. "And could I speak to Gabe again."

Gibble passed the phone over to Arnold and left the desk.

Amélie asked, "How long am I going to be stuck on the base?"

"I'm not sure. But I think I'll get you sent up here to Andrews. I'm sure your father would like you to be close to the White House. What do you think?"

She sighed. "Yeah, I guess."

"Don't worry Amélie, this won't last forever. I'll be sure to let you know when we hear from your parents."

"Thanks again Gabe, I'll be anxious to hear from you."

The Major came out of the office and accepted Colonel Joseph's kind offer. She also talked the OSI into taking her home to get a few things, and of course, Ruthie. As she was driven back on the base she told Christine, "I feel like I'm under arrest."

THE PRESIDENT'S SEVEN-SLED ENTOURAGE CONTINUED TO PLOW through the heavy snowfall. If one of the local residents happened to see them going by, they would see seven headlights flashing wildly up into the sky then down into the snow and jerking left and right. The going was rough and it was just the kind of ride Marc loved. But since this trip had an actual mission to accomplish, and thinking about what was waiting for him in Washington, all the fun and adventure were out of it.

Yvon's focus was intense. As he approached the beginning of the next bridge, his headlight revealed bare pavement with waves of snow eerily blowing snake-like over the entire length of the bridge. This could only mean that a massive snowdrift was blocking the other end; time to stab the throttle.

In seconds he was across the bare pavement, gaining speed and momentum. His sled pounded the drift and sent him steeply toward the top. As he gained the crest of the drift, he saw that it was not only high but at least 40 feet wide! He wondered if everyone would make it, especially the President who was riding double. Sûreté John also saw the spooky bare pavement. He stopped to see how Yvon was going to do. There was a dark moment, but suddenly the entire team saw a headlight beam flashing into the night! Yvon cleared the drift.

Sûreté John slid his butt all the way to the back of his seat, lowered his head as close as he dared to the handlebars, and pushed the throttle. The exhaust roared and up he shot. Once at the top he got off the throttle, almost stopping his sled, then jammed the gas again! The wide track blew snow back 20 feet behind him. His intentions were realized – he reduced the height of the snowdrift thus making it easier for the President, who was carrying precious cargo, to make it up and over. Sûreté John pulled up behind Yvon, both now anxious to see how the President would do.

"You're not going up that!" Leonie yelled into the mic.

"Hang on, and leeean forward!" Marc replied. She leaned as much as possible, tucked her chin to her right shoulder, tensed up every muscle in her body, and closed her lips and eyes tightly. Her mind was saying 'crazy, crazy, crazy!' The VK leaped forward and upward! At the top, Marc was thinking of doing the same thing as Sûreté John did – bang the throttle and reduce the snowdrift – but he knew Leonie would freak. So with an easy hand on the gas he kept his 20-inch-wide track moving steadily forward toward his two teammates.

Next came big Brian, flying his Mountain Max completely in the air over the top of the drift, never letting off full throttle! He too shot snow backward like a jet-propelled snow blower. The top of the drift was again chopped away by yet another foot. He glided his sled smoothly up to his parents. High fives would usually be going around, but there were three more sleds to go – and they were trail sleds, not deep snow sleds.

Jim Martin on his 136-inch track was next. He gave it the gas, gently at first then nearly full throttle. Up he went. At the top he stabbed the throttle to the bar! To his astonishment his sled muscled forward and gained more momentum. Backing off the gas to slow the spinning, he found himself easing up right behind Brian.

Next was Agent Akins, and he didn't like what he saw. He knew his short-track was a real dog in the deep stuff. They were waiting for him up top and there was nothing left to do but follow the President's often-given advice, 'use your throttle,' so he jabbed the throttle hard. His spinning track fishtailed wildly on the loose snow and kept spinning all the way to the base of the drift. He realized his mistake: too much power too soon. Halfway to the top his sled began to bog down. The whirling short-track dug deeper and deeper, slowing his sled and sinking it in the soft snow. The running boards came to rest on the snow, the track now spinning in vain. Akins quickly stood up and waived LaPlante off. LaPlante started scaling the snowdrift on foot; when he got to Akins he saw Brian coming down from the top.

While the three men were assessing the situation, the President, Yvon and Martin snowshoed their way to the stuck sled. Sûreté John stayed with the First Lady. The assessment was universal. Sure they could get the sled dug out but it would take quite a while, then what? From this point it would be almost impossible to get the sled to the top. And there was another short-track behind him. A few minutes of silence passed while everyone was thinking and worrying.

Officer LaPlante broke the silence. "About 100 meter back is de driveway for a pig farm. I know dat guy. I take Mathew wit' me on my sled, and we go dere. We can spend de nuit in da barn. You guys keep going. Okay, Mathew?"

"But what if you don't make it?" asked the President.

"Pas problem. We can snowshoe to da barn if we have to. It's not very far."

Akins was not in a position to disagree, but he hated to abandon the mission. Then he thought maybe he could get to the pig farm on his own. But with his limited French, he could find himself in trouble with the farmer. He was about to ask Jim Martin for advice but LaPlante asked again, "Okay, Mathew go with me to da farm?"

The President reluctantly said, "Okay, but we're not leaving here until we know you are both safe. How will we know that?"

Mathew offered, "Maybe we can come up with a code we can give when we get there." Bertrand said, "Sure. If we get to da farmhouse, I'll say 'Condition Alpha.' If we make it just to da barn, I'm going to say 'Condition Bravo.' If we have to come back, I'll say 'Condition Charlie.' Mais, if we need some help, I'll say 'Condition X-ray.'"

Reluctantly the President agreed. Instantly LaPlante and Akins were sliding on their butts down the snowdrift. The two men made short work of turning LaPlante's sled around and in seconds they were riding double – on a sled made for one – heading back north.

The President asked Yvon, "Just in case, where's the next closest house?" Yvon replied, "About 150 meters back is a road on the right. It is a cul-de-sac with six or seven houses. Ahead, about half a kilometer is the Laframboise family. I know them very well. We can go there if we need help."

The President pursed his lower lip but said nothing. He also knew the family. He wondered what they'd think if he had to set up the Oval Office in their living room in the middle of the night. He also thought about how long of a hike it would be to either place, especially on snowshoes, in the dark, and in heavy snow. Maybe this was a bad idea, but he forced those thoughts right out of his mind. There were still five able sleds.

A few moments later Brian yelled, "There they go!" All eyes turned and saw the lone headlight steadily moving up the farmer's driveway. They all silently watched until the light went out of sight.

The President returned to the First Lady. She had her helmet off and her red tuque pulled down over her ears. As her husband approached she closed her eyes and waited to hear what happened, absolutely sure it wasn't good. The President explained everything to her, fully realizing that all she was thinking was they should never have left the house. She didn't say a word but her worried look said it all.

Brian asked, "Should we go back and start digging out the sled just in case?"

The President advised against it. "We'd just work up a sweat and make ourselves cold. Let's give them a few more minutes." As they waited, an inch of snow accumulated on Brian's sheepskin-covered seat.

Suddenly Sûreté John's radio crackled: "Condition Bravo, Bravo! – vas y, vas y!"

A careful smile came across the President's face as he looked at his wife. "See, I told you they'd be fine."

She wasn't amused and said, "So they are going to spend the night in a pig barn."

Sûreté John chimed in, "Pas problem Madame. Bertrand, he work seven years on pig farm before joining the Sûreté. He goin' to make a lot of friends in dere, and it is plenty warm in da barn." Then he picked up his mic and calmly replied. "Bien. Ont a reçu 'Condition Bravo.' Bonne chance à vous deux."

The President understood: "We received 'Condition Bravo.' Good luck to you both.' The transmission was replied with two clicks.

Helmets and gloves were quietly pulled back on, and in random order the headlights of the five remaining sleds lit up. Yvon moved out and everyone followed. The President turned for one last look at the distant spotlight glowing over the pig barn door and thought, 'Take care, guys.'

LaPlante had pulled up right to the barn door. He reached inside his snowmobile suit and pulled out a can of mace. Akins wondered why. Bertrand said, "Pig farmers don't usually keep dogs in da barn, but you never know." Inside he flashed his light around, and the first thing it hit was a massive pig lying on her side in a tight-fitting cage, nursing nine piglets. Matt whispered, "They sure don't give these poor pigs much room to move around." LaPlante responded, "No, they want them to stay still, make da fat."

To their left, Bertrand spotted the office door and motioned Matt to follow. Inside was a busy desk, a coffee pot, a couple of broken office chairs, and a cot. Bertrand went right to the phone. Matt put his hand on Bertrand's arm, "You can't say anything."

"No problem. I'm goin' to be very careful for sure." Officer LaPlante knew full well that a lot of people, especially the Canadian Press, were aware the Vice President had a winter home in the area, and given the circumstances he knew they would be using every resource available – legal or otherwise – to locate him. He carefully punched in the number for the Sûreté office in Louiseville. When the officer answered LaPlante just said, "Comment ça vas?"

"Un instant!" came the startled sergeant's reply – he immediately recognized the voice of his comrade and barely avoided blurting out his name. He rushed to find the station commander, Richard Savard, who hurried to the phone. Calmly, Savard picked it up and said, "Oui?"

Bertrand recognized the boss' voice and said in French, "Can you believe that UPS is still delivering packages in this weather? They're bringing you five." Commander Savard went along with the ploy and asked, "When are the packages getting here?" The reply was, "In an hour or two. Maybe you can tell the relatives; they will be happy to know their boxes haven't been lost." Savard thanked him and hung up the phone.

Savard quickly used the caller ID to locate the origin of the call, then swung to the map and pinpointed LaPlante's exact location. He wondered aloud, "Why only five?" Surely something happened. "But the packages haven't been lost?" And the 'tell the relatives' comment – he must want him to call Washington.

But first things first. He ordered his sergeant, "Get our two-sled team prepared to meet the President at St. Jacques and Route 349." Pressing his finger on the map of Louiseville he added, "They will escort them into the school parking lot on St. Jacques. Have the cars there ready to pick them up in the schoolyard."

Savard then grabbed the secure phone to call the White House.

When the Secret Service agent at the other end realized who was calling, he immediately handed the phone to Gibble. Savard reported, "Bon, I received a phone call from one of my officers who was escorting your President here to Louiseville." Gibble immediately picked up on the words 'was escorting,' but didn't interrupt. "He said five packages are on their way. I don't know if he meant five people or five snowmobiles."

Gibble couldn't hold himself back, "Is the President one of those packages?"

"They wouldn't be moving forward if the President wasn't part of the group. And he said the packages haven't been lost."

"Do you know where they are?"

"We have the exact location of where the phone call was made, 24.5 kilometers from here, and they are traveling on Route 349. He said to expect them in one or two hours. We'll be ready for them." Gibble took this all in for a moment. Then he asked, "Why only five packages?"

Savard replied, "Well something happened for sure. Maybe a mechanical problem or someone got stuck. But LaPlante didn't ask for assistance of any kind. So I think we can assume that whatever the situation is, they have it under control and everyone is okay."

"So we know where they are – can we call the officer back?"

Savard answered, "I would not advise that at all. We don't know if he is in a house or the barn, we don't even know if the owner is aware he is there. And as you know, every communication we have helps the press locate him. Besides, LaPlante has strict orders. He won't say anything more."

Savard paused a moment before adding, "Don't worry Sir, your President is on his way. We will take care of him as soon as he arrives and we'll call you immediately. They'll make it. He's with experts."

Gibble was recording the entire conversation and knew he could play it back just in case he missed something. Still, he had one more question, "Is your guy going to be okay, and whoever might be with him?"

Savard reassured him, "No one in the entire Sûreté knows survival techniques better than Bertrand LaPlante. Even if he were stuck outdoors in this blizzard, in less than an hour he'd have a shelter built and a fire going. And whoever is with him will be fine. Rest assured as I am, they are inside somewhere and warm."

Gibble repeatedly thanked Commander Savard and said he looked forward to an update, hopefully soon. He then relayed the news to Gabe Arnold.

Gabe said, "Well, he's right. The team certainly wouldn't be going ahead without the President, and the President won't leave the First Lady behind. I think we need to take Savard's advice – let's get ready for the President's arrival."

Gibble decided to agree but with reservations. Turning to the map, he asked, "Okay, once they leave Louiseville they head to Montreal – which border crossing are they going to?"

Gabe replied, "Highgate Springs, Vermont, about a dozen miles from the President's home in Swanton. You take care of getting your people there to pick him up; I'll look into having Air Force One waiting in Burlington."

"Wait a second," Gibble barked. "If we send Air Force One too soon the whole world will know where he's going. It's only a 90-minute flight from Andrews to Burlington. And AF1 is secure, serviced and well staffed right where she's now parked. With the right notifications, we'll have plenty of time to get her to Burlington. It can wait." Gabe nodded in agreement.

While the two men were discussing the matter, Paul Chapel approached them obviously distressed.

"JUST THE TWO PEOPLE I NEED TO TALK TO," THE PRESS Secretary said. "We have a real problem. A reporter from the Canadian Broadcasting Corporation asked to see me away from the rest of the press corps. She told me she knew where President Grégoire is, and she wanted to know if I could confirm her information. I let her talk and it turns out her information is accurate. I got her sequestered but I can't keep her there long. If she acts on what she knows…"

Arnold ordered, "Get her in here and let's see what we're dealing with."

"Her name is Colette Galipeau. I believe she is out of Montreal, speaks French and English like a pro, and she's all business." In a few minutes, Paul was escorting Ms. Galipeau into a West Wing inner office where Gibble and Arnold were waiting. They both greeted her cordially and everyone was introduced. She recognized Gabe – and when she shook his hand, she turned her hand over to the top, a signal of presumed power. Gabe noticed but just intensified his stare into her eyes.

She was the first to speak. "Might I assume the information I shared with Mr. Chapel is accurate – why else would I be brought into the inner sanctum, n'est pas?"

Gibble thought, 'She is all business.' Gabe wanted to be tactful yet polite. "We are indeed interested in your information." Then there was a deafening moment of silence which broke only when Ms. Galipeau laid out her cards.

"The CBC is well aware that the Vice President has a vacation home in St. Alexis-des-Monts. Since he was elected, we've casually kept track of his cabin and established a few sources in the area. When the news broke about President Morris' death, we cranked up our efforts in that area of Quebec, hoping Monsieur Le Vice President was there. One of our sources reported seeing seven snowmobiles leaving the Vice President's home in St. Alexis, heading south on the road. He was certain that Grégoire and his wife were in the group. Right now the mother of all blizzards is raging there – not the kind of conditions for a joy ride." She paused to reposition herself in her chair, causing her to lean closer to Gabe, showing a little cleavage.

"We also learned that the Sûreté in Trois Rivieres has a large SUV, and that vehicle has been sent to Louiseville along with an unmarked car. Furthermore, we're monitoring Sûreté radio communications and they are clearly in a radio-silence mode, a strong indication that something big is going on in Louiseville. Finally, the snowplows are working hard to clear the access road from Louiseville to Highway 40." After a coy moment of silence, she added, "I'm sure you can come to the same conclusions as we have."

She had more. "It's just a matter of time, an hour or two, providing your new President makes it through, before he arrives in Louiseville. We plan to be there."

Gabe gave her a long, stern look. The intensity in his eyes confirmed in her mind that her information was dead on.

Gabe decided to lay it out, "Ms. Galipeau…"

"Please call me Colette."

"Of course, Colette. You are indeed well informed. Here's the situation: The new President has little protection and is very vulnerable. We're not even sure he'll make it through the storm – they've already lost two of the snowmobiles you mentioned. We are doubly concerned because we don't know how President Morris died. It is on everyone's mind that the North Koreans somehow caused his death and will now target the new President. If you report his location before we can get him safely back to the United States" – Gabe's voice became bold, his pointer finger came out and was aimed just above Colette's head – "you and your network will be putting him in grave danger."

Colette rubbed the tip of her nose then slid her fingertips down her raised chin and the length of her throat. Keeping her hand on the base of her neck, she said, "First, you are underestimating the abilities of Canadian

Law Enforcement. They will fully protect your President, even under the conditions you describe. Secondly, we have a scoop that we worked hard for. Just imagine: CNN, Fox, NBC, they have all ignored your Vice President. But we, the CBC, can air an exclusive no one else has. And the whole world will be watching." She hesitated, unsure if she should add something, but out it came, "This will not only put CBC on top, this story will bring in revenues that we haven't seen since the Canadian Olympics."

The proverbial cards were on the table and the room went dead still. After a moment Gabe excused himself to take Paul to another room, leaving Gibble and the Colette looking at each other. She maintained a pleasant smile – he tried on his poker face, but his mind was working on some kind of legal reason to lock her up for a few hours, Secret Service style.

Gabe asked, "How can we stop her?"

Paul's head was shaking, "Maybe a deal, I don't know … an exclusive with the President. Whatever deal we make her, we'll have no way to enforce it. Short of threatening her life, there's no way to stop her. Even if we took her out of the picture, CBC is already all over this. So whatever we offer, it has to be good enough for her to convince CBC to back off."

Gabe replied, "Yeah, and no matter what they agree to, it'll be temporary at best. And CBC won't be the only network figuring this out. Now that we've told the world that the President is on his way back, it won't take but a few clicks on Google for anybody else to figure out where he is or was. But they won't have the informants like CBC has. And another thing, while he was the Governor of Vermont he gave an interview with the local newspaper in Louiseville. He even cut the ribbon to officially open the annual Sarasin Festival. They all know where he is. But the people in St. Alexis have been good to him; if anybody asked where Marc Grégoire lived, nobody knew anything."

After nine of the longest minutes ever, Gabe and Paul re-entered the room. Gabe smiled at Colette, then expressed his agreement that "Canadian Law Enforcement agencies are very good at what they do, but their resources are understaffed." Gibble added, "And probably uninformed about the newest threats and unknown adversaries." Gibble could have easily belabored the shortcomings of the Canadian Law Enforcement Intelligence community but realized it would only poison the negotiations that Gabe was apparently trying to start.

Gabe continued, "You must agree that the new President is very vulnerable. And given the extreme weather conditions, there is just so much anyone can do." Colette just listened; she was sure there was more to come.

"It is of paramount importance that his location and route of travel be kept secret – it is the best defense he has. Nevertheless, I understand the advantageous position you and the CBC have earned, so we have a deal to offer you."

Colette sat motionlessly but was all ears. "A deal?" she asked.

Gabe continued, "President Grégoire took the oath of President of the United States in St. Alexis des Monts – on Canadian soil, a historical first. At this moment we don't know who administered the oath but I believe it was a local official. As soon as we have the name of that person we will give it to you – exclusively."

Colette pressed, "And?"

Gabe fidgeted, assuming she would ask for an 'and' but hoping against it. "Well, with your resources you will be the first to interview him or her. They'll be free to tell you all the details, show you where it happened, and everything else. With the historical significance of this event, Canadians everywhere will want to see your report. In fact, people all over the world will be watching.

"In addition, we'll point your reporters to people who will be able to give exclusive details of the snowmobile ride to Louiseville. As I mentioned the party has already left two people behind. There's been some kind of incident, hopefully not an accident – even we don't know anything about it yet. All these details will be available to the CBC *first*."

Colette held her smile but intensified her glare at Gabe, still waiting for the 'and.' Gabe reluctantly added, "Furthermore, we believe the oath of office was videotaped right inside the President's lodge. No one has that recording yet. I will see to it that it is given to CBC 30 minutes before we release it to anyone else." At this, he leaned back in his chair.

Colette lowered her chin, knowing she was in a position of power. She also realized pushing too hard could backfire. She said, "Good offer. Of course, within 10 minutes of us airing all this, the rest of the world will be rebroadcasting our report, not even giving us an ounce of credit." She waited a moment before asking, "What else is on the table?"

Gabe nodded his chin toward Paul who was reluctant to speak, but he did. "We'll give you – personally – a 10-minute exclusive interview with the President, here in the White House, as soon as he gets settled in."

Colette shook her head, "You obviously haven't cleared this with the President, and 'as soon as he gets settled in' is up to interpretation." She proposed, "How about I make you an offer?"

Several sets of male eyebrows went up.

She countered, "Everything you offered about the name of the minister and the video of the swearing in, and a 30-minute exclusive, not with the President, but with Madame the First Lady. *Within two weeks of their arrival in Washington.*"

Paul was taken aback and asked, "You would rather have an interview with the First Lady instead of the President?"

Ms. Galipeau explained, "Yes. Canadians are interested in the American President but an interview with him is routine news, it would be seen once. Madame *is a Canadian.* An exclusive interview with her will be viewed over and over. She will be on every Canadian television by tomorrow morning and every day for some time to come. Now that's worth dollars." She pressed, "Do we have a deal?"

Gabe's nod gave a 'maybe' signal to Paul. Paul asked Gabe, "Do you think she'd do it?"

"I think so, when we explain everything to her. We might have a deal."

Paul had caveats: "You will have to give us a list of your questions before the interview – nonnegotiable. She's not a politician and will want to be prepared. Secondly, there will be no cutting and pasting."

Colette asked, "What do mean, 'cutting and pasting'?"

Paul explained, "What I mean is, you ask her a question about abortion, she replies, and later in the interview you ask her a different question that causes a giggle. You then cut the giggle and paste it in after the question about abortion, making it look like she's laughing about abortion." His piercing glare sent her a strong signal that he knew she knew exactly what he was talking about.

"Neither I nor any of my colleagues would do such a thing with Madame the First Lady. As I already pointed out, she could become more important to Canadians than the Queen." She glared back. "Do we have a deal? Because we're out of time."

All eyes were on the Secretary of Defense. He said, "We have a three-handshake deal." Ms. Galipeau flashed a grin as she took the first handshake with Gabe. Under the table Gabe tapped Gibble's foot. After Gibble shook with the CBC reporter he kept her hand in his. "As head of the

Secret Service, I am obliged to tell you that we expect you and all of CBC to live up to this agreement." His voice got louder, "Because if there is a breach the repercussions will be grave. First among them will be the permanent absence of anyone from CBC in the White House Press Corps." He took a second before adding, "My apologies for my rudeness but I take my responsibilities seriously." With that he let her hand go.

"As do I," she replied coldly.

Gibble wasn't done. "And one more thing, I need you to give me your passport."

She protested, "But I won't be able to get back to Canada without a lot of hassle."

Gibble thought, 'exactly.' "It's only for a day or less, until the President is safely in the U.S.A."

She didn't like it one bit but reached into her purse and retrieved her passport, then suddenly put it back. She glared at Gibble and demanded, "I want these agreements in writing. Now!" Arnold nodded, "It'll be in simple language because we don't have time to consult lawyers." She agreed but stipulated, "I'll loan you my passport after I see the agreement, and it needs to be done within 15 minutes or I won't be able to stop our crew. We have people who know how to ride snowmobiles too."

Paul escorted her to another room to tap out the agreement. When they were gone Gibble asked Gabe, "Did I get your signal right?" Gabe replied, "You did. But we'll have to see if they live up to this. The CBC has a great scoop; I'd be surprised if somebody up their chain lets this go."

DESPITE THE IMPOSSIBLE CONDITIONS THE PRESIDENT AND party were making progress. They rode through several segments of road that passed through the forest. The tall and broad maples, birches, and pines blocked the wind, just as Yvon had hoped. Sure there were a few snowdrifts to jump but passing through the protection of the forest allowed them to finally pick up speed and make up a little time. Yvon was worried though. He kept thinking about a place in the road where the pavement dropped sharply between two steep hills with nothing but open fields on both sides. He knew even when it wasn't snowing that spot filled in with deep, wind-blown snow – and it was just ahead.

Just nine minutes later he pulled to a stop at the base of a massive snowdrift, exactly what he'd been dreading. With his headlight on high beam he could barely see the top of it. It appeared to taper off gradually versus a sharp facing edge, a small consolation. He wondered if he could make it over the top. Reluctantly he decided there was only one way to find out. White exhaust blasted from his roaring Ski-Doo and up it went. Sure and steady at first, but the steepness of the snowdrift slowed him down to a spinning crawl, and finally to a dead stop just three feet from the top. Suddenly Yvon's sled started slipping backward. Seeing the danger, Brian and Sûreté John clambered up the snowdrift on all fours. Yvon was holding the brake but he was still sliding back; if it picked up enough momentum the sled could go into a roll – with Yvon on it. Jumping off would mean letting go of the brake and making it almost certain his sled would roll several times on the way to a crashing halt at the bottom. Sûreté

John got there just in time to push the back of the right ski down with his strong foot; a second later Brian grabbed the ski hook and pulled it hard straight up. It worked! The ski was now driven backward into the snow like the fluke of an anchor holding the big Ski-Doo in place. Certain disaster was averted.

The three men assessed the situation and it wasn't good. While Sûreté John and Yvon discussed the situation in French, Brian climbed his way to the top. Whipping out his light, he plodded to both sides of the colossal drift. After a quick look he slid down the snowdrift on his butt. As he passed Yvon and Sûreté John he yelled, "Rest ici."

With one sharp pull he brought his 700-triple to life. He shot his sled to the right side of the drift, where it wasn't so high, and throttled right to the top! Everyone watched as his headlight turned in circles, the sled apparently packing down the snow above. Then his light reappeared at the top of the drift where he had gone up – and down he came. At the bottom he danced both feet onto the left running board, U-turned the Mountain Max around on its side and shot right back up the drift. At the top he pushed the throttle to the bar. He was doing what he knew how to do best: break a trail. Over the top, he yanked his sled back around and again rode down the drift. He repeated his climb four times, cutting a path now almost anyone could climb. He returned to the party and waived Yvon and Sûreté John down to the group.

When all were assembled Brian gave his plan. "Dad, you go up first and back your sled as close to the edge as possible. Wrap your tow strap around the rear bumper and throw the rest down to Yvon. Everyone else get to the top with your sleds and stand by."

There was no discussion and no questions. One by one the sleds followed the makeshift trail up the snowdrift. In seconds Marc was in position. While wrapping his tow strap as directed, Leonie held the VK's brake with all her might. Martin and Sûreté John held the tow strap from unwrapping while Yvon tied the other end to his front bumper. When all was ready Brian and Yvon pulled the anchored ski out of the snow, and as the men at the top slowly eased the wrapped tow strap out and down, Brian and Yvon carefully guided the Ski-Doo back to the bottom of the drift. As Brian rewound the tow strap, Yvon drove his sled up the Mountain Max's trail to join the others.

This time the high fives were given all around! Yvon came over to Brian with several "Merci, Merci tres bien." Then he said to Brian in French, "You are the best rider, especially on that light sled of yours; you should go first and make the trail." Brian argued, "No, you are the leader, and you know the road." But Yvon insisted, "We are now close to Louiseville and you know the way as well as anyone else." The President nodded in agreement.

In moments everyone was back on their sleds with Brian in the lead. Brian did recognize the terrain, especially as he rode down Temperature Hill where the houses were closer together. Indeed they were approaching Louiseville, perhaps just two or three miles ahead. This part of the ordeal was almost over.

As ordered, two Sûreté officers were waiting with their snowmobiles at Route 349 and Avenue St. Jacques. Their engines were off and no lights were showing, partly to protect their night vision and partly to keep their presence surreptitious. They both glared ahead into the dark waiting for five headlights coming their way. Fortunately the snow was finally letting up. Suddenly the first officer blurted, "I think I see a light! Yes, there's two, three, there's five. That's them!" He lit up his blue/red lights but only for two or three flashes. Sûreté John replied by blinking his blue and red lights once.

Brian led the group directly to the waiting Sûreté sleds, both started up and turned around. The presidential motorcade of snowmobiles quickly fell in behind the two Sûreté officers. They turned right onto Avenue St. Jacques and right again into the schoolyard. As Brian entered the driveway he noticed that he was now on plowed pavement. Leonie noticed too, and she was very relieved.

Sûreté John, first off his sled, went directly to Commander Savard who led him to the President. Marc's first question to Savard was, "Have you heard from Bertrand and Mathew?" Savard assured, "They are okay. Just a few minutes ago Bertrand made contact with the farmer. Both men are about to be treated to a hot midnight meal in the house."

Out of nowhere appeared a man trudging through the snow, wearing a winter parka but no hat, and casually smoking a cigarette. When he saw the SUV and snowmobiles he quietly stopped, took a long drag off his cigarette, and studied the people and vehicles. Martin immediately moved in closer to the President. Savard jerked his head toward the man. Taking the signal, two Sûreté officers walked over toward him. Now recognizing they were police officers, the stranger cupped his cigarette in his hand and brought it closer to his chest. One officer asked him, "What are you doing here?"

"My wife is sick, she's coughing a lot. I had to go out for a smoke." The man's face was dull but his eyes were taking everything in.

The officer asked, "Where do you live?" The man jerked his cigarette back toward a small apartment building across the street from the back of the cathedral. The officer advised, "You better go back home, your wife may need you. And you should put your hood on."

The man nodded, and with a flick of his cigarette hand toward the vehicles he asked, "What's going on?"

"None of your concern. Everything is okay." Casually pointing to the man's apartment, the officer ordered, "You just go home."

The man turned around toward home but kept his face turned toward the vehicles. He started to shuffle back the way he came and turned his head toward his path in the snow. Suddenly he snapped his head back toward the scene, his eyes fixed on the SUV.

As the officers walked back one asked the other, "You remember him? His name is Rueville, his wife left him when we arrested him last year."

The second officer replied, "Yes, he used to drive a tow-truck. He got six months for distributing child pornography."

"I wonder what he's doing now?" the first asked.

"Probably anything for a buck."

The officers got back to Savard just as the man went out of sight. They told him who he was and added that the man never took his other hand out of his pocket. Savard's eyes squinted when he heard the name and declared, "We must have you on your way Mister President." At this, one of the Sûreté officers went to the SUV and put his hand on the door ready to open it. The President and First Lady took a few steps over to Yvon. They solemnly shook hands and Marc said, with Leonie translating, "Very, very good job my friend." Yvon nodded and replied, "Bienvenue mon vrai ami, c'est de rien."

Continuing in an even more somber tone, the President added, "You know, you will be famous now, you and your Ski-Doo. Being famous might be fun for a while, but it can be a problem. Be careful."

"Merci encore, M. Le President."

The two men shared a hug after which the President said, "It might be a long time before I see you again, Yvon – but I will be back. Take care of yourself, and St. Alexis."

"Bien sure, bien sure."

With that, the President asked Savard, "Can you take care of Yvon, and all the sleds?" Savard assured the President, "M. Matteau will be well taken care of. All the sleds will be transported to a secure garage – they are Canadian history now."

"One more request, my wife would like to use the ladies' room; we have several more hours to travel."

Savard said, "Oui," and in moments everyone was boarded and the motorcade was headed directly to the Sûreté office. There the President used Savard's secure line to call the White House. Ironically, the White House operator wasn't sure the voice at the other end was really the President. She hesitated at first, but out of caution connected the call to Houseman.

Relieved to hear the President's voice, Houseman said, "Mr. President, does this mean you've made it to Louiseville?" The President replied, "We certainly did. We had to leave two people behind, but they're okay and out of the storm. I'd like to speak to Gabe Arnold."

"Yes, Mr. President."

It took only seconds to find Gabe. "Marc! You made it." A clearly audible exit breath was heard on the White House end.

Marc replied, "Yep, a trip like no other. What's the latest on the warhead?"

The Secretary of Defense reported, "It's been separated from the missile and is on a barge being brought out to sea. Once they decide how to make it completely safe, we'll bring it on board one of the ships. But I got to tell you, I'm not sure they can make it safe, it was slapped together."

The President asked, "But it is a full-scale nuke, not just a dirty bomb?"

Gabe hesitated before answering, "It's the real McCoy. Had it gone off over Tokyo ... or Seattle ... it would have destroyed everything. There was silence at both ends of the line. The President broke it; "Does Prime Minister Suko know this?"

"Yes, Sir, he does. He's trying to keep a lid on it, but too many people already know. So the rumors, which are essentially accurate, are running rampant. And there's something else you need to be aware of, the Japanese Defense Forces are all on full alert. Some Japanese politicians, especially Suko's political opponents, are demanding an immediate attack on North

Korea."

The President wasn't surprised; he said, "They do realize that would be fatal. They must know China will come to the rescue of their bastard stepchild. What is Prime Minister Suko's reaction to all the pressure?"

"It would seem that he's between a rock and a hard place, but he knows they can't attack North Korea," Gabe replied.

"I presume Secretary Rikes is in constant contact with the Japanese government?" asked the President.

"Yes, Sir. Jane has had two video conferences with the Prime Minister. She's assured him of our full support, but of course he wants to speak to the President."

"He is aware" – there was hesitation in Marc's voice – "that there's a … new President?"

Gabe's voice grew softer, "Yes, Sir; and Jane is having a hard time convincing him that you are en route … he wants to know where you are."

The President said, "Maybe I could call him from here."

"Jane thought of that. But she and I see several issues. First, he's going to ask where you are and when you'll be at the White House. Then he'll want to know what the plan is for the device, which we can't say yet. Most importantly, he's going to ask you to help them attack North Korea, something I know we're not prepared to discuss yet. So most of the conversation would involve explanations of why you can't answer his questions. The call could do more harm than good."

The President agreed and was somewhat relieved. Indeed he wasn't prepared to talk to the Japanese Prime Minister nor any other foreign official. But he had another idea: "You call him – you and Jane. Tell him you're calling on my behalf. Make sure he understands that it is my firm belief that an immediate attack on North Korea would have dire repercussions. Assure him – guarantee him – that we, the United States, will not permit a second attack. Also, strongly urge him to contact President Taos. China owes an explanation not only to the Japanese but to the rest of the world." The President's voice grew louder, "Taos better be able to goddam explain how he let this happen."

Gabe replied, "Yes, Sir, I agree. Jane has attempted to contact the Chinese ambassador and he isn't responding."

"No kidding," the President replied sarcastically. "They're responsible for this situation as much as anyone else *and they know it.* Okay, Gabe, I want to get on the road. Do you need anything else from me – that I can talk about over this phone?"

"No, Sir. We'll set up the call right away, Jane's in the building. Godspeed, Marc."

"Roger that," the President replied.

Savard asked that the snowplow drivers to come in for a briefing. The first driver entered the building duly clad with insulated coveralls and a heavy, fleece-lined vest faced with orange and white reflective fabrics. He glowed in the dark and the light! The darkness around his eyes indicated he'd been up for more than 24 hours. As he entered the briefing room, the First Lady suddenly jumped to her feet and almost ran – to her brother Bruno. They exchanged customary kisses on both cheeks and a warm hug. Since Bruno spoke little English the conversation went immediately to French. "You're the snowplow driver?"

"Bien oui," he answered, "and Sylvain is driving the other truck; here he comes." Sure enough, in came Sylvain. Again more Quebec hugs and kisses. After the hugs Leonie asked them, "How come you are here?"

Sylvain replied, "Our company received a request for two heavy snowplows to be immediately dispatched to Louiseville, and the trip was to be confidential. I heard the news about the American President, and I thought for sure this had something to do with my brother-in-law and my big sister. I told Bruno we are taking this job ourselves!"

By this time the President and Brian joined them, and rigorous handshakes were shared all around. Sylvain looked up, then looked back at his sister and said, "I think the Commander wants to get started." Everyone took their seats.

Savard explained the plan: "The first truck will lead the motorcade to Montreal where you will be joined by other police and protective forces. The second truck must remain immediately behind the motorcade and keep any traffic from passing. Tractor-trailer drivers and hotheads in big four by fours will all want to pass. It will be Sylvain's job to stop them. The first truck will plow the snow to the right. The last truck will push all the snow directly into the passing lane, keeping only one lane open. That should do the job. Any questions?"

Sylvain asked, "How long do we stay with the motorcade?" Leonie whispered to her husband, "All the way." Savard picked up the whisper and directed, "Right to the border." Sylvain gave a quick, close to the chest, thumbs up to his sister.

Savard added, "If the weather changes and they can get a plane into Montreal, you'll be redirected to the airport. But the forecast is for snow and freezing rain there for several more hours." Savard looked at his notes for a moment, then proclaimed, "Time is of the essence. Are we ready?"

Agent Martin spoke up, "Please explain to everyone – in French – that radio silence is a must. Cell phone communications must not be made either. We don't want anyone to locate us until we are at the border." Savard thanked Martin for the reminder and instructed everyone accordingly.

The President was the first to head for the door – he wanted to see the trucks. "Awesome! Look at these monsters." He brought Leonie to his side. "Two axels in the front."

Leonie asked, "Why two axels in the front?"

"To help support the weight of this truck; loaded it probably weighs 75,000 pounds. All four front wheels turn left and right together." Bending over to look under the truck, he said, "Look at the driveshaft; it's as big as a sewer pipe." Leonie would have been uninterested except that this was her brother's truck.

The President and First Lady were motioned to the middle row of the SUV. Sûreté John slid into the shotgun position, a spot Martin thought he should be in, but he got into the back row with First Son Brian.

Behind them, sitting in the driver's seat of his truck, Sylvain pulled the throttle putting his powerful diesel engine into a deafening roar. He pulled a side-lever which spun around his plow like an airplane propeller, putting the discharge side to the left. The powerful diesel then calmed down to an idle. Several car doors slammed shut and the motorcade was ready to move.

Standing there on the steps, coatless in the snow, Savard somberly watched the first truck move away, the first plow banging away as it scraped the snow right down to the pavement. It was followed by the black unmarked Sûreté car, then the President's SUV, and finally the second snowplow. The only flashing lights were the rotating amber lights on the snowplows. He watched them as far he could, which was to the traffic circle leading to Hwy 40. He lamented forgetting to give the First Lady a blanket to keep her warm, hoping there was one behind the rear seat and someone would find it for her. They were out of sight five minutes before Savard realized he was freezing and his heart was pounding.

When he went inside he saw M. Matteau standing in the window near the radiator warming his hands; his eyes were sad, his face worried. He turned toward Savard and put his fingers over his lips, but said nothing. Softly Savard said, "Don't worry, they'll be okay now. Would you like some coffee?" Yvon nodded in the affirmative, just now feeling how cold he was. Yvon poured himself a coffee and Savard grabbed an empty cup for himself. Suddenly Savard remembered that the security cameras must have captured everyone embarking the vehicles and the motorcade pulling away. Putting the cup down he hurried to a computer to ensure the footage was saved. It was Sûreté du Quebec history, Canadian history, and U.S. history. And it all happened at his station in this tiny city of Louiseville, Quebec. After saving a second copy on a thumb drive, he let himself slowly lean back in his chair, his heart still pounding.

His mind was now slowing down enough to think things over, and he thought about what one his officers said about Reuville, the man out for a smoke: 'he never took his hand out of his pocket.' Picking his chin up toward Yvon, he asked, "Do you remember the guy on Rue St. Jacques, walking in the snow?"

Yvon said, "Yes."

"Do you remember if he was wearing a scarf?"

Yvon recalled, "No, I didn't notice. I wasn't paying attention to him."

Savard rubbed the side of his face in thought. Little did he know that within the next 24 hours, an order would come directly from Ottawa to do everything possible to find that man, and Louiseville would be crawling with RCMP officers from all over the province. But now the immediate business was to notify Washington, then Sûreté headquarters in Quebec City of the President's progress. In moments he was talking to Gibble himself. Savard explained, "The motorcade will be met with reinforcements north of Montreal. I can't say what those reinforcements will be but the Royal Canadian Mounted Police – the RCMP – will be involved. They have a national headquarters in Montreal so they have access to many resources."

Of course Gibble wanted to know, "How long will it be before the President gets to Montreal?" Savard replied, "The earliest, an hour and a half – but more likely two hours." He almost added 'given no unforeseen circumstances,' but he didn't want to give Gibble any more reasons to worry. Gibble thanked him very much and pleaded to be kept constantly informed of the President's progress.

After putting the phone down Gibble spun on his heels and darted over to Gabe Arnold. "They're inside real cars and on their way to Montreal. The Sûreté commander said at least 90 minutes before they get to there. Then it's to the border."

Gibble then swung around to the computer, did a Google Maps check, and learned it was 61.1 miles from the La Fountaine Tunnel in Montreal to the Port of Entry in Highgate Springs, Vermont – but only 44 miles from the tunnel to Champlain, New York. "Which way is he going, chief?" Gabe let the 'chief' remark pass.

Gabe explained, "Highgate. It's the closest to Swanton, his hometown. Most of his family still lives in the area, and he probably would like them to be there when he retakes the oath. I'm going to let the rest of the staff know that the President made it to Louiseville."

When Gabe announced the news everyone clapped. Gabe raised his hands to quiet the group so he could add, "I just checked the weather and we're sure we can't get a plane into Montreal; so they'll head straight for the border, and I'm hoping they'll be there in about two or three hours."

Paul asked, "What's the weather in Vermont?"

"Rain," Gabe answered.

Then Jane asked, "Is the First Lady with them?"

"Yes, she and their son Brian. Dr. Grégoire is on Patrick AFB."

The question reminded Gabe of his promise to Amélie. But it was 'zero dark thirty,' and if she was getting some sleep he hated to wake her. When the meeting was over he sent her a text. It read: 'I have an update, call on secure if you are awake.'

Ruthie saw Amélie's phone light up and vibrate so she licked her mistress's arm. Ninety seconds later Amélie was saying hello to Gabe.

He began, "Sorry if I woke you."

"No problem, I was just napping. You have news?"

"Yes, your parents and brother are in cars and heading to Montreal, then to the border."

"So they made it to Louiseville on the sleds. I knew it!"

"Yeah, they did. And thanks for the information about your mother's brothers. They're driving the two snowplows making the way to Montreal."

"Great! Does my mother know?"

"Yep, she got to say hello to them at the Sûreté office."

"So you're getting ready to meet them at the border?"

"Yes. I expect every news agency in the world will soon figure out what's going on, especially when they hit Montreal. They'll all be at the border waiting with plenty of cameras and reporters. So you'll probably be able to watch it all on TV. There's a FOX affiliate right there in Burlington, isn't there?"

"Yes, and I'll be watching." Her voice softened, "I can't thank you enough for everything you're doing for my parents, and taking care of me."

"No problem Amélie, not to worry. The situation isn't ideal, but it does seem to be 'under control' as your father likes to say."

Amélie asked, "I think I hear Colonel Joseph stirring around. Can I share the news?"

Gabe said, "Yeah, well just tell him your father is safe and will be in the U.S. in a few hours. It's not that we don't trust Woody, but we have strict orders – orders your father himself gave."

After Amélie clicked off the phone she returned to Ruthie. Resting a hand on Ruthie's neck, she dropped her chin and ran her other hand through her hair. Despite her expressed belief that her parents and brother would get through, she realized a colossal blizzard would pose a significant challenge – even for her father.

She wished now she had gone home this past Christmas. It was probably the last opportunity for the family to get together privately and without all the problems of the world on her father's shoulders. She recalled her Christmas Day phone visit with her father and how they discussed who was the greatest person who ever lived. She made the case that Jesus Christ had been a great teacher, humanitarian and leader, and now, over 2,000 years later, still has millions of followers – and conceivably will have for hundreds of years to come. Dad's opinion was that Buddha was the greatest man who ever lived. He was everything Jesus was – four or five hundred years earlier – but did not have any delusions about being a god, had no claims to a kingdom, genuine or otherwise. Her father believed it was Buddha's teaching that created the most golden rule of all – from the Udanavarga 5:18: "Hurt not others with that which pains yourself." It was an interesting chat back then. What they talk about next will probably be on much heavier subjects.

Just then an unexpected text lit up her phone: 'Heard the news, everything ok kid? Geno.'

NEITHER GIBBLE NOR ANYONE ELSE AT THE WHITE HOUSE anticipated what was to happen after Savard notified Sûreté headquarters. The news was briefed to the head of the Sûreté who in turn called Ottawa for RCMP assistance. He accurately pointed out that the President was a national head of state and therefore under the responsibility of the Canadian federal government, not the province of Quebec. He made it clear that he expected total RCMP involvement by the time the entourage arrived in Montreal, and the Sûreté was expecting full reimbursement for their current expenses.

RCMP Headquarters went into action immediately. The shift commander made the required up-level notifications. Not all of these notifications were made with the important caveat that the President's travel was to remain highly secret. It only took minutes before the Director of the RCMP, Donald Clark, was ringing up Canada's Prime Minister to report the news.

The Prime Minister had gone to bed as fully informed as he could be by watching TV news and with a briefing by Canada's ambassador to the U.S.: the new President was on his way home but was still in Quebec. He saw an opportunity for political hay to be made but it could wait. He also knew he wouldn't have to ask anyone to leak this vital information to the media. It'll get done, and it will only be in a matter of minutes.

* * *

The unorthodox yet effective presidential escort of two snowplows and a standard sedan was making steady progress towards Montreal. The monotonous banging and scraping of the plows drowned out all other sounds inside the SUV. It must have been soothing to the First Lady because her eyes were closed and her head lightly bobbed. Marc hoped she would soon be dozing and numb to the ongoing ordeal. He filled his chest and belly with a deep breath and felt … well he couldn't exactly relax, but he no longer had to decide whether his right thumb had to push hard or ease off the throttle, and his left four fingers were no longer in charge of braking hard or feathering through a curve. Yes, he and Leonie were now sitting comfortably in a warm vehicle and others, experts all, were in charge of getting them back to the USA.

He closed his eyes and began square-four breathing: four seconds in, hold for four, four out, hold again, and repeat. As intended, the exercise calmed his mind. When he opened his eyes, he saw the business lights on both sides of the Berthierville exit. Steady progress indeed. His mind was quiet enough now to delineate and examine his pressing concerns.

First on the list was President Morris' death. In review of the few facts he had, Marc recognized that it was very unlikely that Leo was assassinated – not in the White House, and not while surrounded by the seniors of his Cabinet. Intentional food poisoning was a possibility, but nobody else was sick, and the entire White House staff was thoroughly and continuously investigated. In Marc's mind, it had to be a heart attack or a stroke. Time would tell.

He put aside those thoughts and now focused on North Korea, the bastards; in this case, the bastard. Marc was now sure Pak was a lunatic, because only a lunatic would start a nuclear war, one he could never win. And China. How could they have let this happen? The question in his mind was quickly overcome by a realization: China would not have condoned, encouraged or in any way supported the attack, especially not right in their own back yard. But they still bore responsibility; and if somebody's feet were going in the fire, more than just PRC toes would be included.

Marc realized, after three more cleansing breaths, that complex and difficult decisions immediately lay ahead. But he knew he wouldn't need to design all the solutions; they would be provided by professionals at the Pentagon and his senior advisors, Gabe and Jane. What he would have to remember is that solutions come easy to those not responsible for the outcome. Final decisions come hard.

Last of his top three concerns was the potential of a Presidential coup in Washington. Would the Democrats really try to declare the Vice President, now President, as lost or unavailable to perform the duties of President? He picked up his cell phone, noted a two-bar signal which would improve as they got closer to Montreal, and assured himself that if need be, as Gabe earlier pointed out, Gabe could contact him in the clear, killing two birds with one stone: Establishing that the President was indeed in contact with Washington, and purposely exposing his location to the media. If that instance arose, he could actually use his phone to hold a video press conference right there in the SUV as it moved south.

It was all interrupted when Agent Martin suddenly announced to the President, "Sir, I have sat-phone connection with Washington – no secure voice, but secure text. I've told them where we are. Secretary Arnold wants to talk to you." Handing his satellite phone to the President, Martin cautioned, "Unfortunately the battery is about dead; extreme cold is hard on batteries."

The President took the phone and punched in,

- MARC HERE
- RT [ROGER THAT] YOU LL BE MET AT THE BORDER. AF 1 ON STANDBY
- NO AF 1. SEND SMALL JET RIGHT TO HIGHGATE
- WILL DO
- YOU AND JANE BE ON THAT PLANE
- RT, I LL HAVE GREEN MOUNTAIN BOYS TAIL YOU TO DC
- ANY WORD ON MORRIS
- NEGATIVE. MRS. MORRIS WANTS TO TALK W/YOU ABOUT IT, CURIOUS
- IS AMELIE OK
- SPENDING NIGHT ON PATRICK DOING FINE. WILL MOVE HER TO ANDREWS

The President was entering a question about the call to Prime Minister Suko, but was stopped by a red battery symbol momentarily lighting up the dying phone. The President handed it back to Jim. "Well, that was short. They're sending a jet to Franklin County Airport to pick us up. No word on the autopsy. Amélie is staying on Patrick AFB."

The First Lady asked, "Where is she staying on the base? Who's with her?"

"Didn't get that far. She's fine. And, ah, the Vermont Air Guard's jets will be escorting us back to DC." A momentary lump in the President's throat delayed him from saying anything further.

Brian was looking at his phone and saw several text messages from his sister. Martin noticed and quickly ordered, "Don't answer any of those yet. In fact, shut it off."

"But she's asking if we're okay? I got to let her know."

"NEGATIVE," Martin ordered. "Washington will let her know you're okay. One blip out of that phone and the whole world will know where we are. Then we *won't* be okay."

The President quietly said, "Gabe's all over it, Brian" – then a wave of his hand signaled 'shut it down.' Brian complied.

Back at the White House, Gabe once again gathered the staff to tell them about his brief contact with the President. After telling them that the President wanted a small jet to pick him up, Gabe pointed at Jane and said, "You and I will be on that Lear."

Jane nodded and asked, "Is there anything in particular I should bring?"

"He'll want the latest and he's a 'show me the papers' kind of person, so if you have any documents from the Japanese – messages, communications of any kind – bring them. Bring the appropriate maps, too. Do we have anything yet from the Chinese or Russians?"

"Interestingly both governments are acting like this never happened. The Russians must be following the situation minute by minute and formulating several contingency plans." Shaking her head, she added, "The Chinese must be in total disbelief. I can only imagine the chaos in Beijing right now."

"And bring whatever intel you have on the actual bomb. Everything we got," Gabe added.

Jane said, "That's an issue. The Agency is willing to brief us, but providing actual documents – at least to me anyway – is out of the question."

"I'll take care of it," Gabe said.

"How much time do we have before we need to leave for Andrews?" she asked.

"Well, let's look." Gabe glanced at the Google map and guessed, "I think we'll be leaving for Andrews in an hour."

"I'll be back in an hour," and with that Jane left the room to meet with her staff.

Gabe swung toward Tim. "Get me the CIA director on secure voice. Please."

Moments later Tim handed Gabe the phone. "Hello, Derek, Gabe Arnold here. What do you have for analysis on the nuke that landed in Japan?"

The CIA director replied, "The Japanese provided a complete description, photos, everything. The initial assessment is that the detonator wasn't electronically configured correctly."

"The President has asked me to be on the plane that's going to Vermont to pick him up. I'll need the photos and written analysis – he'll be expecting it."

"Well Gabe, I can't release those documents. When the new President gets into the city here, I can bring them over."

"Derek, I can't tell you how imperative it is to have that material when he gets on the plane. It'll be the first thing he'll ask for."

Derek interrupted with a slightly raised voice. "First of all, all the material given to us was highly caveated, caveats I have to respect. Second of all, I can't be sure he took the oath of office as President yet, so I'm going to have to wait. That's it."

Gabe was getting pissed. "Well, in the first place the Japanese are expecting us to take action against the North Koreans. Certainly they expect the President to have access to the information they provided, caveats or not. Secondly, the President did take the oath."

Again he was interrupted. "Yeah, in Canada, by a Canadian. How legal is that?"

"And he will retake the oath at his home in Vermont, before he sees any documents."

Derek boldly replied, "Fine, and right after he takes the oath he'll be on his way to D.C. And I'll be at the White House with everything we have."

Gabe barked, "Derek, President Grégoire doesn't like the CIA, never did. He always thought the CIA acted far too unilaterally without nearly enough oversight. Remember he's worked with you guys before. So I don't want to be a prick about this, but if the Japanese material, every bit of it, isn't in my hands by the time I get on the President's plane – in less than 90 minutes – I can 95 percent assure you that the first official act of the new President of the United States will be to replace the CIA director – at my recommendation. So you got a choice to make. When the President joins me on the plane, do I say 'Here's what the CIA has on the bomb,' or do I say 'Sorry, Mr. President, Windgo refused to give it to me, said something about not believing you were the President yet, and some bullshit about caveats.'"

There was a very long pause. Gabe waited.

Windigo finally said, "But you *are* going to be a prick. Alright. I'll have it in a pouch for you at Andrews."

"Thank you, Derek. Respectfully, I have other arrangements to make." Both hung up without another word.

Gibble and Houseman were quietly staring at Secretary Arnold, causing a little redness to show up in his face. Gabe told them, "He really doesn't like the CIA. He had to work with them back in his Air Force days in Europe. Hated them. I'm not sure he'd have fired him though. The important thing is, I'm getting the material."

Tim broke out a curt smile. "Indeed, Sir. I wish Secretary Rikes could have heard that. I don't think anyone distrusts the CIA more than she does. And she has to provide most of their cover."

Moving on, Gibble asked, "Is anyone else supposed to be on the plane with you two?"

Gabe replied, "Jane and I were the only two the President asked for."

Gibble pointed out, "There's going to be hordes of media there. People from the press office should also go, maybe Paul himself and some of his staff. Are you okay making that call?"

Gabe hesitated as another thought occurred to him. "Tim, would you know where Speaker Glinko is at this moment?"

Tim replied, "I'm sure I can find out." Gabe nodded and Tim picked up the phone.

Gibble asked, "What you got in mind?"

Gabe was wondering about inviting the Speaker on the plane to Vermont. It would isolate him from his party and make it difficult for anyone to plan a constitutional coup, but he wasn't going to say that out loud and especially not to Gibble. He simply replied, "Just trying to think ahead."

Moments later Tim advised, "Speaker Glinko is in San Diego attending his grandmother's funeral. He's expected back in the city by tomorrow noon."

That settled the question in Gabe's mind. He turned to Gibble saying, "Yes. Paul should send people up there now, and he can come with Jane and me on the Lear."

"So why not the big bird?" Gibble asked.

"Probably because it can't land at Franklin County. It's small, no tower or anything. They'll probably have to use trucks to light the runway. In fact, we better make sure we can put a Lear down on that tarmac. It's a short runway."

Gibble asked, "If it's that unsafe, maybe we shouldn't use it?"

Gabe replied, "I'll check. But the President specifically said 'Franklin County' so we're going to do our best to make that happen."

Gibble was working things out on the map and asked, "I was thinking of flying the President's limo to Burlington to securely transport him from his home to the Airport. If Franklin County is that close, is it worth the trouble?"

Gabe looked at the map. "Probably not. What are we talking, two country miles? I know the President wouldn't want us to spend the money – but under the circumstances, maybe we should."

"You need to decide now if we're going to get it done in time."

Gabe decided. "Negative on flying the limo out, but if we have to fly into Burlington the limo goes too."

Turning to General Chaffee, Gabe said, "Milt, notify the Vermont Air Guard about the arrival. Ask them who's in charge of the runway at Franklin County and if we can put a Lear down there. And ask if they can provide an escort for the presidential aircraft back to DC – I'm presuming that will be a yes on the escort."

General Chaffee answered, "I got Colonel Swift already on it."

* * *

As Bruno was leading the way through Repentigny, Quebec, two white police cars suddenly dashed out from a U-turn, just in front of the motorcade. The First Lady noticed them and asked, "Who are they?" The SUV driver turned his head slightly toward the back and pronounced, "C'est la Police Montée, Madame." Sûreté John turned to face the President and added, "The Mounties. Dose are der cars. Dere' going to be lots more of dem." They were in the nick of time too, because Repentigny was the line where the snow was changing to freezing rain and there wasn't much snow left for Sylvain to scoop into the passing lane. His followers could see blood. They were greatly disappointed that the RCMP vehicles, with all their lights flashing and roof signs up, took over the passing and breakdown lanes. It was starting to look like a real presidential motorcade.

Just two miles later the entourage met a rolling roadblock of four Montreal City snowplows escorted by more police cars. The President's entourage was guided through the rolling roadblock, and Sylvain's followers were all diverted off the 40 at the next exit. Now the highway belonged only to the President.

As the motorcade approached the Lafontaine Tunnel, the escort vehicles repositioned themselves for the three-lane entrance like choreographed dancers moving precisely on cue. Once through the tunnel everyone danced back into their original protective positions. The motorcade passed the exit for Hwy 20-north, much to the disappointment of the President. He had hoped to get one more view of the Montreal nighttime skyline. They sped on toward the exit for Hwy 30-north, then on to Hwy 10 eastbound where the rolling roadblock reconfigured for two lanes of travel. They were now officially around Montreal.

When the President saw the sign for the L'Acadie River, he knew the turnoff for Hwy 35-south was just a couple miles away. The President said to his wife, "We should be at the border in less than an hour now."

It was Martin in the back seat who first thought he heard the sound of an approaching aircraft. As it got closer, everyone recognized the thumpa-thumpas of a helicopter. It maintained an altitude of 1000 feet but was clearly following the motorcade. The President said, "That's a news chopper, isn't it?" Sûreté John confirmed it was a Montreal traffic reporter who was called in to catch up on the action. Jim commented, "Well it was only a matter of time. Actually, I'm surprised we made it this far without the media catching up to us."

Sûreté John informed everyone in the SUV that "the RCMP has made contact with the chopper and warned them to keep their distance. They've also enlisted the chopper pilot to keep us abreast of unusual activity. They'll be with us to the border."

They were now passing through St. Jean Sur Richelieu, a city near and dear to Marc's heart. This is where his grandmother used to live, the only grandparent he ever knew. The old road went right by her house, something else he'd like to see one more time. But a new section of Hwy 35 was finally finished, and it took the motorcade away from the old farm and directly south for the border. Had the sun been up, the beautiful view of the snow covered mountains of Jay, Vermont, and Sutton, Quebec, could have been a nice trade-off for missing the sight of Mémère's house. But a January sunrise was still hours away.

⋆ ⋆ ⋆

At the White House, Paul Chapel was watching a TV monitor in disbelief. Out of the corner of his eye he saw Gibble, and without taking his eyes off the monitor grabbed Gibble's sleeve and said, "Look at this!" There on the monitor was aerial coverage of the President's motorcade on its way to the U.S. border. The darkness of the night made it difficult to recognize at first, but when it passed under street lights the six snowplows and seven police cars were discernible.

"Better find Gabe," Gibble said.

In seconds Gabe was trotting toward the monitor. Gibble said to him, "Check this out. The Canadian announcer just said that this is the new U.S. President rushing back to the United States."

Gabe exclaimed, "You're shittin' me! Where are they?"

Paul replied, "All the announcer mentioned was they were heading toward the border at Philipsburg, Quebec."

Gibble added, "The RCMP just confirmed they're now south of Iberville. They said the roads are glare ice and they've had to really slow down."

"What station is this?" Gabe asked.

Other than the fact it was coming out of Montreal, Paul wasn't sure. But he added, "It's just a matter of minutes before it will be on every major network on TV."

The three men watched for another minute or two, then Paul said he better get to the press room. Gabe advised, "No sense denying it but we don't have to provide details. Let the media step all over each other with their own speculation." As an afterthought he added, "Put somebody in charge of the press room and get right back here; we have to leave for Andrews." Turning to Gibble, he asked, "Snowplows?"

Gibble smiled and unwrapped a cigar. Rolling the Romeo and Julieta through his left-hand fingers he chuckled, "Yeah. It's a hell of a setup. They're on the southbound lanes, two police cars in the lead, three snowplows behind them, blocking the two travel lanes and the breakdown lane; I assume the President is in the big SUV, police vans on both sides of him, followed by three more snowplows and more police cars." Pointing the cigar at the screen he said, "Got to hand it to the Kanucks, that's what I call a rolling fortress." But his smile completely disappeared when Gabe said, "And with only one Secret Service agent. We owe the Canadians big for this. The snowplows must slow things down?"

Gibble said, "Yeah but they're moving and they're spreading sand." His mood was picking back up as he added, "You better get your ass over to Andrews. They'll be at the border soon."

Again ignoring Gibble's crass statement, Gabe just walked away to find Jane.

Within minutes Gabe, Jane and Paul were briskly walking toward Gabe's staff car. When they were all aboard, the three-vehicle security team sped toward Suitland Parkway and Andrews Air Force Base. They rushed through all the security checkpoints and right out onto the apron where a Lear was warming up its high-pitch engines. Gabe got out of the car and scanned around for someone from CIA. Suddenly two men approached him, one handing him a hardened briefcase. When Gabe extended his hand in thanks, the other man clamped a handcuff around his wrist! The cuff was attached to a chain which secured the briefcase to Gabe's arm.

"You better be kidding me. Take this off NOW!"

"Sorry Secretary Arnold, if we take the cuff off the case stays with us. Do you want the key to the case?"

Gabe opened his hand, this time keeping it close to his waist. The key was pressed into his hand and the two men left as quickly as they came.

In minutes the Lear was lifting off. Once in the air, Gabe tried the key he was given to see if it would unlock the handcuff. It didn't come close. Jane was thinking of something clever to say but Gabe interjected, "If Derek thinks this shit's funny…"

Seeing how thoroughly irritated Gabe was, Jane decided to keep her comment to herself.

There was one other passenger on the plane, quietly ordered there by Gabe himself: Colonel Lucy Bessette, U.S. Air Force, carrying the bags with the keys to America's nuclear arsenal.

The President's entourage reached the end of Hwy 35, and it was now only 11 miles of county road to Philipsburg. Ms. Fernande Owens, the director of the Port of Entry at Philipsburg, came in to personally supervise what certainly will be an event watched around the entire world.

On the U.S. side authorities had closed both roads and all entry lanes approaching the border. Owens wanted to block all lanes on the Canadian side, too, but didn't have the vehicles. A southbound 53-foot tractor-trailer, covered in ice, was the only vehicle left in the inspection area. She was told it had stalled and the driver wasn't able to restart the engine until just now. She walked out to the driver and using her native French told him he wasn't going anywhere, all the roads were closed. He replied in English. She reverted to her Ontario English and once again told him the truck was not going anywhere. "But I have a favor to ask you. If you back your truck across all the incoming lanes, I will see to it that you will be the first vehicle to go through when the port reopens." After asking a lot of questions, none of which could be answered, the driver finally agreed. He had little choice. After the truck was angled as directed, engine in idle, Owens told him, "Come inside. I'll show you where you can watch history going by."

The presidential motorcade was now reaching the summit of a hill just a couple hundred yards from the port. The spot affords a complete view of both the Canadian and U.S. Ports of Entry and the quarter-mile of 'no man's land' in between. As his SUV crested the hill, the startled President said, "Look at that, there's hundreds of flashing lights!" In fact there were police and border vehicles everywhere, all flashing every light they had.

As the President's SUV slowed, at least a dozen Canadian officers ran alongside of it and guided it to a stop at the granite post that marks the U.S.-Canadian border. Sûreté John jumped out of the front seat and put both hands on the President's door handle. Instantly officers from both countries surrounded the vehicle. Another green SUV pulled up beside them, leaving eight feet between the two vehicles. Surging media crews from both countries pushed and shoved, ready to injure each other to get closer, but they were held back by heavily armed Border Patrol Tactical Team agents. When all was ready, a Secret Service agent asked Sûreté John to open the door, which he did – proudly.

The President slowly stepped out, then helped Leonie. Jim and Brian slid out after them. Immediately the President and First Lady were surrounded by five Secret Service agents, one of them urging the President to move quickly into the other SUV. The President recognized it as the car used to transport the governor of Vermont, a two-year-old Lincoln Navigator. He looked up and saw two Border Patrol helicopters hovering at about 500 feet, and dozens of helmeted officers on the roof of the port building, all armed to the teeth. The sea of flashing police lights was now almost blinding. He nodded to the Secret Service agent and said, "We've had a long ride, let us stretch a second." Spreading his fingers away from his hips, the President added, "Don't worry; this looks like the safest place in the world right now."

Reporters were shouting questions from all directions. The President didn't have to ignore them, they were all yelling over each other – in two languages. But when one reporter managed to break through the barricade of officers, a BORTAC agent jacked a round into his 12-gauge pump shotgun, a skin-crawling clattering noise everyone recognizes. The reporter stopped in his tracks and was arrested by two Vermont State troopers.

Realizing the situation was getting very difficult to control, the President gently guided his wife into the waiting Lincoln. Brian jumped into the back seat again, this time with two Secret Service agents. The President recognized the driver, a Vermont State trooper who had chauffeured him when he was governor. As the vehicle started moving forward past a solid line of officers and police vehicles, the President pushed the button to lower his window but it was locked. "Hey Butchy, unlock the windows."

Butch said, "Sure, Mr. Governor." The shotgun riding Secret Service agent cringed, but he knew this was the President's turf and wouldn't be able to countermand the President. The President said hello to several officers he recognized and somberly thanked them for their help. When he saw the port director he tried to apologize for all the rigmarole his arrival had caused. The only thing the port director heard was 'sorry.' He managed to get off a curt salute which the President unfortunately didn't see. The vehicle began to speed up and the President's window glided closed.

"Home, Butch," the President ordered.

"On the way, Sir. Twelve minutes."

The President looked out and saw that he was entirely surrounded by police vehicles. They were even paralleling him in the closed lanes of I-89 north and the adjacent U.S. Route 7. He thought aloud, "Wow, what the hell caused all this?"

Noting that Brian was banging away on his cell phone, the President drew his phone and dialed his sister, and when she picked up he said, "Anna!"

Flabbergasted, she exclaimed, "Yes! Where are you?"

"Coming into Swanton. Can you call the other sisters and tell them that if they want to be there when I retake the oath they need to be at the house quick, in less than an hour."

"I'll call them right away," she anxiously replied.

Next, the President called Gabe. "Where are you?"

"On final for Franklin County Airport, should be on the ground in five."

"Good, who's with you?"

"Jane and Paul."

"Alright, I'll ask the Secret Service to send a car over to get you. You can be here to witness the oath."

"Well Marc, ah, Mr. President, I'm sure somebody can give us a ride."

The President explained, "There's no taxi stand there. I'll send someone – they'll be able to get you right through all the security. And man, they sure went overboard with protection – we're in the middle of a rolling Fort Knox."

By now the Lear was low enough for Gabe to see the massive glow of flashing red, blue and white lights moving into Swanton. Gabe said, "Yeah. Well, everybody's kind of wound up, you know, with the back-to-back events."

"Okay, we're coming into the village, see you shortly."

The motorcade slowed to pass through a roadblock at Spring Street and Kane Avenue. Moments later the Lincoln was turning into the Canada Street driveway. The President stepped out to a group of waiting federal agents – Secret Service, FBI, Homeland Security Investigations, even a few from ATF – just about every federal officer available for 200 miles. In just four steps he was on the porch he was so familiar with. He entered through the kitchen door, passed through the dining room, and into the splendid living room. The red marble and double-mantle brick fireplace was adorned with black and white pictures of his parents. The lower mantle was simply decorated with a carved antique wooden clock with matching candlesticks, a wedding present from long ago. Leonie went straight up to the master bedroom. For just a few moments Marc was alone. Getting closer to his father's picture he said softly, "Well Dad, I should have listened to you." The moment caused Marc to think about the time he told his father he was going to run for governor of Vermont. He clearly remembered Dad's reply: "I hope you stay out of that stuff."

A Secret Service agent came in and asked, "Mr. President, they want to set up for the oath, may we let them in?"

The President took a breath, lowered his head, and replied, "Sure."

Two of Paul's staffers came in and saw the President in front of the grand fireplace. One asked, "Sir, would you like to take the oath here in front of the fireplace?"

The President slowly turned to the aide and said, "Yes, that'll be fine." He solemnly looked back at the top mantle, "But do not remove anything from the mantels. Nothing." After a few more moments of reflection he turned back to the staffer and said, "Open those two large sliding doors to the parlor." When they did they found a beautifully furnished sitting room with a bay window looking out onto Canada Street. The President said, "You can find some folding chairs in the closet. There won't be enough for everybody. I'm sure the others won't mind standing as this will be short."

⋆ ⋆ ⋆

There was an unusual figure standing in the Burlington Airport control tower – Bird Colonel Steven Swift, Commander of the Vermont Air National Guard. A no-nonsense kind of officer who did two tours in

Afghanistan. He was there to oversee the arrival of the Lear in Swanton, its departure, and the launching of the six Green Mountain Boys F-35s that would accompany Air Force One back to Washington. As he was picking out a stool to sit on, he heard a call on the controller's radio: "This is Special Air Mission 51. We're on the tarmac at Franklin County." The controller responded, "Roger that, SAM 51."

Two Border Patrol vehicles pulled up to that Lear, and once Gabe, Jane, Paul and Colonel Bessette were all belted in, the cars sped toward Swanton, red and blue lights flashing. After easing through the roadblock at Broadway and First Street, the vehicles pulled up to the President's residence.

Marc had already changed into a suit and was standing in the parlor. He smiled when he saw Paul, Jane and his friend Gabe come in. They all greeted him as "Mister President," and each, in turn, expressed how glad they were of his safe arrival. Marc spied the pouch locked to Gabe's wrist and asked, "What's in the bag?"

Gabe got closer to Marc and told him of the contents. Both decided it shouldn't be opened now. Then Gabe asked, "Can we get the video of the inauguration in Canada – right away?"

Marc answered, "Brian should have it – I'll get him."

Brian walked into the room with his camera; he was still in his Yamaha snowmobile shirt and jeans. Paul asked if he could take the camera and extract the video. After getting a nod from his dad, Brian handed it over saying, "I haven't had a chance to make any copies. You are holding the one and only original." Paul replied, "We'll take good care of it," then casually handed it to one of his staffers. Brian pointed a finger at the staffer and cautioned, "Take *damn* good care of it."

Gabe gave Marc a quick explanation on the deal they made with CBC, leaving out – for now – the part about the First Lady giving an interview.

Paul, noting that Brian was not yet dressed for the occasion, asked, "Do you have a suit to put on?" Brian explained, "My wife apparently didn't get my text about bringing my suit. So what I have on is it." His father looked him over and said, "Well I can fix you up with a shirt and tie, but I don't have a coat or pants to fit you."

Paul took his suit coat off and said, "Try this on." Brian slid it on and stood there with his arms half outstretched. Paul observed, "It'll work if you don't button it. Okay, here's what we're doing. Brian, get a shirt and tie.

You'll stand behind the podium so that only your upper body will show to the cameras. After you administer the oath" – then turning to the President – "Mr. President, you will kiss your wife, then take a few steps toward your guests to accept congratulations. The cameras will follow you. Brian, you exit to the right. Then, Mr. President, you can return to the podium for a few words."

The President agreed but asked that things get in motion because as soon as his family arrived he wanted to take the oath – and get to Washington. With that, Gabe broached the subject of an approximate departure time. After taking a moment to consider, the President announced, "We leave this house in 45 minutes. Make it happen." Gabe excused himself to make notifications. Colonel Swift was among the first to get the word.

Various members of the press were near the porch and trying to get in. Paul greeted them and began laying out parameters. "First, the President will not have time to take any questions." The press was not happy – and there was more to come. Paul added, "Since we don't have a metal detector, to get inside you'll have to be searched. No cell phones, cameras or electronics of any kind will be allowed inside. Everything will be fed real-time to the video bus, and the official photographers will make photos available to you immediately."

Cell phones and microphones started coming out of pockets and bags. While they didn't like the rules, none of the press was about to give up the chance to personally watch the President take the oath of office. Each eagerly lined up for their search hoping to get the closest spot possible.

Inside, the President was now alone in his 'office,' immediately off the living room. In his childhood, the room was a playroom and later his temporary bedroom. He recalled how on one particular Christmas Eve, he and two of his sisters sat on his bed and sang Christmas carols – at the top of their lungs. His mother came and shut the door but otherwise didn't discourage the singing/screaming.

Years ago, when he was elected governor, he turned the room into an office and furnished it with a large, solid-maple desk – at which he was now seated. He was here to collect his thoughts about what he wanted to say after taking the oath. Not a speech per se, but he knew he had to address the nation, however briefly.

Another memory came to mind – this was the room he was sitting in when he heard a TV bulletin that Lee Harvey Oswald had just been shot.

He recalled running into the living room in time to see the first replay of the actual shooting. He remembered the terrified look on Oswald's face, eyes closed, mouth wide open, arms trying to protect his torso. A tender youth at that time, Marc had never seen anyone shot before, for real.

Marc took out a pen and, in outline fashion, wrote:

Condolences to Morris family
America lost a great President, leader, etc
Alice lost her hero
Will personally monitor investigation
North Korea's attack on Japan w/deadly nuke
Unprovoked
Obviously the action of a lunatic
Have authorized further military reactions and movements
Earlier ordered the destruction of any new NK missiles
Spoken with Cabinet by phone – all standing by at the White House
Will have more to report in the next few hours
First took oath in Canada, after consulting w/chief justice
Thank the Canadian government for all their help, especially SQ
Immediately departing for the White House

While looking over his notes, he heard a knock on the door. Leonie stuck her head in and announced, "They're ready."

Marc folded his notes and slid them into his shirt pocket, figuring he'd wing the rest as he knew he was not good at endings. He rose to his feet and drew his wife inside the room and closed the door. He gave her a kiss and whispered, "I'm really sorry about this. It was never the plan. I was supposed to retire, travel, we were going to enjoy life."

But in his youth Marc thought that someday he could be President. The boyhood notion went away with adulthood. And after serving as governor, he'd had enough of politics and all its pitfalls. He often wondered how he was ever talked into running for Vice President.

And now here he was …

Leonie could almost read his mind. She took a deep breath, hesitating a moment, not really sure what to say. "Yes, well, you better come in – everybody's waiting."

He took her by the hand. Before opening the door, he twisted over to his bookshelf and pulled out a book entitled *The Constitution of the United States Explained.* They walked out together. He took his place facing Brian, handed the book to his wife and raised his right hand. Taking the unrehearsed cue, Leonie held the book out so her husband could rest his left hand on it.

Brian began, "I do solemnly swear…"

It was all over in 25 seconds.

There was another kiss for his wife and a handshake with Brian. The President then handed the book to him and whispered, "I'll sign this for you later." Brian looked somber and about to cry. The President took a few steps toward his sisters, giving each a warm hug. Eva whispered in his ear, "I hope this is what you want."

He stepped back to the podium and began his remarks. "I want to express my deepest, deepest sorrow to Alice Morris and the Morris family…"

11

OUTSIDE, IN A HEALTH CENTER PARKING LOT DIAGONALLY across the street from the now historic Canada Street residence, a state trooper, Skip Richards, was working his dog around the TV trucks. Tippy showed a lot of interest in one particular truck so Skip let her off the leash. She went wild running back and forth the length of the truck, but no alert. The trooper called over a Secret Service agent and explained that his dog was quite excited about the truck.

The agent said, "I see that. Is your dog trained for drugs or explosives?"

"Both. She sits for drugs, barks for explosives."

The agent could see Tippy's excitement. He looked over the unoccupied truck and noticed it wasn't running. All the other network trucks were running or had generators running to power the equipment. The agent noted the truck was from Montreal, recorded the company name and license plate, and called in for the usual checks. While waiting, he called over a Border Patrol Canine unit. The second dog, Jay, reacted much the same as Tippy, but Jay's wildly wagging tail showed more interest in the driver's door while Tippy was keen about the rear cargo door.

Skip climbed the two steps to the cargo door and pounded four or five knocks. There was no response. He said, "They may have some left-over weed in there."

"Maybe," replied the agent, in an otherwise occupied tone. Then looking toward the Border Patrol agent, he asked, "Can you check when this rig came through the border?"

"Sure." Three minutes later, he reported, "The truck came through

Champlain, New York, at 12:06 this morning." The Secret Service agent's right eye tightened as he said, "That was well before anyone was supposed to know the President was on his way here."

Skip added, "Yeah, and the engine is cooled off, so it's been sitting here quite a while."

The agent ordered, "Run this truck in every system we have, DHS, FBI, State, all of them. Skippy, call this company, CFTV. Ask them about this truck. The phone number's right on the door." He then barked into his radio. Less than two minutes later, Supervisory Secret Service Agent C.J. Davis arrived on the scene. He was briefed by the first agent and was informed about the checks being made. C.J. asked, "Where's the driver?"

Skip loudly interrupted, "The company claims they dropped the truck off at a garage late yesterday afternoon. It was in for an oil change and check engine light. And they said they have no reporters in the U.S. at this moment."

"We need to get the President out of here," C.J. ordered. "But we have to be careful because we don't know who this asshole is or where he is." The first Secret Service agent started reciting a series of codes over the radio.

The Border Patrol agent said to C.J., "There was one reporter who did not go in the residence. Apparently he didn't want to give up his phone."

C.J. said, "Or he didn't want to be searched. Where is he?"

The Border Patrolman brought C.J. to the edge of the parking lot and nodded across the street toward a man right in front of the residence. He was holding a microphone in his hand and talking toward a tripod-mounted news camera.

C.J. said, "Come with me, we'll pay him a visit." While walking over, C.J. instructed the Border Patrolman, "Just make nice, don't get too close and don't spook him." As the pair approached the reporter, the President's SUV suddenly started up. As casually as he could, C.J. called out to the reporter, "Hey, we're going to switch out vehicles here, you may have to move." The reporter didn't interrupt his soliloquy but made eyes that he understood.

C.J. and the Border Patrol agent kept moving toward and into the house. The SUV slowly moved around the back. Inside C.J. found that everyone had been moved to the office, as far away as possible from the front of the house.

The President himself demanded to know what was going on.

Agent Davis motioned the President into the bathroom; Gabe went with them. After the door was closed, Davis cautiously explained his suspicions and gravely added, "I just walked past the reporter outside, and he has a lot of bulging under his winter coat, and it's not reporting equipment."

Gabe asked, "Could the driver of that truck already be in the house?"

Agent Davis said, "If he was, he would of done something by now, especially when we rushed the President out of the room. I think that if we have a dangerous person here, it's the young man outside just 15 feet from the front door – who doesn't realize what's going on inside." He let that sink in for a second or two, then with authority he ordered, "So Mr. President, let's get you and your family out of here. Now."

The President asked, "We're not overreacting?" Davis looked the President straight in the face, "No Sir." The President looked back and saw years of experience talking to him; time to follow instructions.

As the bathroom door reopened, the President himself raised his index finger to his lips and motioned everyone to follow him. There was a door on the other side of the bathroom which led to an attached shed and into the backyard. The driveway circulated around the President's house to Webster Terrace. The Lincoln was in the back, idling and waiting.

The President and his wife were to be first out and into the SUV. The First Lady resisted, "What about my brothers – they don't understand what's going on! Where will they go?"

In her Gore-Road French, the President's sister-in-law, Jacquie, told Sylvain and Bruno, "Vien avec nous autres." Then the President's sister Isabel piped in, "Don't worry, Leonie, we're going down toward the river and back up the other side, right to my house. They'll come with us. Now you go with Marc." It sounded like an order. Once the President and First Lady were aboard, the Lincoln moved to Webster Terrace thus putting a large four-apartment building between them and the residence. There was only one way out of Webster Terrace and that was onto Canada Street.

Everyone else followed a state trooper on foot to the end of Webster Terrace. There the state trooper directed the party downhill to a level area behind an old home. After a few minutes Anna said, "Isn't this where Godfrey had his chicken coop?" Isabel replied, "Yes, and I'm not standing around here freezing my frigging ass off. We just have to go up the other side and we're practically at my house. Come on." She started walking to the edge of the hill but the trooper stopped her. "We have to wait here,

Ma'am."

She snapped her head towards him and barked, "You guys might have to wait here but we don't!"

At this point, Kim, a Special Agent with Homeland Security, stepped forward. He told the trooper, "I know where she lives, I'll go with them. It'll be farther away from here and warmer." Without another word, Kim was leading Anna and Isabel, who were helping their sister Eva along, down the hill toward the river. The rest of the family followed.

Secretaries Arnold and Rikes, Sûreté John, and all the reporters waited with the trooper. The reporters were beside themselves because none of them had cameras or cell phones to record all this activity – just their pens and pads.

C.J. went back in and consulted with his fellow agents. "If he's wearing a bomb, the switch could be in his pocket or on the microphone itself." Suddenly he said, "Look, he lowered his mic and stopped talking. He knows something's up!"

"Two shots to the head. We got a sniper 20 yards away. Andrew, our best." The suggestion by a fellow Secret Service agent was clearly heard, but Davis said, "We don't have enough to warrant that. We'll have to go out there, casually, and grab both his hands before he can do anything. Anybody want to come with me?"

Rory Kidder, ATF, stepped forward. "Stay put. We'll do it." Rory knew something had to happen quickly and he was the best qualified person to get it done. He headed to the door and right behind him was his longtime partner, Ken Takahara. Before opening the door, Rory grabbed a sheet of paper left behind by one of the other reporters.

Davis said, "Wait!" Rory stopped. Davis asked, "Is everyone else out?" He was told that the reporters and the President's family were down an embankment, well away from and below a blast, if there was one. "Well shit, that's where the President should be." The original speaker assured C.J. that the President was safe from anything except a nuke.

The other officers moved to the office, which put the massive fireplace chimney between them and the street. C.J. held his place in the living room as did Skip and his dog.

C.J. gave the nod to Rory.

Rory headed through the porch and, holding the paper at head level, called to the suspect, "Hey, you're probably the only one that didn't get this press release, you want it?" He and Ken kept a steady pace and were only two steps away when the reporter put out his hand to take the paper.

Rory pounced! Driving the man to the ground, he seized his right hand and forced it over his head. Ken was a split second behind and seized the left hand. C.J. flew out to assist, and right behind him was Skip with his dog Tippy snarling and barking and just begging for the order to attack. More agents ran out to assist Kidder. One produced a needle which he drove into the struggling suspect's neck. In seconds he was unconscious but everyone maintained their firm holds. Instantly Rory produced a small, sharp knife and began to carefully cut the man's coat away, exposing a vest – holding 11 sticks of dynamite.

C.J. yelled a code into his mic; it translated to – 'Bomb, move out!' In seconds the 32-inch tires of the President's Lincoln were squealing as they hit the pavement of Canada Street. Sirens were blowing everywhere.

Gently and carefully Rory cut away at the duct tape holding everything together. He could see where the trigger wires entered the mishmash of tape. He made a gentle slice here, a careful tear there.

Agent Davis said to everyone, "Rory and I have this guy. Everybody else move away." No one moved. In seconds Rory announced, "Okay, I got it." Gently he pulled away a flap of several layers of tape revealing two 9-volt batteries. Very carefully – and one at a time – he disconnected the batteries by snipping the wires to them, and gently pulled them out and away. He then cut four other wires to ensure the circuitry was disrupted.

Rory said, "We're good now. Even if he had a back-up power source, it's all disconnected. Man, this thing is as crude as they come." He now felt safer about cutting away more clothing and tape, but he wanted to keep as much intact as possible for the forensic bomb examiners.

Looking things over he explained, "This dynamite is the type they use in quarries. The markings are in French and English, so it was probably stolen in Quebec. At least it's stable, not like some of the shit these idiots use." He looked at Davis and added, "Be careful with the truck – could have more explosives in it, and it will be loaded with evidence. Watch for booby traps." C.J. Davis stood up; his first order was to evacuate all the neighbors. Secondly, the officers around the truck were ordered to keep it secured but not to touch anything. And, "Call the Mounties – they're going to be heavily involved."

* * *

Colonel Swift suddenly jumped to his feet. He yelled, "Every aircraft within 300 miles: TO THE GROUND!" The supervising air traffic controller protested, "That would include Boston, New York, Newark." Swift yelled even louder, "GODDAM do it! They found a bomb! The only planes allowed in the air right now are those six F-35s." The controllers went to work. In four minutes the F-35s were rolling down the runway for takeoff, two at a time.

Swift was on the phone with the Green Mountain Boys: "How many more birds can you put in the air?"

"Our three backups can be airborne in 10 minutes."

"Do it!"

The 2.6 miles from the Canada Street residence to the waiting Lear took only three minutes. Butch knew the way. The Secret Service whisked the President and First Lady onto the waiting jet, then started securing the hatch. The President intervened, "We can't go until Arnold and Rikes are on this plane."

"We have orders, Sir, and they are to get you to Washington."

The President said, "Orders, eh?"

He walked up to the cockpit where a lieutenant was guarding the door. The Commander-In-Chief greeted him nicely and said he'd like to meet the pilots. "Yes, Sir." The astonished lieutenant punched in a code, swiped his ID, and the cockpit door opened.

The President saw a surprised Air Force lieutenant colonel and a major at the controls. He shook the major's hand first; the major nodded and said, "Mr. President." Then the President turned to Lieutenant Colonel Lester Watterson and took his hand saying, "Looks likes the weather is breaking up."

"Yes, Mr. President."

"Yes, but we're not taking off until you get directions from me personally. Shall we consider that an order."

"Yes Sir, Mr. President."

The President simultaneously tapped both men on the shoulders and said, "Thank you, gentlemen, for coming up here to get me. I'll personally let you know when we're ready to go. Then it'll be full afterburners."

With that he retreated to the passenger area and told the Secret Service,

"This plane isn't moving until I say so."

Back on Spring Street, the President's sisters and entourage had made it to Isabel's residence. There were two bathrooms in her home and both now had lines waiting.

One thing Franklin County, Vermont, has plenty of is Border Patrol agents. So it was no surprise that it was the Border Patrol once again who transported Arnold, Rikes, Chapel, and the colonel to the President's waiting aircraft. Once aboard Gabe informed the President about the bomb. To say Marc was shocked would be a gross understatement. He stared at Gabe for a few seconds, then asked somberly, "Eleven sticks of dynamite?" Gabe just nodded. The President turned his head, lowered his chin and raised his eyebrows in the direction of the First Lady, and said, "Let's keep that to ourselves for the moment."

"Yes, Sir."

After a few questions, and a quick but reassuring phone call to his son, the President walked forward and gave the crew the okay for takeoff. Everyone took their seats and buckled in. The security vehicles moved away from the jet and pointed their headlights to light up the dark runway.

The engines of the Lear grew ear-busting loud as it turned to taxi toward the north end of the runway. The pilots took it right to the edge of the pavement, wanting to make sure they had every inch of runway 19 to lift off.

But there it sat with the engines back in idle.

Marc and Gabe presumed the pilots were going through their takeoff checklist but the wait was getting longer than expected. It wasn't like the Lear was ninth in line for takeoff or something. Arnold suddenly pulled off his safety belt, double-timed it to the cockpit and grabbed the intercom. He couldn't believe his ears. BTV air traffic control was not allowing them to take off. The only aircraft allowed in the air were nine F-35s. "And us, those idiots!" Gabe closed his eyes to think, then grabbing his phone he started through his contacts, praying he had Swift listed.

Colonel Swift felt his phone vibrating but was so busy giving orders he wasn't going to answer. Fortunately he looked to see who was calling. Seconds later he yelled at the controllers, "Let the Lear go in Swanton, that's the goddam PRESIDENT!" Not only was his face raging-red angry, so was his bald head. Apparently the pilot of the Lear had forgotten to change his call sign from Special Air Mission 51 to *Air Force One.*

Gabe barely had time to retake his seat when the Lear's engines were winding up to near full throttle again. The brakes were released and in about 30 seconds the wheels left the tarmac. Marc and Gabe recognized the familiar bumping and thumps of the landing gear folding away inside and the closing shields. In minutes they were at 10,000 feet and still climbing – now en route to Andrews AFB, Maryland. In moments they were swarmed by F-35s.

When the seatbelt sign went off the First Lady was first to get up to go visit the ladies' room. The President also rose and waited for her. When she came out he gave her a long, tender hug and said, "Everybody is all right, even the suspect," tactfully avoiding the word 'bomber.' But she could read his face like a book. "He had a bomb, didn't he?" she asked. He bowed once and turned his face away from hers. She wiped away a few tears. He took her hand as they walked to their seats. They sat there quietly. After a few moments she asked, "Everyone is okay, really?" Marc nodded. She barely choked out, "You're not just telling me that?"

He replied, "The suspect is unconscious from a sedative they gave him but he'll be okay, too" – but he thought to himself, 'until I have him hung by the balls.'

After a few minutes he softly asked, "Will you be okay for a few minutes while I talk with Gabe?" She only nodded and slowly released his hand.

The new President finally had the opportunity to discuss matters with two of his top advisers. He, Gabe and Jane moved to a rear office area. Marc leaned forward in his seat and demanded, "Well SHIT! What other surprises do you have for me?"

"Mr. President, nobody knew there was an assassination threat," Gabe said.

The President barked, "Somebody must have known something! I haven't seen this much security since Trump was inaugurated."

Hesitating, Gabe replied, "All the security is the result of President Morris' death and the attack on Japan. If we had known about the slightest threat, we would have never let you go to the residence. You can probably thank Director Gibble for the additional security. And it was a Vermont trooper and his dog who led them to the guy with the bomb."

"Okay, I've been President for what, five or six hours. And I've already had enough of it to last me a lifetime, a fucking short lifetime." Then the President was silent for a few moments. Finally, looking at Gabe, he sharply said, "So let's see what's in the goddam bag."

Gabe explained, "It's a CIA report on the nuke. I'll get it out." The pouch was finally opened and the contents laid out. The most telling document was a photo of the insides of the bomb, with CIA notations on overlays, clearly indicating it was a clone of an old Soviet nuclear warhead. The material was carefully studied by the President and the two Secretaries. The President commented, "We certainly don't think the Russians made it for the North Koreans, do we?"

Gabe agreed, "No. The Koreans got most of it right, except the detonator," somberly adding, "fortunately for Japan."

The President leaned back in his seat and lowered his chin to his chest in thought. The reality of it all – especially the fact that the whole world was counting on him to right this wrong – was taking over his mind and body. He took a deep breath, raised his head and, staring at his joined hands, cleared his mind of all thoughts. With each breath he down-counted to himself, from ten to one. When he got to one, his head lowered again. He could feel his heartbeat, sharp and strong, and remained in his mind-neutral state for about a minute.

Calmly the President collected the various documents and handed them to Gabe. While Gabe was placing them back into the bag, the President asked, "Whose idea was the handcuff?"

Gabe replied, "It wasn't mine, and the cuff is starting to chafe."

"Really." The President looked it over, called a Secret Service agent into the office, and asked him for a handcuff key. The agent handed the President his standard-issue, long shaft key. The President unlocked the cuff, much to Gabe's relief. Gabe used the occasion to inform the President of the 'discussion' he had with the CIA director, and while he was at it, he reluctantly provided the full details of the arrangement with CBC News.

The President asked, "You've been a busy man. Did we burn any other bridges?"

"No, but I'm sure I started a couple other fires."

After a moment the President asked the burning question, "So was Japan the actual target or was the missile heading toward San Francisco?"

Gabe answered, "We're still not sure, but it was likely Tokyo. Regardless of the intended target, I hesitate to say it – but *he was crazy enough* to do it once, he'll try it again." Lowering his head he added, "And this time he might get it right."

"How soon?" asked the President.

"Could be days or a couple weeks. But it won't be months," Gabe surmised.

"But we'll get it before it gets off the ground, right?"

"Yes, Sir."

Turning to Jane, the President asked, "So what was Morris putting together?"

She said, "First, he wanted to make sure that before we reacted – militarily – that we had all the appropriate confirmations: the source location of the launch, course verification, and confirmation that the weapon was, in fact, a nuke. All of those confirmations have since been made.

"He believed there was no need for an immediate response, and when the response occurred it needed to be a coalition response, getting other countries involved. He also wanted an emergency meeting at the UN. While we were discussing it he got up to go to the men's room – so we presumed. And, well … he didn't come back."

The President was silent for a few moments. Then he raised his chin and said, "Regardless of where the missile was heading, it landed in Japan. The appropriate action needs to be initiated by Japan. We can't take – and we don't want to appear to be taking the lead in responding to this … situation. It's up to the Japanese to ask for the UN meeting. Naturally, we're going to end up leading the way, militarily; but the coalition plan is not only a good idea, it's the only way to proceed."

After a pause, the President added, "This event has now made Pak everyone's problem, not just ours. China, to say the least, has as much at stake as we do, probably more. The Russians – all of Asia – and Europe … they're as scared as everyone else is right now." Pointing his finger up he added, "We're not the only ones holding emergency high-level meetings."

Turning again towards Jane, the President asked, "So the Chinese? Have they contacted anyone yet?"

Jane reluctantly reported, "Still not a word. Their ambassador is allegedly unavailable, and no one in Beijing will put our call through to an actual official, just staffers – all with the same answer, 'everybody is busy.'"

The President reacted, "Busy cleaning their shorts. Pak just put World War III on China's doorstep. I'm sure they have no idea what to do!"

Jane replied, "They have only themselves to blame, Mr. President."

The President raised his head and agreed, "Damn right. And they better figure out how to fix it and fast." Calming down by just a notch, he said, "I'm going to call Tim and have him schedule a Cabinet meeting two hours from now. Will that give us time to get to the White House?"

Gabe answered, "Yes, Mr. President. I'll have Marine Corps One waiting."

The President nodded. "Good. My message at that meeting will be to emphasize that Japan is in charge diplomatically. Now, should the North Koreans be linked to Morris' death – or to the attempt we just had in Swanton" – the President's face revealed the anger of his thoughts – *"the shit will hit the fan."*

MARINE CORPS ONE WAS IN FACT STANDING BY WHEN THE President's plane landed at Andrews. The Lear taxied as close as possible to the waiting helicopter. Marc was first down the steps closely followed by his wife. He took her hand into his left, keeping his right free to return the numerous sharp salutes he was receiving.

Once all were aboard the blades of Marine Corps One began to spin, and in what seemed like only a minute or two the chopper – with its most precious cargo – was moving forward for liftoff. Less than ten minutes later Marine Corps One was landing on the White House South Lawn with the new President and First Lady.

Mrs. Grégoire had seen the White House before and had received several private tours. But this time she was seeing the White House from an entirely different perspective. Now she saw it as the ultimate source of stress for her husband, the kind that can cripple and kill. No matter how confident, or how strong, or how resilient a person can be, the job of The President of the United States takes its toll on all those who hold the office. She could see that in just a few hours the penalties of the office were already extracting payment. But this is all the result of his choices, not hers.

She also knew that although it was a magnificent mansion, it was merely a living quarters attached to the most important government building in the world. She thought about how her husband loved the outdoors, the freshest of fresh air he experienced at his fishing camp deep in the northern woods; how he loved bouncing across steady waves on Lake Champlain; the excitement he had for a good snowstorm; and of course the thrill of a fast ride on one his snowmobiles. How will he ever endure three years here, possibly seven, and as many as 11 years? She knew that the additional time in the White House was a distinct possibility because her husband was not one to abandon a ship in trouble, and if he genuinely thought he was needed he would likely run and re-run for re-election. Perish the thought.

Her ruminations were abruptly interrupted when Marc gave her a gentle tug. The helicopter steps were down, and all eyes inside the White House were anxiously awaiting their first look at the new President of the United States. Some of them, like Tim Houseman, Ronald Gibble, and Alice Morris herself, were greatly relieved to finally lay eyes on the President and his wife, now safe and sound. And here they were, about to enter the mansion as the new occupants.

Houseman and a few staffers went outside to greet the President. General Chaffee was there to greet his boss, Gabe Arnold. Several other staffers were there, envelopes in hand, to meet Jane Rikes.

The Grégoires were led inside, and after formalities and handshakes were exchanged Houseman attempted to move the President to the business side of the building, the West Wing. They were immediately encountered by Mrs. Morris. Marc hugged her gently and told her, "Alice, there are no words to express our deepest sorrow."

Alice sobbed softly into a white hanky. Gaining her composure she said, "I'm very sorry to hear about the incident in Swanton. I've been praying for you ever since I heard the news." The President graciously thanked her for her prayers and tenderly suggested, "I'm afraid I'm going to need a lot more prayers."

"You certainly will," she agreed.

She told Marc she really needed to talk to him and asked if he could spare a few moments now. Marc turned toward Houseman, who was almost moved to tears himself. Tim said, "We can … we'll make time, Sir."

Alice led Marc and Leonie to a private sitting room and began her sorry business. "Well, first, I understand they're ready to release Leo's body from the hospital. They gave me several funeral homes to choose from but I've never had to plan a funeral. I have no idea what to do. I don't know what to ask, who to ask, what would be right, or wrong. I just don't know." She dabbed another tear before going on, "Here in the White House they're planning a huge funeral, processions and a long memorial service. And I understand they are planning to bury him in Arlington Cemetery, if that would be okay with me." She sobbed some more and cried, "I don't want him in Arlington."

Marc waited a few moments before he gently said, "Alice, funerals are just as much for the living as they are for those who have gone. Do you know what you want?"

"Well yes, I do. I don't want anything here in Washington." Suddenly her voice became stronger. "I want him to be transported as soon as possible to Kokomo, Indiana, where we can have a simple ceremony for him. No military people, no dignitaries, and no long speeches."

"I, uh, I didn't realize Leo was from Indiana?" the President asked.

"He's not. Kokomo is my hometown. And that's where I'm going to go live. With him there I'll be able to visit him every day if I want to. He'd like that." There was a pause before she added, "And when it's my turn, I can be right next to him."

Tears ran down Leonie's cheeks. She had met Alice many times during the campaign last year, and had gotten to know her well enough to recognize she was a kind, down to earth soul and always beside her husband no matter what.

The President lowered his chin even more. He said, "Alice, I'm going to make sure that everything will be just the way you want it. Nobody will pressure you for anything else. Now I'm going to get someone here, a funeral director, his name is Arthur Choinière. He'll give you all the guidance you need. He'll help you choose a funeral home and the services you want. Nothing more, nothing less."

Alice sighed. She paused some more before she had one other thing to add. "You know I said I didn't want any dignitaries – I'm afraid that includes you. I'd like to have you there. But if you come they'll lock Kokomo down. Block every street and arrest people. I don't want to do that to Kokomo."

Marc didn't have to think long to remember what they just did to Swanton, so all he could say was, "I completely understand, I truly do."

The room was silent, and Marc was thinking about the waiting Cabinet meeting. But Alice put her hand on Marc's arm and said, "Now the most important thing to tell you, only you."

Leonie rose, gently hugged Alice's shoulder and said, "I wish you peace, Alice," then quietly went toward the door. Alice looked up at her, "Oh,

Leonie, I didn't mean to offend you. You should know though, that I'm leaving this building immediately with no intentions of ever coming back. Never. I've collected my things; they're all ready to go. And Tim told me he can have someone here this afternoon to have everything else moved out. They have a suite all made up for you so you can both spend your first night here. Now, this prison is all yours." She sobbed, regretting using the word 'prison,' but it was out now. Leonie was ready to tell her there was no rush, no hurry at all … but she understood what Alice was saying, and more importantly what she wasn't saying.

After Leonie was out of the room Alice turned to face Marc directly. She twisted her lips side to side; she really didn't want to say what she had to say but now was the time. "About Leo's death. He had a quirk you should know about. He never told his doctors about it because he thought it would ruin his political career." Marc was intrigued. He just looked at her silently with eyes that said 'go on.'

"You see, sometimes when Leo sneezed his heart stopped. I understand that isn't unusual, but sometimes it wouldn't start up again. He would actually stop whatever he was doing and give himself a hard whack right in the middle of his chest. In the past his heart always started beating again.

"Yesterday during the meeting I came over to check on him. I knew he was under a lot of stress and I was worried. You know he didn't drink enough water, especially when he was under pressure. Anyway, I didn't see him – but I heard his very familiar sneeze, a loud one. When I got to him he was on the floor." She sobbed again, more intensely now. Marc moved in closer to comfort her. After a few more deep sobs she was somewhat composed.

"The North Koreans didn't get him. His heart just stopped." She broke into heavy tears. Marc waited her out.

When the tears slowed down he asked, "When was the last time his heart stopped?" More composed now, she told him, "It was at Michelle's wedding, right after we moved into the White House. He had just walked her down the aisle and was turning to join me in the first pew. He sneezed – and stopped straight up in his tracks. He looked at me with wide eyes and then gave himself a good whack. Then he just slid in next to me, like nothing ever happened. The next day I begged him to get it checked out. He wouldn't hear of it."

"And you think this is what happened yesterday, but he didn't whack himself in time?"

She replied, "Either that or the whack didn't work." She sobbed quietly. After a moment she continued, "I don't want a media frenzy about this, he doesn't deserve that. So I'm counting on you to deal with this information with prudence. Leo deserves that much."

"He certainly does. I'll handle it with the discretion it deserves." After saying the words, Marc knew that a 'media frenzy' couldn't be avoided, just delayed. So he carefully avoided making any more promises.

There was more silence. Alice broke it by telling Marc, "You have an important meeting to go to." She looked directly at him and said, "It's very important for the staff to see you in the flesh, hear your voice, and know that the new Commander in Chief is in charge." She further advised, "They're a good bunch, most of them. But Leo always said there was one or two to watch, and others with their own agendas."

Marc was now sorry that Alice was leaving the White House – he was sure her brain had plenty to pick. He knew that her husband entrusted her with information no one else had. Pillow talk was often the best medium for the exchange of frank information.

Alice gathered up her hanky and leaned forward in her chair. The tears were slowing down but her eyes were red with deep sadness. Marc said to her, "If you ever change your mind about coming to the White House, you are always welcome." She told him, "I don't think so. But you never know, we did have a lovely Christmas party last month."

"You are always invited, Alice, and you'll be the star of the show."

"Perhaps. But make no mistake, Marc" – she looked straight at him – "all eyes will always be on you. They may be diverted for a moment if they catch you dancing with a pretty girl, but they'll always go back to you."

With one more hug and a gentle handshake, Marc rose to leave.

The Chief of Staff was waiting for the President, ready to accompany him to his first Cabinet meeting. He said, "I know you must be beyond exhaustion, Mr. President. After this meeting there are three priority phone calls to return; after that the rest can wait." Tim wanted the President to get some sleep even if it was just a couple of hours. "After all you've been through, Mr. President, you really deserve the rest of the day off. But of course…" The President thanked him and said, "I doubt there will be time for a nap today."

The two men arrived at the door of the Cabinet meeting. As Houseman opened the door he announced:

"Ladies and Gentlemen ... The President."

Everyone was already standing and the room went silent. For a split second Marc was nearly overcome with emotion, but after a quick breath he walked right to the chair at the head of the table. He said, "Please, take your seats." He looked around the table and recognized most everyone, but there were a couple of faces which didn't bring in a full name. He knew everyone was waiting for him to speak and somberly he began, "Good morning. I want to thank each of you for being here, especially on short notice." After a moment he continued:

"I never thought that I, nor anyone else, would be having a meeting like this, under the circumstances our country – and the world – find ourselves in. A nuclear attack; the sudden unexplained death of the President; and a nearly successful attempt on the life of" – he paused, having a hard time to say it – "the new President. All in less than 24 hours."

Pausing to rub his hands up and down in front of his face, a sign Leonie would recognize as an indicator that Marc's thoughts were intense, the President went on, "Here we are, not just our country but all the nations in the world, still working hard to knock out the Covid virus, and now we're dealing with another threat to mankind." The President was silent for a few moments and every set of eyes in the room were now riveted to his face. "It would be easy to think that a higher authority wants to put an end to mankind, and give mother earth a chance to recover from millions of years of human occupation. But we humans keep fighting back," he turned his head and lowered his chin and said, "and we're going to do it again; with great minds and cool heads.

"Before we proceed there is a great deal of information we need to gather. Every step we take must be carefully calculated so we're going to take all the time we need. Above all, our objective will be to resolve the situation without going to war. It remains to be seen if that's possible.

"At this point in time, I think it is important to let you know what my position – the official position – of the United States government is. I know North Korea's missile could've been on its way to the U.S., but it landed in Japan. So we need to let Japan take the lead in the response. The *Japanese* must be in charge of rallying the world behind them. *They* must be the ones demanding action at the UN. We won't be behind Japan, we will be beside them in every way. And if there is a military response, the

United States will be at the forefront – doing the heavy lifting."

Dargun Yashuka, the Secretary of Education, could barely wait for the first pause to ask, "Exactly what are we willing to do, Mr. President?"

The President, somewhat taken aback by the interruption, reiterated that North Korea and 'Pak Jr.' – as the President would come to refer to him – "was everyone's problem, and if there is military action, and there probably will be, U.S. forces will have the lion's share of the action," but he gave no further details.

The President turned to again address the entire Cabinet. Gravely he pointed out, "China is a major factor, *the* major factor, in the sequence of events. We and our allies are not holding all the cards here." The President paused for reaction. Heads bobbed in agreement.

Marc sensed some uncertainty in the room. He couldn't tell if the Cabinet members were unsure about his ability to do the job, or concerned about the back-to-back events and the possibility of a major war. He felt compelled to add, "The situation with North Korea will be dealt with without nukes. Everyone can be sure of that." In a lowered voice he added, "Time is on our side. Tonight we'll all go to bed under nice warm blankets, knowing we are safe and sound. *But not so in North Korea.* Imagine what is going through the minds of their senior staff. How scared they must be. A good night's sleep isn't in their future for some time to come. They know we're coming, they just don't know when or how. And they don't know if they will survive the attack that they're certain is on the way."

After a few moments of silence the President decided he had said enough for the moment; his key message had been delivered. All he added was, "I've said it before, we have here assembled around this table the best team in the world. That is what's going to allow me to sleep tonight. That's all for now; we'll all be getting together again very soon."

The President rose and everyone jumped to their feet. As he walked toward the door he told Houseman, "I'd like Gibble, Billings, Jane, and Dr. Green in my office in ten minutes." On the way out Gabe asked the President if he wanted him at this meeting and the President replied, "That goes without saying."

Marc left the room but wasn't sure where the Oval Office was. The Vice President had an office in the White House but he was never able to use it because Morris assigned it to one of his advisors. Marc was relegated to pass his time in an office in the Executive Building; it didn't even have a view, supposedly for security reasons. He gestured to Tim to lead the way. Tim picked up on the President's cue and led him directly to the curved door of the Oval Office. On the way he told the President that Morris' effects had all been removed and the only things in the desk were pads, paper, and pens.

During the walk Gibble caught up to Gabe. "Am I about to get fired? Because if I am…" Gabe held Gibble back, stopping him in his tracks. He put his long arm around Gibble's shoulder, looked him straight in the face and said, "What did I tell you before, cowboy? If he was about to fire you, it wouldn't be in front of all these people. Just keep cool and relax."

When they got to the Oval Office Houseman opened the door for the President. Marc walked in trying to look calm and collected, but he was in awe. There was the Resolute Desk. Made in England from timbers of the HMS Resolute, the desk was a gift to President Rutherford B. Hayes. Marc wasn't emotionally ready to sit at that desk. Not yet.

Tim asked him if he wanted everyone at once. Marc said yes, and took the chair immediately in front of the desk facing the horseshoe arrangement of chairs and couch. Everyone was soon seated.

After the customary greetings the President said to Gibble, "Ron, your people did an outstanding job in Swanton. I don't have all the details, but from what I've been told the actions of some were heroic."

Gibble cleared his throat and said, "Thank you, Mr. President. Fortunately we had assistance from a lot of agencies. Clearly the people of Vermont and the State Police still think of you as their Governor simply on loan to us. They expect us to take very good care of you."

"Well I, ah, I'm not sure that's how all Vermonters feel, but I thank you, and my wife thanks you, sincerely and dearly."

The President took a moment before getting down to business. First came strict instructions: "Nothing we discuss in this meeting leaves the room until further notice." Everyone nodded in agreement. He told them about Alice Morris' belief that her husband died of cardiac arrest brought on by a sneeze. He then looked at the Surgeon General and asked, "Dr. Green, have you heard of such a thing?"

Dr. Green, not as accustomed as the others at being in the Oval Office, was a little uneasy but her reply came out with confidence. "During a sneeze, the chest builds up a lot of pressure which increases the blood flow to the heart. The heart may react by skipping a beat, and there could be a delay before the heart resumes its rhythm. I would presume that is when President Morris slapped his chest to restart his heart, so he thought. But the body's electricity restarts the heart. His slap was coincidental.

"I'll add that extreme stress does bad things to us. It puts the body in a mode of 'fight or flee,' and if the brain overrides the body's overwhelming desire to flee, or we feel cornered, the repercussions can be serious. The heart becomes the most affected. We know that stress and fear can trigger a heart attack, and I'm sure we would all agree that at that moment President Morris was experiencing extreme anxiety. In my opinion it went right to his heart."

The President thought this over for a few moments, then responded, "I'd like you to go over every word of the autopsy report and talk with the doctors. See if we can come to a conclusion, an honest, supportable conclusion, that Morris died of natural causes. Because if we can do that we can put the whole world at ease. We could significantly ratchet down the tension and fear our country is going through. Many are wondering why we haven't already annihilated North Korea for killing President Morris and trying to kill me.

"By no means do I want the death certificate falsified in any way. But if we can officially eliminate foul play, at least in Morris' case, we'll be doing ourselves a great service."

Dr. Green replied, "I've read the preliminary autopsy report, and indeed the only cause of death identified was cardiac arrest, and there was no presence of unusual substances – except for a trace of Viagra." The President asked, "Can't that cause low blood pressure or something?"

"Clinically speaking, only slightly and often not at all. Mixing with nitrates, though, can cause the blood vessels to relax and lower one's blood pressure. But there were no nitrates present in the President's body. I will study the final autopsy report again and talk to the doctors."

The President said, "I don't mean to press, but, well, you can understand," rubbing his hands in front of him again, "the sooner this is done…"

"I'll get right on it, Mr. President. Will that be all?"

"Thank you, Dr. Green. Please get back to me as soon as possible. Tim will see that you'll get right in." Tim nodded toward her. Dr. Green rose and smartly walked to the door, unsure if she had the right one. But it didn't matter; for the first time ever she had an urgent mission of national importance.

The President turned to Gibble and Billings and commented, "You can see why I wanted you both here for the revelation of that information." They nodded in agreement. "We needn't let our guard down nor should we back off on any investigative leads. But soon we might be able to lower the national stress level. Half of the networks on TV have some asshole talking-head making a case that the North Koreans killed Morris and tried to kill me. We need to put those fires out, dead out.

"Now on the subject of leads, can either of you give me more details on the attempt in Swanton?"

Gibble responded, "The bomber's name is Carol Bebabeau, born in Bécancour, Quebec. He had press credentials on him, but the station he worked for fired him three weeks ago for fraternizing with the boss's live-in girlfriend."

"His name is Carol?"

"Yes Sir, the proverbial boy named Sue."

Gabe blurted, "Do we know if his station was affiliated with a bigger company, like CBC?"

Gibble shot back, "I know exactly what you are thinking and I'm all over it."

Gabe said, "Time to drag Ms. Galipeau in for another chat!"

"Not yet." It was Billings' turn to speak. "The RCMP is on it. They've been briefed on the deal you had with the CBC and they are working it. We need to give them time to do their job. If we call her in it'll mess things up."

The FBI director continued, "Mr. President, every minute that goes by new information is being gathered. Most of that is being done by the Canadians because everything is on their side of the border, except the truck and dynamite which we have."

The President asked gravely, "And the asshole, Carol Bebo – whatever. You aren't telling me we turned him over to the Canadians?"

Billings continued in his trademark official-ese, "Absolutely not Sir. He's in the infirmary of a Vermont state prison in St. Albans, recovering from the sedative he received. As soon as he's well enough to travel we'll be bringing him to a facility in Virginia. The vest and dynamite are being transported to our lab for examination. The ATF said it was crude, like a kid put it together trying to follow instructions from an internet site. But the explosives were real and the batteries were fresh. We think he was waiting for you to come back outside to get in the vehicle." With a bowed head Billings added, "It would've done the job."

Marc took a chest-deep nasal breath. After a moment he asked, "Who was the ATF agent that went out there and grabbed this guy?"

Gibble answered, "Rory Kidder and his partner Ken Takahara."

The President said, "I hope someone puts them in for medals. What they did was like jumping on a live grenade. And I personally want to present those medals."

Gibble responded, "Yes Sir. I'll get C.J. Davis to write the justification as he was right there, then it'll go up the chain. I'll personally monitor the progress."

"Thanks again, Ron." Turning back to the FBI director, the President asked, "Shawn, can I get an update on the investigation tomorrow morning?"

Billings promised he would make himself available. "Just give me a time and I'll be here."

"Thanks, Shawn. Now on to the situation at hand, North Korea. We need to look at all the options and remain flexible." Shaking his head he added, "The situation is very dynamic. As we gear up for one thing, something will happen which may dictate an entirely new approach.

"And contrary to what the rest of the world may think, the key players here include China – and Russia, but primarily China. But the Russians are watching this whole situation very carefully – and they're looking for opportunities. The fact that both the Chinese and the Russians are silent speaks volumes. I am most interested in knowing what the Chinese are thinking, what they're saying, and what they're willing to actually do."

Realizing he wasn't prepared ... not well enough informed ... the President took a moment before cautiously stating, "You all heard what my position is, the Japanese have to take the point here. We need to relay that to them immediately. Under normal circumstances we would probably use our ambassador to Japan. I believe his name is Felix Howard?"

Jane helped him out: "Felix Craig Howard, Sir."

The President said, "Wasn't he appointed by a Democrat? And if so, why wasn't he replaced when Morris came in?"

Jane answered, "In short, the Japanese wouldn't let him go. When Morris came to the White House, the Japanese informed him that it would be a great insult if Howard were replaced.

"I'm afraid there's more, Sir." She then made eyes, nearly unnoticeable, toward Gibble and Billings. As slight as her gesture was, the President picked up on it. He looked over at them and said, "Gentlemen, we'll be talking again soon. Keep me posted. Shawn, I'll see you tomorrow. Ron, please keep taking good care of us – you'll find me very cooperative from now on."

The men recognized a cue when they heard one and exchanged the usual but somber pleasantries as they rose to leave. When the door shut Marc peered at Jane and said, "Am I not going to like what you're about to tell me?"

Jane lowered her head. Hesitatingly she said, "Ambassador Howard made a statement about an hour ago, assuring Japan that the nuclear forces of the United States will completely and utterly destroy North Korea as we know it. It was carried on Fox News. It's probably on all the networks by now."

The President started working both hands like he had a stress ball in each one or he was about to start a boxing match. He thought hard for a moment and asked, "Before I react let me ask you, did you or did you not inform all our ambassadors that we would not be resorting to nuclear weapons in this emergency?"

"Yes, Mr. President. The cable went out Ops Immediate."

"So he either didn't read it or ignored it?"

"So it would appear, Mr. President." She hesitated before adding, "Even if he hadn't seen the cable," bowing her head again and speaking softer, "I would have expected him not to make such a … a statement without checking with me."

The President crushed his eyebrows together. "Tim said I had a couple of calls to make – one is to the Japanese Prime Minister. Exactly what am I supposed to tell him now?" Jane didn't move a muscle. The President joined his hands together, interlacing his fingers but keeping his palms apart, still exercising his fingers. Suddenly his hands went down and he leaned way forward toward Jane and ordered, "You call Howard. I don't care if you have to get him out of bed or the bathtub. Tell him to have his ass on the next plane to Washington. Upon his arrival he is to report to you immediately." A curl to his upper lip betrayed the President's anger. "And if he gives you the slightest indication that he can't make it or some other bullshit, you can tell him that he has an emergency of his own."

"Yes, Mr. President." Glancing down at her phone then back up to the President, she said, "I just got a message from my Chief of Staff. Apparently Howard realizes he may have spoken out of turn."

"Yes, I'm sure he has. So he won't be shocked when he gets your call, will he?" The President sat back in his chair. His eyes went off into a distance. Jane took the pause as an opportunity to carefully point out, "Mr. President, under the circumstances, I might suggest this is not an opportune time to pull our ambassador from Japan."

Thrusting forward and almost yelling, the President said, "He's no goddam ambassador, certainly not mine. He's a frigging loose cannon!" The President realized he was taking things out on Jane which he didn't want to do. He ordered, "Get his ass back here and pick somebody there who can act in his place. If we have to send somebody over there we will. But you're right, I don't want it to look like I'm firing the ambassador. The media can be told he's coming here for consultation."

After a deep breath, he said, "Jane, I need to talk with Gabe. You're welcome to stay."

"Thank you, Mr. President. I have some urgent calls to make."

"If you hear anything official from the Chinese or the Russians let me know immediately. And let Tim know when Howard gets in, not that I want to talk to him myself. But just in case. He may have some insight we need."

"Yes Mr. President," and with that she rose to leave the room, but before getting all the way through the door she heard the President ask Gabe, "So we have the Seventh Fleet on full alert?"

"Yes Sir, and another task force on standby. We haven't moved the second one yet, without your order. I was concerned about the message it would send. And of course, there's the cost of such movements."

"Good call. No, I certainly don't want to signal the beginning of World War Three. Though the burning question still is, if Pak Jr. takes another shot at us can we knock it out of the air – if we don't get it on the ground?"

Gabe answered, "Absolutely. We'll get it. We just have to be careful about *where* we knock it down."

"Does he have a missile that will reach us?" asked the President.

"He might but accuracy is his primary problem – and they haven't figured out re-entry."

"Re-entry?" the President asked.

"Yes, Sir. In order for their missile to travel as far as our West Coast, it has to go into space and then re-enter the atmosphere without disintegrating."

"We don't think they've solved that yet?"

"No, but maybe they think they did, and if the Russians or Chinese are so inclined they can easily help them."

The President nodded in understanding, then asked, "What should we be doing, proactively?"

"The order of battle for this situation has been established for years. The Joint Chiefs know who should be preparing and what deployments are needed. And they are aware of your order of no nuclear engagement."

The President stressed, "No engagement at all – until I give the word."

"Yes, Mr. President."

Marc sat silently. Momentarily he added, "Time is on our side. The longer this goes on, the more the North Koreans will dizzy themselves with fear, all while we are calmly planning and preparing. The Chinese have to be frantic about damage control. They're between the proverbial rock and a hard place – and they know it."

Gabe's head bowed in agreement. Marc said, "Well, I'm forcing my eyelids to stay open and I know my brain doesn't function well under these circumstances, so we'll talk some more later. I'll have talked to Prime Minister Suko by then; we'll have more to discuss. Tim, make sure Jane is invited."

Gabe was heading to the door when the President asked Tim about the phone calls he had to make. Tim went out to get the information.

While no one was in the room, Marc gingerly moved around to the back of the desk and slowly sat down in the chair. He let his fingers touch some of the carvings. It was a gift by Queen Victoria in 1880, nearly 150 years ago. He experienced a few moments of silence and was in awe of all the Presidents who sat here before him.

Tim re-entered. The President slowly looked up from the desk toward Tim who said, "Sir, Suko will not be available for two hours. And there's a note to return the call of someone saying he is your brother, Albert. I don't know all your family yet, so I thought I better bring this in."

The President was shocked. "Two hours? What the hell is Suko doing? Is he in a hot game of poker or something?"

Tim replied, "I'm not sure; I'm certain he's meeting with his staff, it's about 2 AM there. The opposition government is all over him, he's under unbelievable pressure. Also, we believe he's trying to make a call to President Taos."

The President looked directly at Tim, "That is the most important step right now."

Tim answered, "But we don't think Taos is ready to talk with Suko just yet."

Nodding gently the President acknowledged, "When they do talk, the realizations will sink in on both sides.

"And yes, my brother Albert is in Malaysia. He must be worried sick. I'll call him later today. What else do you have?"

"Ah, well, Sir, I have this handwritten letter from Secretary Yashuka."

"What's it about?"

"He's resigning effective immediately."

The President read the letter – the handwriting was rather challenging. He asked Tim, "Do I have this right, he's resigning immediately because of my lack of immediate action against North Korea?"

"Apparently so. His lineage is Japanese. He's probably still in the building, we might be able to explain things to him – he may be just waiting to be asked to reconsider."

The President slammed the letter to the desk and whipped out his G2 heavy ink gel pen and wrote 'Approved' and scribbled his 'MzG' initials under it. He turned to Tim and said, "If he can make such a dumbass decision on the spur of the moment then I don't need him on my staff. Make sure we get all his government i.d., and that he's cleared out of his office by the end of the day. Immediately means immediately." The President hesitated before adding, "It seems like my staff is conducting some self-cleansing. That's not a bad thing."

Tim was just short of shocked. "Yes Sir, Mr. President. Shall we start a search for a replacement? We have a list of party donors from which, I'm sure, we can find several qualified candidates for Secretary of Education." The President thought for a moment, his bulldog expression gently softened. "No Tim, that won't be necessary. I think I have someone for the job. And she's not even a Republican."

The President sat back in his chair to take stock. Everything at the moment that should be in motion was in the hands of the staff. After reflection he looked back at Tim and asked, “Did you say I had time for a 40-wink festival?”

Tim half-smiled. “Right this way, Mr. President. The front gate just opened for you.”

THE PRESIDENT'S LATE-NIGHT SNOWMOBILE ADVENTURE through the Canadian blizzard by itself would have been enough to exhaust the fittest of the fit, and at this point he'd been up 39 hours. So the President was glad to follow Tim to the private residence of the White House and into a nicely appointed bedroom. The bed looked very comfortable and was tempting. He looked around the ornate room and whispered to his wife, "This isn't the Lincoln bedroom is it?" Tim overheard and answered that it was not. Marc turned to Tim and said, "If I get in that bed, I'll be out for the count for hours. I just need a nap. Don't you have a nice Lazy-Boy I can crash on?" Leonie smiled. She knew her man often got his best sleep on a comfy recliner. It took less than three minutes before one was being slid into the room. The President removed his suit coat, loosened his tie, kicked off his shoes, and plopped down on the chair, declaring, "This will be okay." Leonie threw a light blanket over him, making sure his feet were wrapped in the blanket, and gave him a peck on the forehead. As she and Tim were leaving the room the President ordered, "Remember to wake me up in an hour, and see if the cafeteria can grill me a cheeseburger or something." Leonie said back to him, "No cheeseburgers on your diet, Big Boy. Nighty-night."

Once outside the room, Tim informed the First Lady that two hours will be okay, everything can wait. "Things are happening fast. The more time we let him sleep, the more information we'll have for him when he wakes up. If he's needed immediately I'll come and get him. I'm sure you could use some sleep too."

She replied, "I never sleep during the day."

Tim said, "As you wish, Ma'am. Also, the chef would be glad to prepare something for you and the President. Just give them your instructions." Then he asked, "Are you sure he's going to be able to sleep, Ma'am?"

She replied, "Like a rock. He has this little meditation/self-hypnotizing routine he does if he can't sleep. In five minutes he'll be out like a light."

"Is he a student of meditation?"

"He was but couldn't find the time to dedicate to what he called proper meditation, so he's into mindfulness. He thinks it is the answer to most personal issues. Give him time, he'll tell you all about it."

"Hey, this is great. All that's missing is a Sip of Sunshine." Marc and Leonie were sitting at a nicely appointed table for two – white tablecloth and napkins. On Marc's plate were a perfectly cooked sirloin steak, baked potato, brown-sugared carrots, and side salad of mixed greens – no tomatoes – with 'red' dressing on the side. The First Lady was enjoying the same sides but with sage-rubbed salmon. Her salad had lots of grape tomatoes, her favorite, and her dressing was raspberry vinaigrette. She said, "You can't have a pint of beer, especially that high-test stuff, not before calling the Prime Minister of Japan."

"Yeah, but it might be just what I need to keep me steady. Besides, he may not want to hear what I have to say. So I presume you didn't get all this from the cafeteria."

"Now you know very well that Clément is a world-renowned chef, and the White House is lucky to have him. So when you see him make it a point to lavish him with compliments. I want to make sure he stays so I can learn a few things from him." The first thought that came to Marc's mind was 'messing with the President's wife is a hanging offense,' but decided even though the 'messing' pun was perfect, he'd save that line for another time. She was still shaken over the incident in Swanton. Marc might have been also except his mind was too preoccupied with other affairs. His little jibes here and there were a means of keeping his stress under control.

* * *

"Al-bear, how are doing? So good to hear your voice!" The President was on the phone with his brother in Malaysia. In a very serious voice Albert curtly responded, "Never the hell mind about me, what about you."

It wasn't a question.

"Well hey, ca-ca occurs. All's well that ends well," responded the President.

"Yeah, but the little bastard is still alive. Why didn't they just shoot him on the spot and save the taxpayers a bunch of money?"

"True. But we're a civilized country. Besides I'm sure he has information we can use."

"Like he's going to tell you anything."

"You never know. Under the right conditions he might. Anyway, I've got bigger fish to fry."

"Yes, you got your hands full. Just two days ago you were probably breaking a hundred on the 'racetrack' in St. Leon de Grand. Now you're wondering what you're going to do with China."

Marc was impressed with his brother's foresight. "Yeah, China is the problem for sure. Just means we have to do a good job lining up our ducks before we act."

"Well, I'll tell you what you have to do with the Chinese. Hit 'em in the breadbasket. Sanctions and high tariffs! They've gotten rich thanks to the rest of us. Go after their economy."

"Yes, I know. But you remember Dad's favorite expression: 'talk is cheap.' Don't get me wrong – we can put the hurts on the Chinese economy but not without damaging our own. Besides, sanctions wouldn't have time to kick in. And if they decide to react badly they won't give a damn about the economy."

The conversation turned to how everyone was doing otherwise. Marc broached the subject of Albert's security as the brother of the new President. Albert acknowledged the concern: "Well, I'm damn sure keeping a low profile and I'm certainly not advertising the fact. My wife may be a problem. She wants to tell the world. It's just a matter of time someone will find out."

"Well, you call me immediately if something comes up. The staff here now knows who you are – they'll put you right through as soon as they can. But I got to let you go. I have to call the Prime Minister of Japan."

Albert joked, "Sure, blow me off so you can bullshit with some big shot." In a more serious tone he added, "Just remember, Marc, you *are* the Big Shot. Don't let any of them forget that."

"I'll try to. Hey, we'll talk again soon."

"Yeah, and try to stay safe will you?

It was now indeed the appointed time for the call with Prime Minister Suko. The President found a pad of paper to jot down his thoughts. He preferred yellow, legal size pads over the government standard white, but only white pads were in the desk. He didn't have to look for a pen because his two-dollar black gel pen was always in his pocket. At that moment Tim pushed his head through the door and announced Secretary Arnold. The President called both Tim and Gabe in.

Without any of the usual greetings Gabe took a chair, leaned forward towards the President and announced, "Sir, before we talk with Suko, I have some important information on the missile." President Grégoire raised his eyebrows slightly and focused intently on the Secretary of Defense. Gabe said, "We have data strongly indicating North Korea's missile was targeting Tokyo, not the U.S."

The President joined his hands on his desk and leaned forward, a signal for Gabe to continue. "Sir, as soon as the missile was airborne it established a course of 113 degrees, east-southeast from the launch site, directly towards Tokyo. Had the North Koreans intended to strike a west coast city, the course would have been to their northeast."

The President leaned back slightly and asked, "Do we know why it didn't reach Tokyo?"

Gabe said, "It ran out of fuel. We don't know why, maybe they miscalculated."

The President asked, "Given the short distance that's a significant miscalculation, isn't it?"

Gabe agreed, "Yes, Sir, about 25 percent." Gabe waited for a reaction.

The President tightened his chin and almost unnoticeably nodded. He asked, "Does Prime Minister Suko know about this?"

Gabe replied, "I wanted you to know first, but Jane is informing his staff now. I presume that by the time he's on the phone he'll know."

The President lowered his eyes to his desk. "This changes things but not by much." His mind was working hard. After a quick rub of his chin he added, "Not enough fuel and an improperly programmed detonator. Errors maybe, but I wonder" – flashing his eyebrows up and down once – "if one or both of these 'mistakes' were on purpose. Is there someone" – mechanically clasping his hands together – "who followed Pak's orders but purposely sabotaged the mission?"

Gabe sat still and momentarily acknowledged, "It's possible, Sir."

The President nodded in the affirmative, possible indeed. He said, "Well, let's see what Suko thinks." He asked Tim if an interpreter was going to be used. Tim explained, "Suko is rather proficient in English, although sometimes awkward, but he does have an interpreter next to him in case he draws a blank."

"Does the interpreter listen in?"

"Absolutely."

"Well Gabe, I'd like you to listen in, are you good with that?" Gabe had no problem with it but turned the question to Tim. Tim assured him and the President, "Suko will have at least two other advisors listening in and the call will be recorded, transcribed in both Japanese and English, and the transcripts on Suko's desk within an hour."

The President remarked, "Japanese efficiency. Gabe, you're on the call. And we can record it?" Tim gave the President a sideward's glance and a serious nod in the affirmative. The President looked back at Tim and ordered, "Okay, but let's remember to revisit the issue of what gets recorded in this office and what doesn't. I don't know what the hell Nixon was thinking."

The President asked, "Are we calling them?" Tim replied that it was agreed Prime Minister Suko would initiate the call. The President seemed perplexed and Gabe noticed. He explained, "It may seem trivial, Mr. President, but he's the one who needs help, not the other way around." Tim added, "If I may, Mr. President, we need to let him do the asking. No one knows more about protocol than the Japanese Prime Minister." The President understood what was being said. He knew the politics involved but he wasn't sure he liked it. Just then a staffer opened the door and brought in a tray of coffee. As the President was getting back to his desk with his cup, Tim announced that Prime Minister Suko was on the line.

Marc quickly pointed at Tim and gestured for him to sit down and pick up a phone. Tim was surprised but quickly sat and slowly picked up the phone. So did Gabe. Marc looked at the phone set on his desk; there was only one light lit so he pushed it. "Prime Minister Suko?"

"Yes, Mr. President. How are you, Sir?"

"Fine, Prime Minister, and yourself?"

"We are well, Mr. President, considering the circumstances."

Suko offered his sincere condolences on the sudden passing of

President Morris. The President accepted and assured Suko that Morris' death was from natural causes.

"And your horrible experience, Mr. President – just hours ago?" Suko asked.

"Frightening – for everyone. But it turned out alright." The thought of it caused a temporary numbness in Marc's throat but he managed to add, "We are all okay."

Suko got right down to business. "Mr. President, I'm sure you realize that North Korea's attack threatened the lives of millions of Japanese. It is an unprecedented act of war. We must react decisively and punitively." In a tone of agreement the President said, "Yes, the reaction must be strong. It was an unbelievable attack, not just on Japan but on the entire free world. Indeed the response must be decisive and it will be." But he held back regarding the 'punitive' comment. Not wasting time, the President said, "Since the missile was targeting Japan, and landed in Japan, it is important that you take the lead in organizing the response."

Suko agreed. "And we are. I have asked for an immediate meeting of the UN Security Council." The two leaders discussed the proposed meeting with the President pointedly asking Suko about his thoughts on how the Chinese might react. Suko responded, "The Chinese will support their rogue North Korean friends. They will certainly veto any military action. But behind closed doors, both in New York and Beijing, they know that Pak has foolishly put China in a great deal of danger. They are as angry as we are, perhaps more." Then Suko's voice deepened. "To Japan it doesn't matter what China thinks, decisive action is required. My people demand it. The world expects it."

The President said, "Despite our anger, our shock, and the desire for retaliation, we must not forget that initiating a war with North Korea" – he hesitated – "may well start a war with China. And that could quickly turn into a World War."

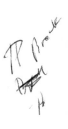

The softer tone in Suko's reply suggested agreement. "Yes, Mr. President. But this attack can't go unanswered." There was a moment of silence, broken by the President: "There are options, Prime Minister. Prudence dictates that we take time to consider them all – and the ramifications of each. For the moment I am confident that Pak will not make a second attempt. If he is foolish enough to try we will destroy his missiles before they can be launched. He realizes we can do it and knows we *will* do it." The President then asked, "Have you talked with President Taos yet?"

"I have tried. His people keep giving my people various excuses, none of them acceptable. Therefore I believe he and the party are 'scrambling,' to use an American term. I'm certain they are shocked with Pak's action and disagree with each other on what to do."

The President agreed. "I suspect there is a lot of disagreement within the party leadership. Until there is consensus, the only people we're going to hear from are staffers under orders to say nothing." He returned to the subject of the United Nations Security Council meeting. The President emphasized, "It is important that you make an unquestionable case that the weapon was indeed a nuclear device and intended for Tokyo."

Suko quickly pointed out, "Only the United States has such evidence. So I must ask, Mr. President, will you present your information to the Security Council?" The President looked over at Gabe. Gabe gestured by holding his eyes wide open, rocking his head side to side. Taking Gabe's cue, the President told Suko he would look into it immediately but didn't make any promises. Of course he knew the material existed – it was the exact material Gabe showed him on the plane. The President also knew the CIA didn't want to give it up. Again though, he assured the Prime Minister the issue was being worked.

The President changed course and asked, "Mr. Prime Minister, how could we avoid military action and the deaths of many innocent North Koreans?"

Suko responded, "I see no way to avoid military action." His voice rose as he emphasized, "For many years negotiations and sanctions have failed. This act of war has ultimately shown that North Korea will understand only one thing, and that is harsh retaliation."

The President appreciated the sentiment, had the missile landed in the U.S. the demands would be the same or worse. Still, the President pressed the issue, "What could North Korea do to avoid a military attack?"

"I can't think of anything, Mr. President. That is, nothing they would be willing to do."

As realistic as this response was, the President was determined to explore any possibilities. He asked Suko to consider the question seriously and he would do the same. The President pointed out, "Military action will cause the deaths of many North Korean soldiers, airmen and sailors, all of whom are just following orders of a madman. And many innocent civilians will also die, some of them already starving because their leader would rather feed a nuclear program than feed his people. Mr. Prime Minister, none of those people deserve to die."

Suko hesitated. His response was thoughtful in tone: "Yes, Mr. President, I understand. But had their bomb hit its target thousands of Japanese innocents would have died. We cannot, and will not, give North Korea a second chance. They must be stopped now, however painful the lesson may be."

"Yes, Prime Minister. I would only ask you to make the loss of their capabilities your first priority, and the lesson the last priority."

"Well stated, Mr. President. I shall honor your humanitarian concerns with great respect."

Suko then broached the subject of America's commitment to back Japan. The President was reassuring, "You are aware of our naval movements and the elevated alert status of our forces worldwide. Our nations are in this together. There's no question." Suko was grateful. The President wanted to start his next sentence with 'But,' but he didn't. "Now we must rally the free world – even the 'not so free' – to be part of this, to back us in every way, because the Chinese will not allow the destruction of North Korea. China doesn't want to get involved, but they have no choice but to protect their neighbor. The war could quickly escalate. Neither side wants that, especially with the weapons available to … the countries involved. So we need the rest of the world on *our* side."

Suko took a deep breath. He wondered whether the President was trying to back off on his commitment to Japan. Although he knew little about yesterday's unknown Vice President – today's leader of the free world – he knew President Grégoire had little experience in international affairs. His prior political experience was that of governor of a small rural state. Was he genuinely prepared for the job? Suko's thoughts caused a moment of silence in the conversation. One of his aides, perhaps reading the Prime Minister's mind, quickly jotted a note in front of Suko's eyes: "He suggests extreme caution – WW3," then bowed his head in respect to his Prime Minister. Suko nodded.

"You are right Mr. President. Anyone can plot revenge; it takes a leader to consider the ramifications and show restraint. I will keep an open mind to a non-violent solution, but the Japanese people will not be patient for very long."

The two agreed to continue the conversation after the UN meeting. Suko expressed his wish to meet the new President in person in the not too distant future, and the President said he looked forward to such a meeting. They exchanged cordial best wishes and good-byes.

When the President hung up the phone, he joined his fingers and thumbs into a loose fist, obviously in thought. After a moment he gently gestured his hand toward Gabe for comment. Gabe gave his chin a small twist and said, "Well, no surprises here. They want to act – decisively – and they don't want to wait for everybody to be on board, but cooler heads must prevail."

Tim added, "Just think, if Israel had been the target and Iran the offender, Iran would already be a giant sandbox of smoking ruins. And the Israelis wouldn't give a damn about what the UN thought."

The President nodded and said, "Yes but Iran doesn't have friends like China willing to come to their rescue. North Korea does."

"Speaking of China..." Tim had something to say but seemed to want the President's permission. The President turned directly toward him and pointed his forehead. Tim accepted the cue. "Mr. President, my wife was born in the Philippines; her grandmother still remembers gruesome details of the Bataan Death March. Grandma's father was a Philippine Scout and one of the few survivors of Bataan. His fellow soldiers got their heads cut off just for having a Japanese coin in their pocket."

At that moment Secretary Rikes was announced. The President invited her in and gestured toward a chair. She quickly advised that she still had not been able to reach anyone of consequence in the Chinese government. The President grimaced, then asked Tim to continue.

Tim said, "Well, four years before Bataan, during Japan's invasion of China, the Japanese captured the capital city of Nanking." Tim's head lowered as he continued, "Japanese soldiers tortured and murdered 300,000 Chinese prisoners and civilians, and" – his voice softened – "they raped more than 25,000 women. Other atrocities – are unspeakable." Tim had everyone's attention. He adjusted himself in his chair before saying, "If Grandma still remembers the horrors of Bataan, I am sure there are still Chinese ... who haven't forgotten the rape of Nanking."

The President was starting to see the point but let Tim make it. Tim asked, "Is it just possible that ... perhaps China welcomed Pak's action – or at least, didn't discourage it?"

The President unpleasantly puckered his lips and said, "My first boss in the Air Force, Chief Master Sergeant Johnson, was the son of a missionary who worked in the 'Safety Zone' of Nanking. The Safety Zone was miraculously established to protect civilians from more atrocities. The Safety Zone didn't stop the Japanese from beating and whipping Chinese soldiers to death, and those were the lucky ones. According to the Chief, the Nips – as he called them – invented torture, like electrical wires to the testicles. The Chief's stories were so gruesome… I couldn't repeat them. After the attack on Pearl Harbor he immediately signed up for the Army Air Force, wanting to kill every Japanese soldier he could, especially officers. He went from a missionary's son to a B-25 bombardier, and was proud to say he was one of the first to drop bombs on Japan in 1942. The only thing good he could say about Japanese soldiers was that they never gave up and fought to the finish.

"Every time I think about Harry Truman's decision to drop the big ones in Japan, I think of Chief Johnson's stories. Truman knew what Chief Johnson knew, the Japanese would never give up and would continue to slit throats to the very last man. Truman knew that the only way to end the war and save a lot of American lives… was the bomb. Truman said he hoped no human would ever have to make such a devastating decision again." With that the President lowered his eyes towards his folded hands. His horrible thought moved from the back of his mind to the front. In fact, he could be the next President to be put in the position of having to use the 'bomb.'

When the President lifted his eyes and checked the faces of everyone in the room, he stopped at Jane's. She lowered her head and said, "Today's Japanese school books don't acknowledge the rape of Nanking." She hesitated, then added, "But the ancient Japanese didn't invent torture; China's Genghis Khan prided himself with how cruel he could be. He's quoted as saying: 'If you had not committed great sins, god would not have sent a punishment like me upon you.' She turned her head towards her left shoulder and said, "All the same, I can't believe China would risk a war, a major war, over…"

The President agreed, "I don't either. But we still don't know if Covid-19 was an accident or an experiment gone bad, and," his voice becoming even more serious, "there are some who think the virus was an experimental attack that went almost as planned."

"For years now they've been building artificial islands, and basing military equipment on those new islands – to what purpose?" The discussion continued for a few minutes and concluded with the unanimous agreement that China would not have condoned Pak's attack. Nevertheless, the dialogue left a measure of doubt in the back of everyone's mind.

Moving on, the President asked Jane, "You haven't received anything official from the Chinese yet?"

She answered, "Nothing tangible, Mr. President. And I have to wonder what they are waiting for to denounce this terrible attack."

The President offered, "Well, while they and the Russians are staying silent, we are avoiding a war of words. Shouting and tossing accusations at each other may seem harmless, but when shouts turn to shoves ... the fight begins." The President pointed his left finger up and said, "We don't want to fight until we have to. And when we do, it will be only when we are best prepared and on our terms. So the silence, although aggravating, may in fact be golden."

After more reflection the President said, "Well, no matter what, the Japanese, our close ally for decades now, need our help, military and otherwise. And Pak has to go." His chin dropped to his chest, and after he raised it again he turned to Tim and said, "Tomorrow morning at seven, have Windigo, Lee Roberts, and General Chaffee here – and the four of us."

"In the Situation Room, Sir?"

"No, here." The President wanted the meeting in the Oval Office, his official 'turf.' The President had one more order: "Now the three of you get out of this building and go home. I'll see you at seven."

The three left the Oval Office, leaving President Marc Z. Grégoire alone again at THE desk. Marc rose to his feet, looked down at the polished oak, and quietly said, "Well, Mr. Kennedy, nothing is as bad as it seems – sometimes it is worse."

By 6 AM Marc had already devoured his bowl of oatmeal and blueberries, but no Vermont maple syrup. He asked Leonie to call their friend Phil to see if he could ship some to the White House. His mind was shifting into gear for the 7 AM meeting. At his desk he found a morning report which was an outline of overnight news, and a second document with a list of legislative bills soon coming to a vote either in the House or the Senate. Momentarily, President Morris' personal secretary poked her head in the open door and said, "Mr. President?"

"Come on in, Marilyn."

"Sir, I know we haven't had much time to meet – but Mr. Houseman said that I would be staying on for the near future. I know new presidents usually bring in their own assistants. I'm just … well, I was wondering how soon that would be? I hope you will excuse my being so forward."

The President stood erect so he could properly face Marilyn. He knew her of course, having met her during his few visits to the White House. She was worried about her job for good reason. The President told her, "I can assure you, Marilyn, I'm going to need all the help I can get to do this job. I'd be lost without people like you. You can be sure I will always need you right outside that door. You can expect to be here for the long term."

"Thank you very much, Mr. President. Also, Michelle Donaldson is here to see you, and she said she can wait here as long as she has to."

"Michelle. You mean Morris' daughter? At this hour?"

"Yes, Mr. President."

Marc asked, "You know what she wants?"

"I'm afraid not Mr. President, but she seems quite distraught."

The President moved around to the front of his desk, stood by a chair, then said, "Send her in."

No sooner did Marilyn leave the Oval Office, Michelle was rushing in. She hadn't yet reached the President when she blurted, "You can't let my father be buried in Kokomo, Indiana!"

The President was taken aback. Using his funeral-home-visiting-hours voice, he said, "Hello Michelle, I am so sorry about your dad."

A bit calmer, she replied, "Yeah. Me too. He had a bad heart, Mom and I both knew it … but he can't be buried in Kokomo."

Still in his funeral-home voice, he asked, "Why, why not?"

"Have you ever been to Kokomo? Really?"

"Well, yes, I passed through there on a Sunday once. I thought it was a pretty respectable little city."

"It's dullsville! My father didn't exactly hate it, but he was sure glad he didn't grow up there! And he would be very much beside himself if he knew he was going to be buried there."

"Well … where would you have him interred?"

"Arlington. But Mom won't hear of it."

The President's tone was turning more business-like, "Where did your father grow up? I know it was in California, but where?"

"That's the point, Mr. President! He was born and raised in Temecula, on a vineyard!" Michelle's voice turned into a swoon. "He grew up playing in the hillsides, watching the grapes ripen. He loved stomping them and getting his feet purple. His first drunk was at 12 years old, on a wonderful Merlot. He used to tell me about the beautiful sunrises in January, climbing the hill behind their villa to see stunning sunsets, wonderful evenings dancing under the stars. Temecula, Mr. President. If not Arlington, he belongs in Temecula."

"Have you talked this over with your mother?"

"She won't listen."

The President paused for thought then looked straight into Michelle's pleading brown eyes. "I'm afraid I can't interfere. What happens to your father now is the decision of the family, not the government. Did he have any last wishes, because if he did they should be respected?"

"My father never gave it a thought. If he did he never told us."

Marc lowered his chin and was back into his funeral-home voice, "Did your father have any brothers or sisters? Maybe they can help you – with your mother."

"He had one older brother, Richard, who died of a stroke. He has a younger sister who lives in L.A. She and my mother never saw eye-to-eye."

"I do recall now, him mentioning his sister. I'm very sorry." After a moment the President added, "There's nothing I can do. But I have a couple of unusual questions to ask, if you don't mind." She looked away utterly discouraged but managed to say, "Okay."

"Has your mother picked out a casket yet?"

She picked up her eyes to look at the President. "Yes, I have to admit, it's pretty fancy – bronze or something."

"So it is metal."

With a curious inflection, Michelle said "yes."

"And the vault, it's solid cement, sealed?"

"I have no idea, Mr. President." Now her face revealed pure curiosity.

"Well, Michelle, in time, maybe six months or six years, your mother may change her mind and she'll want him in Arlington. If your father is in a steel casket, inside a sealed vault, it will be an easy ... a clean job, to have him moved. Wood caskets tend to crack which can make the task, uh, tedious. So if your mother decides to move him, it can be done by just slightly disturbing your father. Abraham Lincoln was moved five times." Slowing down he continued, "And if she doesn't change her mind, someday you'll be making the decisions. You'll have the wisdom of many years by then and you can decide. There'll always be room in Arlington for your father, I promise you."

The President was ready to end the discussion. "If your father had any final wishes, I'd consider talking with your mother. But apparently he didn't." With a voice of regret he advised, "All I can say is, support your mother. She needs you now."

The room was silent for a minute while the two just looked at each other. Michelle finally stood up, raised her chin and looked toward the window. Looking back at the President she quietly said, "Thank you anyway, Mr. President. I know you're busy trying to avoid World War Three. I'm sorry my father couldn't finish the job. He would've done a splendid job. But now all he's going to be famous for is being one of the presidents who died in office after being here only a year."

The President softly said, "You'll also remember him as a great father, and a man who one day became President of the United States."

Her lips and eyes went into a pout, a tear appeared, and after a moment she put out her hand for a gentle woman's handshake; instead she got a presidential hug and the President's best wishes.

Tim Houseman was the first to enter the Oval Office after seeing Michelle leave. "Anything I can help with, Mr. President?"

"Well, first you can tell the office staff that everyone is staying on as long as they're loyal. And you can ask one of them to get the particulars on Morris' funeral. Find out what the family will allow from the White House. A President of The United States deserves at least a military honor guard at his funeral. But don't push. Alice is doing things her way and that's how it has to be. I'll ask my wife to send flowers specifically from us."

Tim said, "I've heard there were a number of foreign diplomats who sought invitations to the funeral, but Mrs. Morris is adamant that none be allowed. She won't even allow senior party leaders to come. She says they only want to be there for the publicity."

The President was surprised. "She's blaming politics for her husband's death. Leo died of a bad heart and a hard head. It's a common combination. All the more reason for me not to get involved. So, is anyone here?"

"Yes Sir, Jane and Gabe are waiting outside. The others are in the building and will be here momentarily."

"Well, as everyone arrives have them come in. They don't have to wait out there."

Tim left the Oval Office and soon returned with Jane and Gabe. Lee Roberts, the National Security Adviser, General Chaffee, and Derek Windigo soon followed. Marilyn brought in a pot of regular coffee and one of decaf. She quietly learned from the First Lady that the President only drinks decaf, and likes it strong with just a splash of half-and-half. It was all on the tray. Tim poured a cup of the hi-test and handed it to the President. Marc waived it off saying, "The pot of kids' stuff is for me." As he poured his own decaf the President said, "Have you ever been behind someone in line at Starbucks whose coffee order was a whole paragraph long? Double-shot this, flavored that, extra something. I always thought the longer your coffee order is, the bigger the asshole you are."

There was light laughter, just what the President wanted. He knew this was going to be a serious meeting and he wanted to loosen things up. Everyone settled down and waited for the President to speak. He wasn't quite sure how to begin but the small assembly was waiting.

"Well, you all know the situation. I asked you here to get your thoughts and ideas, but also to get the proverbial ball rolling." Giving his head a little sideways twist, he said, "I had a telephone discussion with Prime Minister Suko. There's no doubt the Japanese expect military action." He took a moment to look each and every one in the eye and added, "It's now our job to make sure this doesn't turn into World War Three."

The President turned his chin slightly and said, "I know the DoD already has a plan for a military reaction to an attack by North Korea. But that plan is all us. I want to put together an action plan with as many participating countries as possible. First, I want Jane and Gabe to lead the effort to get as many nations involved as possible. The entire world needs to send a message to Pak and the Chinese. China needs to know in no uncertain terms they can't get away with backing Pak any longer. To do that we need to get everyone on board – all our friends and maybe some foes. And I want those countries to be ready to put not just skin but actual flesh in the game. That's where you come in, Gabe, getting participants to dedicate military resources. Once they commit, your people will assign them tasks according to their capabilities. Use all the persuasion at our disposal, if you know what I mean."

"I do, Mr. President."

Looking at Gabe, then Jane, the President added, "It's time to call in all our chips, maybe even make a few threats to ensure involvement." He gently pointed his upside-down right hand at Gabe and Jane. They both nodded their understanding. The President nodded back.

"Milt, I'm going to ask you to design the order of battle. We'll have to be careful with the Yongbyon Complex. We don't want to create a Korean Chernobyl disaster, but we do want to put Yongbyon out of commission. Simultaneously, we'll also have to take out all the chemical weapons aimed at Seoul, and do it before any of them can be used."

Here the President paused for a sip of his decaf and reaction from General Chaffee. The General put down his coffee and said, "So Mr. President, you want the U.S. to plan and carry out the military attack."

"I want the U.S. to design the attack but I want as many countries as possible participating. I know it's a tall order, but your team will decide what our allies, old and new, are capable of and what they are willing to do. Some of them will conduct maritime interdictions, while others will fly air cover. It'll all be part of the tight noose we're going to put around North Korea." Looking at the Chairman of the Joint Chiefs, he said, "But we'll reserve the precise work, like Yongbyon, for ourselves."

The President continued, "Of course we'll coordinate all this with Japan. But we need to temper their thirst for pure retaliation because that is what causes more retaliation." General Chaffee nodded as he and Gabe rapidly scribbled notes.

"Next, the United Nations. Suko wants us to present the material which proves beyond doubt that the bomb was North Korean made."

Shaking his head, Windigo didn't hesitate: "That information comes from highly sensitive sources that are still active." The President didn't hesitate either. He fixed his eyes directly on the CIA director. "If the identity of the sources, human or otherwise, becomes important, then you and I will have the appropriate conversation." The President's expression was intensely serious.

Windigo gently leaned back in his chair. Undaunted he added, "At the risk of being argumentative, Mr. President, if we release the details about North Korea's nuclear weapon, it will help Iran perfect their nuclear weapons. And it could give a head start to all the nuclear wannabes out there." With that Windigo folded his hands on his lap, as if determined not to say another word.

"Noted," the President replied. "So your job now is to prepare something we can present to the UN Security Council. Protect the information you need to, but provide enough information to do the job. I want to see it first and I want to see it by noon." He wanted to add, 'Is this something the current CIA director can handle?' But there was no need to get confrontational – yet. Windigo just sat quietly without responding. The President glared at him and said, "So, by noon. You'll be here?"

"Yes, Mr. President." Windigo had a thing or two more he wanted to say but wisely kept them to himself, remembering what Gabe had told him about the President's dislike for the CIA.

The President went back to addressing the group. "Now, a crucial aspect to all of this: From this moment on we must not use words like 'retribution,' 'payback,' 'retaliation' or any other similar terms. What we do from here on out will be described as 'defensive,' nothing else. We have to let the entire globe know that any military reaction is just that, defensive. I'm sure you all understand why." There were a couple of nods but no verbal reaction.

The President leaned forward in his chair. "Now, before we engage in an attack, I want to give the North Koreans alternatives. I don't think they will do what needs to be done – but, for many reasons, we have to offer them a way out." After a sip of his decaf he added, "Of course, the optimum would be the removal of Pak, Jr. That probably won't happen, but" – the President raised his finger to chest level – "not impossible. Then we'll insist that North Korea end their nuclear program and allow international inspectors in." He paused for reaction.

Jane went first. "It is important to show that we're not warmongers. And I can't agree more that we need to offer options." She raised her head before adding, "No country that's ever made any progress making nuclear weapons has ever stopped developing such weapons. They just do it more secretly. So our plan must be nothing less than thorough."

The President nodded in agreement and waited for more feedback. The room was silent. The President said, "Well Jane, I'd like your people to formulate an ultimatum. Consult whomever you need to, obviously the UN. In fact, the UN should issue the ultimatum. What concerns me is they can't do anything quickly. You'll need to hold their feet to the fire because it needs to be done today."

Jane cautiously asked, "And the ultimatum will be … that Pak is removed?"

The President raised his chin and said, "That Pak is removed and his nuclear missile program is dismantled."

Jane responded, "Yes, Mr. President."

The President then turned to the subject of China. He expressed his concerns about China's decades-long takeover of the South China Sea: artificial island building, increased military presence, and their new control over major shipping lanes. "We know very well that their new island bases were built for one reason, to assure full military control of the South China Sea. Japan, the Philippines, and even Vietnam are all very concerned. Taking everything into consideration, I'm certain China will engage if North Korea is attacked. The question remains, how will they react and how far are they willing to go? We need to figure that out," declared the President.

The otherwise-quiet Lee Roberts offered an observation. "I believe the Chinese want Pak eliminated more than we do. A war in that area will severely disrupt China's trillions of dollars in exports which is now just recovering. And if a nuclear disaster should occur" – he paused for a somber moment – "the holocaust could undermine the entire Chinese government, or what would be left of it." Roberts paused another moment before adding, "It seems to me the Chinese would be most anxious to work with us."

The President listened carefully. Looking at Roberts he asked, "So you don't think they condoned this attack?"

"Absolutely not, Mr. President. They're building up but they are not ready for war, nuclear or otherwise. I believe the Chinese are ... stunned, and not sure what to do next."

The President bowed in agreement then announced, "I'll be talking with President Taos today. Apparently he's agreed to take my call. Our first conversation could speak volumes or might be just an exchange of threats." The President moved his hands together in the church and steeple position, resting the steeple on his chin. "I agree with you, Lee, he has more than just lives on the line. If this becomes a major war, it will begin and end *in his front yard.*"

The President was once again alone at his desk now perusing the list of various bills which could show up for his signature in the very near future. One particular item caught his attention – the National Carbon Footprint Reduction Act. He was familiar with this proposed law, better known simply as the Carbon Tax, a 99-cents a gallon tax on all carbon-creating fuels, from gasoline to propane with no exceptions. He made a mental note to further inquire about the progress of this bill.

"Sir, Dr. Green is here."

"Thank you, Marilyn. Send her in and please call Director Billings and ask him to come over."

"Yes, Mr. President."

The Surgeon General walked smartly into the Oval Office. One would have to study closely to recognize that her Public Health Service uniform was not that of a Navy Vice Admiral. In her left hand she carried a Holey Joe envelope full to its capacity. She delivered a sharp, "Good morning, Mr. President." The President smiled and slightly bowed his head. "Good morning, Dr. Green. Please sit down." The doctor nervously seated herself in the chair on the President's right. She politely declined a cup of coffee. The President reached for a fresh cup of decaf and mentioned, "Well, mine got cold during that last meeting, and since I think you'll be doing most of the talking I'm going to try to enjoy this one. Would you like tea or water?"

"Thank you, Mr. President. I'm fine."

He slid back into his chair and flipped his pad to a fresh page, noted the date and time, then wrote in 'Dr. Green.' Not being adept in small talk, the President turned his smile toward the doctor and said, "Looks like you have some material to discuss."

"Yes, Mr. President. I believe we have conclusive evidence that President Morris died of cardiac arrest, and that he was well aware of his serious heart issues." She began to unstring the Holey Joe and remove its contents. She noticed the President was watching the envelope. "I would have brought the material in a briefcase but was told briefcases are not allowed in the Oval Office."

The President's smile went away. "I had no idea. Must be a Secret Service rule. Well, they're a little edgy right now," and he brought back a half-smile.

She said, "I can understand why. I was instructed to leave mine in the outer office. They did offer to secure it for me." While she was arranging her documents the President mentioned, "You know Hitler narrowly escaped assassination when a briefcase bomb went off during a meeting. A thick oak table leg saved his life. There were two briefcase bombs in the room, but the detonator was never set on the second one. Had it gone off Hitler would have surely been killed." Dr. Green was now quite still in her chair and was staring at the President. He noticed and explained, "Well, I, ah … studied the whole thing while I was in the Air Force. So you mentioned you have conclusive evidence," then he leaned forward toward her with great interest.

"Yes, Mr. President. If you'll indulge me I believe the best way to present this is in chronological order." The President unfolded his fingers and folded them back. She took that as a signal to begin.

"As you know, President Morris was found on the floor about four feet from the restroom. His wife was the first to reach him, quickly followed by a uniformed Secret Service officer. The officer saw the President wasn't breathing and after calling for help, promptly began CPR. Other agents and staff arrived in just seconds. EMTs continued CPR while bringing him to an ambulance. Once in the ambulance, an EMT deployed the defibrillator. They gave him four shocks even though they couldn't get a pulse. It's a common misnomer that electric shock can restart a stopped heart; it can't. They went back to CPR. I'm sure they were just trying anything and everything."

The President softly asked, "He was already dead?"

Doctor Green simply nodded yes, waited a quiet moment, then continued. "At the hospital, the ER did all they could to resuscitate to no avail. One doctor simply refused to give up but the senior doctor called it off." At this point her voice lowered, "He was officially pronounced dead." After a brief pause she looked back at her papers. Intently looking up at the President she continued, "I asked to see the President's clothing. I was surprised when I found a pair of compression socks, full length, thigh-high. I spoke with the two technicians who undressed the President, and they said the President had the socks on and pulled all the way up to his groin. They had to cut them most of the way down to get them off."

"Compression socks?" the President asked.

"Yes, Sir. These types of socks can be worn for various reasons, varicose veins for example, but there was no evidence of varicose veins. These particular socks are the type worn by patients who have undergone coronary artery bypass surgery, but he never had bypass surgery."

The President asked, "So you think he was wearing them hoping it would help his heart?"

"Yes I do, and there's more." After taking a deep breath and a moment to compose, she continued, "The only thing he had in his pockets was a bottle of sublingual nitroglycerine. Five of the 20 pills were missing. However, there was no nitroglycerine present in his system, which means he must have taken the pills at least 24 hours before his death. We don't know if he took them all during one episode or over the course of days or weeks. But we can presume, because the label was worn, he had that particular bottle for some time, well before the North Korean missile incident."

"Interesting. So he had chest pain in the past. He *knew* he had heart problems?" the President asked.

"Very much so, Sir." Dr. Green took a moment to review her notes; she had a lot more to add, but the President interrupted.

"You said earlier that he had a trace of Viagra in his system; what if he took all five of the nitro after taking the Viagra?"

"Well, if he took all five within the same day it could have been a problem, but there was no trace of nitro noted in the autopsy. The Viagra-nitro combination is not a player here."

The President nodded his understanding and motioned for her to continue.

Dr. Green continued with her report, "I went to Bethesda Hospital to see if I could get a look at President Morris' health records. It appears that even I need a search warrant to get into those records. But I was directed to Dr. Edward Terrier, the Navy Flight Surgeon who conducted Morris' last physical, just two weeks ago. What he told me was ... nothing less than shocking."

The President leaned forward in interest as she continued:

"According to Dr. Terrier, President Morris was given the usual pre-exam checks: height, weight, blood pressure, and pulse. The RN who conducted the preliminaries made some notes and quickly ushered the President into Dr. Terrier's office. They shook hands, exchanged small talk, and were seated.

"Dr. Terrier reviewed the notes with what he described as utter shock. Morris' blood pressure was 210 over 144, and his pulse was 102. He watched the President's breathing and noticed he was using short, quick breaths. He asked Morris how he was feeling, and Morris said – quote 'Terrific, and anxious to get back to work' unquote. Dr. Terrier listened to his heart and lungs and detected the possibility of at least three arterial blockages.

"He told the President about the blood pressure and pulse readings and the possible blockages. He then informed him that he was setting him up for an immediate EKG. Morris said, 'You mean right now?' Dr. Terrier told him yes, and after the EKG there would be other tests.

"President Morris told Dr. Terrier he didn't have time for any tests and needed to return directly to the White House. Dr. Terrier told the President he would not release him until the tests were completed. The discussion got heated and the President finally stood and said" – looking at her notes, Dr. Green quoted, 'I've got two armed Secret Service agents right outside this door that say I'm leaving now.'"

Dr. Green paused for a reaction and she got it.

The President blurted, "He actually said that? A frigging threat!"

"So it appears, Sir. But Dr. Terrier was not intimidated. He asked the President how soon he could come back for the tests. Morris told him he would have his assistant mix it into his schedule, could be a week, could be next month. Dr. Terrier shook his head and told Morris that he wanted him back at the hospital by the end of the week. Morris told him there was no way. So, Dr. Terrier swung around in his chair, pulled a blank sheet of paper out of a printer tray, and using a large black magic marker wrote the numbers 210/144, pulse 102. The numbers took up the entire sheet of paper. Holding it up to the President's face he told him that there wasn't just Secret Service agents outside the door, several members of the media were also waiting to hear the results of the President's physical examination. Dr. Terrier claims he leaned in toward Morris and said, 'If you're not back in this office by NOON Friday, I'm releasing these numbers to the press.' Then he lowered the paper to look Morris straight in the eye."

President Grégoire's eyes were wide open. "This Dr. Terrier has a set of balls! Uh, sorry, Doctor. So after Terrier got in Morris' face, what'd he say?"

"Morris calmed down a bit and asked him if he thought he was a heart attack waiting to happen. Dr. Terrier said no, you're a heart attack *about to happen*."

Dr. Green nervously looked at her papers and took another deep breath. After a few moments she went on. "Apparently Morris had nothing further to say and simply started opening the door. Dr. Terrier remained in his chair and told him, 'Remember Mr. President, by noon Friday,' and once again raised the sheet of paper toward Morris's face. Morris went out, broke into a big smile and said, 'Come on fellas, a clean bill of health, let's go home.' And he walked out waving like he was in the middle of a campaign in downtown Des Moines."

The President said somberly, "And Morris never went back."

"No Sir."

"And Dr. Terrier didn't follow through with his threat."

"To some degree he did. He told me that at 12:01 that Friday he turned in his written report in to the hospital commander. The hospital commander wouldn't talk to me. Well, I should say his assistant said he wasn't available. I think the FBI or Secret Service should subpoena that report."

The President assured her, "Director Billings is on his way here; I'll tell him that we need to get that report immediately. Can you stay and give him the details? He's going to want to go over all of this with you."

"Yes indeed, Mr. President."

After a few seconds of reflection the President said, "Actually, we need to release this information immediately." Raising his finger in a slant to indicate a pause, he got up and walked toward the door and called for Marilyn. She and the President met just inside the doorway. He gently pointed at Marilyn and ordered, "Get Paul in here right away, find Tim, and when Billings gets here send him straight in. And Gabe too."

Returning to his desk, still standing, he placed both palms flat on top of the desk, and leaning toward Dr. Green he said, "The whole world needs to know – immediately – that there was no plot to kill President Morris. He was not assassinated and the North Koreans had nothing to do with his death. But before I move forward, what else do you have?"

Without looking at her notes, she announced, "The autopsy confirmed that there were three major blockages to the heart, one 90 percent, the other two 65 percent each."

The President said, "Deadly. And we can say that he knew about the problem and was ignoring his symptoms. Maybe for now we'll leave out the part about ignoring his symptoms."

Dr. Green's mind was starting to assess where the President was going with this, and her uneasiness was sharply increasing. Suddenly she realized she needed to get rid of the coffee she drank on the way over to the White House. Exactly how does one ask the President for a restroom break? As apprehensive as she was, ask she must! "Mr. President, while we are waiting for the others, may I step out for a moment?" The President looked up from his notes, "Certainly. In fact, that's a good idea." With no hesitation but with all the composure she could muster, she walked out of the Oval Office, taking a moment to ask Marilyn for directions. The President headed for his private facility, and as he opened the door he strangely remembered the stories of how Lyndon B. Johnson used to make people give him briefings while he was sitting on the toilet!

Minutes later Marc was back at his desk and Dr. Green was back in her chair. Tim and Gabe soon walked in with Paul on their heels. Behind them was Marilyn to announce that Director Billings was in the building and making his way to the Oval Office. The President smiled at the new arrivals and said, "I guess you gents weren't able to get too far before you were hauled back here."

Tim replied, "No problem, Mr. President. I trust Dr. Green has important news."

"You're damn right. Very important."

At that moment Director Billings walked in and everyone was seated. The President eagerly summarized what Dr. Green reported. With even greater enthusiasm the President reiterated the need to release the findings right away. He outlined his plan for an immediate press conference with Dr. Green being the briefer. Of course, some time would be needed to go over precisely what was to be said.

He addressed Director Billings: "Can you get your people over to Bethesda and secure a copy of Dr. Terrier's report?"

"Right away, Sir. I'll see to it that they have a verbal search warrant from the installation commander so they can get what they need."

"They're not going to ransack the place, are they?" the President asked.

"No. If they get any resistance they'll get the warrant, and they'll get what they went for professionally."

"Okay. It'd really be good if they find that sheet of paper the doctor wrote the blood pressure and pulse on."

"Indeed it would, Mr. President."

"Okay, why don't you step out and get that ball rolling, then come back and we'll talk about, uh, the other matter."

"Yes, Sir." And with that Billings left the Oval Office.

The President fixated his glare on his Press Secretary. "Alright, Paul, how do we make this happen, how do we make sure this gets the widest and fastest dissemination? We need to put an immediate stop to all the rumors and theories that Morris was assassinated. We got a fire here that needs to get put out."

Paul was ready. "First, you want Dr. Green to make the announcement?"

The President said, "Yes."

In a business-like tone Paul described a plan. "So we'll use the White House press room. Who do you want standing behind her while she gives her briefing, Billings, Gibble?"

"Yeah, that reminds me." With a loud voice he called out, "Marilyn, get Ron Gibble on the phone – better yet, ask him to come in here."

Turning back to his guests, the President said, "Sorry Paul, you were asking who should be standing behind her. Yeah, I'm familiar with the technique. She gives the briefing and other officials stand behind her, giving the impression that they are there to back her up." The President hesitated a moment, twisted his chin, and commented, "I never cared much for that setup. It almost looks like the government – in this case, Dr. Green – is telling the press some kind of story, and to make sure everyone believes it she has these other important people behind her. It's like saying, 'this is our story and we're sticking to it.'" He pronounced, "Let's have Dr. Green do it solo."

Paul replied, "Okay, Mr. President. As soon as we're done here, I'll call in the press corps and inform them that a cause of death has been determined, and a White House announcement is imminent. They'll gather immediately and pepper us with questions. I'll string them along, and about every 20 or 30 minutes by throwing them a bone; the first will be the fact that the Surgeon General is making the announcement. They'll make assumptions based on that fact alone. When the time is right I'll tell them the FBI is making some last-minute inquiries. Network anchors will be called in early. They'll be interviewing every 'expert' they can dig up and analyze it to death."

Turning to Dr. Green, Paul enthusiastically continued, "You'll be carried live, then they'll replay the tape at least every half hour. Given our time zones, I'm guessing your announcement will be on TV somewhere every 15 to 30 minutes, completely around the world."

Turning back toward the President, Paul asked, "Will that do the job, Sir?"

The President didn't immediately respond. He looked at Dr. Green and noticed she was a bit pale, so he directed his comment to her. "What do you think, Dr. Green?"

"Well, I've never been … never made a, ah, a nationwide press announcement. I'm concerned about saying the wrong thing, or misspeaking. If I do, I could lose all credibility. That's my concern."

Paul was quick to respond. "Doctor, we're going to rehearse this many times over, you'll do fine. I'm judging that your part of this will take three or four minutes. In fact, we'll keep it to that. When the press starts asking their usual follow-ups, I'll step in and handle it from there." Dr. Green was only somewhat appeased. She realized that for better or worse, by midnight tonight she could be the most famous doctor in the world, and she didn't want to be famous. But the situation appeared to be a 'fait accompli.' The President of the United States wanted this done.

But the President wasn't quite ready to call it a done deal. Addressing Paul, he said, "You said the press will analyze this to death; expound on that for us."

"Well, since Dr. Green is the expected speaker, the press might presume the cause of death was health related. They'll dig up every medical official they can find, especially any former Surgeons General, and interview them ad nauseam. But if I told them the Director of the FBI was making the announcement, they'd assume the worst. And if we told them – which we won't – that Gabe and the CIA director will also be at the briefing, the media would go wild with speculation. They'll practically have war all declared. Today's media are intense. There are no more Walter Cronkites." After a short breath Paul continued, "So back to Dr. Green" – looking toward her – "you, Ma'am, are the right person to make this announcement." Paul waited for everything to sink in before he asked, "Does this meet with your approval?"

"Well, I have some reservations." The speaker was Gabe.

"Yeah, so do I. But go ahead, Gabe," said the President.

Gabe was about to point out that a lot of things could go wrong with this, but decided for Dr. Green's benefit he'd temper his comments. "What if the FBI isn't able to retrieve official documentation and all we have is Dr. Terrier's oral statement? And the question about the compression socks, what if they turn up missing? I think these are just a couple of considerations that need to be nailed down before we tell the world we have this solved."

Tim, who was doing all the listening, piped in, "Why would the hospital commander not produce the report? What would compel him not to cooperate? Just being rhetorical."

"Dereliction of duty!" boomed a voice from the Oval Office doorway. It was Gibble, in the flesh. He strolled into the meeting, stood in front of a chair, and asked the President, "May I?"

"Of course Ron, and please, tell the group what you think." Before Gibble could speak, Billings came back in the room to take his chair. The President looked at Gibble and ordered, "Go ahead, Ron."

"When the Bethesda director, Brigadier General Hayden Johnson, who prefers to be addressed as 'General' versus 'Doctor,' received Dr. Terrier's report, he may not have been too keen about blowing the whistle on his President's health. The General likes his job and wants to keep it. He could have buried the whole thing, even going so far as deleting the computer records, and ordered Terrier to keep his mouth shut." Without turning his head Gibble pointed at Billings. "Let's see what Shawn's people find out; they're probably on their way there now." Then he dramatically turned his head toward Billings. "I assume you sent the A-team." The room went silent. Billings was never a fan of Gibble's, but now a bad taste was developing in his mouth. Gibble bent toward the tray and asked, "Is this fresh coffee?"

The President gave Gibble a moment to pour a cup of coffee, then asked Billings, "So, are your people on the way?"

"Yes, Sir. NCIS is also sending a Special Agent over who specializes in medical records. She apparently knows where and how to drill down for data. I think that when General Johnson sees the entourage of agents coming into his office he'll be fully cooperative."

"Okay, let's tie up a couple of loose strings," the President ordered. "Dr. Green, when did you see the compression stockings and the nitro?"

"Yesterday about 1500 hours."

"Shawn, has all of President Morris's clothing – what he had on when he arrived at the hospital – been retained as evidence, and anything he had in his pockets?"

"Yes, Mr. President. In fact, I'm surprised somebody at the hospital let Dr. Green see them." Turning toward Dr. Green, he said, "No offense to your office, Doctor." Looking back toward the President, Billings added, "But I'll ask immediately and make sure everything picked up at the hospital was brought to our evidence vault. As soon as I have that confirmation I'll inform you." And he thought to himself, 'and *somebody's ass is grass*,' an expression learned from his late father but something he never said aloud.

The President ordered, "Do it. Now, how soon can we reasonably expect an update on how things are going at Bethesda?"

Billings was busy furiously texting. He stopped long enough to say, "That will be my next text."

"Okay. So, Paul, you see where we're going with this? I don't think we should lather up the media too much just yet, especially the knuckleheads on cable news. All we might be saying is that the cause of death was cardiac arrest caused by heart disease and that President Morris was aware of his heart problems. I really want this done by prime time, but depending on what happens at Bethesda we may be forced to throttle this back. Get to work getting Dr. Green prepared but wait until you hear from me personally before you go live."

"Yes, Mr. President," Paul promised. "You know, as long as we get this in by 8 PM Eastern, it'll be all over the news right through the night and into tomorrow."

As Dr. Green and Paul left the Oval Office, the President asked the others, "So are all our ducks in a row?" No one answered but the President assumed it was a yes.

"Shawn, let me be the first to know about the Bethesda progress. Now, I think you have some information for me regarding the Swanton attempt?"

"Yes Sir, I do."

"I'd like Gabe to sit in, is that okay?" asked the President.

"Yes, Sir."

"I would like to hear this report firsthand if I may, Mr. President." Gibble was sort of asking, but his tone was more of a demand.

"Sure Ron," replied the President.

THERE WAS SOME SHIFTING AS THE GROUP GOT SMALLER. THE President asked if anyone needed a break. Gabe and Shawn gestured that they were okay; Ron sat motionless with eyes forward on the President.

"So what do we know, Shawn?" asked the President.

The FBI director had a small pad resting on his lap. Without looking at his notes he began. "Carol Bebabeau is currently on a DOJ aircraft en route to Virginia. He has asked for a lawyer so we are not questioning him any further. Even though he's not talking, the Canadians have made progress in their investigation. As previously reported, he was carrying on a relationship with the station owner's girlfriend and they were caught in the act. When he was fired he managed to keep his press credentials. The girlfriend's name is Nikki Deemer, originally from Windsor, Ontario. The RCMP established that she's the one who informed Bebabeau that you were on the way to the border."

Gabe interrupted, "Did Deemer get her information from CBC?"

Billings reported, "She did not. Her source was probably a government official in Ottawa."

Gibble nearly came out of his chair! "I knew those goddam Canucks couldn't be trusted." His face was turning red with rage – when he suddenly felt a sharp poke to his side from Arnold. The President raised both of his palms in the air to signify calm.

After a moment the President asked, "You mean somebody from the RCMP called this Deemer person, like they were giving her a news tip or something?"

Shawn bowed his head, "Or something, Mr. President. Actually, they still don't know if it was an RCMP employee. It could have been the Sûreté, Canadian Intelligence Service, or someone else. Several agencies have representatives in the RCMP command center. They're very concerned that the Ottawa caller … may have been part of a conspiracy."

"Conspiracy?!" shot the President.

"Yes, Mr. President. The Mounties … think … that there was a conspiracy to assassinate you, then the Vice President of U.S. Because the group had no access to President Morris, you were the next best target. They knew you were often in Quebec and believed you were accessible. Suddenly, when they realized you were about to become the new President, and currently in Quebec, you became their immediate and urgent target."

Billings took a breath and then continued, "The sequence of events, as the RCMP currently has it, is as follows: The RCMP in Ottawa was notified by the Sûreté de Quebec that your motorcade was on the way to the border, and the Sûreté was seeking RCMP assistance. Much as we would have done, up-channel notifications were made, right up to the Prime Minister. Over 50 people, most of those working in command centers, quickly became aware of your movements and your destination, the U.S. border at Highgate Springs, Vermont.

"Someone, not yet identified, used a common line at RCMP headquarters to call Deemer. She was sitting right in front of the wire center in her studio watching every piece of news as it came in. When she got the call from Ottawa she put Bebabeau in action. They believe she told him where he could get the station truck that was out for maintenance. The garage that had the truck had no way of knowing Bebabeau was no longer a station employee and released it to him.

"The RCMP searched Bebabeau's apartment and found no trace of bomb-making material. No residue, no remnant of tape or wires, nothing to indicate the bomb was made there. A search was done at Deemer's apartment with the same negative results. Our search of the truck showed the bomb was transported in the back of the truck, but there is no evidence it was assembled there.

"The RCMP has three major investigative 'fronts' if you will. First, find the bomb maker. Two, identify their inside source. Three, ascertain whether the source was merely providing a news tip or is in fact part of a conspiracy, and if there is a conspiracy, find the other members." At this point Billings paused; he had more information but he wanted to give the President a chance to ask questions about what was said so far. He got his wish.

"What the hell?" the President said loudly. "Who are they? Why were they targeting me? What was their motivation? Are they frickin' radicals or what?" The President's French-Canadian short temper began to surface.

Billings had the possible answers and continued with his professional but somber voice. "Bebabeau attended college in Sherbrooke, Quebec. According to a classmate, Bebabeau met a Muslim girl, a refugee to Canada from Iran, and they started living together. Her family had huge problems with Bebabeau not being a Muslim. To try to appease the family, he began attending services at the Mosque.

"Bebabeau became radicalized. So much so he actually worried the Imam there and was forbidden from further attending the Mosque. But he and the girlfriend continued to play house." Billings took a moment to dampen his lips, then went on. "She had a brother who was particularly distressed about his sister's infidel boyfriend, even more so because she was married to one of his best friends when she was 14 years old. The brother, an asylum applicant, lived in New Hampshire and had not yet received all his documentation – and therefore would have a difficult time re-entering the U.S. if he left. Now, according to the classmate, the brother went to Canada anyway, kidnapped his sister and brought her to a remote location in Quebec." Here Billings took a deep breath and his 'official voice' crackled as he said, "The brother and his friends dug a hole, forced his sister into the hole, and ... stoned her to death." Billings stopped long enough to wipe his lips with his knuckle. "Apparently stoning is the prescribed penalty for her crime. Bebabeau was sent a video of the stoning, and according to the classmate he went out of his mind with rage. He couldn't find the brother and wasn't even sure of his full name. It seems the brother returned to the U.S. With retribution against the brother becoming improbable, Bebabeau turned his anger towards the U.S. To possibly answer your question, Mr. President, they think Bebabeau was motivated by misguided but strong anti-American sentiments."

The Oval Office was silent. After a few moments the President asked, "And what was Deemer's motivation?"

"The Canadians are working on that, Mr. President. I have to say that reluctantly – I think the Canadians are over their heads with this. They are competent but they don't have the resources to pursue the many tentacles of this investigation. As it evolves more and more leads will develop. They need help. So I'm putting a contingent of six FBI agents together, and a bomb expert, and sending them to Canada. They won't be able to conduct investigations on their own but they can assist and advise. And of course, they'll be able to keep me better informed on the progress of the investigation. I've already made the offer to the RCMP and indications are they will gladly accept our assistance."

The President asked, "So what about our guy Carol? He's the key to all this, isn't he? He knows where he got the goddam bomb, probably knows the son-of-a-bitch who made it, and knows who else is involved. But he lawyered up, correct?"

"Yes, Mr. President."

Gibble boomed, "Send his ass to GITMO! One, he came across an international border to conduct terrorist activities; and two, he wasn't acting alone – which puts him within the definition of an international terrorist. Using GITMO methods we'll get everything we need out of him."

The President leaned heavily forward on his desk, elbows spread apart, "Shawn?"

Billings gave a cocked grimace. "I think we should give the investigation some time before we resort to such measures."

Gibble shot, "And lose valuable information while we're waiting," his empty coffee cup came down hard on the table. "Look, send his ass to GITMO. And make damn sure he knows ahead of time where he's going. He might piss his pants just thinking about what's going to happen to him, and sing like a bird before he even gets on the plane."

The President unconsciously raised his eyebrows. Gibble and Billings perceived the President might be in favor of the idea. The President said, "It would take a day or two to get him there, and maybe while he's cooling his heels or feeling the heat, so to speak, he just might talk. Move him to GITMO tomorrow, but let's wait four or five days before we actually use any 'techniques' on him – just to see where the investigation goes."

Billings bowed his head and said, "So ordered, Mr. President."

Gabe, listening carefully, pointed out, "I heard a group was organizing a movement to have Bebabeau returned to Canada. They think he can't get a fair trial in the U.S."

Gibble pounced, "The only thing they have to worry about is the length of rope we'll hang the little bastard with. It has to be the right length given the height and weight of the prick being executed. The Army still has manuals on it!"

Silence again. Then Gabe interjected, "Well, I'm in favor of sending him to GITMO. Because who knows who else this group is targeting? I'm just saying there will be fallout. Can we do it without a presidential order? Shawn, can't you make that determination unilaterally?"

Billings thought for just a moment. "I suppose I could. If I'm asked though, I'll have to admit I consulted the President."

The President curtly ordered, "Shawn, do whatever you got to do. And let me know if the Canadians turn down your offer to send the FBI up there to help. I'll call Trudeau myself. AND" – the President was fully riled – "you can tell them that we're going to want Deemer extradited to the U.S. Don't tell them we're sending Bebo to GITMO. Otherwise, we'll never get her here."

During the latter part of the above discourse, Billings received several texts marked urgent. He announced, "The agents at Bethesda have a copy of the report on Morris' exam. Essentially, all that's in it are the results of the preliminary checks and a written comment by Dr. Terrier noting that Morris refused further tests." Scrolling though the text Billings added, "They do not have the paper that Terrier wrote the BP and pulse on. General Johnson told the agents that he saw it but shredded it. He is willing to provide a signed, sworn statement to that effect. Apparently he is cooperating fully.

"Also, Mr. President, I have a photo of the compression socks here on my phone; may I forward it to you?"

"Yes, that'll be fine … MARILYN!"

Marilyn stuck her head in the door. The President ordered, "Call Paul and tell him full speed ahead for Dr. Green's announcement. He and Dr. Green can plan on discussing it over lunch with me, 12:30." Turning back to the group he abruptly announced, "Gabe, hang here, we need to talk about China. Otherwise that will be all for the moment, gentlemen."

As the men rose to leave the Oval Office the President said, "Great job Shawn, thank you. And Ron" – with a lowered voice and a pointing finger he added, "don't worry, we're going to get every one of those bastards. *One by friggin one.*"

"Mr. President, you greatly overestimate our influence with Pak Jung-ho. He is not a puppet on strings we can control. North Korea makes their own nuclear weapons, and he develops rockets and builds missiles using resources entirely available in North Korea. China has nothing to do with North Korea's nuclear program." It is China's President Zhong Taos on the phone with President Grégoire.

"It was the Soviets, not China, who gave North Korea its start with nuclear weapons. North Koreans sought atomic weapons during the Korean War because your Harry Truman admitted that a nuclear attack on North Korea was a possibility.

"As for doing something about Pak, we're doing what we can. We have greatly reduced trade with North Korea. But all that will do is further starve its citizens, and strengthen Pak's resolve." With that, President Taos paused to let President Grégoire react.

"Are you indicating, Mr. President, that China has done all it can to rein in Pak Jung-ho?"

"No, Mr. President. We are pursuing several options, one of which looks promising. We need time though."

"How much time? Hours or days?"

"Ah, Mr. President. Such things take time. I believe it will take days – perhaps weeks. You know it is against the law for a nation to target the leader of another nation, a principle you may well appreciate."

"So you have a plan to take him out, but it may take weeks?"

"Sir, I would certainly not indicate that we intend to eliminate Pak

Jung-ho."

"But it's going to take weeks?"

"Mr. President, our objective will require us to 'tie up some loose strings,' as you Americans say. We have to get the right people in the right places. We're making progress, but it is impossible to rush."

President Grégoire replied, "We don't have weeks, Sir. We barely have days. And I must add, respectfully, that China has had years, Sir – YEARS – to deal with Pak Jung-ho, and has done nothing. Now it is past the eleventh hour – and you are asking for more time. No Sir, we don't have time. An international coalition of military forces is in motion, and in hours, President Taos, not more than 48 hours, they will act."

President Taos assumed an even less-pleasant tone of voice. "Yes, Mr. President, you have swarmed the Yellow Sea and the Sea of Japan with war vessels of every kind. Not one but two carrier strike forces are off our shores. Britain, Germany, and even France are sending military aircraft to your bases in South Korea and Japan. One could make the assumption that you, President Grégoire, and your 'coalition' intend to destroy more than just North Korea."

"President Taos, you are well aware that Seoul is less than 30 miles from North Korea's massive military forces. As soon as hostilities begin the North can destroy Seoul in an hour. Pak's chemical weapons near the DMZ must be completely taken out first. That will take a lot of firepower."

Taos knew this was all true; he was also quite sure it would be impossible to destroy all of North Korea's missiles before some of them reached Seoul. "Mr. President, no matter how you conduct this war, regardless of every effort you make – tens of thousands, even hundreds of thousands of people will die. Some North Koreans, some South Koreans – most of whom will be innocent people just going about their daily lives. And when it is all over, who will be blamed for firing the first shot?" He was hoping the question would have an effect on the new, backwoods President of the United States.

He was wrong. Grégoire quickly answered, his voice rising, "The first shot has already been fired, and it was by North Korea – a country led by a lunatic who threatens the security of all of Asia. History will well record the fact that China did nothing to prevent it. Nothing. In fact, Mr. President, while the rest of the world has attempted to impose and enforce sanctions on North Korea, you have been keeping Pak well supplied with all the oil and other essential resources he needs to keep his military running – usurping our efforts to reign him in. Please don't insult me with denials." It was a direct hit to Taos' breadbasket and Grégoire knew it. He gave Taos a moment to respond but there was just silence on the other end. So the President of the United States moved on:

"As for protecting Seoul and the rest of South Korea, we are moving more defensive equipment toward the DMZ. As I already pointed out, we know where all his firepower sits. It will all be destroyed in a massive coalition attack, which will take less than 60 minutes." The President paused for a moment before adding, "Regretfully, North Korean soldiers, men and women who have no other choice but to follow the orders of a mad dictator, will die. Such are the unfortunate rules of war. But make no mistake, Sir, it will be done."

Taos' staff had done their research on Grégoire and had labeled him just a 'hick from the sticks' with zero experience in international dealings and wars. What Taos was hearing now seriously contradicted that assessment. He asked, "What about his nuclear missiles, President Grégoire? He keeps them on trucks constantly moving from one hiding place to another. What will you do about them?"

"As long as he's hiding them he can't use them. As soon as one is set up to launch we will know, and it will be immediately destroyed. You, Sir, know we can do it. So I must state…" – President Grégoire's voice reached a grave and measured tone – "the time has come to act decisively, and when I say 'we' I mean the collective 'we' of the United Nations."

"Not all the United Nations, Mr. President."

"That's true. The world has noted China's absence in the solution phase of this problem. The silence of your ambassadors screams volumes. The Russians appear to be sitting on the sidelines but they are closely monitoring every move by all sides. What do you think their plans are? We know the Russians never miss an opportunity to take advantage of a situation." Grégoire took a moment to readjust his voice, toning down the anger he knew was showing through. "Corrective action is required; we're going to deliver it."

The line went silent as both Presidents held their peace. President Grégoire broke that silence in a calmed-down, acquiescing voice. "Sir, I'm the new guy here in the United States, you're the new guy in China. One of us is about to go down in history as the President who took defensive action to stop the nuclear deaths of many innocent people. The other will be seen as the one who did nothing to curb those deaths. It's rather plain who is who."

Although an insult wasn't intended, it was assumed. Taos therefore knew that further discussion would only degenerate so he cut to the chase. In a business-like tone tainted with anger, Taos asked, "Mr. President, you called me. *What do you want*?"

Now it was President Grégoire's turn to cut to the chase. "First, I want your assurance that when hostilities begin China's military will stay out of it, meaning you will not militarily aid North Korea. In turn, I will assure you that the minimum amount of damage will be done to North Korea, only what is necessary to put their nuclear program out of commission. I can also assure you that Chinese airspace and waters will not be violated."

"The first thing, Mr. President, there's more?"

The abrupt question almost caught President Grégoire off guard but he was ready. "President Taos, you have intelligence, on-the-ground intelligence. Your people could be of great assistance to the coalition. You could *save lives* with the information you have if you are willing to share. It can be done at the lowest levels without political or diplomatic red tape. Your people know how to put 'information' into our hands. Make that happen, Mr. President."

Once again there was a moment of silence, now Taos broke it. "China will certainly not stand by and watch the destruction of North Korea's defense force. If that were to happen South Korea would only need to wait until you all went home, and in one fell swoop take over all of North Korea. We cannot permit that and we won't."

Grégoire understood and appreciated Taos' concerns, and he was prepared with an answer. "The United States will guarantee that South Korea will not make such moves. I've already made it clear to them that we will not allow any sort of aggression, and will not stop China from intervening should South Korea act against our direction."

"Mere words, Mr. President, just words."

"Yes, President Taos, but they are *my* words and my promises. Now I'd like some promises from you."

President Taos' tone suddenly softened. "Unlike you, Mr. President, I can be replaced on a moment's notice – by the party. One hastily called meeting, a quick vote, and I'm removed. Therefore I cannot make promises without seeking the concurrence of the party. I know your Congress has already voted to support you. But most in my party continue to support North Korea unhesitatingly, and under no circumstances will they permit the destruction of North Korea's socialist government we've worked so hard for.

"Pak Jung-ho is temporary. Like you and I, the party believes the sooner he is replaced, the better. But it must be done correctly. If we are given time we will remove the menace."

Terseness returned to President Grégoire's voice. "You've had time. The Pak family did not come to power last month. Your 'best' hasn't been good enough and your resolve is questionable. The time to act decisively is now!" Easing up a bit, Grégoire continued, "I recognize the position you're in but that does not forgive your party for years of inaction. If China wanted to protect the socialist government of North Korea, they should have acted long ago to remove the series of lunatics running that country. Now they've threatened *your* way of life and your security, not just there but throughout the entire region. China failed to act when it could have. So now someone else has to act. I called hoping you could be part of the solution."

President Taos recognized the conversation might be ending. He hated to see it close with no real resolution. But more gravely, he didn't want the dialogue to end before making one more attempt to stop the destruction of China's neighbor and ally. "Mr. President, you have your finger on the trigger – a trigger, if pulled, may well start World War Three. Are you truly ready to accept that responsibility?"

President Grégoire's voice deepened and slowed, "The only way this will turn into a world war is if China intervenes, and that war will start and end in your part of the world." Grégoire gave it a moment to let his statement take effect, then he calmly added, "There's still time for China to act. But not long – 48 hours."

Taos took the cue, intended or not. He had 48 hours. "Thank you for the call, Mr. President. I appreciate your willingness to discuss our respective positions. I hope we have the opportunity to talk again before irrevocable actions begin."

"You have my word, President Taos. We will talk again. Good evening and goodbye."

As Marc put the phone down he raised his eyes toward Gabe, then over to Tim and Jane – all of whom were hanging up their receivers. He asked, "Well?"

Gabe went first. "He's in a big jam. He knows we're right. He knows that if China gets involved they have everything to lose. Yes, he has a determined Chinese government, but they certainly recognize the precarious position they're in."

Tim was next. "I wonder what their plan is to remove Pak. Have they sent in assassination teams? If they did I could see why they need more time. Pak is running so scared he lives in underground bunkers, frequently moving from one to the other. He trusts no one, allows only two or three people to get close to him, and changes them out as needed. He's a tough target to find – and hit."

Jane interjected, "I have to believe Taos is meeting with the party leadership at this very moment. They're between the proverbial rock and a hard place. In the end they're going to have to recognize things as they are. Here and in Beijing none of their spokespeople are giving consistent answers, very unlike the Chinese. They really don't know what to do. And I might add, they're scared."

The President was deep in thought. After rubbing his lower lip with his thumb and forefinger, he questioned, "Tim, how do we lean on the banks that do business with China? Could we impose a surcharge on all transactions with Chinese banks?"

"Probably," Tim answered. "It could add up to billions of dollars in just a few days. Wall Street won't like it though."

The President said, "The market is going to tank no matter what happens. It'll recover. But if we impose fees China would really feel the added heat."

"Indeed Sir. But at a cost to the U.S. also."

"I'd like to see some written discussion," the President stated. "What agency can put a proposal together? I don't want to enact tariffs immediately, but I want the Chinese to know we're considering it. We need to show them that we intend to use all the tools at our disposal."

Tim said, "I'll have Commerce draft up a proposal."

"Yeah, but just a draft – basic actions we can take and the ramifications. Do you think they can have something for me to look at by first thing in the morning?"

"Ah … Yes Sir."

The President was now rubbing his cheek with his finger and thumb. "Okay, but I don't need anyone here to make a presentation and I certainly don't want a 50-page dissertation. Just a 'what if' plan."

"I'll see to it, Sir."

The President was ready to move on and with a deeply exhaled breath declared, "Alright, let's have a three o'clock meeting in the Situation Room. I want General Chaffee, Shawn, Windigo, Paul, Roberts, Senator Duerr, and Speaker Glinko at this meeting, and of course the three of you. Also, ask the Director of Homeland Security, Woods, to attend. His first name..."

"Roger, Sir. Roger Woods," Tim answered.

As both men were leaving the Oval Office, Marilyn stuck her head in the door and announced, "Mr. President, you have a visitor."

THE PRESIDENT WASN'T EXPECTING VISITORS AND ASKED, "Who?" Marilyn just replied, "I'll send her right in." The President's eyebrows crunched down. Who would Marilyn 'send right in' without his okay?

Suddenly appearing in the doorway was Dr. Amélie Grégoire, sharply dressed in her USAF Major's uniform complete with medical indicia, knowing he would be pleased to see her in full uniform. She took two or three steps in, and abruptly stopped, 'This is the Oval Office,' she thought, and there was Dad at the President's desk!

The President rose. He managed a smile but his eyes were a little sad. "Am-mi!" he said. With a big wave of his arm he said, "Come in, come in." His face brightened as she moved toward him, and gave her a big hug, customarily lifting her off the floor. "I can still do it, he told her."

With her feet back on the floor, but still in awe, all she could say was, "Hi, Dad." With a huge grin, Marc asked, "Are you here for a few days? How long can you stay?"

"Well Dad, you know how you always say, there's the right way, the wrong way, and the Air Force way. Well, the Air Force way is to transfer me to Andrews indefinitely."

"That's okay, isn't it?" he asked.

"I suppose," she replied. "I have Ruthie here, but curiously they said my car will follow in due course but I won't need it much. What does that mean?"

"Well, it probably means they'll be transporting you around, with security, for the time being. But hey, when you do get your car you can come over here and I'll go incognito; we'll go for a crazy ride to Front Royal or someplace."

"Yeah, like that's going to happen. I can't even walk my dog alone."

The President smiled, "Bring her over here. I'll see that you get to walk her all by yourself."

"Okay, but how can I go on a date with a team of sunglasses not letting anyone near me?"

The President gave her a sad smile. "This will pass Am-mi. I hope it will all be over in a few days, then we can reassess."

"I can go back to Patrick?"

"We'll have to see," he responded. "There are a lot more resources here to keep you safe. Here, have a chair." Once they were seated he told her, "Let your mother help you pick out a bedroom here in the White House. Stay anytime you want. It's a little creepy at first, but it's an amazing place."

She was getting a little more comfortable, now glancing around the room. She asked, "Dad, you aren't going to waterboard the Swanton bomb guy, are you?"

Marc was astounded and his face showed it. "Now who would have told you a thing like that?" he asked her. During his hard-fix stare the unpleasant answer occurred to him: 'The spy who loves me is *not* keeping all my secrets safe tonight.' A mental note was made – be careful with the pillow talk.

Leaning closer to his daughter he explained, "Amélie, let's say your mother, you, your brother, and your beautiful little niece Angela are all on a plane from Denver to L.A. The FBI calls me and says there's a bomb on your plane and it is rigged to go off when the plane goes below 10,000 feet – in other words, on final approach into L.A." Slowing his pace down, Marc went on, "The FBI says they're doing everything they can to find it, but right now they think the best thing to do is to direct the plane to stay aloft as long as possible for more time to look for the bomb. But when they're running out of fuel they should drop below 10,000 feet out over the Pacific near San Diego. If the bomb doesn't go off they can land. If the bomb does go off there'll be plenty of rescue boats already on scene to pick up survivors, if any. This way there will be no deaths or damage on the ground. They also give me another option, attempt to land at Edwards AFB, where there is lots of open space for a plane to crash, if..."

Marc gave it a moment for that scene to form a picture in his daughter's mind. "Now they also tell me they got the little bastard who put the bomb on the plane, but he refuses to tell them where the bomb is or how to defuse it. They ask my permission to waterboard him to get the information out of him. Of course time is of the essence." After another short pause for effect, he asked, "Am I supposed to say, 'No, we can't violate that poor guy's rights. I guess we'll send the plane over the Pacific.' Do you think that's what I'd say?"

Amélie sadly shook her head. Softly her father said, "Of course I wouldn't. I'd tell them to do anything they want to the little ... until they get everything they need out of him. Terrorists break all the rules of humanity so sometimes we, in special circumstances, have to break a few rules ourselves."

The President leaned back in his chair and continued, "Now the Bebo guy in Swanton was ready to kill not just me, but your mother, your brother, your little niece, most of your aunts and uncles, and a large number of law enforcement officers and reporters. For what?

"He's just one of the nuts in a terrorist group operating out of Canada. They have some leads on other members, but the Canadians ... well, the Canadians haven't lost as many people to terrorism as we have – they need our help. One of Bebo's cohorts may be in a high place in Canadian law enforcement. They need to find out who that bastard is, immediately.

"And Bebo's group, they're going to strike again. We don't know who, when or why. What I do know is we got a key player in our hands. He's going to talk. We can't let his gang succeed in their next hit; and, I might add, it's the bastards like him that stop us from letting you walk your dog where you want."

The President wasn't done. "And what about all your aunts, uncles, and cousins who live in Quebec – who's protecting them? While the Bebo gang is on the loose, can they leave their homes without being afraid? The Mounties can't protect them all." Turning his head away from Amélie for a moment, he firmly added, "We might not get them all but we'll get all we can, by whatever means it takes. The gloves came off in Swanton."

The President knew he had drilled his point home, maybe a little more than he needed. Now to change the subject. With a partial smile he asked, "Are you coming to the dinner tomorrow night with the Dalai Lama? It's one of the perks of knowing somebody in the White House." Amélie's grimace turned to a pucker, then almost a smile and she responded, "Who'd miss a chance like that?"

"That's my girl." The President's face lit up. "Let Mom help you pick out something to wear – there's some kind of etiquette on dress. Now I have to call someone to offer them a job, then get ready for a meeting, but I will take time for supper. Will you still be here?"

"Sure Dad, I can stay. Clint Eastwood or somebody is not coming too, are they?"

Marc smiled, "Just you and me and Mom. Later, maybe you can ride out to the airport with the Secret Service – they're going out there to pick up Brian."

"Might as well, they won't let me do anything else."

"Keep smiling Amélie; you know 1600 Pennsylvania Avenue isn't exactly a shabby address."

* * *

Winter mornings are rather routine in the Acer home in St. Albans Town, Vermont. Beth Acer is tall and slim with features resembling her Dutch ancestry: blond hair and pretty blue eyes. Her husband Joe is local stock, barrel-chested and fit, always ready to run a marathon. He just came in from blowing a big snowdrift out of the double driveway and Beth was putting on a second pot of coffee.

The TV was on but nobody was paying attention to it – until the phone rang. Beth turned her head to see who was calling and she was more than surprised to see 'The White House' in the bottom corner of the TV screen. With some excitement she asked, "Could it be?" Joe, rather suspicious of telemarketers, said, "It could be him. You'd think he was too busy to be checking in with us." Beth asked, "Should we answer it?"

Joe said, "Well we better, that's the fifth ring, it's about to go to the answering machine." With a quick stretch of her long arm, Beth snatched the phone and said hello. The polite female voice at the other end said, "Good morning, is this the Acer residence?"

"Yes, it is."

"Could you please hold for President Grégoire?"

Beth's eyes went wide open and her jaw dropped down to her neck. She turned toward Joe excitedly and jabbed her finger to the mouthpiece of the phone. She tried to hand the phone to Joe but he waved her off. The next voice she heard was all too familiar.

"Beth my dear, how the hell are you?" Now she knew it was him.

"Marc! Um, I mean Mr. President! How are you?"

"Doing okay. We'll have to discuss the part about you calling me 'Mr. President.' So, are you staying warm, getting any skiing in?"

"Not much skiing, the hip still nags me. But at least this year we have enough snow. Joe is starting to wish we could spend more winter months down south though."

"Funny you should mention that."

"You know, I bet you called to talk to my hubby; let me put him on."

"No actually. I called to talk with you."

"Do tell. What could I possibly do for you?"

"Well, I have a position open here in Washington and I think you'd be perfect for it. So I'd like you and your old man to catch a plane to D.C. and come see us. And, if you come tomorrow, you can join us at a dinner in the Dalai Lama's honor right here in the White House."

"What do you mean 'a position'? What kind of position?"

"Well I can't discuss it over the phone, so I'd like you to come visit me. I'd love to go visit you two but I'm a little, uh ... tied up right now."

"Tied up is putting it mildly isn't it?"

"Things are under control," he replied.

"You know Marc, we're finally both retired and neither of us is looking for a job. We're looking forward to doing some traveling now. So fess up, what's the deal?"

"All I'll say is that it is an executive position, with a tremendous amount of influence in the future of our country, and ... it pays very well. You'll get to do all the traveling you want, meet interesting people, and get the red carpet treatment everywhere you go. And you are eminently qualified for the position."

"Sounds intriguing but I'm sure I'm not qualified – and I'm certainly not an executive, not even close."

"You don't need to be an executive – you'll have a huge staff to do all the administrative stuff for you. And you'll get to live here, where the winters are much shorter and there are lots of nice marinas for your boat. Now I've got to get ready for a meeting, so just say you'll both come and see us. How often do you get to have dinner at the White House and meet the Dalai Lama?"

With a tint of sarcasm, she replied, "Nah, I wouldn't have anything to wear."

"Don't give me that crap, you look terrific in anything."

"Can I call you back? You know I'll need to talk with Joe about this."

The President's reply was sheepish, "Well you could … but you'll have to talk to a lot of other people before you ever get to, you know, actually talk with me. I'll probably be too busy to take your call. So just say you'll come. I'll give you a number to call back, you tell the nice lady who you are and when you'll be getting to DC. She'll make sure someone is at the airport to pick you up and whisk you both to Blair House, then to the party. You can't tell me you don't want to come?"

"But a White House party – we don't know anything about high-brow parties."

"You'll be seated with Amélie, Brian and Lori – you know Brian's wife. Now come on. Tell me you two are on the way."

After a long, deep breath, she reluctantly said, "Okay, we'll come. But don't count your chickens before they hatch!"

Marc hung up smiling and thinking, 'and Brian, Lori and Amélie will be sitting with the next Secretary of Education.'

THE NEW PRESIDENT DOESN'T LIKE GRAND ENTRANCES, SO HE chose to be in the Conference Room ahead of everyone else. Once he was seated and had time to review a few of his handwritten notes, he gave the okay for everyone to come in and take their seats. First in was Tim, quickly followed by Lee and Jane. When Glinko and Duerr entered, the President invited them to sit on either side of him at his end of the table. In less than a minute everyone was seated with their heads pointed at the President.

The President welcomed everyone and thanked them for being there. He commented that the meeting probably constituted a war council, but he had every intention of avoiding a war. He started business by recounting his phone conversation with President Taos, reluctantly emphasizing that Taos did not, and probably could not, guarantee China would not come to North Korea's defense should there be an attack. He focused on Taos' request for more time to resolve the situation, and how he, President Grégoire, gave him two de facto days.

"Now in actuality, we're going to give China more than the two days but Taos won't know that. He needs to pull out all the stops to get rid of Pak immediately. While we certainly don't have two weeks, I believe we can string two days into five, maybe seven." He explained that the U.S. and the allies would put a choke hold on North Korea, first by establishing and enforcing a no-fly zone, then sealing off their seaports. China will be an unwilling partner in that they will close their entire border with North Korea to stop refugees from coming in. "This 'seizure,' if you will, of all of

North Korea will be accomplished in days rather than hours, giving China more time to do whatever it is they are planning."

Jane questioned, "What do you think they're trying to do, Mr. President?"

"There are several possibilities; foremost in my mind is a hit." He then looked up at Windigo, "Am I correct in thinking they have a team on the ground?"

"Yes Mr. President, we think they do. Although as we discussed, their team will have a hard time getting anywhere close to Pak. They may have to do something remotely – a bomb or a missile in the right place at the right time. It'll be tough."

The President nodded in agreement. He continued, "There aren't many other options. Of course we are all hoping for a peaceful solution. But it's been three years now since we stopped most of our joint South Korean–U.S. military exercises. We've even reduced the U.S. military presence in South Korea, all negotiated with Pak. And instead of curtailing his nuclear program as promised, he has expanded it. And now…" – tilting his lowered chin – "time is of the essence. I'm presuming Pak will need time to fix what went wrong on the Japanese nuke – could be a slight adjustment or just a change in personnel. In any case, we can't have any miscalculations on our part. We have to presume he's ready to launch another nuke.

"On the plus side, the attempt on Japan has caused Japan to go all-in with us, and most of the rest of the world recognizes and appreciates our need to act and act fast. But if the Chinese come to North Korea's defense it will turn into a major war. We have to persuade them not to do that. So we're going to tighten the screws."

Turning first to Glinko then to Duerr, "I understand Congress is on the verge of passing a carbon tax." Both men bowed their head; Duerr explained, "It's nip and tuck in the Senate. Constituents are giving plenty of feedback and both sides are vehement with their opinions."

"I'm sure they are," commented the President. "As I understand it, it raises all fuel taxes by 99 cents a gallon."

With a straight face Duerr replied, "Yes Mr. President. It is a hefty increase, it would be implemented in phases over four years. The proponents say that the people who use the highways should be the ones paying for them."

"Is that so?" Getting animated, the President demanded, "Then I want a goddam refund on my school taxes. I haven't had a kid in school for over 25 years!" The President took a breath and then turned to Speaker Glinko, "And this tax would also apply to heating fuel, is that right?" Glinko could see the President wasn't buying the carbon tax idea so all he did was nod. The President eased back a moment while he asked, "And what is our frugal government going to do with all these new dollars?"

Glinko explained that the roads and bridges would be improved, more money would be available for fuel efficiency research, grant money would be given to improve home insulation, etc.

The President asked, "How does that help the couple in Idaho who live in a trailer and heat with a pellet stove? Or those who either don't trust the government or have no idea how to apply for a grant? And how does a gas tax affect the local plumber who has to drive his truck to all his calls with the parts and tools he needs? Or the single mother who lives in Highgate, Vermont, and has to drive to Burlington every day for a decent job? And how does the carbon tax affect the price of everything that moves by truck, from the shirt on your back to a bag of carrots?"

Calming his voice but just by a notch, he said, "I know the super-leaning liberals want everyone to ride their bikes to work. They want the people who live in the sticks to move to the city. Well, the folks in Cheyenne, Wyoming, can't ride a bicycle anywhere this time of year, and there are no commuter trains for a hundred miles. Before I digress further, let me make it clear I will veto the carbon tax the second the bill hits my desk. It is a punishment tax, not a righteous tax to fund the government." Relaxing a bit, but rubbing his hands, the President pointed out, "I asked for some statistics, and learned that since 2005 the U.S. carbon dioxide emissions have declined by 758 million metric tons – annually! That's almost as much as the 770 million metric ton decline for the entire European Union." Raising a finger to head level he added, "During the same period China's carbon dioxide emissions grew by three billion metric tons."

Calmer, the President said, "Now we get back to China. Why do all the people in Beijing still wear surgical masks when they go outside? Because the air is polluted. Their factories burn the lowest forms of fuel they can find. All over the country their trucks and equipment burn stuff that is nothing more than low-grade kerosene. They're doing it so they can get rich providing the rest of the world with cheap goods. And we happily buy everything from them with total disregard of what it's doing – what

Chinese industry is doing – to the environment and our health."

The President leaned way back in his chair, stretched his arms out and laid the palms of his hands down on the table. After a long pause he continued, "I know there's a lot more we can do in the U.S. to improve Mother Earth. But our environmental protection measures have been the benchmark for most of the world to follow – except China."

Turning first to Senator Duerr then to Speaker Glinko, the President ordered: "You gentlemen go back to Congress, and – immediately – write a bill that puts hefty carbon taxes on imports from China. By buying Chinese goods Americans are doing far more harm to the environment than they can ever imagine. Call that the new carbon tax. And at the same time you'll notify the government of China that we, the people of the United States, have more than missiles at our disposal."

Duerr let a small smile escape to his lips. Now he knew why he and Glinko were sitting so close to the President. The President asked, "Are you picking up what I'm putting down?"

Glinko replied, "I certainly am, Mr. President."

Duerr nodded in agreement but pointed out, "China will retaliate, Sir."

"Yeah, I'm sure they will, but who will suffer most, them or us? The price of goods in America will go up but not by as much as your damn 99-cent fuel tax. Remember, some tariffs can be imposed with just my signature. We should explore those immediately. Now while we're on the subject of taxes and duties, Mr. Woods – Roger!"

"Yes, Mr. President."

Just then a door opened slightly and only a face could be seen; the eyes were looking for General Chaffee. Once found, the man behind the door pointed to his forehead then used his thumb and forefinger to form a U and placed it over his chin. The General nodded and the President waited.

"Mr. President, I have an urgent message, may I take a look?"

"Yes, go ahead."

General Chaffee opened his cell phone and read the message; his eyebrows flashed up and down and his hands came together in the yin-yang position. "Mr. President…" All eyes turned toward General Chaffee whose grave countenance indicated heavy news.

"Yes, Milt?"

"Mr. President, approximately 30 minutes ago a Chinese predator satellite" – his voice hesitating – "destroyed one of our satellites heading into deep space."

The President jumped to his feet so violently his rolling chair bounced off the wall behind him.

"They – did – what?"

The General was re-reading the message; he wanted to be absolutely sure. "They pursued one of our retired satellites and destroyed it."

The President was still on his feet, the anger in his voice fully displaying his French-Canadian temperament. "What do you mean, a 'retired satellite'?"

General Chaffee quickly composed himself – he well noted the President's anger and didn't wish to fan the flames. He explained, "When one of our satellites is running out of fuel we either let it fall back to earth where it burns up before it hits the surface, or we send it deeper into outer space where it becomes space junk. The Chinese chose one of our satellites heading into deep-space and blew it up. There was no great loss to us but they're clearly sending us a message."

The President was speechless but just for a moment. "The sons of bitches want to start star wars?" All eyes, some fearful and some wondering, were now riveted on the standing President. Putting his left hand over his mouth, he turned toward the world map. Then his right arm rose to wag a pointing finger at China. "Well, we're going to send the bastards a message of our own. Gabe!"

"Yes, Sir?"

Turning just his head toward Gabe, "Can we jam the GPS system over the entire country of China?"

Gabe rose to his feet and went to the map. "Well Sir, China's borders are jagged. I'm not sure we could turn it off precisely over just China." Gabe remained at the map. He could see where the President was going with this and pointed out that the simplest thing to do was jam the GPS coverage in a big round hole over most of China. But Gabe quickly regretted his suggestion; he knew that this would escalate tensions. "Sir, if we shut off GPS coverage over China, that will mean most of their aircraft, especially commercial aircraft, will lose directional guidance. They rely on GPS to find the destinations and plot courses. Some of those will be U.S. companies. The confusion could cause a crash. If we do something like this it shouldn't be for more than 20 or 30 minutes."

The President retorted, "They certainly don't rely on GPS alone, they'll resort to their other instruments, but I see what you're saying." The President lowered his eyebrows and pursed his lips indicating he was thinking, but in this case, plotting.

"Alright" – turning to face Gabe directly – "jam the GPS system for a full 30 minutes over the largest portion of China we can, but give all the airlines a warning about when it's going to happen. Jane!"

"Yes, Mr. President," she answered in a hushed voice.

"Call the Chinese ambassador and let them know we're shutting down the GPS over China for a little while. Let's say 7 o'clock tonight our time, and you can tell him why. And if he's shocked, you tell him his President should be calling me with a full goddam explanation of the stunt they just pulled."

"Yes Sir, Mr. President." Jane lowered her nose almost to the notebook in front of her while she scribbled away. Gabe headed back to his seat but quietly rolled the President's chair back in place so he could retake his seat.

Marc knew he had exposed his temper and once again demonstrated that he was a rough-around-the-edges boy from the country, so he decided to look at his notes to buy a few moments of composure. When he looked up all eyes were riveted on him. With a calm voice but serious face he said, "I think we need to adjourn and let you get to work. I've got a few things to do myself." With that the President rose. "I'm sure we'll meet again very soon," he added. The Cabinet members began to leave but as usual there were a couple of stay-behinds who wanted to speak to the President. First was the Attorney General.

"Sir, we have word that some cities, Seattle in particular, are issuing parade permits to some unsavory organizations. They are purportedly anti-war groups, but in fact, they're just highly organized troublemakers looking for legal ways to loot stores and burn police cars. These parade permits are nothing more than permission to riot. Frankly I don't know what the mayors are thinking. I know they're ultra-liberal there but this is downright foolish."

The President considered the information for just a few seconds, then asked, "Isn't the mayor of Seattle some young kid, like 22 years old or something?"

"I believe that's true, Sir, Joseph or Josh Dumont. Not sure which."

The President's sharp order came quickly, "You make a few calls to the mayors and governors involved. Tell them what you think about the permits. No need to ask them for an explanation. Just tell them that if they have to call out the National Guard, don't expect the federal government to reimburse them for their expenses. I will not have the American taxpayers paying for stupidity on the part of some local politicians. They'll be cleaning up their own messes on their own dime. Make sure they understand that. And yes, you can quote me."

"Yes, Mr. President."

"You like that answer?"

"I surely do, Sir."

Next was Jane. "Walk with me, Jane. I know you have lots of concerns." The two went out the door with Gabe and Tim trailing by a few feet. "Just one for the present, Mr. President. Ambassador Howard has arrived. Shall I bring him over?"

"Absolutely not. We are not going to reward his insolence by giving him an audience with the President." He stopped to face her. "I want you to have a carpet session with him. Let him know in no uncertain terms where he screwed up and what is expected of him from now on. He needs to fully understand how reckless – no, dangerous – his statement was. Even the Japanese saw that and I'm betting they won't be surprised if he is recalled. Fortunately for him this is no time to be swapping out ambassadors. But I will if I have to. You can tell him by my order that until further notice, any future contact with the Japanese government is strictly dictated to him from here. And as soon as you are done with him he is expected to have his ass on the next plane back to Japan. No hanging back here in the U.S., *the next plane.* If he has a problem with any of this he can consider himself removed immediately. And who can we ask in the embassy to keep an eye on him, to make sure he's following the letter of the law – my law?"

Jane was taken aback. Have him watched – the ambassador? Gulping down her shock she replied, "Well there is Monique Norman, the First Secretary. But she is not a State Department employee though, if you know what I mean."

"She's a spy. That makes her perfect for the job. Make it happen." As they continued to walk, the President had one more instruction. "Start looking for a replacement for Howard, a temporary ambassador if needed ... just in case. Somebody actually qualified, not some major donor. And make no doubt about it, when this is over there will be a new ambassador to Japan, but Howard doesn't need to know that yet."

Jane nodded. "Yes, uh, yes Sir." With that, she fell back to talk with Gabe and asked him, "What's a carpet session?" Gabe stopped walking and held her back. "That's where someone stands at attention on the carpet in front of your desk while you read them the riot act. You're not..."

"No, he wants me to have one with Ambassador Howard."

Gabe nodded in agreement. "Yeah, well his status as ambassador is on the edge. And that's the first thing you might tell him when he's standing on your carpet. If I were the President I'd have fired him on the spot for making such a reckless statement. As we just witnessed this is a no-nonsense President. And don't let his colloquial mannerisms fool you. He may not have the diplomatic sophistication we might expect our presidents to have but he is a man of action. Now he will cool down but he doesn't put up with foolishness, not for long."

Changing the subject Gabe inquired politely, "Didn't you and Marc know each other a few years back?"

"Several decades ago ... yes," Jane replied. Gabe detected something in her answer; he wasn't sure what it was. Somehow he felt a strange need to ask, "Back in college or something?" Fortunately for Jane she had reached her exit in the hallway, and as she turned she said, "No, nothing like that," and kept moving. But Gabe's questions momentarily stirred in her good thoughts of a hotel room in Africa.

THE WALLS OF THE INTERROGATION ROOMS AT RCMP Headquarters in Montreal are all painted institutional blah, and here in room two sat the now notorious Nikki Deemer. She wore the standard prison-grey pants and shirt 'outfit' with her own socks but no sandals or shoes. Her shoulder-length brown hair was tied up in a haphazard bun ready to fall apart. She sat in a straight-back metal chair which is bolted to the floor, and both of her wrists are shackled to the table. She had been sitting here all alone, for two hours, gagged and shaking like a leaf, and she has to pee something awful. The only window in the room is the one in the door, which she knew was a one-way mirror. Suddenly she saw some shadows moving on the other side of that window.

In walked a stout, 50ish man with a Molson-X belly, white shirt and tie, just about bald and sporting a first class, walrus-style, salt and pepper moustache. Behind him was a younger man in perfect physical condition, also in shirt and tie – both of them apparently unarmed. The younger man went and stood near the wall in a relaxed parade-rest stance, while J. F. McNeil pulled up the only other chair in the room and turned it around backwards so he could rest his arms on the back, yet still be face-to-face with the prisoner. He carried a legal size, manila envelope which he placed on the floor against a table leg.

McNeil greeted her, "Bonjour, Mademoiselle Deemer." Not being able to answer she shivered even more. McNeil said, "Ah, you would probably rather speak in English, eh? Easier for me, too." He looked at her straight in the eyes for a moment, then said, "The guards here say you've been giving them a really bad time." She shook her head once. McNeil said nicely, "No, eh?" He waited a few seconds before asking, "Then why are you cuffed to the table ... and you're gagged, too?" With exaggerated motions he bent over to look under the table and saw that both of her legs were strapped to the chair. Returning upright, he looked at her again and cocked his chin. "Are you sure you haven't been naughty?" he asked. She just glared at him.

RCMP Chief Inspector J. F. McNeil was glad she was gagged because up to the moment she had been throwing a lot of tantrums but had not yet asked for a lawyer, and he was hoping to get some vital information from her before she lawyered up. All she had to do was utter words like "I want a lawyer" or "Where's my lawyer?" and this interrogation was over. He didn't want that to happen. Somehow he had to get through the rights advisement without her asking for an attorney, so the gag was staying on for the moment.

He produced his police credentials and introduced himself, then pointed an open hand to the other gentleman, "and this is Special Agent George Fiske. He's an FBI agent from Washington, D.C." Fiske robotically pulled out his credentials, gave Nikki about three seconds to look at them, put them back in his shirt pocket where just the top of his gold badge still showed, and resumed his parade-rest stance. McNeil then reached for the envelope and pulled out a legal looking three-page document, but a complete forgery. "This is an extradition order," he told her. "Special Agent Fiske is here to take you back to the U.S." Brandishing the paper in front of her face, he taunted, "It's all signed. All it needs is my okay to release you, right here on this line," pointing to a blank line at the bottom on the last page. Then he hesitated. Over the next few seconds his stare softened and he told her, "Do you know what, Nikki? I really don't want to hand you over to the Americans, because they're going to take you directly to an old U.S. military base in Cuba where they 'incarcerate' terrorists." She raised her eyebrows. He added, "Your boyfriend Carol is already there." Her head fell backwards in shock.

"Yes, the Americans have branded you a bloody *terrorist*." McNeil hesitated for effect; Nikki just shook her head 'no' vigorously. "The Americans have had a lot of trouble with terrorists, and they especially hate assassins. So when they get you to Cuba," he leaned forward and in a low, frightening voice said, "they're going to do to you *whatever* they have to to get all the information they want." He leaned back in his chair slowly and added,

"The American President, the one you tried to kill, ordered it himself. He said you're all going to hang." He turned towards Fiske for a moment and then looked back at Nikki. "I can save you from all that, Nikki. You and me, working hard together, can keep you here in Canada where you'll be treated fairly, and eventually returned to your home. But you'll have to be forthcoming with me, Nikki. I'm your one and only hope, and we have only this one chance, right here and right now." She glared at him with moist red eyes. He asked, "Do you think we can work together? Protect you from the Americans?" She nodded up and down profusely. "Good. Here's what MUST happen. I'm going to take the gag off, then I'll advise you of your rights. At the end, I'm required to ask you if you want an attorney. If you say yes … then this talk of ours is over. Because attorneys presume anyone in a prison suit is guilty; they won't let you say a word. Then you and I won't be able to talk things over. I'll have no choice but to bow to U.S. pressure and sign this extradition order. You'll leave this room in the custody of" – he turned slowly toward Fiske – "this American FBI agent. So I'm telling you that you do have the right to ask for an attorney, really. But if you do – it's over for you here in Canada. Do you truly understand everything I explained to you?" She nodded.

"And you're ready to work with me?"

She nodded again.

"Okay then." McNeil got up and went around to the back of her head and gently untied the gag, saying, "Remember, you can ask for a lawyer but if you do…" He didn't have to finish the sentence. Nikki was an experienced reporter and she knew exactly what he was saying. Once the gag was off he stuffed it out of sight in his back pocket and went back to his chair, again facing her directly. She sucked in air like it was the first time she ever breathed. She blurted, "I have to pee – right now! I've already made a puddle on the chair!"

McNeil looked at her solemnly and said, "We'll get you cleaned up. But when you leave this room you have to be either in his custody" – turning his head toward the official-looking Fiske – "or mine. You and I both want you to stay with us." Taking a card out of his shirt pocket, he explained, "Now I'm going to read you your rights; remember what we talked about." She nodded. He pushed a button on the corner of the table and announced, "We are now being recorded."

He read her her rights under Canadian law: told her she had the right not to say anything, then informed her that she had the right to speak to an attorney or have one present during this interview. Looking up from his card with his head slightly cocked and an eye half shut, he asked, "Do you wish to call a lawyer at this time?" She shook her head no. McNeil said, "For the record, Ms. Deemer is shaking her head no, indicating she does not wish to speak to an attorney at this moment." Under normal circumstances he would have asked her to say it aloud but he wasn't going to push it.

They got down to business slowly. He started by getting her full name, date of birth, and a few other details he already knew. Then he asked about where she grew up and she mentioned several places in Ontario and Quebec. McNeil used her answers to gently delve into her childhood with questions such as, "What was it like for a seven-year-old girl to move from an English province to a French province?" She answered casually and began to relax ever so slightly. He asked her how she got into the news business, etc., and soon the two of them were talking about her job at the station. Easing closer to the harder questions, they talked about the rigors of news reporting and the events of the last few days.

Now it was time to get down to brass tacks and McNeil wasn't sure which question he wanted to ask first: who the bomb maker was or the name of the source in Ottawa. Since he hated traitors himself, he went for the Ottawa source question first.

Nikki was aghast and blurted, "I can't tell you that! He is a confidential news source; I can never reveal his identity."

McNeil expected pushback so he said, "Nikki, what do you think we brought you in here for?" He went quickly over everything they knew so far, especially the phone call from RCMP headquarters in Ottawa, then told her, "I need that name; if you can't give it to me … you're leaving with Agent Fiske," and leaning hard towards her he warned, "he'll get it out of you down in Cuba. By tomorrow night."

She cried, "But he's a news informant, that's all. If I tell you he'll lose his job!"

Fiske bent forward towards McNeil, pointed at the envelope and demanded, "I knew she wouldn't tell you jack-shit. Now, just sign it. I'll take her from here."

The Chief Inspector crunched his chin making his moustache look even larger. He pulled the fake extradition order off the floor and laid it on the desk with a slap. He pulled a pen from his pocket and loudly clicked it open, then cocked his head and said, "Nikki, give me his name."

She leaned back into her chair and tears started coming down both cheeks; with a big sob she cried, "Cal Kinney. We were co-joints at one time" – the Quebec way of saying they shacked up – "and he's just a clerk in the Operations Center."

McNeil nodded. "How long has he been a member of your gang, your organization?"

She turned furious, "He's not a part of any gang. He's just a clerk who gave me news tips. When we were living together *I'm* the one who moved out and broke things off with him, and he has been doing everything he can to win me back. So whenever he could he sent me information, things I might get a news story from."

McNeil looked at her directly and probed, "But he knew you were plotting to get the American Vice President."

"NO!" she yelled. "He had nothing to do with that, he was just a news source."

Just down the hall from Nikki's interrogation was another room, this one packed with RCMP officers listening in on Nikki's interrogation. With the revelation of Kinney's name they were all immediately on their phones or mashing away on laptops. Suddenly the senior officer nearly dropped his phone and announced, "Kinney signed out on sick leave yesterday. How the bloody hell did they let him go? They knew he was on the short list. God DAMN!" Shaking his head in anger and pointing at the computers he directed, "All points bulletin on Kinney – Canada-wide." One of the officers mumbled "yes sir" and frantically changed screens on his computer. The senior officer went back to his phone and yelled, "Find his ass! Go to his house, check with all his relatives." Even louder he yelled, "Get him! You know what to do."

Indeed Kinney was on the short list of suspects, and as such they already had all the bio data they needed. They knew his car, his address, and that he grew up in Brossard, Quebec, where his parents still lived. He also knew police tactics, so if he was running it was to anywhere but Brossard.

In fact Kinney was on the run, and he believed that the best place to lie low was with an old school chum in Roberval, Quebec, on Lac St. Jean – 150 kilometers north of civilization. He had already driven the secondary roads over the north side of Montreal, then northeast to Three Rivers, and now it was straight north toward Roberval. He had to stop in La Tuque for fuel and some beef jerky; it was still another two hours to Roberval. As he got back in his car at a gas station on the north side of La Tuque, he noticed a Sûreté du Quebec police car parked across the street. It was three in the afternoon and already getting dark; the officer was out of his car and dealing with a couple of teenagers on the sidewalk.

Cal Kinney had already seen several police vehicles during his long ride from Ottawa, and none of them took notice of him. So as cool as possible he started his car, pulled out to the intersection, and waited at the traffic light. By the time it turned green the Sûreté officer was back in his car. After Kinney passed him the screen on the police console lit up! The license plate reader mounted on the cruiser's trunk had picked up Kinney's plate number and displayed the BOLO in red! Instantly the officer pulled a U-turn and started after Kinney, deciding not to turn on his red and blue lights until he could get closer. He got on his secure radio to Sûreté headquarters. Instructions came fast, 'Do not attempt to apprehend without backup. Maintain surveillance.' The La Tuque station commander was mortified as he listened in on the radio. Half of his officers were in Quebec City for mandatory training. The only officers he had available were two detectives working a theft at the church in Lac Edouard, over an hour away, and a snowmobile team running radar on the Rail Trail towards Rivière-a-Pierre.

Kinney noticed the police car was now behind him and he was getting nervous. Was he following him or just happening to be going the same way? He had to find out. Using his turn signal, Kinney indicated a left turn into what appeared to be a small, road-side restaurant. Pulling in he was disappointed to see the *casse croute* was closed. In fact it was just a summertime French-fry stand. The Sûreté officer passed on by but quickly backed into a driveway with Kinney just out of sight. Not wanting to get caught going south if Kinney continued north, the officer got out of his car and trotted about 30 feet to where he could observe Kinney, just in time to see him pulling out to head south again back toward La Tuque. Back in his car, the officer was soon six car lengths behind Kinney, petrifying the now indecisive Cal Kinney.

Kinney tried to think things out quickly while studying his GPS. He surmised he could never lose his follower in the tiny town of La Tuque, so as he was entering town he abruptly turned right on the only road toward the tiny settlement of La Croche. From there he could take logging road number 10 towards the Barrage Gouin, over 150 kilometers away. He hoped that somewhere in between he could lose his tail long enough to hide his car; but given the January weather, there was no way he could go on foot – and survive. In great dismay he saw the Sûreté car turn the corner with him. What he didn't know was that the two detectives in their unmarked Ford Explorer were racing back from Lac Edouard.

The Sûreté officer radioed in the situation. He pointed out he was driving a sedan and Kinney had a Highlander, and it might be possible for Kinney to lose him on the logging road. Orders came back fast: 'Stay on him at all costs,' and in unprecedented English a voice came across the radio, "Don't bloody lose him." Obviously someone in Ottawa was connected into the radio transmissions. The Sûreté officer considered several scenarios: if Kinney did stop and go on foot he could pursue, especially since he was already dressed for cold weather and deep snow. If Kinney pulled off onto a rougher road, the Sûreté's AWD Dodge would take a beating but could probably keep up as long as it didn't bottom out in a deep rut or a washed-out culvert. All of the side roads were 4x4 only, unplowed, and came to an abrupt end at a closed-up hunting camp or logging point, something Kinney probably didn't know. So the Sûreté was actually hoping he would be foolish enough to take one of those random turns. He would be easy to track in the snow and wouldn't get far on foot.

Kinney continued northwest, now on logging road 10, a desolate road with no electricity, no houses, and now just darkness. The Sûreté eased back knowing he could easily follow Kinney's tire marks in the new snow, and by not pushing him the detectives would have more time to catch up.

Sixty-five kilometers into the moving surveillance, Kinney suddenly saw a light, then several lights, then the large driveway of the Relais 22, a hunting and fishing outfitter with a restaurant and a motel – the only semblance of civilization between La Tuque and the Barrage Gouin. He slowed to see if the Sûreté was still behind him. The Sûreté officer knew the place well, and as he approached the narrow bridge just before the 22 he slowed to a stop and turned off all his lights. Sure enough Kinney pulled in. Having had the last 65 kilometers to think things over, Kinney quickly went in and asked for a room, making up a story about his car battery being bad. When he was told the mechanic at 22 could replace it tomorrow, Kinney asked if they could put his car in the garage for the night so it would be warm in the morning; otherwise it might not start. The 22 employee readily agreed. Kinney went back on the porch to look around and there was no sign of the Sûreté or anyone else. After parking his car inside the repair shop in the back he went directly to his room in the adjacent single-story motel. He knew he wasn't safe but this was his best option. He figured he'd cool his heals for an hour or two, and if the Sûreté didn't show up he'd get some gas and keep heading north. It also occurred to him that maybe the gig was up.

The Sûreté officer called the situation in. He was informed that the detectives were 45 minutes out. Knowing the snowmobile trail went right to 22, the station commander ordered the two snowmobile officers to get to 22 as soon as possible. When they got the call they were just congratulating themselves on giving an American on a super-charged Arctic Cat a ticket for going 102 MPH in a 45 zone – double the speed limit, triple the fine. After quick deliberation they decided it would be faster to get there by snowmobile, and headed their Ski-Doo Summits for Relais 22, balls to wall. They intended to make the three-hour ride in 90 minutes. On the way they learned who they were going after and why. The news made them take more chances than they should have.

By 7 PM the plainclothes detectives had arrived. They sauntered into the Relais 22 restaurant, took a table where they could keep an eye on the small motel and the garage, and ordered coffee and burgers. By 7:30 they were informed that the snowmobile officers had arrived but were holding their position in the woods just out of the lights of 22. The senior detective, Serge Lacoste, took charge. His plan was as follows: The uniformed officer would guard the back entrance of the motel building while the two detectives went to Kinney's door for the arrest. The two snowmobile officers were to station themselves right outside his bedroom window.

Kinney had taken a shower and was lying on his bed in his skivvies, trying to come up with a better plan. He looked the part of a turncoat: skinny build maintained by chain smoking handmade cigarettes, prematurely thin, sandy colored hair balding from the forehead backwards, and beady brown eyes that always looked half-closed. He was scared. He knew they wouldn't give up, not when they were after one of their own, and not for what he had done. His heart was pounding. Momentarily he got hold of himself and started assessing what was going right. His car was well hidden and it had been about two hours now and nobody had come after him. He didn't know what had happened to the Sûreté car that was following him but it didn't show up at Relais 22. All the same he wished he could get his hands on his cousin's snowmobile, because the trail went from 22 directly to Roberval. It would be a long night ride all by himself; he'd freeze but he'd make it.

It was all spinning in his head when the silence was crashed by two bangs on his door! His head jerked up and he instantly panicked. He went straight for the window, flung it open, and dove into the snow … right at the feet of the two snowmobile officers. Seeing the two massive-looking officers in their black and brown snowmobile suits, he didn't resist and just let himself drop. Knowing who they now had in their grasp, the officers each took an arm and dragged him on his back unceremoniously through the deep snow to the front entrance where the detectives were waiting. His tighty-whities had slid down all the way to his ankles and his bare butt was now rosy red. Lacoste pulled him to his feet and handcuffed him while the other detective pulled up his underwear. Minutes later he was dressed, double-cuffed in the back seat of the unmarked Explorer, and on his way back to La Tuque. Now the marked car stayed close behind.

While all the above was put in motion, McNeil was getting ready to ask Nikki about the bomb maker. He was expecting a lot of resistance from her, but when the question was posed Nikki only slightly hesitated: "Ricky Boucher," she announced. Boucher – pronounced 'Boo-shay' – was somewhat known to the police but only as an anti-government noise maker who had one time marched with a group known as Black Block. The police had no idea he made bombs.

"Who did Boucher get his instructions from?" McNeil asked.

"Me."

Surprised, McNeil asked, "You? But who's in charge of the organization?"

She said again, "Me, you chauvinist. I'm the leader." Her inflections showed clear pride yet pure indignation. McNeil surmised that the insult may induce her to tell all, and if an insult was all it took to push her buttons, he'd try another one. "But you're a girl!"

She would have slapped him if she'd had a free hand. She leaned as far back in her chair as her cuffed hands would allow, sat straight up, squinted her eyes and pursed her lips. McNeil realized he had found the right button but he may have pushed it too hard. He tried to backpedal: "You're the mastermind behind all this? You had an excellent plan." The sideways compliment didn't work; she asked him, "Have you ever heard of Madame Marie-Madeleine Méric?" McNeil shook his head. She explained, "Madame Méric was the head of the underground French Alliance during World War II. She organized and led the entire organization all across France. A woman! She was arrested by the Nazis and escaped several times, but she continued to run the organization right to the end of the war, a war in which she helped kill a lot of wicked Germans."

McNeil wondered if perhaps Méric was some kind of role model for Nikki. He let that possibility float to the back of his mind because he wanted to get back to Boucher. He asked, "So you are the one who recruited Boucher?"

"I *found* him," she answered. "He lives in Chambly and works in a mine – I think it's a copper mine – near Granby."

McNeil pressed, "That's where he got the dynamite?"

"He was in charge of the inventory; whenever they were over by a stick or two, he brought it home."

"His home?" McNeil asked.

"Yeah. He has an old farmhouse on Chemin des Patriotes." Her voice still had anger in it but she was talking.

"How did you meet him?" McNeil asked.

She hesitated for a moment, not sure why, then answered, "He was in Quebec City protesting a world bank meeting. The protesters were running from the water cannons; he bumped into me and fell, scared as hell. I helped him up and told him I wasn't a cop, I was a reporter. I ended up taking him someplace for a meal and found out about his job with dynamite."

The RCMP officers in the room down the hall had just gotten the ball rolling on Kinney when Deemer spilled Boucher's name. RCMP officers with plenty of backup from the Sûreté were sent to stake out Boucher's home. More officers were sent to his place of work in Granby. The immediate plan was to apprehend him either at his job or before he got home. They certainly did not want to have to go into his home to get him; the place could be totally booby trapped by a guy who had access to lots of dynamite.

In fact, Boucher was running scared and left work early. His plan was to get home, pack a few things, and use his new passport to fly to Brazil or anywhere else in South America he could get a ticket to. When he parked his Nissan Sentra behind a hedgerow at his house, he was swarmed and seized by five RCMP officers with several others coming out of nowhere. In minutes he was handcuffed and chained to the inside of a special police van rolled to the scene moments after his arrest. He said only one thing to the police: "I want my lawyer and I want him now."

Back in room two, McNeil had a lot more to ask. He was wondering why Deemer gave Boucher up so easily. If he could draw that out he was sure more incriminating information would surface. He also realized Nikki had wet herself a little and could bring this interview to an end at any moment. Indeed, Nikki said something that almost made McNeil wet *his* pants: "You know, maybe I should talk to a lawyer." McNeil let his guard down by wiggling his huge mustache up and down. There were a number of things he could say but he chose silence. Nikki's keen reporter's observation skill clearly noticed McNeil's poker face was broken. McNeil was thinking of countering by invoking the Agent Fiske threat again but he had already pushed her to the edge once, barely avoiding a huge backfire. He didn't want her to say the actual words so to prevent that he said, "Nikki, you and I have made some excellent progress this afternoon. I just have a couple more questions, then we'll get you cleaned up and something to eat." Still anxious for her not to say anything more about a lawyer, he pushed on.

"Boucher screwed up, didn't he?

Nikki's eyes narrowed and apparently forgetting about the lawyer, she acknowledged, "He didn't put the bomb together right." This was her first clear admission that she knew about the bomb. There was silence – but at this point McNeil didn't want any silence because that allowed for thinking. He didn't want Nikki to think; he wanted her to talk. He asked, "He didn't?"

Nikki's anger was back. "No he didn't. If he had, for the first time in history the United States wouldn't have a President." It was another important admission.

"What happened?" McNeil asked.

"I don't bloody know. What I do know is that Carol called me while he was standing in front of Grégoire's house, said he noticed some movement inside and that he had pulled the trigger several times and nothing happened." The association between Bebabeau, Deemer, Kinney, and Boucher was now complete and all on tape.

McNeil turned his head and pressed, "So you told him…"

"I told him to be cool, pack up and get away, but not to come back across the border with the bomb. Just then," pointing her thumb to the perfectly still Fiske – "these guys grabbed him. If they hadn't, I would have told Carol to throw the bomb off the Rouses Point Bridge and get back to Canada."

Suddenly Deemer sat back in her chair, leaned to one side, and pissed in the chair. She let it all go and it could be heard running down the chair leg onto the floor. The small room was instantly putrid with the acrid smell of urine. When she was done she leaned forward and declared, "This interview is over. You got all you need. There's no one else involved. And remember, Cal had no idea about my plans to kill the American president. Let me out of here or I'll demand a lawyer."

Stunned, McNeil decided to end it for the moment. But they would continue tomorrow, and somehow he would have to find a way to coerce her into taking a polygraph exam. Even though she said no one else was involved, it had to be verified. He also wanted to ask about other targets the group had, their motivations, and much more.

McNeil said, "Okay, Nikki. We'll talk again later. We have some lose ends to tie up but we can give you a break. Now I'm going to go out and tell them you're helping us and you deserve a shower, a meal, and a place to rest all by yourself." Pointing at her he directed, "Don't screw that up by giving them a hard time, because when we meet again I hope you won't be strapped to a chair, and maybe we'll both be able to relax with a coffee." He was thinking of giving her the standard speech about her not being a bad person, just misguided, but realized it wouldn't work with this Nikki Deemer.

As J. F. McNeil rose to leave with his colleague, Nikki said, "Just make sure you lose this American goon," nodding her head towards Fiske, "and bring some donuts; you coppers know all about donuts, right?" McNeil smiled inside; Nikki probably intended both comments as insults but to him they were strong indications that the interview would continue. What he didn't know was that during the next interrogation, Nikki would admit that Canada's Prime Minister was also on their hit list.

Fortunately the polygraph she eventually agreed to take indicated that all the members of her group were now in custody: Deemer, Kinney, Bebabeau, and Boucher.

A PIERCING CHILL, THE KIND THAT GOES RIGHT TO THE BONE, pressed to the earth by low hanging January clouds, made the coming dawn almost unnoticed to two dozen Chinese soldiers on bivouac by the banks of the Yalu River. The cold rapids could be heard forcing their way around and under ice shelves frozen to the river's marshy shores and rocks. The soldiers arrived 20 hours earlier from Baishan, China, about 15 kilometers east-northeast of their present encampment. The cold was made worse by the fact they were ordered not to pitch tents, and no open fires. The conditions made for a long, cold night. But these soldiers were Leishen Commandos and cold meant nothing to them. With just 15 centimeters of snow on the ground, they considered this bivouac a walk in the park. Bent over bushes were their tents, heavy clothing their warmth.

An obscure truck had turned off Chinese Provincial Road 303 and was making its way southwest to the bivouac area. It was a 10-wheeler heavy cargo truck with an eight-meter cargo box. Its military affiliation went unnoticed except for the unusual array of communication dishes collapsed on the cargo box roof. Indeed it was a mobile command post, stricken of all its military markings. The forward six meters of the cargo box was all electronics and well-muffled generators. The remaining two meters was a 6.5-foot by 8-foot office. When the truck came to a stop in the bush it was surrounded by the waiting commandos.

It was a long 40 minutes before the cold, still air was disturbed by the whoop-whoop of three approaching helicopters crossing the river from the south. They were coming in hot just feet above the treetops. The first helicopter circled the bivouac area once, then landed. The second went directly toward the truck and settled down in the snow. The third remained in the air hovering, obviously surveilling the general area.

When the rotors of the second helicopter finally came to a slow stop, two figures exited and trudged through the snow toward the rear of the command post. The stairs were down and commandos were posted at the base. The two from the helicopter began to climb the steps but only one was allowed to enter; the other was ordered by the commandos to wait outside.

Standing inside the truck waiting for the visitor were two men, both in uniform. The senior's uniform was devoid of rank and name tags, but the insignias on his sleeve and collar disclosed his status as a senior ranking Chinese military officer. The second man was a heavily armed commando, garbed in winter gear and clearly ready for anything. When the door closed, standing in front of them was their visitor: none other than Pak Jung-ho.

"Sit down, fool," ordered the Chinese officer. Pak half-smiled thinking the order was for the commando. But it wasn't. The officer sternly repeated, "Sit down," and pointed to the chair behind Pak. Pak's indignation caused him to hesitate a moment, then he instantly turned toward the door, pointed at the officer, and cursed "*Shi-bal-nom-a*" the Korean equivalent of 'F you.' But the door wouldn't open. Pak struggled with it then resorted to banging. Nothing happened. Once again the Chinese officer ordered, "Sit down, or I'll have this man shoot you right between the eyes, doing the entire world a great favor." Pak was in shock. He slowly turned back; the officer half-stepped to his left so Pak could get a full view of the commando, who was holding a large semi-automatic pistol tucked tightly against his chest with the barrel pointed right at Pak's head. Pak saw the scared face and intrepid look in the commando's expression and correctly concluded that this man has killed before, and would kill now if so ordered.

The officer ordered, "For the last time – sit down." Pak bent slowly toward the chair, barely letting his buttocks touch the seat and not letting his huge torso touch the backrest.

The officer barked, "Do you know how much trouble you have put us all in? I suppose not, being the imbecile that you are." Pak opened his mouth to protest. "Not a word from you!" shouted the officer as he pointed the full length of his arm and index finger at Pak's face. Pak jumped to his feet and tried the door again. When he realized his attempts were futile, he once again half-turned toward his accuser.

The Chinese officer glared at him and said, "Listen carefully, idiot. It is only because I have been so ordered that I make you this offer. Return here within 24 hours. Bring one other person with you if you wish. I don't care if she's your grandmother or your favorite concubine – just one." The officer's cold stare radiated with revulsion, yet he continued, "From here we will take you to the interior. You will be housed comfortably. We will move you from place to place as needed for security. Do you understand?" Pak glowered; after a few moments the officer tersely stated, "Remember, I would rather shoot you than protect you." Then pointing his head towards the noisy chopper circling above he added, "And your men in your helicopters, they would be glad to leave without you because they know you're going to get them all killed by the Americans. So for the last time, do you understand my offer?"

Pak's lower lip puckered out. His eyes opened widely. His angry voice finally spewed, "Go to hell." He took a breath, his right hand turned into a fist, his eyes now narrowed, then he barked, "I was told I would be protected like the hero I am." Both men stared each other down. Making a bulldog face, Pak demanded, "When would I return to North Korea as Supreme Leader?"

"Never!" came the quick answer. "Your time is up." The officer intensified his angry stare. "We will be back here in 23 hours. In exactly 24 hours, not a minute longer, our generous offer will expire." The officer leaned closer toward Pak and said, "If you are not here, you might as well put a bullet through your head, like Hitler. Because if you don't, somebody else will, somebody close to you. Remember that."

The stare-down continued for a few seconds then the Chinese officer loudly ordered, "Now get out!" and on the officer's signal the door flung open, letting the cold in and Pak out. Pak was quickly down the stairs, and with 27 giant goose steps he was at the helicopter door. As the chopper lifted off, Pak angrily looked over the area and the truck below. Under his breath he said to himself, 'I shall *not* be back.'

He had no way of knowing that in days, not many, just three or four, this very area will be packed with North Korean refugees escaping to China.

The three helicopters were quickly back across the Yalu River, now back into North Korean airspace.

'THE PRESIDENT'S OWN' MILITARY BAND WAS PLAYING SOFT chamber music in the Center Hall of the White House. Guests were arriving for the banquet in honor of His Holiness, the Dalai Lama. The President was in the Map Room receiving updates on diplomatic communiqué's and military movements – some in person, some by secure phone. When the Secretary of State and her husband arrived, she immediately reported to the President: "The Chinese informed me, Mr. President, that they hit our satellite by accident. They were – essentially – target practicing, and had no idea the satellite was ours."

The President lowered his chin and said, "And you told them that was the biggest load of shit you ever heard, right?"

"Well, yes Sir, but in slightly different terms. They had some very terse remarks about us jamming the GPS over China."

"And you told them it was just an accident."

"No Sir, I didn't. But I did relay in the strongest terms that Taos should call you personally with an apology and an explanation. I was led to believe that he will call tonight. But I wouldn't count on an apology."

"Good. I got a few things to discuss with him. Anyway, the Dalai Lama should be arriving any moment. I better go check my hair."

"Just one more thing, Mr. President. Howard is on a plane back to Japan. He has strict orders."

Several thoughts came to the President's mind, but he knew he didn't have time to discuss it at the moment. So all he had to say was, "Good. Now let's see if he can follow those orders."

The President arrived at the Diplomatic Reception Room in time to greet Beth and Joe coming through the Center Hall. They had just enjoyed a private tour of the China Room with the First Lady. Beth was giddy and nervous; Joe was collected but clearly out of his comfort zone. Leonie walked them up to the waiting President. "Hello Beth, my dear!" he said, and with that came a hug. Then a presidential handshake with, "Joseph, *mon homme*!" All Joe could do was smile and say, "Nice to see you." He too was quite stunned to be standing at the grand entrance of the White House. Beth quipped, "This is ... just surreal." She didn't want to make it obvious, but her head was turning in all directions trying to take it all in.

Marc said, "Yeah, it's a nice place, you know, once you learn your way around. But it's a little too – uh – pompous for a kid from the sticks like me." The President had a big smile as he said it, and it was obvious that both he and Leonie were glad to see their good friends from home. Joe finally mustered a question, "Any of your brothers or sisters coming to this shindig?"

"Nah. After the situation in Swanton, they probably want to stay as far away from me as possible." The President's smile faded. At that moment, Marc was informed that the Dalai Lama's car was approaching the steps. Joe presumed they needed to get out of the way and certainly didn't want to be in the background of any pictures. His wish was granted by a White House butler who escorted the Acers to the East Room and their table. They were glad to see Amélie, Brian and his wife Lori there. Otherwise, they'd have been totally lost in a sea of some very important looking people.

The Dalai Lama opened his own door of the black Lincoln Town Car the White House had provided. He wore a heavy, full-length parka from LL Bean, with the logo removed. Once inside the White House, the parka was taken and he swapped his boots for thick-soled sandals to protect his feet from the cool floors. His flowing robes, which usually exposed at least one shoulder and arm, now covered as much skin as possible. Over his robes he wore an oversized, rust-colored wrap of soft, felted wool squares sewn together in a random pattern, regal in color, artistic to the eye, and warm to the Dalai Lama's shoulders.

The President, who hadn't had much time to be briefed on the etiquette of greeting the Dalai Lama, except to learn that His Holiness did not allow women to touch him, put his hand out for a handshake. Protocol or not, the Dalai Lama took the President's hand and shook it. 'Welcome to the White House' and 'I'm very honored' and other usual and customary greetings were exchanged. The two men were escorted to the Vermeil Room, or Gold Room, where two podiums were set up close together. To the President's displeasure, portraits of former First Ladies were temporarily removed for the occasion.

The two men stood at the podiums facing several cameras which were streaming everything to the outside in real time. The President was adamant that the whole world, particularly the Chinese, were well aware of this grand reception, because he knew that China did not approve of White House visits by the Dalai Lama. He also felt that the visit would convey a sense of normalcy at the White House – versus panic – which Americans in particular needed to see.

The brief speeches at the podiums were all politeness and the warmest of wishes. Neither of the men mentioned politics. And since the Dalai Lama didn't specifically request a private audience with the President, he wasn't going to have one. He would, though, be dining at the same table as the President and First Lady.

As the entourage was making its way to the East Room, the President was informed that President Taos was on the phone. The President decided this was a good time to take the call, as it would take about a half hour for the Dalai Lama to make it through the reception line. The President begged his pardon.

As expected, Taos was calling to offer an excuse for the destruction of the U.S. satellite. It was the same excuse that was relayed through diplomatic channels. President Grégoire listened respectfully, and when Taos was apparently done the President bluntly asked, "So who got fired?"

Taos was confused and asked, "What do you mean, Mr. President?" President Grégoire explained, "If someone in my government shot down a Chinese satellite, or anyone's satellite – through a grievous mistake – somebody would get fired. It would be anyone from the Secretary of Defense on down. So I'm asking you, who did you fire for this mistake?"

It was almost like the line went dead. The best Taos could come up with was that they were still investigating the matter. In an attempt to get on the offensive, Taos tried to scold the President for jamming the GPS system. He even claimed it had caused several deaths, then added, "I suppose you're going to tell me it was a mistake?"

The President jumped on it. "No, there was no mistake. I personally ordered it. But how did it cause deaths?" Taos explained that when some truckers lost their GPS signal, their confusion caused numerous traffic jams causing several fatal accidents. Without apology the President remarked, "That's unfortunate."

Eager to move on, President Grégoire asked if the Chinese had made any headway in removing Pak. Taos said there were several irons in the fire and that he expected results, possibly in less than 24 hours. President Grégoire was impressed and commented, "Apparently you've been able to move things up. But 24 hours is just about all you have left before corrective action begins."

Taos asked, "I understand, Mr. President, that you have ordered the evacuation of Seoul?"

President Grégoire responded, "I suggested that the South Koreans evacuate the city and any other areas in the range of Pak's chemical weapons. The South Koreans, although extremely reluctant to do so, have begun the evacuation. The city will be patrolled by a coalition of security forces, and it's all being coordinated by Canada National Defense. Speaking of evacuations, Sir, I've been informed that you have placed all your military forces on top alert, even your nuclear delivery systems."

Taos was direct. "Well, what do you expect? We certainly are not going to let you surround our part of the world with the largest military force ever witnessed by mankind, and just sit idly by."

President Grégoire genuinely understood but still asked, "But the nukes, Mr. President – you aren't thinking of starting a nuclear war, are you?"

"If a nuclear war begins, Mr. President, it will be at the hands of the United States and you, its President."

"What about the Russians, President Taos, they have over 80 percent of their forces on high alert. What do you think their intentions are? Could they be looking for an opportunity to realign the Russian-Chinese borders, especially around Mongolia? I'm sure you are aware that they've moved equipment and forces closer to their border with China. How much does that concern you?" There was no answer, and President Grégoire didn't really expect one. He knew Taos was well aware of the Russians and their movements, and was sure the Chinese were gravely concerned.

Assuming a more conciliatory tone, President Grégoire pointed out,

"As we discussed before, there are two Presidents – you and me – who are in charge here. Neither of us wants war. If we both keep our eyes on the ball, the objective could be reached with little or no death and destruction. I can do my part. What will history record about you?"

Taos answered, "I'm warning you, President Grégoire, if you initiate hostilities on our close ally, we will react."

President Grégoire was disappointed but not surprised by this response. He replied, "Have it your way, Mr. President. Once again I believe our conversation has come to an end. I will advise you that when hostilities do begin, the GPS system may go down. So you better teach your truck drivers how to drive and your pilots how to fly."

"Our pilots know how to fly – and how to win, as your pilots may so soon have an opportunity to learn."

Grégoire didn't want the conversation to end this way, and realized he may have been more the antagonist in the dialogue. He offered, "We both have the same goal, President Taos. Let's make it happen as peacefully as possible."

Taos was also repentant, "Indeed, Mr. President, I agree that Pak must be removed. But you are not allowing enough time for things to occur as they need."

"We don't have more time. If Pak manages to get a nuke off toward San Francisco, I can't guarantee that we'll intercept it or where it may errantly go. I didn't move up the time frame, Pak did." President Grégoire paused for effect, then added, "You have my phone number, even my personal cell phone. Let's stay in touch, for the sake of mankind, and for the sake of history."

Taos agreed and the telephone conversation ended.

Gabe, Tim and Jane were listening in on the call. As they all put down their earpieces, Jane asked, "Do you really think he will resort to nuclear weapons?"

The President was rubbing his open palms up and down again as he replied, "No. It's all about saber-rattling. He knows there would be no winner in a nuclear exchange. He has to thump his chest right now for everyone to see, especially the leaders of the Chinese communist party. Fortunately for him, I recognize ceremonial chest-thumping." His left hand was stroking his lower face and chin now, but he didn't give any hints about his thoughts. Momentarily he said, "I guess we should attend to our honored guest." With that he rose to his feet, as did the others, and they quietly walked to the reception. Just before reaching the entrance, Jane leaned toward the President and informed him, "Sir, we just learned that India has placed their nuclear forces on alert."

Incredulous, the President snapped his head toward her and asked, "Why?"

"We're not sure."

"Call them. Ask them what the hell's up."

"Yes, Mr. President, right after I greet the Dalai Lama."

The President forced a smile and cautioned, "Remember, no touching."

The President forced a bigger smile as he entered the grand East Room, splendidly decorated and appointed for the gala event. The Dalai Lama was impressed, and his first words to the President expressed wonder and gratitude for such an extravagant reception. After more pleasantries, the party took their seats.

At first, it was idle chit-chat between the President, First Lady, the Dalai Lama, and his aide. Naturally their table was the first served. The Dalai Lama waived off his plate and asked that everyone else be served first. The confounded waiter looked at the President, who gave a sideward 'yes' nod. The waiter moved his cart to another table and passed on the appropriate instructions.

This gave the President an opportunity to give the Dalai Lama a good look in the eye as if to say, 'so why are you here?' The Dalai Lama picked up on it. He told the President that his original reason for coming was to ask President Morris for more assistance in freeing Tibet. "But now, Mr. President, I'm here on a new mission and that is to beg you for peace. Peace with North Korea and peace with China."

The President thought for a half moment before he replied, "I know that you teach and practice nonviolence. Sooner or later though, one must fight or flee." The President was going to remind the Dalai Lama how America's CIA helped him escape Tibet, and that escape involved violence, but decided there was nothing to gain. He continued, "Unfortunately North Korea – well, I should say Pak Jung-ho – has crossed the line. It is one thing to build bombs, yet another to use them. Pak has attempted to use nuclear weapons on people who mean him no harm. He promises to launch more." The President hesitated before pointing out, "He has to be stopped."

"But nuclear war, Mr. President."

"There will not be a nuclear war, Your Holiness."

"But how can you be sure, Mr. President?"

"Because I have my finger on the trigger and I'm not pulling it. True, the Chinese have nuclear weapons, but they will not use them unless we use ours first – and we won't. We don't need nuclear weapons to neutralize North Korean's arsenal."

At that moment the waiter placed a beautifully arranged plate of food in front of the Dalai Lama: edible flowers, hand-carved vegetables, and a succulent square of wild caught salmon on a bed of black and white rice. Simple food, elegantly presented. The Dalai Lama's eyes widened, "Such a feast! We must pray." With a bowed head, he said his solemn invocation:

"I offer this to the highest teacher, the precious Buddha. I pray that he bestow his greatest wisdom on President Grégoire.

And I beg of the great Buddha, a supreme warrior himself, to give special guidance of peace to all the leaders of the world, especially at this hour." The President was touched and solemnly responded, "And may I be worthy of these blessings." He opened his hands with kindness and said, "Let us enjoy the fruits of the labor of our farmers, fishermen, chefs, and servers." With that, he picked up his fork.

The remaining discourse was of neutral subjects, which included teasing the Dalai Lama about coming to Washington in January. His Holiness was not offended. He commented that he rather enjoyed the warm coat he was loaned and joked about keeping it. The President told him, "Please accept it as a gift. I'll be sure the owner is compensated." He then complimented the Dalai Lama on his rigorous activities traveling the world, particularly at his age, then regretted saying anything about his age.

The allotted time for the Dalai Lama's visit was coming to an end, and he was so informed by his aide. He gracefully walked with the President down the Center Hall toward the Diplomatic Reception Room. The President thanked him for coming, and before they parted he assured him, "Don't worry about nuclear war, Your Holiness."

The Dalai Lama purposely turned his head directly towards the President and responded, "It is not just nuclear war, Mr. President, it is war of any kind." Now turning his whole body towards the President, he warned, "The world – yes even your enemies – recognize you as the most powerful person in the world. They rely on you alone to keep this dire situation from turning into … a war … one that could result in many deaths and unprecedented destruction." The Dalai Lama paused a moment, canted his head, and added, "It is all in your hands, Mr. President."

The President didn't appreciate the fact the Dalai Lama was putting the entire situation on his shoulders. There was much he could explain to the Dalai but he held back. He simply responded, "I know you will pray for me, Your Holiness, which I appreciate. You must also pray for other world leaders, especially those not considered worthy of your prayers. Pray for them also, Sir."

The Dalai Lama blinked his eyes hard in deep thought, as if something just occurred to him, or perhaps he was insulted. Canting his head in the other direction, he replied, "They are the ones I pray the hardest for, Mr. President."

After more handshakes and best wishes, the suicide doors of the Lincoln soon slammed shut and the Dalai Lama was rolling away from the White House. Jane approached the President to tell him she had reached the Indian ambassador and was informed that the Prime Minister would like some assurances directly from the U.S. President. Marc said, "If that's what it takes, set up the call."

She then asked, "Will that be all, Mr. President?" He turned toward her and saw the face of a very exhausted Secretary of State.

"Yes, that will be all. Go home, and let the staff do their stuff." Marc remembered the last time he saw Jane so exhausted. It was the early 1980's in Odienne, Cote D'Ivoire. He was in the Air Force, she was …

MARC WAS IN ODIENNE BECAUSE A SOVIET GRU AGENT WANTed to defect, but would only meet with an Air Force counterintelligence officer. He was to meet the GRU officer at an inn near the Odienne train station – if the proper signals were made. The GRU agent, whose cover name was Boris Ramper, was to place a piece of tape on a certain pillar near the tracks. Marc was instructed to put another piece of tape across the first, making an X. When both marks were made they were to meet at the inn at 2 PM the next day. If the meeting didn't happen, the back-up time was 8 PM.

Marc was on the train platform, trying not to stand out as an American, when he spotted a disheveled blond woman, fresh off a train and asking how to get to a hospital. She was carrying a small bag on her right shoulder, which looked like a terrible burden, and her left arm was hanging noticeably limp. No one was paying attention to her questions about the hospital. Marc approached her and in obviously American English, said, "Howdy little lady." She looked at him suspiciously at first but was desperate enough to say 'Hi' back. Her face was white as a sheet and her pale green eyes could barely be seen between her nearly shut eyelids. Marc asked her, "You need a doctor?" She said yes, that she was bitten by a monkey four days ago, and was sure the bite was infected. She also knew she had a bad fever. He slowly raised his hand and gently touched her over her left eye. "You're burning up alright. I got a taxi next to the station; I don't know where the hospital is but the taxi driver should. Here, give me your bag." She looked him over; he was wearing regulation jungle pants and web belt, with a dark blue fishing shirt that almost matched his eyes. On his head was a desert-sand Castro-style cap. He looked ridiculous and quite out of place. Under other circumstances she probably would have said no; but he was obviously an American, and well, in her present state she just decided to swing the bag toward Marc's hand. He guided her towards the taxis and asked her name.

"Jane. And don't tell me you're Tarzan, I've heard it a million times."

"No, I'm Marc. How'd you get bit by a monkey?"

"I'm a Peace Corps volunteer. I teach grade school in a commune south of here, and the people there are supposed to provide me food. A few days ago a guy came into my hut walking a monkey by the hand and said he was my dinner. I told him no way! He just said it was his turn to feed me and the monkey was mine to eat. I tried to give the monkey back but the guy refused, saying his obligation was met. Off he went. When I bent down to pick the critter up, wondering what I was going to do with him, he bit me. The native 'witch doctor' stuffed the wound with spider web and covered it with mud. Told me I'd be okay. By last night I was feeling so sick I spent my last dime buying a train ticket to here."

They arrived at the hospital and Marc helped her walk inside. He told her to sit and let him deal with getting her seen. To his shock, the only doctor on duty was a German gynecologist, and it would be at least three hours before she could be seen. Marc figured that even a gynecologist would know how to treat an animal bite, and three hours would have to be okay. He explained the hospital situation to Jane; she said, "Only three hours? I figured it would be 24; look how crowded this place is."

Marc was glad she understood, then told her he had some things to do and should be back to check on her but couldn't promise. "In case I can't come back, good luck," he told her. "And don't worry, they'll fix you up. Where are you going from here?" She said she had wired her dad for money, something she hated to do, and if it came in time she was hoping to stay the night in the city. She was also considering taking the next flight back to the states. Softening her voice, she said, "There's nothing in my hut I can't live without, but I hate to abandon the school."

Marc looked at her pitifully and said, "I promise I'll be back. I don't know when but just wait here for me." She only nodded.

At 2 PM Marc was at the inn. His instructions were to wait 30 minutes, no more. If Boris didn't show up, use the back-up time. At 2:30 he checked his watch and left the building. A no-show for a first meeting was quite normal. He couldn't find Jane at the hospital and thought perhaps she had left. Fortunately the nurse saw him and told him Jane was still in with the doctor, but should be out soon. She was, and when she came out she had a large white bandage wrapped around her arm and a small bag of pills. She was very glad to see Marc waiting. He asked her how it went.

She said, "It's infected alright, I got two shots. I have to come back tomorrow to get the bandage changed. The doc said it was too late for stitches and scolded me for waiting so long to see a real doctor. He said I should see a plastic surgeon when I get back to the states. And he said never let anyone put mud on an open wound. I should have known better."

"So you're going to be okay?" Marc asked.

"Yeah."

"Are you going to spend the night here?" he asked.

"Yeah, but I don't know where. I tried to get them to admit me so I'd have a place to stay. No dice."

"Well, I know there's more rooms available where I'm staying. It's an okay place by African standards."

She grimaced and said, "Looks like a bench for me inside the train station. I've done it before."

"That's dangerous – don't you have a credit card or something?" he asked.

"I lost my credit card a couple of weeks ago. When I asked the bank to send me a new one to my African address, they said sure, we'll get right on that! So they are sending it to my dad and he'll activate it and send it to me. In the meantime, I'm broke."

"Well, come with me. I'll get you a room and you can send me the money when you have it. Don't worry, it will be your *own* room."

She asked, "Will I be able to take a bath?"

"I don't see why not, they don't have showers."

"With hot water?"

"Yeah, as long as it's not seven in the morning."

Her face was a window to her mind and it was clear she was a little suspicious, maybe rightly so. But a bench at the train station wasn't looking good at all. She finally said, "Okay. As long as you leave me an address to send a check." She looked up into his blue eyes, waited a second, then asked, "How about some food? I'd suggest going to the market and picking up some fresh stuff, but they're closed now. Have you checked out any restaurants here?"

"I don't eat in restaurants in this … corner of the world." He was thinking of the word 'cesspool,' but refrained. He added, "I make exceptions for breakfast, if I can watch them cook the eggs."

She laughed, "You're kidding me. You only eat one meal a day?"

"Nooo. I come prepared. I bring granola bars, cheese, and stuff. And as a matter of fact, I have time before my next meeting. Let's get you checked in and I'll share my grub."

"You bring food in your luggage?" she asked.

"This ain't my first African rodeo."

She offered, "Well, Odienne isn't a bad little city. They have most everything one could need, especially a hospital. They are friendly and politically they seem neutral, or they want to be."

Her use of the word 'politically' piqued his curiosity. He responded, "I can tell you that the politics here are controlled by the religious fanatics with the most guns."

His answer made her ask, "What exactly do you do?"

He could see that was eventually coming, but he still wasn't prepared. Honesty being the best policy, he answered, "I'm in the Air Force."

She squinted and said, "The American Air Force? What would you be doing here?"

He laughed it off with, "You know that old cliché, I'd have to kill you if I told you."

"Okay. You don't want to tell me." She decided to let it go for now. A gift horse was a gift horse, as long as there were no strings.

Thirty minutes later they were sitting on her bed; he served crackers and cheese which he topped off with a nice piece of ham, right out of the can. She loved it. He said, "I even have a bottle of wine. But I can't have any now, still have work to do."

She said, "Well whatever you do, you come prepared. You don't carry a gun do you?"

"Noooo. Carrying a gun in a place like this would just get you in a lot of trouble." Wanting to change the subject, he asked, "How'd you wind up in the Peace Corps?"

"I went to Indiana State and earned my degree in forensic science. After graduation I couldn't find a job, well except for one, the Cook County

Coroner offered me a position. I wasn't too sure about it so I went up to Chicago and checked it out. They brought me into this big room in the basement of the hospital where eight autopsies were going on at the same time, seven men, one woman. It was table after table of some poor soul with their scalp pulled back, brains hanging out, their chests cut wide open, and their guts going into a black plastic bag. Two had been shot, another was stabbed, and two were found dead in an alley. Two more were suspected drug overdoses, and the last was found dead at home of no apparent cause. The stench was overwhelming, but the scene of it all was worse. One of the victims had been shot in the middle of the forehead, and it looked like there was sawdust around the entrance wound. I wondered how sawdust got there so I got closer to see. It wasn't sawdust … it was maggots.

"I went back home thinking, if I was on a date after work, what would my conversation be about? 'How was your day?' he'd ask. And what would I be thinking about when I went to sleep at night? Anyway, that job was definitely not for me. After checking things out I realized the best jobs in my line of work were with the government. The Peace Corps was a door into the federal government, and I liked the idea of helping where I was needed. So I signed up. That's my story; you still haven't told me yours."

"Which reminds me, I have work to do," he dodged. "I may be able to check in on you later, but it might be in the morning. Enjoy your bath, should be plenty of hot water this time of day."

She frowned, "I must look terrible, and speaking of 'oh-dors' I suppose the doctor is used to stinking patients."

"You're fine. I'll see ya later," and in seconds he was passing through the door. As he closed it, a portion of his brain momentarily thought about the cute blond who was about to get naked for her bath. The anxiousness of the imminent encounter with a real GRU agent quickly shorted out that and all other thoughts. Every cell in his body was intent and focused. He was going over the plan in his mind: during the meeting he must convince Boris to defect in place, that is, keep his position in the GRU and report vital information to the U.S. But first things first, he wanted to recheck the signal on the train station pillar, and that's where he headed.

The X was gone! Shocked, he thought sure he had the wrong pillar! He double counted again and now he was sure he had the right pillar. Almost in a state of panic, he checked all the pillars. None had the taped X.

What did it mean? Was the meeting off? If so, was it because he or Boris had been compromised? Was somebody watching him? Did the Soviets get to Boris first? If so, Boris was a dead man. Marc found a train bench to sit on and calm his thoughts. He scanned all who walked by but no one stood out. After contemplation he decided there were several reasons the X could have been removed and he must go to the meeting point as planned. As he entered the dining room of the inn he made sure to get a good look around. He took a table where he could watch both the door and the kitchen. Eight PM came, then 8:15, 8:25, and finally 8:30. He waited until 8:45, then paid his check and left. He walked around outside, hopefully inconspicuously, just to observe. There was nothing out of the ordinary, and with fewer and fewer people on the streets he decided it best to head back to his room. Anxiously he checked at the desk for a message – and there was one. It was from Mike, the project manager at Headquarters back in Washington. It simply said, 'call ASAP.'

Marc went straight to his room to place the call. Mike was at his desk, way past quitting time, waiting for Marc's call. It was short and included several two- and three-digit code numbers, and the word 'zeros,' the office slang for CIA. Marc knew the numbers well; it all translated to, 'CIA picked up Boris.' Marc was ordered to return to London.

Shocked! He was robbed!

His shock quickly turned to anger, but as upset as he was he had orders to follow. There probably was one more train that evening to Félix-Houphouët-Boigny International Airport, but that would mean an all-night train ride with lots of stops and spending a few hours on an airport bench. Then it would be an Air France flight to Paris, and another to London. Too stunned to even think about such an exhausting trip, he decided to catch the 7:10 express in the morning. Wishing he had a brandy, he just sat on his bed in a cloud of intense frustration and anger.

It was probably too late to check in on Jane, but if she was up for a chat, it might be a temporary diversion to the crushing thoughts swirling in all directions through his mind. So Marc walked to her door and saw light barely shining under it. She could have fallen asleep with the light on, so he knocked gently. He heard her ask, "Who's there?"

"Me. Marc. Is it too late?"

"No. Hang on."

After a few moments her door opened. "Come on in," she said with a happy face and her hair still wrapped in a towel. As he did she started to ask how his meeting went, but the look on his face stopped even the first word from coming out of her mouth. Instead she asked, "Are you okay?"

"I'm hot enough to …"

"I see that," she said.

"But I got to shake it off. I'm okay."

"Are you okay, are you okay really?" She even started to look him over for wounds or injuries.

"Yeah, I will be. How about you, was there enough hot water for your bath?"

"Wow, yes. And thanks for the grub. But are you going to be okay?"

"Yeah, but I have to catch the early train in the morning and I wanted to give you the cash I promised you."

"Loan me," she corrected. "I promise you'll get it back."

"Okay, loan." He started to unbutton one of his many cargo pockets, then removed a safety pin. In fact all his pockets were full of 20, 50, and 100 dollar bills. If it was all there, it would equal 20,000 U.S. dollars in flash money. Under each button was another safety pin double closing every pocket. Marc found the pocket with twenties and handed her ten, "Will a couple hundred dollars see you through?"

"More than enough," she said and gently raised her good arm to take it. "Now write your address down for me." Marc scribbled his name and address on a piece of paper and handed it to her. She noticed it had an APO address and raising her head she said, "You really are in the military."

"You didn't believe me?"

"I believed you, I just can't figure out why you're here, but I'm glad you are." Gently shaking the cash, she said, "Thank you very much, and … well, thank you for everything."

He still looked very upset and she was thinking of asking him to go get his wine, but that might send a signal she wasn't ready to send. She asked him to sit, but he declined saying he had to get packed. He put his hand out for a hand shake, which he got, followed by a tender hug. She said with a pleasant smile, "You really are my Tarzan. I can't thank you enough."

"Hey, well, at least my trip here wasn't a total waste. Make sure you get back to the hospital tomorrow."

"I will. I'm already feeling much better."

"So, does this mean you're going back to your Peace Corps job?"

"Yeah, I love those kids. It's the tribal leaders that are a pain. But the kids – they can be so mesmerized by the simplest science experiment."

He opened the door and waved at her one last time. "Good for you. Always get back in the saddle, otherwise…"

"Safe travels," she said, "and thank you so very much."

And he thought he had seen her for the last time.

* * *

It was 29 years later – soon after Marc and Leo won the election, when Marc was meeting proposed members of the new cabinet, there she was – the petite blond from a dark corner of Africa. The President-elect didn't know what to think when she and Marc shared a quick hug. Marc and Jane chatted long enough for Marc to learn that back in Africa she was actually approached by the CIA, and they wanted her to stay another year but in a different location. She declined but did help them out a few times. When she got back to the 'world' she talked herself into applying for a job with the State Department. She was accepted and over the years she moved up through the ranks. Helped along by doing well in some unsavory assignments, particularly Somalia and Afghanistan, she rose to Deputy Secretary of State. A few days ago she became President-elect Morris' choice for Secretary of State in the new administration. Plus, she and Alice knew each other from high school days and occasionally kept in touch. Marc also learned she was married, no children, and lived in an upscale D.C. high-rise rather than the traditional colonial in a Virginia suburb. When he got her aside, he said, "Never figured you for a Republican!"

"Far from it." With a wink she added, "But don't tell Morris. I want this gig; I've earned it." Marc smiled and was impressed because Leo had actually picked someone for Secretary of State based on her qualifications, not her politics.

Since that meeting he met Jane during the two or three Cabinet meetings President Morris allowed him to attend. There were also the rare quasi-social events where they could chat. One of them, held in the Pentagon, gave her the chance to ask Marc if it were possible to tell her why he was in Africa where they first met. Gabe was now part of the conversation and was also curious.

A little uneasy about the question, Marc said, "I cannot; and other than running into you, it was an episode I'd rather forget."

She smiled sadly.

And Gabe detected a little chemistry between the two.

WITH THE DALI LAMA OFF ON HIS WAY, THE PRESIDENT SAID, "Alright, now that the formalities are over, come on up to the rez. I may be able to find us something to drink." Leonie followed with Beth and Joe, Beth still holding her chest as if every breath was precious. Soon the four old friends were alone in a room the President referred to as his bar. Once the door was shut behind them, the President swung around to Beth and ordered, "Anytime we are on this side of that door, you shall call me Marc! Got it?"

"Yes, Mr. President."

The President raised his hand and joked, "Now I just got a speech from the big guy about nonviolence, don't make me…"

"Yes, Mr. President," she quipped.

With a little laugh Marc threw his hands in the air and went to the fridge. "Wine for the ladies, Pinot Grigio?"

"Sure," came Beth's reply, "and something tells me I'm going to need a double."

"Joe, a beer? A real beer, none of that light stuff?" Marc asked.

Joe said, "I'll have whatever you're having, as long as it's cold." To everyone's surprise, Joe – who hadn't said more than 10 words all night – asked, "Did he really give you a speech about nonviolence?"

"Yeah, well you know, it's his job. He has his job, I have mine." With that, Marc plopped down in an overstuffed armchair and pulled the tab on a large can of Sip of Sunshine.

Joe asked, "They sell that stuff here in DC?" After a good gulp, the

President said, "I don't know where it came from or how it got here, except I'm sure my wife here had something to do with it. I just hope the Air Force isn't flying special missions to Vermont to get it." After another gulp, he proclaimed, "Ah, the nectar of the beer gods."

Joe had one more question about the Dalai Lama. "I'm surprised you have time to…" he couldn't quite find the right words, "well, entertain the Dalai Lama – and us for that matter – during this crisis? Your brain must be in overdrive."

The President had another quick sip before saying, "Well, as for His Holiness, he had been begging Morris for months about a visit to the White House. Morris tried to put him off by scheduling him during the winter. When I got here I could have cancelled it, but I thought – why not? It would get everybody's mind off all the other shi … crap going on. And for a couple hours, it did.

"As for you guys, that's easy. Next to clean lakes and rivers, nothing is closer to my heart than education and training. I need – the country needs – someone in charge at the Department of Education who can make some badly needed changes – and fast. And besides, I knew you are tired of blowing snow."

There were some more chuckles and warm regards. Indeed the four good friends were happy to be together again. After a few more cracks about snow, Beth broke the ice: "So before you suck down that pint of hi-test you're holding, how about telling us about this mysterious 'position' you have for me."

The effects of the eight-percent alcohol were already kicking in as seen in the President's reply: "Is that any way for the future Secretary of Education to talk, especially to the goddam President of the United States?"

With genuine curiosity, Beth asked, "Who are you talking about?"

"You, Madame Secretary. I'm talking about you."

She was stunned. It took her a moment or two to collect her thoughts. When she did, her reaction was plain, "Are you nuts?"

Marc playfully put all 10 of his fingertips on his chest and said, "Another insult. You know, I may go back to making you call me Mr. President. Of course I'm talking about you."

Joe took a long swig of his beer, looked a little shocked, but didn't say a word. Beth mustered up the strength to say, "I'm not the least qualified to be the Secretary of Education. I wouldn't know where to begin."

With his finger in the air Marc said, "Well, I'll tell you where to start. After the Senate approves you – and they will – you'll go to work at a nice building on Maryland Avenue. Everyone will call you Madame Secretary and treat you with the respect you deserve. You'll assess things, establish your own priorities, figure out who on your staff can get those priorities done, and reorganize accordingly.

"Although Morris wanted me to keeps my hands off everything, I used my position to quietly keep track of the Department of Education, and I can tell you that the staff there needs a shake-up. That's not something you'll do the first week you're there, but it will be a top priority. Your good sense will tell you who you need as your closest advisors, and who needs to find another job."

"Sure, simple as all that. And I have to appear in the Senate, answer questions?" she asked.

"So what do you have to hide, Miss Snow White? When they check you out, they'll see that you are a Progressive and wonder how you got the nomination by a Republican. That will actually work for you – you'll have support from both sides of the aisle."

Her reply was quick, "The Senate will see right away that I'm not qualified. I've never been a college President or even a school principal. I'm just a retired first-grade teacher."

"Exactly, and they'll like that. All you have to do is answer their questions truthfully, and they won't have a thing to criticize."

"You know what's really scary about this? I think you're serious."

The President leaned forward in his chair, "Well, I wouldn't have dragged you two down here if I wasn't serious. You are the next Secretary of Education."

Beth took a deep breath and looked at Leonie. Leonie recognized the look and told her, "I really didn't know. What I do know is that you wouldn't be here if he wasn't serious."

Beth took another deep breath and said, "So let's say I was interested, which I am, but I'm still sure I'm not qualified. What would you expect of me? What would you want accomplished?"

Marc took his last swig and put the empty 16-ounce can aside. "Well, first, I want you to identify future mass shooters." Beth tucked her head down and raised her eyebrows. They both stared at each other for a moment, the President reading the '*say what?*' question all over her face.

"Yes," he said. "Teachers have ways to pick out kids who are being bullied, or kids that are being ostracized, the misfits, and the underachievers. They need to be identified and helped." He took a moment for Beth to absorb what he was saying, then continued, "I'm betting these sorts of things start showing up by the fourth grade, maybe even sooner. And I'm certain we can train our teachers to spot them." He waited for her reaction. It came.

"Most of the time we can, but not always. Do you have ideas how to…?

He replied, "Well, if your questions is, do I have ideas on how schools can spot the troubled kids, I do. I've read about some innovative techniques, something referred to as 'Grade School Survivor,' already being used by some pretty forward thinking educators out there. So that wheel has already been invented. You and your staff will need to examine these techniques and work with test schools around the country to see if refinements are needed. Then figure out ways to get every school to use them.

She replied, "I've read about Grade School Survivor; it's very interesting, but it's asking a lot of teachers who are already … well, a lot is already expected of them."

Marc said, "My father was drafted in the Infantry in 1944. His military training consisted of three basics: obey orders, shoot straight, and throw grenades hard. He was issued uniforms, helmet, boots, rifle, and a web belt to hold his extra bullets and a canteen. Today's soldier is equipped with so much apparatus and electronics it would boggle your mind. And training – they're constantly training. Like the modern-day soldier, our teachers are going to have do more and be more. They too will need help and constant training."

Pointing his shoulder towards Beth, the President added, "The need for change is urgent and we don't have years to experiment; you'll need to make some changes fast. Determine what's working and make it work everywhere it can."

Beth leaned back in her chair, her eyes blinking faster. Marc couldn't quite read her thoughts. In fact, she had very mixed feelings, especially about her abilities to make this happen. But something was welling up inside her. Could this be a terrific challenge that she could meet? Maybe she *could* do it, and very well.

After some thought she pointed out, "Identifying troubled students is just the start; we're going to need more family outreach councilors. Most problem kids come from troubled homes or no home at all."

Marc only nodded in agreement. Clearly, the subject would require a lot more discussion which she was sure the President didn't have time for at this moment. She had another question, "What would your other priorities be?"

He was ready: "This country desperately needs electricians, plumbers, welders, carpenters, and masons."

Beth nodded and asked, "How would you encourage students to seek that kind of training instead of going to college?"

"Ah, that's my next point: student loans." Marc leaned back as if he were about to start a dissertation, "We have to target who we're giving student loans to. Now if kids want to go to college thinking they can be screenwriters or some other pie-in-the-sky job, they need to be doing that on their own dime, not the taxpayers'. Another of my favorites is all the kids who think they can be special trainers for some big-time NFL team. And do you know how many people with degrees in stuff like Ancient Greek Literature or Oceanography are back living with their parents, delivering pizzas, and not paying back their student loans? Too damn many. Under you, Secretary Acer, I want that to change. The only people who will get government-backed student loans are people with realistic plans. Someone who knows how many job openings there are in their intended fields, and knows where they are going to have to live to get those jobs. Do you know that millennials earn 20 percent less than their boomer parents did at the same age – even though millennials are way better educated?"

There was a pregnant pause before Beth asked, "What about a cure for cancer?" She hesitated before further pressing, "Or the shortage of nurses?"

Marc cocked his head, almost insulted, but realized her questions were not only legitimate but heartfelt. In a lowered voice he replied, "Of course we'll support students of science – to the highest degree. In fact, another of your priorities will be to implement ways to reduce the costs of medical degrees." His answer was followed by silence. He gently broke it by asking Joe if he'd like another beer. It was declined. Marc decided one was enough for him too, mentioning "I'm expecting a call from the Prime Minister of India."

Regaining his momentum, Marc pressed forward. "And when a kid tells his school counselor that he wants to be a mechanic or go in the Army – that councilor better say, 'great idea' and not try to talk him or her out of it." Marc looked right at her but took a moment before pointing out, "Your experience is from the ground up. You know what it's like to deal with kids of all kinds. Little kids that come from abusive homes, kids that are hungry, or dirty, or just plain lost. There's too many of them out there. Yeah, all the geniuses who'll seek the Secretary post will all have a Ph.D. or two, lectured at some high-priced ivy league school somewhere – but never spent a single day teaching first graders – where it all starts. The last Secretary of Education didn't know his ass from his elbow."

Joe muffled a laugh as Leonie rebuked, "Mister President!" Her stern look had just a mild effect on her husband.

Marc was now glaring at Beth, "And somehow, Madame Secretary, you have to teach kids more respect. Respect for their peers, respect for adults, and respect for the rules. Maybe we would have fewer school shootings. You know, often it is the parents' fault, not teaching about consequences and, most importantly, how to accept and learn from failure. When kids mess up *they need to know they messed up*. They need to understand that Peter Pan is a fairytale, and Never Never Land doesn't exist – AND as a goddam matter of fact you *do* have to grow up!"

Beth put the wine down. Was this a great opportunity or a sure path to disappointment? She was sort of warming up to the 'Madame Secretary' possibility, but it just seemed…unreal. Her mind was grinding gears, shifting widely with lots of questions. Suddenly her eyes narrowed in thought and she asked point blank, "What would your top priority be – for the new Secretary of Education?"

Marc nodded his head gently up and down, "That I can answer. I believe – I know – that our school systems are indoctrinating our kids, at all levels, towards a liberal form of government. Yes, they want to turn this country into a giant socialist experiment. That's got to stop." He paused, but never took his eyes off Beth's face. He continued, "I get it, you know. Our educators want us to be a big happy country where no one does anything wrong, just misguided. And anybody can do whatever makes them happy, whether it pays the bills or not. Unfortunately, that's not the way things work. We can't all have an equal piece of the pie, whether we worked for it or not. Not in this country. We became the greatest country in the world through hard work and the freedom to pursue as good a life as we are willing to work for.

"Being number one in the world has its costs. Namely, everyone expects us to right the wrongs all over the globe. Just look at the situation we're in now. We are who we are because we earned it. Sure, I wish we could be like Canada or Switzerland, relatively neutral countries with no enemies, and therefore no need for a major defense force. But they're not number one. No one is jealous of them." With that Marc realized he was getting off-track and probably boisterous. He took a moment to pause.

Beth realized the President was under a little alcoholic influence but that's usually when the truth flows forth. This last but first priority sounded political to her so now was the best time to ask, "As you already pointed out, Marc, we're of different political persuasions. What happens when we disagree?"

"We'll work it out," he replied. "Steering the nation's education isn't about Republicans or Democrats, it's about the kids. That's all I'll expect from you: make it *about the kids.* I know that some of it will seem impossible, but I also know your motivation will come from your heart. And you'll know that you'll have full backing of the Oval Office. Not every cabinet member enjoys that."

Silence ensued, but Marc and Beth were looking hard at each other. He could only guess at her thoughts. Turning to Joe, Marc asked, "She can do it, right Joe?" Joe had several serious reservations; of the top three he worried about the extreme stress the job would put on his wife, and the potential for physical and mental health issues. Secondly, the President's orders were tall, and he knew failure wasn't in Beth's vocabulary. It was improbable, more like impossible, to meet all the President's objectives; how would she deal with failure? Thirdly, she truly didn't have executive management experience. Would the lack of such cause her high-level embarrassments and humiliations? Wisely he decided not to say any of this out loud, not here. He didn't want his wife to think he was against the idea, or worse, that she couldn't handle it. But Marc's stare was expecting an answer.

Joe obliged, "It's her call." Turning to his wife, he said, "I believe you can do it."

"So how long do I – we – have to think about this?" she asked.

Marc settled back in his chair. "Well, I expect to be pretty tied up for a few days. Events will overcome events. I think you'll have at least a couple of weeks to think it over. When I'm ready, I'll give you a call. I just want to emphasize that I'm sure you can do this, and do it very well. Don't worry about running the department. There are a slew of undersecretaries there that will take care of that for you. All you'll have to do is take charge, apply your good common sense, and," turning his head to look at her straight in the eyes again, "make the changes that need to be made.

"And we'll have some good times together when you move to D.C. I want to take full advantage of the peace and quiet at Camp David. We'll need you two to join us frequently."

Beth took a deep breath. Her inclination was actually just to say 'no' now. But she really was intrigued and felt highly honored just to be asked. It all made her mind swirl. She was about to speak when a phone rang. The President was informed that the Prime Minister of India was calling. Marc began to excuse himself and the Acers took the occasion to quickly say their goodbyes. Giving him a quick hug, Beth said, "Thank you, Marc, I'll give it some hard thought." As Marc started through the door, Joe gave him a half-salute and a curt bow; Leonie got two heartfelt French-Canadian-style hugs.

* * *

After the phone conversation with the Prime Minister, President Grégoire put his left hand over his breast and began gently tapping his right-side collarbone with his fingers. While his right hand reached for another beer the other went back to pick up the phone. Seconds later he said, "Hello, Gabe; Marc here. I just spoke to Prime Minister Archarya; he said that he had sensitive information that for unclear reasons, the Pakistanis elevated their nuclear force alert level, and he was under pressure to do the same. He was willing to rescind the order if I could assure him there would be no nuclear war. I reassured him as best as I could.

"He reminded me that if the stuff hit the fan, Pakistan might side with China, as there's no love lost between the U.S. and Pakistan since we withdrew foreign aid. Then he tersely reminded me that we haven't followed through with some of our promises to him; of course I have no idea what those promises entail. Then he threw a really low punch by telling me if there was war, some of his staff believe they may have to rely on Russia and Israel for assistance."

Gabe reacted! "To use one of your favorite terms, Marc, 'the bastard.'" He quickly added, "He better realize this isn't just another pissing-contest over who controls Kashmir; a nuke was actually launched. This is real, this is nuclear. He needs to sit down with his staff and really think this through. If he visualizes the chain reaction under nuclear involvement, he would see a lot of Indians dying. Neither he nor the Pakistanis want to be in a position to have to choose sides. *But* – he may have done us a favor."

"A favor?" the President asked.

"Yes, he has increased tensions. China must be wondering if Pakistan would really come to their aid with their nuclear force; and if they did, how effective could they be? And right now China can only hope that India isn't a player. In sum, the whole thing adds anxiety to Taos's decision making."

The President said, "I see," then added, "fear of the unknown is the worst kind of fear there is." Heavy thoughts were stirring around in his mind; he hesitated – then somberly he asked, "If China was foolish enough to launch a nuke ... where would they hit first?"

Gabe let out a deep breath. "Probably Tokyo, maybe Seoul. It would be someplace close to them. They've already calculated it out; they know that an ICBM heading towards the U.S. has to travel a long distance which gives us time to knock it out. Yes, they have submarines, but we know where each and every one of them is. If their subs get orders to launch, we'll know it as soon as the subs do; and we'll take 'em out. The important thing is, Taos knows we can do it and then the shit would hit the fan, *their* fan."

Marc asked, "So you think they wouldn't gun for us, they'd start with an easy target ... someone who can't retaliate?"

"Yes, Sir. And if they hit Tokyo, what would they accomplish? Besides destroying a city full of innocent people, they would incur the wrath of the entire world; they'd be the scourge of the earth. They would be wracked with fear about retaliation. Their businesses and production plants would come to a halt. Marc, I just can't see them doing it. They have nothing to gain and everything to lose."

The subject still weighed heavy with Marc: "If they hit Japan, it would be *my* ultimate decision on how we react."

"Yes, Mr. President, it would." Gabe paused before somberly adding, "But you would listen to your own gut. As hard as it would be, we would *not* retaliate with nukes."

"We wouldn't launch our nukes," the President said softly, almost asking.

"No, Mr. President. We would respond by neutralizing any of their subs within range, and take other steps to protect ourselves and our allies, steps already well laid out." There was silence on the President's end of the phone. Gabe waited it out.

Marc asked, "But what if they actually take out New York or San Francisco? We'd have to retaliate."

There was silence on Gabe's end; he wasn't pausing for thought, he was pausing for effect. "Marc, I'll ask Admiral Dickinson to put together a brief on our military response should either Russia or China launch a nuclear attack. It will give you peace of mind. You'll have it by noon tomorrow. It'll be something you can read, and when you're ready, we can bring you over to the Pentagon for an in-depth video briefing which will include a number of scenarios, particularly the one we're in."

Marc responded, "These are things I should already know." After a moment he added, "Thank God I have you; the whole damn world is lucky we have you."

Gabe was touched. He simply said, "Don't worry about nuclear war. Other than Pak, nobody wants to start one, and we're going to put that asshole out of business."

"Well," the President eventually said, "as long as level-headed people remain in charge in China..."

"Marc, don't let this rattle you. It won't happen. But ... if it hits the fan, you will confer with your advisors."

"And I am surrounded by the best."

Gabe's voice softened, "Yes, Mr. President. You are."

Both men were silent again. After a minute, Marc said, "Thanks, Gabe. See you tomorrow."

Gabe simply replied, "Yep. Good night."

After putting the phone down, Marc put the unopened can of beer back in the fridge.

It was President Taos' turn to be in the War Room. Also revered as The General Secretary of the Communist Party of China, Taos was the supreme leader of his nation, in total control of its vast military. With him in the room were several generals, military advisors, intelligence officers – and representatives from the National People's Congress – the entity that could remove him with a simple majority vote. Stakes had never been higher and Taos was feeling the heat.

He was questioning one of the generals about the 'invitation' China had made to Pak. The general was unhappy to report that the 24-hour window had closed and Pak had apparently passed on China's offer. He added, "Perhaps we should have sent someone more suitable to make the offer to Pak," then he wished he had never said it.

"Why?" demanded Taos.

The general's face struggled to hide a cringe as he said, "Immediately after the offer was made, Pak cut off all contact with us." What the general wasn't saying was that he knew the officer who made the offer hated Pak. But that was history. In retrospect, China's government should have ordered Pak's arrest while he was on their soil. There certainly were plenty of charges that could be made against him. China could then wash its hands of the entire affair by turning Pak over to the UN for prosecution. The world could be at peace now.

Taos was grim-faced and asked, "What about our people on the ground in North Korea, are they making any progress?"

The general replied, "Pak is moving from hideout to hideout, but remains in communication with his forces. He keeps one senior officer with him at all times, but only one. Every time he moves, he dismisses the attending officer for another. He's very afraid and his tactics make it difficult to track him down. However, one of our team of advisors is with a Korean general who they believe will eventually lead them to Pak."

"Eventually will be too late!" yelled Taos. He was furious, and he certainly had much to be angry about. Taos took a few reflective moments; he knew everything was being done to find Pak. After another moment he asked, "What is the U.S. and allied military situation?"

An intelligence officer lit up a massive TV monitor that displayed the Korean peninsula and the surrounding seas. He subtly cleared his throat and began, "The *Carl Vinson* and *Ronald Reagan* carrier strike groups are in these locations" – pointing with a laser – "*Vinson* here, *Reagan* here. Accompanying them are practically all of Japan's Maritime Self Defense Force ships. They are in total control of North Korea's west coast. All shipping has ceased passing through the area."

Taos demanded, "They are not stopping our ships?" The intelligence officer turned toward his superior to give the answer. The general rose to say, "Sir, to avoid a confrontation, our vessels have been ordered to temporarily stay clear of the area." Taos didn't like that answer, and his furrowed brows amplified the anger now revealed in his bluing lips. But he knew it was indeed wise not to let an inopportunity turn into a disastrous sea battle. He curtly motioned for the briefing to continue.

"Aircraft from the U.S. Air Force and Navy are enforcing a no-fly zone over most of North Korea. They are augmented by the air forces of other counties, most notably the UK. North Korea has made some minor attempts to shoot down enemy aircraft, but the U.S. response has been the total annihilation of the ground unit which initiated the attack. It appears Pak has ordered his forces to 'allow' the Americans to control the skies."

"And their nuclear forces?" Taos asked. Another general stood and said, "Sir, we know on what ships the Americans have nuclear weapons readied. But we've noticed that they have stopped conducting exercises."

"Stopped what exercises?" Taos demanded.

The general explained, "Nuclear launch readiness exercises, Sir. They were routinely conducting them but they have stood down." Taos looked perplexed so the general explained further, "During an exercise, the alarm is sounded and the launch crews rush to their stations unknowing whether it's the real thing – or another exercise. They go through all the launch procedures, sometimes right up to the point of turning the launch keys." The general waited a moment, then said, "They've stopped those exercises, Sir."

"How do we know that?" Taos asked.

"Sir, we have various sources, particularly an asset on one of their destroyers."

Taos opened his eyes a little wider but otherwise kept his stoic look and asked, "Are we in regular communication with this … spy?"

"We have been communicating with him more than prescribed, making him more susceptible to discovery. But we felt the situation warranted the risk. Further communication with him will only be for emergency purposes."

Taos paused, then turned his chin slightly toward the general, "Do we know why they stopped the exercises?"

"No, Sir. There could be several reasons; one is that they want to intimidate us, or…"

Taos asked, "Or what?"

"Or, they have no intentions of using nuclear weapons and they are trying to let us know." The general was anxious not to be further questioned on the subject, so he sat down and turned his head to the original briefer. It didn't work, Taos had one more question to ask about the spy.

"So they might already know about your asset, and they are using him for their benefit, not ours?"

The general bowed his head and said, "We are always cognizant of that possibility and remain vigilant."

The original briefer waited to see if Taos had more to say on the subject, but Taos slightly jutted his chin. The briefer took this as a signal to move on so he immediately changed the map on the screen to the area of the Demilitarized Zone. He pointed out the location of Pak's chemical weapons and stated that the missiles carrying those dreadful weapons were all in a 'ready' status. As for South Korea, most of the border area had been evacuated including all of Seoul. All military air bases in South Korea were full to capacity with aircraft from the U.S., Britain, France, Japan, Australia, Italy, and Spain. More aircraft were expected from Chile and Argentina." Lowering his voice he added, "The Saudis are continuously shipping fuel and other supplies in."

Taos yelled, "The Saudis! They've chosen sides?"

"Yes, Sir. Apparently they've decided who is going to win … if…"

Taos lowered his chin in disappointment. It was becoming somberly clear to him that most of the free world had taken sides, and done so unhesitatingly … and under a new, unknown American President. He was realizing that while China may be the only friend North Korea had at this time, China may not have any friends at all. He hoped the party members in the room also understood and recognized the position China was in. Momentarily he raised his head again and signaled for the briefing to continue.

The senior officer stood and reported, "We firmly believe that the Americans are planning an all-out, instantaneous air and naval attack on North Korea's chemical and nuclear weapons. It is called 'Operation Global Blizzard.' They have divided North Korea into 15 sectors and assigned each sector to one air wing or another. On command there will be one massive air attack; Pak's nuclear plant will be the priority target."

Taos asked, "When do we expect this to happen?"

"They could have done it hours ago. We're not sure why they are holding off. They have all the firepower they need. Now." The reply took Taos aback, but he gestured for the briefing to continue. The briefer was reluctant to change the screen because the new map displayed China's border with Russia. When the slide was up he said, "Russian forces are in motion to these locations on our border." Fourteen red dots lit up on the map. "We think the Americans may be hedging their bets by giving the Russians more time to move in to intimidate us."

Taos knew the Russians were not purposely aiding the U.S. and its allies, but he also knew the Russians were extremely concerned about the massive instability now occurring in Asia. The Russians by no means wanted war, but if there was one they wanted to be in the best position possible to capitalize on it. If Taos was rattled by the Russian move, he didn't show it. He decided he would ask more about Russian intentions later. For now, he asked "Who is in command of the Allied attack?"

Another Chinese general stood, changed the monitor screen to that of a portrait of a U.S. Navy admiral, and said, "Sir, this is Admiral Kevin Sears, U.S. Navy, Commander in Chief of allied forces. He is quartered on the *Ronald Reagan* where he maintains his command post."

"What do we know about him?" asked Taos.

"Originally from Utica, New York, he began his military career as an enlisted Marine. He eventually earned an appointment to the U.S. Naval Academy. He was promoted twice 'below the zone' to Lt. Commander and Commander. He's 61 years of age, somewhat older than his peers, and will likely retire soon. He is married with two daughters, both adults now, no grandchildren. He prefers black cigars which he occasionally smokes on the flight deck.

"He sleeps four hours a day and spends all remaining hours 'on duty.' He saw some action while commanding a destroyer, but otherwise has little combat experience. He's a believer in Naval Air superiority.

"He is known to have a keen sense of humor, but when it comes to the military, he's all business and by the book. We know he will not act without direct orders of the President. The Japanese wholeheartedly supported his selection as supreme commander. As an aside, he and Secretary Arnold and General Chaffee all attended the War College together. They are all on a first-name basis. We presume, however, that President Grégoire is not well acquainted with him."

The briefer changed the screen to a formal portrait of Chairman Mao, suggesting the briefing was over.

But Taos wasn't done, "You said we had several teams on the ground looking for Pak, and one of them might be close?"

27

IT WAS 5:45 AM. PRESIDENT GRÉGOIRE WAS HALF AWAKE, HALF asleep, and definitely not ready to rise. He thought he could hear his cell phone vibrating on the nightstand and opening one eye wider, he noticed the phone was indeed doing a little jig on the bare wood. It finally stopped. He stirred himself up out of bed and toward the coffee pot and pushed the 'on' button. After his first sip, he went back to his bedside to check the phone. There was a text:

I AM GENERAL HOING. ACCESS TO PAK. NEED HELP TO KILL HIM.

The President was pissed. He wondered how some jerk got his cell number. Against his better judgment, he tapped in,

WHERE DID YOU GET THIS NUMBER.

He nearly spilled his decaf when the response came back,

TAOS HE SAID YOU GAVE HIM

He raised his head toward the ceiling and said out loud, "Is it possible?" He looked at his phone again and typed in

STAND BY.

He picked up another phone and crushed '0'; Marilyn answered. He ordered, "Get Tim, Gabe, Jane, and General Chaffee here right away." Marilyn informed the President that Tim was already in, and Gabe was on the way, then she hung up. He called her back and told her, "Get Billings,

Windigo, and Lee Roberts here too.

"Yes Mr. President," she responded.

In moments he was dressed and in Marilyn's office. She informed him everyone was on the way, and Tim was waiting for him in the Situation Room but could come to the Oval Office if needed. The President ordered, "Have everyone meet me in the Situation Room." As he rushed there, Marilyn in tow, his phone vibrated again.

Another text:

HURRY. WINDOW CLOSING

Realizing there was some kind of emergency, Tim rushed to the door and held it open for the President. The President explained the situation to Tim, who immediately responded, "It has to be a hoax. The person sending this text is using a U.S. phone number." The President said, "Maybe. But I did give my cell phone number to Taos."

Just then Gabe and Billings came through the door. The President gave them a quick rundown and asked Billings, "Can you figure out who the phone belongs to?" Billings went to work, and in just moments he announced, "It's a Chicago number, belongs to Wilfred A. Pleverbs. I'm getting everything we can on him right now." By the time Billings' inquiry came back, Jane, General Chaffee and Windigo had arrived. They all watched Billings as the information came in:

'Wilfred Arthur Pleverbs, DOB 06 24 1987, born in Jackman, Maine. Current address: 39873 Carly Ave, Chicago, Illinois. Employed by Chicago Bulls.' The data also included his vehicles and plate numbers.

Gabe pointed out, "Carly Ave. That's a high-price neighborhood. This guy must be a little bored to be pulling shit like this."

"Run his passport," ordered the President. In just a few moments DHS information came back indicating that eight days ago Pleverbs flew from Chicago to Beijing, with onward travel to Pyongyang, North Korea.

Shocked, the President demanded, "Is he still there?"

Billings reported, "He hasn't used his return ticket from Pyongyang to Beijing. But that doesn't mean much – the system in that part of the world isn't always up-to-date."

Looking up from his computer Billings added, "The phone on the other end is an Iridium satellite phone, not a typical cell phone;" now Windigo started pounding away on his device.

The President pointed to Billings and ordered, "Call the Pleverbs' home and neighbors. Don't stop calling until to you get somebody. And contact the Chicago Bulls, get everything you can on Pleverbs' whereabouts."

The President then turned to Milt. "Do the Koreans *have* a General Hoing?"

A monitor suddenly lit up; there was a picture of General Hoing Chi, second in command of the North Korean military. He was in full uniform, his entire coat covered with metals. His date of birth and other particulars were also displayed. The President noticed that he went to school in Shanghai for two years and in New Zealand for 15 months where he learned English.

Tim tried to calmly point out, "Sir, we still don't know who that really is on the other end."

"But we can confirm that phone is in North Korea, and we have the exact coordinates!" Windigo announced. The President sucked his lips against his teeth. Suddenly, without asking anyone's advice, he tapped in on his cell:

IS OWNER OF THE PHONE WITH YOU?

In moments the response came back:

NO. UNDER HOUSE ARREST.

Gabe rushed to point out, "Sir, if this is for real, they are going to intercept all this and – whoever is holding that other phone is a dead man."

Windigo pointed out, "True. But since it's a satellite phone they can't triangulate on him like an ordinary cell phone. We can because we have plenty of satellites over that area. But they may figure it out, and when they do … and the Chinese have to be listening in."

"Yeah. I know." The President went back to reading General Hoing's bio, and noted, "He was an intelligence officer," and quickly typed into the cell,

DO YOU KNOW FIVE AND DIME CODE?

The response was,

YES.

Windigo asked, "Isn't that an old substitution system any 12-year-old can break?"

The President replied, "An oldie yes, but effective as long as you keep the message short. The only way to break it is to find some common words and start plucking in the substitute letters. But it takes lots of words, and we won't use many."

General Chaffee protested, "But Sir." The President cut him off, "Do you know how it works?"

"No, Mr. President."

The President looked at everyone, "Does anyone else know how it works?" No one replied. "Then we'll use it. It's all we got."

Back to his phone, he started typing,

USE THE OWNER S FULL NAME, CITY OF BIRTH, FULL DOB. SEND TEST.

OK.

The President knew what was going on at the other end, and he needed to do the same. He needed a plain sheet of paper. "Marilyn!"

The President turned his sheet of paper into the landscape orientation, and about a quarter of the way down he printed:

WILFREDARTHURPLEVERBSJACKMAN06241987

He explained to everyone, "Now we have most of the alphabet, and for the two missing numbers we add them on to the end."

WILFREDARTHURPLEVERBSJACKMAN0624198735

"That's the first line. For the second line, skip the first 10 characters."

1. WILFREDARTHURPLEVERBSJACKMAN0624198735
2. HURPLEVERBSJACKMAN0624198735WILFREDART

"And so on, for five lines." Windigo was copying the President's work on his computer.

1. WILFREDARTHURPLEVERBSJACKMAN0624198735
2. HURPLEVERBSJACKMAN0624198735WILFREDART
3. SJACKMAN0624198735WILFREDARTHURPLEVERB
4. 24198735WILFREDARTHURPLEVERBSJACKMAN06
5. LFREDARTHURPLEVERBSJACKMAN0624198735WI

"Now you simply number across the top. You automatically add 1 for the 10's, 2 for the 20's, etc. Take your first character from the first line, second from the second line of code, and so on."

```
12345678901234567890123456789012345678
WILFREDARTHURPLEVERBSJACKMAN0624198735
HURPLEVERBSJACKMAN0624198735WILFREDART
SJACKMAN0624198735WILFREDARTHURPLEVERB
24198735WILFREDARTHURPLEVERBSJACKMAN06
LFREDARTHURPLEVERBSJACKMAN0624198735WI
```

Billings pointed out that each line had several duplicates. For instance, there were three e's in each line. The President confirmed, "Yes, and you use them randomly making it harder to break the code. But with computers..."

The President's cell phone popped up a text:

```
10 6 1 18
```

Excitedly he transcribed it. It came out 'test.' He threw his arms in the air and said, "This guy's the real thing." Although there was still skepticism among the others, they were starting to hope.

Suddenly Billings interrupted, "We made contact with Pleverbs' wife in Chicago. She said he was in North Korea to arrange a basketball game. When the missile landed in Japan, some general came to his room and ordered him to stay in the hotel and posted armed guards. They took his cell phone and passport. She hasn't heard from him since. She's worried sick. I have two agents on the way to interview her. Haven't reached anyone with the Bulls yet."

The President began rubbing his lips in thought. The rubbing stopped but his hand still covered his lips. As he barely nodded his head up and down, he announced, "Let's ask Hoing what the deal is."

Using the code, he typed in:

```
SITUATION?
```

It took over three minutes to get a reply, which was not surprising for the President. He knew it takes time to do the substitution by hand, and it took the President time to translate the response:

```
I ONLY 1 WITH ACCESS TO P. HE MOVES IN 6 HOURS
BUT NOT ME
```

The President sent back:

HOW WE HELP

The Situation Room was dead silent. Billings quietly connected the President's cell phone to a wall monitor so everyone there could see.

SEND COMMANDO W BOMB TO MIX WITH LAUNDRY

"This is bullshit!" declared Windigo, "we can't verify any of this." He pushed himself into the back of his chair and folded his arms.

The President almost lost his cool. "And how do we do that, Mister CIA? If you got ideas, spit 'em out!" 'Or shut the hell up' the President wanted to add, but resisted. Windigo held his peace, but he wasn't the only one who had doubts. Jane thought things were moving too fast – more specifically, the President was moving too fast. She recognized that some of the puzzle pieces fit: the phone call was coming from North Korea, whoever was calling knew the owner of the phone's name and etc., Pleverbs was confirmed to be in North Korea, the caller did have the President's cell phone number – a closely guarded secret – and there is a General Hoing in North Korea. What wasn't verified: was it really General Hoing at the other end, and if so, did he really have access to Pak? While she was assessing it all, the President spoke to Windigo again, "You confirmed the source device is in North Korea." Pointing toward Windigo's computer, he ordered: "Show us where it's coming from." Windigo started typing on a keyboard. In seconds a map lit up with a blue dot seven miles east-south-east of Changrim, North Korea. According to the map it was in an area of rugged mountains and twisting roads. As the President studied the satellite photo he pointed out, "It looks like an ideal location for caves, and we think Pak is hiding in a cave." Heads began nodding in the affirmative, except Windigo's. The President's confidence was getting stronger, his resolve more determined. With his fingers covering his lips again, he looked back at the map.

Lee took his glasses off and asked, "What I don't get is, if this guy has access to Pak, why does he need us? If he wants to kill him, he ... well, he must have a sidearm."

Windigo abruptly answered, "Pak trusts no one. He may not allow anyone near him with weapons. He's probably holed up in some kind of vault."

"Well I think we should ask him," said Gabe.

The President nodded in agreement but cautioned, "The more we use this code, the more fodder we give someone to break it." After a moment of thought, he went back to the code and fingered in:

Y DO U NEED US

The reply came back:

NO TRUST ANYONE 2 HELP ME

General Chaffee said, "That's a legit answer. Imagine him asking someone there to help kill Pak? It's a sure way to execution."

The President had a thought, if the PRC gave him the number …

CAN PRC HELP U

In moments the reply came back:

NO CAN FIND NOW

The President raised and furrowed his eyebrows, thinking hard.

General Chaffee offered, "Well, if we are thinking of helping this guy, we should send a team. If one becomes incapacitated, the others can finish the job … if we are even thinking of doing this." Then he looked straight at the President.

The President simply said, "I'll ask."

WE SEND CMDOS TEAM?

The reply came back quickly:

CAN ONLY PROTECT 1 MAN

Gabe said, "He can only protect one?"

Jane suddenly interjected, "Do the radium phones, or whatever, have cameras? Could Hoing take a picture and send it to us?"

Windigo turned toward her and said, "Unlike a typical cell phone, the Iridium satellite phone doesn't have a camera; but I like where you were going with that."

The President abruptly ordered, "Get Admiral Sears on the secure phone."

"Yes Mr. President," replied the general, turning to pick up a green handset. In moments Admiral Sears was on the line. General Chaffee explained who was calling and from where, and indicated that the President wanted to talk with him direct. He also told the Admiral who else was in the room, he then handed the green phone to the President.

The President began by apologizing for the unorthodox call, and then warned him that he had a very unusual and Top Secret request. The Admiral assured the President, "We're here to serve, Sir," and in his normal skip-the-bullshit style he went for the question: "What can we do for you, Sir?"

President Grégoire explained the situation in detail. He acknowledged the skepticism of all those there in the Situation Room, but laid out the question: If a volunteer could be found, and only a volunteer, could the Admiral drop a Navy SEAL, with all the gear he would need, on exact coordinates in North Korea?

The Admiral explained the delivery would be no problem. It would take at least two, possibly three hours after a volunteer was identified. There were about 30 SEALs onboard the *Ronald Reagan*; he would summon the SEALS' commander and ask him for a volunteer. The President reiterated that the SEAL had to be a volunteer, and added, "We know how he's going in, but we have no idea how he's getting out. This has 'suicide mission' written all over it." The Admiral understood. Naturally, he had many more questions but surmised the President had already told him all he could.

The President had one more instruction: "Just find your volunteer, and get the aircraft ready – but nothing else goes into motion until you hear directly from me. I'm still not convinced about this."

No sooner did the Admiral's phone go down, another one came up in his other hand. The intercom rang out throughout the ship with the Admiral's voice, "Commander Stevens to my cabin, double time."

The President lowered his chin and gently scratched his forehead. General Chaffee was looking at him and after a deep breath asked, "So, we're doing this?" The President looked back but didn't answer right away. He thought about going around the room and taking a vote, but he decided against it for two reasons: first, he didn't want to start a precedent of making presidential decisions by vote. Second, if the majority was against him, he didn't want anyone to think less of him because he didn't go along with the general consensus. But the decision weighed heavily. He felt like he was aging a year by the minute. He let his thoughts slowly come out in words, "If … we attack North Korea," he paused and brought his hands together, one inside the other, "which we've committed ourselves to do, perhaps too hastily, China will retaliate. I received an intel report late last night that a Chinese Type 94 submarine was moving from the Kuril Islands toward the Aleutians."

Gabe said, "I read that report. They carry nukes, and from their present location they can hit most of the U.S." Turning his head to address the President directly, he added, "We have a lock on it. We have an X-37 watching it, and we can take it out in minutes."

The President said, "I'm sure we can. Then all hell breaks loose."

Gabe tried to reassure the President, "We're watching it closely. But you know, they're just trying to screw with our decision making."

The President took a deep breath and replied, "And it's working."

Jane more than understood the President's hesitance. During a moment of silence she asked a burning question, "How can we verify who's on the other end, before we send people in harm's way?"

The President said slowly, "Yeah, I know. It all sounds too good to be true, and you know what they say..." Momentarily he picked up his cell, and in the clear, fingered in,

HOW WE VERIFY YOU?

In fact the piece of paper Hoing had with the President's cell number written on it also had a phrase written on the back of it. Hoing fingered it in – also in the clear...

THERE ARE TWO PRESIDENTS IN CHARGE, YOU AND ME.

The President sat straight up in his chair; he recognized 'bona-fides' when he saw them! "That comes straight out of the conversation I had with Taos!" Not wanting to appear that he just rushed his decision, he took a couple of deep breaths and momentarily said, "I think that although I don't want to risk anyone's life," he hesitated further, "risking the life of one SEAL is worth the chance of saving the lives of thousands, maybe millions. I'm going to step out for a minute; if Sears calls keep him on the line. I'll be back in a moment."

As the President left the room, there was Amélie right outside the door waiting to see if Dad had time for breakfast. "Not right now Am-mi," he said, "I'm looking for a very courageous volunteer." Then he went into the men's room right past the very spot where President Morris was found. When he came out Amélie was still there. "How courageous does your volunteer have to be, Dad?" she asked.

He replied, "Well, he needs to be just this side of crazy."

"Then I got the man for you."

The President wanted to get back into the Situation Room, but his daughter seemed to have something genuine to offer. He took his hand off the doorknob and turned to face her, assuming he had a few seconds to spare.

She explained, "I went through Officers' Training School with this guy who was in the top of the class for everything: academics, leadership principles, and of course PT. You remember those practical exercises we had in problem-solving, like getting six people across a 25-foot-wide stream with a 10-foot plank? Well, he was always the one figuring that stuff out. Anyway, he became some kind of counterintelligence agent, a 9Q or something. But it wasn't exciting enough for him. So he actually resigned his Air Force commission to become a Navy SEAL. He made it in, and as of our last text, he's on the *Ronald Reagan*. He's very capable, and he's probably … just short of crazy. Whatever you want him to do, he'll do it – and do it right."

"Well Amélie, if uh, you're attached to this guy … you know, this a very dangerous mission, I wouldn't want to ask ...."

"No Dad, we could never be. I'm a feminist and he's married to the military." She took a moment before adding, "After OTS we ended up at Lackland Air Force Base together for a few weeks. Nice guy, a real gentleman most of the time, but like you, he prefers vernacular over fancy words. We had some good times, nice dinners on the river walk in San Antonio and stuff. Then he went off to the Navy, and I was . . . history." She gently waved her cell phone in her hand and added, "We're just distant friends who occasionally keep in touch. Honest."

The President remembered her talking about a boyfriend she had at Lackland last summer, one of the few relationships she ever told him about, but she was leaving more than a few details out.

Yes, they were at Lackland AFB together, both in officers' training. One Saturday afternoon after commander's call, she suggested they go into San Antonio for dinner; she had a car, he didn't, so she'd drive. It was a date. They walked along the beautiful San Antonio River Walk, easily the most romantic place in Texas. The coolness of the air; the sidewalk tables of quaint restaurants; tall cypress trees offering peaceful shade; the beautiful arched bridges; tourist boats floating by with mesmerized passengers; and of course the pubs, some rowdy and fun, others quiet and intimate. Who wouldn't fall in love on the San Antonio River Walk? It was such a wonderful evening they didn't get back to the base until Sunday afternoon.

For every weekend after that they were together. Sometimes they went back to the river walk, other times they just drove out into the country. By now she was letting him drive her baby, a light blue BMW Z3, her first new car. One time they went to Fredericksburg for wine tasting, then spent the night at a bed and breakfast on a local ranch. Her favorite outing was a hike through the Natural Bridge Caverns. He always held her hand tightly as they stepped from stone to stone, and when they came to a wide puddle, he suddenly swooped her up in his massive arms and firmly carried her across. When he started to let her down on the other side she didn't want to let go. Back on her own two feet she felt his hand take hers again and got this overwhelming sensation of being safe with him, like in one of her favorite movies where Crocodile Dundee says, "That's not a knife, THIS is a knife." It was an amazing feeling and she never wanted it to end.

An extra-long weekend was coming up because the Fourth of July landed on a Tuesday. He told Amélie he decided to go home to visit his parents for that weekend – and surprised her when he asked, "Would you like to come with me?" After a few excited moments to think about it, she said "Yes, sure. I'd love to."

'Going to meet the parents,' she thought. Was this the first step to something big? Will this be an ordinary visit or is she up for approval by the parents? She got a little anxious thinking about it, but then remembered other relationships she'd been in with millennial men. They liked having a good time but settling down wasn't their style. And there were flags with Gene – not red, but one was bright orange. She clearly noticed that he loved guns and the military more than anything else. It was almost all he talked about. He wasn't even finished officers' training and he was already thinking the Air Force wouldn't be exciting enough for him. He was very disappointed when he found out most Air Force officers didn't carry sidearms. The more she thought about it the more convinced she was that this trip to meet the parents would just be routine.

Things went very well for the two of them in Salem. The first hurdle of meeting the parents was a piece of cake; his parents were very warm, charming and most welcoming. His mom said, "We've heard a lot about you." What Amélie didn't think about was that being the Vice President's daughter made her somewhat of a celebrity and therefore more 'researchable' on the net, so his mom and dad already knew just about everything they wanted to know about her, *besides* what their son told them.

There was a picnic, and restaurants, and other delightful outings, especially a magnificent evening with the Boston Pops. The last morning they were there, Amélie found herself alone in the kitchen helping his mom with breakfast. She let Mom lead the conversation but it was routine, no probing questions, no secret girl talk. After breakfast mom showed Amélie some boyhood pictures of her son which brought on a laugh or two. Several pages into the album came the prom pictures. His mom could see that Amélie was focused on Gene's date: a brown eyed beauty with jet black hair and olive skin.

Mom said, "Her name is Elena Caruso; well, that's what it was back then. Her parents emigrated from Calabria, Italy, just a year before she was born. She's married now but I don't know who to." Amélie looked up from the picture with a hard stare at mom; her eyes said, 'And?' Mom read the signal and obliged, "They were inseparable in high school. But in his senior year Gene took a job she hated. He was what they called a 'roof walker.' He worked for a steel company and his job was to walk along six-inch-wide beams with a bucket. The bucket was basically a trash can for the steel workers. When a worker cut off a piece of steel or a bolt, they couldn't just throw it down 20 stories below; that's why Gene was there – with his bucket. It was crazy dangerous work and he loved it. He didn't tell us much about it but I hated it. Gene's father wasn't crazy about it either but didn't want to interfere. Anyway, one day Elena was walking by the construction site where Gene was working. There he was, about four stories up, walking along the beams with his bucket. No safety harness, no net below. She freaked." Mom took a deep breath. "She demanded that he immediately quit. He joked about it and refused. She gave him an ultimatum, if he didn't quit by the end of the week, they were through. It wasn't a joke anymore. He tried to convince her he'd be careful, but she wasn't buying it a bit. The following Monday there he was, back on the beam with his bucket." Mom paused again before saying, "That very evening Elena's sister came to our door and handed Gene his class ring. They never spoke again. I tried to get him to talk with her. We really liked her, so sweet and cheery. Everything she did was to make someone happy. He tried to call her a few times, sent her a big teddy bear, but she ignored it all like he didn't exist. She moved on, but Gene didn't, at least not until he went off to college." At this point Mom felt she had said enough; anything else Amélie wanted to know she'd have to get it from Gene himself. They turned more pages and laughed at photos of Gene with his cowboy suit on, a toy six-gun in each hand.

That afternoon Amélie and Gene went for a walk around town and came upon the memorial for the Salem witch executions. She touched the top of one of the granite benches and in a soft voice asked, "How many witches were burned at the stake?"

"They weren't burned at the stake, they were hanged," he replied. "They burned people at the stake in England." Then, in a somber voice he asked, "But imagine being burned at the stake. Just think about watching them piling wood around you, then someone lighting the fire, the flames getting closer to you, reaching your legs, and up to your torso … the excruciating pain, burning and burning until you mercifully passed out." He turned away from her and softly added, "No one deserved to die in such a barbaric way." They were both quiet for a moment, then he turned back toward her and in a serious tone said, "You know, that's what hell's supposed to be like, constant burning for eternity." This surprised her because it was the very first time he had ever brought up anything remotely religious. She reacted by just looking back at him blankly. He said, "That's why I don't believe in hell. I don't know how long it took to die being burned at the stake, but it had to be one of the worst ways..." He let out a soft breath, "So burning for eternity for whatever sins we committed, as defined by some religious leaders, is just too much for me to believe. I don't believe in hell, and I don't believe in heaven. And I just can't believe a lot of other things they taught me in Sunday school. Adam and Eve were told by God they would "suffer and die" because they ate an apple; what was so goddam special about one apple? All that story is about was their God putting them to a test, with damn serious consequences. Why did he even tempt them with a 'forbidden apple tree' in the first place? They were set up to fail."

Amélie wasn't sure she wanted this conversation to continue, so when he glanced at his watch she asked, "What time is our flight tonight?" He replied, "2150, and I want to take you to a special place for an early dinner – just the two of us, no parents. We better get going, too; those black clouds over there are full of rain."

After walking back home to get the rental, he drove her to a restaurant in Boston's Back Bay. Once they were seated Gene was a little disappointed to learn that because the place was closing early for the 4th of July, they would have to rush dinner.

They were the last people to leave. After the bill was paid she pointed out to her boyfriend that the waiter was acting strange; he had turned out all the lights in the kitchen and most of the restaurant, and was locking the doors. He had taken off his tie and unbuttoned his shirt all the way down to the last button. Her boyfriend said, "Looks like he's anxious to go, probably a party somewhere," but he too thought that it was quite peculiar for the waiter to unbutton before everyone was out.

It was raining hard and they didn't have an umbrella, so Gene said to Amélie, "I'll go get the car, stay inside near the door, I'll drive right up to it. I'll be RIGHT back." As soon as he was out the door, the waiter came from behind Amélie and locked the door! He quickly grabbed Amélie's arms and yanked her away from it. She tried to kick him but couldn't deliver the kicks to the right place. He had her almost to the floor when she screamed long and loud. Suddenly, a size 11-wide black chukka-boot came crashing through the locked door! In rushed Gene who charged at the waiter and instantly put him into a choke hold. Quickly losing oxygen, the waiter began to release Amélie and as he did, both of his arms were yanked behind his back. Two distinct cracks were heard and the waiter dropped to the floor gasping in pain and terrible agony.

"Are you okay, Amélie?"

She choked down two or three sobs and said, "I think so." Gene ordered, "Then let's get out of here." As they headed through the smashed door, Amélie asked, "Shouldn't we call the police?" Gene answered quickly, "I broke both of his arms. Let him call the police."

Now back at Lackland AFB their training was coming to an end. They hadn't talked much about 'after graduation.' The big day came, and they both fervently told each other how much they would miss the other. She was very disappointed but not surprised when he just made the usual promises to stay in touch and they could visit each other when possible. A few days before graduation she had thought about telling him about the Air Force having a policy of trying to put married couples together on the same base; but his casual goodbye made it clear that her decision not to bring that up was a wise one.

The President presumed that *that* guy, and the one she was now telling him about, was one in the same. In fact, he was sure of it.

Looking somberly at his daughter, Marc asked, "What's your hero's name?"

Without hesitation she answered, "Gene Berks, Lieutenant."

"Are you sure, Amélie?"

"Yeah, I'm sure, that's his name."

The President lowered his chin almost to his chest. "You know what I mean."

"I'm sure, Dad. I don't know what you want him to do, but all you'll have to do is ask and he'll get it done."

⋆ ⋆ ⋆

On board the *Ronald Reagan*, Lt. Commander Wynn Horton was just "reporting as ordered, Sir," to Admiral Sears. As soon as Stevens dropped his salute, the Admiral asked, "Do you have a man with you on board, Lieutenant Gene Berks?"

"Yes, Sir. He's on deck leading the men in calisthenics."

"Get him up here triple time."

Horton made a call, and in two minutes Lieutenant Berks was standing tall in front of Admiral Sears. Berks looked the part: 6'3", in awesome physical condition, large square head, exposed muscular arms, scars and bruises from past missions, piercing blue German eyes, focused face, and his mind open but wondering. He didn't have to wonder long. The mission was explained to the two men, everything the Admiral knew. The Admiral then stated, "The President is looking for a volunteer."

Without hesitation Berks snapped to attention and clearly stated, "Lieutenant Eugene W. Berks, U.S. Navy, volunteering for the mission, SIR!"

The Admiral got up from his chair, looked Berks straight in the eye, and said, "There's everything wrong with this mission. Unverified information, deep into enemy territory, no backup, no extraction plan, and we're putting all our trust in an enemy general – or so we think. Those are just the starters." Pushing his face closer to Berks, he demanded, "Are you goddamn sure?"

Berks hesitated the required second or two before giving his answer, "Yes, Sir," then courageously added, "as long as I have the discretion on what explosives and equipment I bring with me." The Admiral turned his body partially away but kept his eyes on Berks. "Yeah. Take everything you need."

"Thank you, Sir."

The Admiral turned to Horton and ordered, "Coordinate with Air Ops, make sure the bird bringing him in is well escorted in and out. We want enough firepower above and below the one-thirty to totally discourage any ground fire. The last thing we want is a shooting spree with our man here trying to float down through it all."

Horton suggested, "Or we could do it quietly, with a glider."

The Admiral went back into his bulldog face. "And where the hell does the glider land after being released over North Korea? And what if he has to go around for a second or third attempt? Our man here," pointing his thumb toward Gene, "must land on a dime. C-130 gunship will be the delivery vehicle. With heavy escort." Horton replied, "Sir, yes Sir."

The Admiral took another bulldog look at Berks and Horton. "Okay, you both have your work cut out for you. I'll give the appropriate orders." Turning back to Berks, he said, "The President wants to make sure you are a 100% volunteer."

Berks nodded, "Assure him that I am, Sir. But may I ask, how did my name come up?"

The Admiral turned away. "Apparently you know his daughter, which I hope has no bearing on your decision." He sharply turned his head to watch Berks' reaction.

But Gene's face didn't flinch. "It does not, Sir." The Admiral had his doubts.

Nevertheless, he turned toward Berks and shook his hand. "Good luck, Lieutenant." Then he ordered, "That will be all, gentlemen." Horton and Berks came to attention and saluted sharply. With all the seriousness of a heart attack, the standing Admiral slowly saluted back. When they were gone, he unwrapped a Macanudo Maduro cigar and started gently tapping the end of it on the top of his desk.

BACK IN THE WHITE HOUSE SITUATION ROOM, GENERAL Chaffee was just finishing a call. After putting the phone down he informed the President, "Everything is in motion on the *Ronald Reagan*, just awaiting your orders, Sir." The President acknowledged General Chaffee, but his mind was still roiling. Among other things, he wondered aloud, "How did the Chinese contact Hoing surreptitiously, what was said, and what was the agreement?"

Jane turned toward the President and inquired, "Yes, and how did they know Hoing was their man?"

"That's the million *lives* question," the President said.

Jane asked, "Maybe Hoing contacted *them*?"

The President said, "Possibly ... but that would have been very risky. Pak doesn't allow many people under him to have contact with the Chinese." He shifted in his chair and stated, "I believe the Chinese want no official association with the death of Pak. Millions of North Koreans – and much of their military – still support Pak. Some idolize him. If they believe China had anything to do with taking him out, relations would become very strained between the two countries." With a twitch of his chin, he added, "And that could turn out to be a good thing for us." Turning his head to address Jane, he continued, "Taos realizes this all too well. So even if one of his hit teams does get close enough to Pak, will they get the go-ahead to do the job?" There was another pause before he added, "I think not. Taos wants a North Korean to do the job. If that can't be done, then he wants us to do it, but *his* hands must remain clean."

The President's eyes moved right, then left, then sharply right again obviously in deep thought. Without warning, he abruptly turned to General Chaffee. "We're wasting valuable time. Call Admiral Sears," lifting his eyes toward the monitor, "and order full speed ahead." Turning back to General Chaffee, "Get the SEAL in the air – and tell us when they expect him to touch the ground."

"Yes Sir," the General's replied. Once again, he lifted the green phone.

The President turned to his makeshift code and lettered a short message to General Hoing:

ON THE WAY

Hoing responded:

LAND 50 MTRS E OF MY POSITION. NEED 10 MIN WARNING.

General Chaffee directed, "Tell him to go outside and count to 20 over the phone, on the exact spot he wants us to land."

Gabe asked, "So we can get an exact fix?"

Milt nodded.

The President understood and transcribed the instructions. In about two minutes, he was fingering in the code to Hoing.

Hoing responded:

OK

The wheels were indeed put in motion. Lt. Berks was soon flying cargo in an AC-130 gunship en route to the drop zone. Accompanying him were four other SEALs helping him check and re-check his gear. When the time came for Lt. Berks to suit up for the jump his fellow SEALs were there to see that nothing was overlooked. His brother SEALs were geared up and volunteered to jump with him without even knowing anything about the mission. But the orders were clear, so the only satisfaction they would have was to see their lieutenant successfully jump – to who knows what – over North Korea. Privately though, the four decided if their lieutenant got into trouble on the ground, they were jumping – orders or not – and they were geared up to do it. Lt. Berks noticed they were all geared up and had their chutes strapped on; it was reassuring, but he hoped they wouldn't put their lives and careers in jeopardy. He decided to make it official, and turning towards them he ordered, "This is a one-man job. No matter what happens on the ground – no one else jumps." Using his thumb to point at the rank insignia on his uniform, he added, "Consider that an order." The men stared at him almost in disbelief – Lt. Berks was not one to pull rank lightly.

The AC-130 wasn't alone, to say the least. In order to deter any interference with the mission, there were three Air Force F-35's from Osan Air Base, and two F-35C's from the *Ronald Reagan*, all flying escort. Below them were two A-10s, brought in from their routine patrol, ready to attack anything or anyone on the ground who tried to interfere. Flying high up and well ahead of the group was an Airborne Warning and Control Systems aircraft, or AWACS, ready to detect and direct interdiction if necessary. Keeping its distance but shadowing this flying armada was a KC-46 air refueling tanker. When Berks learned about the extensive air escort, he joked to his SEAL buddies that even the President didn't get this much protection in the air.

They were approaching the drop site, just 20 minutes to go. The night was black with only a few stars here and there poking around slow-moving clouds; but the clouds were above 2,000 feet, so as far as Berks was concerned it was all-systems-go for the jump. Everything was checked and double checked. He had a few moments now to review in his mind what had to be done. But his mind wavered. For the first time, he actually thought about the danger of this mission, how he could be jumping down into a trap, one that could result in him being tortured and executed. There were other possibilities; for example, he could jump and no one would be there. But then of course, if this all went as designed, Berks could save millions of lives by averting a major war. All these thoughts were flashing in and out of his mind but he forced himself to refocus. There was one thought that didn't go away though: why did Amélie volunteer him to the President?

On the *Ronald Reagan*, Admiral Sears was listening to all radio transmissions from the C-130 and its escorts – something all the pilots and crew knew. What they didn't know is that everything was being fed directly to the Situation Room and to the President's eyes and ears.

Admiral Sears was sure that Chinese radar couldn't possibly miss such an unusual formation of aircraft approaching from the sea … yet they hadn't transmitted a word about it to the North Koreans. If the Chinese were going to warn the North Koreans, something would have been done by now. Why hadn't they? Then it occurred to him – somehow the Chinese knew about the mission and wanted it to succeed. He hesitated at first, but then lifted his secure cell and texted General Chaffee, pointing out the Chinese inaction. He chose not to include his opinion on why.

Back in the Situation Room, it was Jane who pressed a new question, "If this all happens according to plan, Mr. President, wouldn't General Yi be next it line – to take charge of North Korea?"

General Yi Sung-ki, North Korean Military Chief of Staff, was the only military officer above Hoing in rank and authority. He was well known to be a hard-line anti-American and dedicated supporter of Pak. Jane asked, "How will Yi react to … ?"

The President understood the unfinished question. "We don't know. I have to think, though, that Yi is just as scared as all the one-stripers in the North Korean military. 'Scared' may not be the right word, but he knows what he knows, and that is most of the North Korean military strength is on the brink of destruction. Yi is counting on China to come to North Korea's aid, but what if they don't? If he examines things realistically, he'll recognize that North Korea might be in this all alone. As for his reaction to a coup," the President lowered his head, "we'll have to see."

The mood was suddenly changed by a radio call stating they were 15 minutes to the drop site. Lt. Berks was all suited up, all the zippers and closures were tied and tight, and the temperature was just above zero degrees Fahrenheit at the current altitude.

The President picked up his cell, and in code he typed:

```
14 MIN
```

Eleven minutes later the mission commander flying in the lead jet started a roll call of all observers. All answers were affirmative, all systems go. Suddenly a door was slid open on the AC-130. The wind and cold grabbed ahold of everything and everyone. Berks moved to the open hatch, got the awaited tap on the shoulder, and with a giant leap *he was gone.*

His four comrades wondered if they would ever see him again. One of them bowed his head, whispered a little prayer, and crossed himself as he pulled the cargo door closed. After the lever was pulled tight and secured, they hung together near the sealed hatch. One, a Petty Officer Second Class, finally said, "I wonder what dumb-ass decided to send only one?" Another answered, "Had to be one of the idiots in Washington," then started loosening the straps of his parachute. The first one asked, "What are you doing?"

"You heard the lieutenant, we have to stay put."

The first one declared, "If we listen to all the orders lieutenants give, we'll never win this war. That's my lieutenant going down there, and if he needs help I'm out of here." And with that he pulled his parachute straps tighter.

One of the Navy jets was sending guidance signals for the lieutenant, ensuring his glide path would put him right on a dime. Berks was scanning the ground with his helmet-mounted NOD, better known as night vision goggles, but there was little ambient light on the ground to amplify so all he could barely make out were darker clumps he presumed were bushes and trees. He picked what looked like a clearing and steered his chute towards it. The wind was next to nil below 500 feet but Berks felt he was falling faster than usual. He knew SEAL parachutes were designed to drop faster, but his increasing velocity was making him uneasy. Perhaps it was the extra weight hanging below him, a duffle bag filled with the tools of his trade personally selected by him for this mission. It was the first thing to hit the ground with a solid thump. Berks was prepared and landed on his feet just behind it, forcing himself backwards to land on his butt, then shoulders, then helmet. His special SEAL landing was effective. He was quick to his feet and was pulling his parachute into a bundle when an arm suddenly reached out to help. Berks shoved the muzzle of his HK VP .40 caliber pistol hard into the muscle-covered ribs of the intruder. The helper stiffened up straight and said, "We must move quickly." He raised his arms away from his waist indicating he was unarmed.

Berks demanded, "You are … "

The intruder answered, "General Hoing," and now had his hands over his head. Berks kept his HK tight against the purported General's chest, then put a soft green light on his face. After quickly scanning the rest of his body, Berks was satisfied that this person matched the picture etched in his mind, lowered his pistol and ordered, "Okay. Grab the end of the bag," which the General did. Berks grabbed the back and with the chute bundled under his arm, followed the General to the entrance of a cave, hustling in the cold dark at a quick trot.

Inside the cave, to Berks' surprise, was an Airstream-looking capsule with rounded roof edges, painted midnight black, and about eight feet wide and 20 feet long, resting on what looked like cinder blocks. It was hard to tell in the darkness, but it looked like a bunker made of hardened criss-crossed steel, certainly bullet proof and probably resistant to bombs. He could see only one small window and it had a metal plate covering it from the inside. There were cables and hoses attached to the capsule, all in one bundle, most likely providing power, water and communications. The air smelled heavy of raw sewage. Instead of wheels there were two large lengthwise skid beams attached to the bottom of the capsule. Berks surmised that in order to be moved the capsule was set up to be lifted and skidded onto a truck, much like a large construction dumpster.

Berks presumed this is where Pak was hiding, and for a moment he was breathless.

Now standing inside an adjacent but smaller capsule, Berks asked, "You are General Hoing?"

"Yes, Sir," the General replied.

Berks gave him a quick salute but didn't wait for a return. They shook hands vigorously but quickly. Berks whipped out a phone, pushed a few buttons and handed it to Hoing saying, "The President of the United States."

Hoing gently picked it up and put it to his ear, but hesitated. Berks nodded, "It's secure."

"Mr. President, General Hoing here."

Of course the President wasn't holding up a phone – the line was connected to a speaker for him and his audience to hear. Upon hearing General Hoing's greeting in a heavy Asian accent, Jane slapped her right hand to the top of her chest, heart attack style. Her left hand followed to cover her right. The 'audience' was spellbound and breathless. Momentarily the President answered, "Good evening, Sir. I trust our man is with you?"

"Miraculously, yes Mister President."

The President asked, "And Pak is nearby?"

"Yes, Mr. President, just a few meters away from us."

The President took a deep breath, then asked, "Can you tell us a little more?"

The General spoke so that Lt. Berks could also hear. "There is an armored capsule next to mine where Pak lives and issues orders. He takes nothing directly from me; everything passes to two women in the rear of the capsule with their own living area. They examine everything, prepare his food, taste it, and make sure everything is safe before he handles it. I believe they are his cousins. I make sure his capsule is supplied and powered up and I carry out his requests, but I can't see him and he can't see me."

The President listened intently. "Go on."

"There is a chute that I pass everything through to the women. He touches nothing – except his underwear. The women will not touch it; it is the only thing he allows me to pass to him directly. We must hurry, Mr. President – a special truck is coming to get him and his capsule in an hour, sometimes they come early but never late. Once his capsule is lifted onto the truck, I am relieved of my special duties – and my access."

"Where does he go from there?" the President asked.

"To another cave, equipped like this one, with another General officer to assist him."

Although the President wanted badly to ask more questions, particularly about the arrangement Hoing had with the Chinese, and how Hoing was going to protect Berks, he realized time was of the essence so at this point he just said, "I'll let you get to work." After a second, he added, "Good luck to you both." General Hoing returned the phone to Berks who stuffed it in a pocket and zipped it closed.

The President himself hit the button closing the line and then turned away, very solemnly. Jane perceived something but wasn't sure. She softly asked, "Sir?"

The President took a deep breath, turned towards Jane, and with a measured tone said, "A man is about to be killed, on my order. A man who … must be stopped. But still a person." Another thing was bothering him, a U.S. Navy SEAL was about to execute the President's – his – orders to kill another. He knew it was all necessary – the only way to save countless lives, but nevertheless …

Berks asked Hoing, "His underwear?"

Hoing replied, "Yes, here it is back from the laundry ready to deliver to him. I've been holding it. He has already asked for it. He likes to take a shower before he is moved."

Berks looked at the underwear. "Calvin Klein. Really?"

Hoing whispered, "Yes, can you get a small bomb in the bundle."

The lieutenant looked through the underwear and was appalled. He thought to himself, 'He really doesn't know how to wipe his own ass.'

Speaking lowly he said, "Yes I can. I'll use the string around it as the trigger." Quickly Berks opened his bag and drew out several components and the explosives. Hoing was shocked! "You let this hit the ground under you?"

"No sweat, Sir. It's C-4, I packed it myself." Back on the ship Berks had already flattened a half-pound of the clay-like brick of C-4 into a large pancake, breaking all kinds of regulations against modifying C-4, especially on a ship. He had thought about adding shrapnel like nails or screws, but there weren't any handy and he didn't have time to find some. Besides, he was quite sure a half-pound of C-4 was more than enough to do the job. Getting right to work Berks said, "I have to make things feel pliable so he doesn't feel anything strange when he gets the bundle." He started connecting components, hiding miniature electronics in one pair of the skivvies and the explosive in another. Then he attached the trigger. "I'll put in a remote control trigger in case he doesn't pull the string. But we'll have to try to pick the best time to detonate; we need to kill him, not just injure." Finally, he inserted a bullet-shaped cylinder of gas in the clothing and wired it in. Less than a minute later the bundle was ready.

Suddenly the radio squawked with foreign voices. The startled General said, "They are coming to get him, just ten minutes!"

Berks calmly handed him the finished package saying, "It's okay. Tell him his underwear is ready." The General took it and shivered as he turned toward a tube. Berks cautioned, "Careful."

Hesitating, Hoing let the bundle gently slide down, wincing and ducking when it hit the trap door. He turned on a microphone and told the women, "Inform him his undergarments are ready."

The General thought he heard the other end of the chute opening, and ducked down below the level of the tube. The door closed and … nothing.

"DAMN! HE DIDN'T OPEN IT!" BERKS LOOKED AT THE General, "Why didn't he open it?" Not waiting for an answer he pulled a small remote from his pocket and armed it.

Hoing stopped him. "Wait, he's taking a shower." He could hear the water rushing through the pipes. He grabbed Berks' sleeve and warned, "The shower is made of steel – if you blow it now the steel wall might deflect the blast." Thinking quickly Hoing added, "Let's wait 30 seconds after the water stops."

Suddenly they heard a truck approaching the cave, horrifying Hoing. Nearly yelling, he said, "Damn it, get out of the shower!"

Putting his ear to the pipes, Hoing heard the water still rushing through. The sound of the truck was getting closer. He looked at Berks, looked at the chute, and then suddenly bolted out toward the entrance of the cave.

He slowed to a walk as he came to the surprised truck driver and said, "It's not ready to move. Go back out and wait for me to call you."

The startled driver didn't recognize Hoing, but could see he was a high ranking officer. He switched from reverse to first, grinding the gears of the heavy truck. The truck was almost out of the cave when the officer riding shotgun ordered, "Stop. We have our orders, and not from him. Back up." The nervous soldier once again grinded the gears, putting the 10-wheeler in reverse.

Then there was an explosion! Smoke puffed from every seam and corner of the capsule. The officer in the truck screamed, "Get out of here!" The truck revved loudly as it changed direction and jerked forward.

Hoing rushed back to his station. Berks was lying face down on the floor, hands over his ears, the remote beside him, switch still in the ready position. When he saw Hoing he said, "We got him, Sir, nobody survived that."

Hoing said, "Are you sure?"

Berks replied, "If the explosion didn't get him, the gas in the secondary will – in less than a minute." Hoing decided to take Berks' word for it. He took a deep breath and looked down, and stared at the floor in a maze of shock.

Berks tapped Hoing on the leg and asked, "What do we do now?"

"We get out of here. You and your gear must hide in the trunk of my car." In seconds they were running out of the cave, just in time to see the truck lights rushing out of sight.

Berks climbed into the trunk of the General's car, but he wanted to see and hear what was going on. He pulled the bulb out of the socket of the taillight and drew a small knife to bore a hole through the outer lens, just in time to see Hoing running back into the cave. He came running back and quickly let Berks out! "The women are still alive, and crying for help. Hurry!"

The two men ran back into the cave. There were the two women – desperately banging on the armored door of the capsule, pleading to get out but quickly losing strength. "Can't you let them out?" shouted the lieutenant. The General yelled, "No, the only release for their door is on Pak's side of the capsule. The gas is killing them! Blow it open. Blow it open!"

Berks quickly examined the lock and hinges. While reaching into his vest he ordered, "Tell the women to get away from the door, and pull a mattress over themselves!" Hoing got on the intercom and instructed the women accordingly. They barely had the strength to move away from the door. Hoing told them again to cover themselves, but only one of them had the strength to pull a simple blanket over both their heads.

Berks barked, "OK, get away and watch yourself, this is a 10-second fuse." In precisely 10 seconds a small blast went off and the door thrust open, but only about four inches. The two men rushed to it and working together pulled it open wide enough to get a person through. Berks squeezed through with Hoing right behind him. Berks pulled the nearest woman up and across his shoulders in the fireman's carry position and headed for the door. As they passed the bomb-proof window to Pak's compartment, Berks popped his head up to take a quick look and was shocked at what he saw. There on the other side on the window was Pak, flat on his back, half of his head missing, and his hands and arms so covered with blood Berks couldn't be sure the extremities were still there.

They carried both women out of the cave and laid them in the snow. Hoing headed back to his capsule to get them blankets. Berks was right behind and told him, "We definitely got him. Here, take this mask and go look through that window." Hoing grabbed the gas mask, pushed it over his face and squeezed back into the women's capsule. Slowly raising his head to look through the broken window, he was in disbelief of what he saw. After staring for a few seconds, he rushed back out.

With blankets, they headed out of the cave to fresh air. They covered up the two women and tucked the blankets under them against the cold ground. "Do you have an antidote for the gas?" Hoing asked. Berks shook his head. All that could be done for them was fresh air and a hospital. Hoing looked down at them then looked back at the cave, not sure what his next move should be. Suddenly his radio crackled; he listened carefully. When the transmission ended Hoing said, "The men in the truck reported the blast. A security detail is on the way."

"We're not waiting for them, right?" Berks asked.

"No, but the women..." Turning his head toward the road Hoing said, "They'll be coming from Changrim, they must not find us. There's only one road. We'll have to hide along it somewhere until they pass. If they find you, you will be shot on the spot."

"We're leaving the women, right? The soldiers will help them?" Berks asked.

Hoing nodded but he was concerned about what they might say when the detail arrived. Again Hoing's radio crackled. Hoing said, "I can't believe it, they're almost here, we don't have time to hide. Get in the trunk!"

Hesitating, Berks got into the trunk. Once inside, he ripped off the military insignia from his uniform, including the camo-color U.S. flag on his shoulder, and shoved it into a crevice inside the fender. He knew he couldn't pass as a civilian but if he was discovered, the lack of immediate identification might buy him time, maybe just seconds, but enough to take out his aggressors. He grabbed a small tool and with a mighty slam of his fist punctured another peephole right through the sheet metal of the trunk.

He was barely done when Hoing came over to shut the trunk. Berks threw himself flat as Hoing pushed the trunk closed and flinched when he heard the lock double-click shut. He heard vehicles approaching and moved to his peephole to see what he could. After the slamming of several doors there was shouting and soldiers rushing around. It was chaos because nobody seemed to know why they were there. The captain of the guard found Hoing and asked what happened. Hoing was collected and with authority told the captain there was an explosion, but he didn't know what caused it. The captain looked at the smoke coming out of the cave then looked back at the General. Hoing could see that the captain was trying to piece things together, probably asking himself what would a high-ranking General, practically alone, be doing outside a cave billowing in smoke. He *must* know who or what was inside.

Hoing took the offensive, "Secure the entrance of the tunnel. There's gas so no one inside. Search the area, look for saboteurs. Do it!" The captain started giving orders and the soldiers, using flashlights, moved cautiously towards the cave but heeded the warnings not to go inside.

The women. Hoing now realized it would have been best if these witnesses had died with Pak; but there they were, on the ground. He thought about shooting them as escaping prisoners, as horrifying as that was, but they were hardly escaping. He quickly walked over to them and realized that one of them had passed out, and may be dying. The other was moving just her head and unable to speak. He was relieved. He wouldn't have to kill them after all. He made a decision. "Captain!"

When the captain approached, Hoing ordered, "These women are your prisoners; shoot them if they try to escape. Hold them for the SSD" – the North Korean version of the Gestapo – "I'm returning to the base. I'll send reinforcements."

Facing the General full on, the captain spread his stance and demanded, "What blew up inside the cave – Sir?"

Thinking fast, the General said, "Warfare chemicals. They were about to be removed. Don't go inside until I return. Keep searching the exterior."

That was good enough for the captain. He wasn't going inside and neither were any of his people. With that Hoing came to attention waiting for a salute. The captain brought his heels together and saluted. Hoing returned the salute and hurried to his car, greatly relieved that his escape now appeared possible.

When they were a few minutes down the road, Berks got his secure phone out. It was Jane who hit the button that opened the line. She wasn't sure how to answer so she just said, "Secretary Rikes here."

"This is Lieutenant Berks, I have a report."

The President rose to his feet! He asked, "Are you all right?" Berks wasn't sure who was asking, but the answer was the same, "Yes, Sir." Then he announced, "Mission accomplished, Sir. Mission complete."

The President's eyes widened. After a moment he said, "This is President Grégoire. Did you say you completed your mission?"

"Yes, Sir. The target is deceased."

"Are you certain?" asked the President.

"Dead sure, Mr. President."

The President was stunned. With widened eyes he looked around at the others in the room; they were all equally shocked and silent.

"Where are you now?"

"In the trunk of Hoing's car, on the way to a base, probably Changrim."

The President brushed his hand over the top of his head to the back of his neck, more shocked than before. Jane had both of her hands over her mouth, elbows tight to her body. Gabe bowed his head with a deep grimace. The worst was feared. But Berks added, "He's trying to hide me for the time being, and Sir?"

The President answered, "Yes?"

"He said he was going to seize power."

The President's eyebrows flashed up and down. Just then the line started breaking up. Berks quickly added, "I'll call back when I have more." After hanging up, Berks hooked up the phone to an auxiliary power booster on his belt.

The Situation Room was silent. The President looked over at the monitor with the map of Korea. He finally spoke. "Gabe, inform Admiral Sears. And Tim, ask Paul to come in."

The President's lips wanted to smile, but his worried mind wouldn't allow it.

GENERAL HOING HAD GIVEN THE PROPOSITION OF A COUP d'état some previous thought, but up to seven or eight hours ago didn't believe it possible. Now it was a fait accompli! As he drove, reality was settling in. Now it was time for the hardest part – successfully taking control of the country and, most importantly, the North Korean military. His highest priority was to stop the impending war and put an end to any further destruction. With the death of Pak, perhaps that priority was achievable. During the quick drive to the base, several thoughts plagued him; chiefly, could he actually survive his attempt to take over the military?

The hour had drawn nigh. He quietly made peace with the fact he could soon die, but his accomplishment was worth it.

Once within the gates of the small Changrim military installation, General Hoing immediately began giving orders. He found the installation commander and ordered that no one, without exception, was to enter or exit the base until further notice. As the base was being secured, he went with the commander to his office. He asked if a video camera could be brought in for a live announcement to the entire world.

All of this was very unorthodox to the installation commander, and he was wondering. Suddenly he stopped in his tracks and waited for General Hoing to notice – and he did. "What are you waiting for, get the equipment!" the General ordered.

The commander was direct: "What are you, Sir, about to announce?"

Hoing took two steps back toward the commander, looked him straight into both eyes, and told him point-blank: "Pak Jung-ho is dead. I, General Hoing, am taking over the military."

The commander's eyes and mouth went wide open. General Hoing gave him two or three seconds to absorb what he had just said. "Just think – our certain destruction is avoided. At least it can be if you help me." The commander regained his faculties and put his praying hands over his nose and mouth. Could it be true?

Then it suddenly occurred to him, "But Sir, General Yi would now be in command!"

General Hoing was quick to reply, "And he fully supports Pak's insane desire to have us all killed! Yi must be arrested." The commander froze in shock and Hoing could see the indecision in the commander's eyes. He told him, "The U.S. and all their allies have control of our country. And I know, personally, that the Chinese are not coming to help us. So you must choose now: Are you on the side of peace – or the side of total annihilation of North Korea's military?" Hoing stood fast for a reply.

The commander knew which side he was on; he wanted to preserve North Korea, but more importantly, his own hide. His wavering mind was full of questions, chiefly, how did Hoing know 'for a fact' the Chinese weren't coming to help? Although wracked with indecision, he finally asked, "What are your orders, Sir?"

Hoing hid his sigh of relief, nodded, then said, "I must announce to our people that Pak is dead, and that I am assuming command. Time is of the essence!"

Under the base commander's orders everything went into high speed. The equipment, simple as it was, was placed in front of the commander's desk, but General Hoing decided this announcement must be made standing up. In moments the video operator was ready; Hoing was not. Regardless, it was time. The General ran his fingers through his hair, put on his military hat and moved to the front of the camera. Not waiting for instructions, the video operator pushed buttons and a red light came on. Hoing remained dead-still, looking into the camera. The operator 'shot him' with an index finger and nodded. Slowly and with heartfelt words, the General began:

"North Koreans everywhere, be at peace. Pak Jung-ho is dead."

He paused after every sentence.

"We can now be at peace with the world.

"We may no longer face total destruction at the hands of our many enemies.

"Those who were poised to destroy us, might now be our friends.

"Together we can bring civility to North Korea, rather than reckless aggression,

"Food instead of missiles, embraces instead of threats."

General Hoing's voice was becoming almost presidential, but still humble.

"I want to address all who are bravely serving our military forces. You no longer face certain death in a war forced on us by a deranged man.

"You have served obediently and honorably. You can be proud of your loyalty.

"Now, your service to our nation is still required – but for peace, not war – and protection, not aggression.

"Now we can shake hands with our new allies, those next door and those far away from our borders. We will make them all our friends, not enemies."

Still anxious, he took a moment to look slightly above the camera, then back at it. "I, General Hoing Chi, will assume … I have taken control … of North Korea until a new leader – one selected by you, the people – is fairly elected. I won't allow it to take more than six months. In that time I will begin the process of rebuilding a government that supports peace, not war.

"In the past hour, I have spoken directly with the new President of the United States. Although many see him as the designer of our total destruction, I am confident he is now our new friend. He and the rest of the world do not hate you and me, but they despised Pak Jung-ho who foolishly initiated a war he could never win. You will soon learn how the United States has already helped us as a nation.

"My next communication with President Grégoire will be about demobilization of militaries, ours and theirs. I am sure he will reopen our skies and our seaports."

Looking hard into the camera he insisted, "I need *your* help. Our future as a peaceful nation relies on you and the support you give me. It will be only as difficult as we make it *ourselves*. Remember those words.

"I am offering us peace – the peace we dream of, the peace we deserve. I will do my part. I ask that you do yours."

With that he nodded, and the camera went off. The video operator was moved. The General asked him how soon he could get the statement uploaded. The operator was already typing rapidly on a laptop. "If I can use your American satellite phone, Sir," recognizing the phone attached to the General's belt, "in seconds your speech will be sent to all the major news agencies. It will quickly be picked up by Xinhua, the BBC, FOX, Google, and many others; and I dare say, within minutes it will be on every device in the world. But it will take North Koreans a little more time to hear the good news."

General Hoing nodded and gave him Pleverbs' phone. He realized speech-making was the easy part. He knew that General Yi would now be coming for him. He decided that his next step must be to get to Pyongyang as quickly as possible. He thought of his car – which caused him to recall that Berks was still locked in his trunk.

What he didn't know was that Berks had been in car trunks before. He had already disengaged the latch and was able to free himself immediately if needed. He had made air holes through the back seat, and drilled more tiny observation ports in all directions.

Indeed General Hoing's speech was 'on every device in the world,' including the large monitor in the Situation Room. All present watched speechlessly. The President had his right hand stretched across his collarbone. Shaking his head, he said, "Hell of a speech, right off the cuff. Now, I hope he can survive long enough to carry through. So where is General Yi, and what about Lieutenant Berks?"

General Chaffee provided both answers. "We have a lock on Yi – he's at the cave where Pak died. As for Lieutenant Berks, we've been in touch. He's still hiding in the General's trunk and reporting his observations."

The President slowly sat, and turning his eyes toward Paul asked, "Paulo, when should we make a statement?"

Paul replied, "It depends on what you want to accomplish. If you are confident that Pak is dead, and you want to support General Hoing – then the sooner, the better."

The President rubbed his chin. "I don't know … we don't know enough about Hoing yet."

With a serious look Paul said, "But he did take Pak out. I'm not trying to sway you, but if we take that and his speech at face value…"

The President nodded, "I wish I could talk to him again before we go public." He looked around the room to see if anyone had anything to say.

His eyes stopped on Gabe.

Gabe took his cue, "I don't think we have much choice. Hoing has said he's spoken with you; we can't deny it. As I see it, we can delay making a statement, see what happens next, then react. I think we could … should back him for the moment, and keep our options open. We can back off if need be."

The President cautioned, "Yeah, but if we back him too soon it could be his death sentence. He still doesn't know what Yi is going to do. Whatever it is, it'll be…" After a pause he turned back to Paul and asked, "What should we say?"

Paul replied, "We say that we have confirmation that Pak is dead. Our forces remain on high alert, but pending further communications with North Korea, adversarial military operations are on hold. We might elaborate a bit more, but keep the statement short." Then he asked, "What do you want to say about our involvement in Pak's demise?"

The President's answer was curt, "Nothing – yet."

Tim, who had been just an observer for the past 30 minutes, pointed out, "The world, Mr. President, is sure we are on the verge of World War Three. Everything has stopped. From Main Street diners to Chinese factories, all are empty … in anticipation. An announcement like this, made as soon as possible, will change lives."

The President was now looking at Tim, his face showing agreement. Before he could react, Jane posed a question. In a tone as serious as a heart attack she asked, "What if Yi goes straight for the nukes and orders the launch of everything they have ready?" She knew Gabe would say they'd all get taken out, but her burning question still was, "What if we can't get them all?"

Looking around the room it occurred to Gabe that Jane's question resonated with everyone, including the President. He responded with all the seriousness the question deserved, "First, we are very certain that, at most, he has no more than two with nuclear warheads that might actually work. He needs to get them out of hiding, move them to a suitable launch site, then fuel and program them. We'll know immediately if any of that is put in motion. Day or night, they'll be eliminated."

Jane reacted privately, 'So this war isn't over, by any means.' She pushed further, but went with a different question. "What about the chemical weapons on the DMZ?"

She didn't realize that earlier, while working with the five and dime code, the President had also handwritten an order and passed it to Gabe. Gabe gave it to General Chaffee who issued orders from his secure phone. Knowing those orders had been carried out, Gabe was able to say, "Britain's RAF is flying over those weapons right now and monitoring communications on the ground. If it is detected in the slightest way that those weapons are about to be used, the RAF will take them out. All of them." Gabe lowered his voice and added, "But we would rather seize them intact, that would be the safest thing."

Jane felt a little more comfortable, recognizing that everything that could be done was probably being done. She still had her worries but no more questions.

Paul was writing away and only taking in the salient points Gabe and Jane made. He stopped for a moment and looked at his notes, then lifted his head towards the President. "Are we ready, Sir?"

To Paul's surprise, the President said: "Do it."

Paul kept his gaze on the President for a few moments, then put his pen down as if something suddenly occurred to him. His face became intent, "Sir, you need to make this announcement. It will have far more impact if you announce it in person." Knowing the President's aversion to speeches and cameras, he added, "Simply say what we just talked about. Then add something in support of Hoing's speech – then stage right. I'll take it from there. I'll alert the press that you won't have time for questions."

Marc cringed. He knew, though, that the world would want to hear it from him, not the press secretary. Surprisingly he ordered, "Notify the press bureau to stand by for a statement by the President. We'll give them time to assemble. Write me some notes to work from."

With great satisfaction Paul replied, "Yes Sir, Mr. President."

Ten minutes later Paul was warming up the press bureau. Suddenly, without warning, in came the unshaven President with one small page of printed notes in his hand. Paul moved from the podium knowing an introduction was not needed. The room went silent. The President nodded to the group, and having lost all track of time, he began by just saying, "Good day."

As planned, he confirmed the demise of Pak Jung-ho, and added that he had ordered most of the forces to a standby mode. He also confirmed that he had spoken with General Hoing, and hoped to talk with him again very soon. The President cautioned, "Trouble in North Korea isn't over yet. Claiming control and actually achieving control are two very different things; in fact, it may be impossible."

He wrapped up by saying, "We, all of us, can be grateful that certain war *appears* to have been averted, but your thoughts and prayers are still very much needed. Thank you." With that he left the stage under a barrage of questions, none of them heeded.

OCCUPYING THE SEAT AT THE RIGHT HAND OF NORTH KOREA'S dictator afforded General Yi certain privileges. One of those was instant access to the internet, and hearing just the first few sentences of General Hoing's speech sent Yi into a violent fit of rage. He knew Pak was dead because he was, at that very moment, standing in front of the cave watching Pak's burning capsule. His anger had no bounds. To Yi, it was imperative to find Hoing and conduct his immediate execution. He sped to the base at Changrim.

From his concealment in General Hoing's car, Berks suddenly heard approaching vehicles – two, maybe three. He moved to his peephole with a view of the main gate. The gate was closed and locked, and there were several guards posted – none of whom had heard General Hoing's announcement. An officer got out of the first vehicle and demanded the gate be opened. His repeated demands were refused.

Suddenly a second officer got out of the vehicle and angrily approached the gate. "I am General Yi, your supreme commander. I order you to open this gate!"

The soldier standing at the gate lock was wracked with fear and again refused, but told Yi he would immediately send someone to seek permission to open the gate. General Yi suddenly pulled his sidearm and shot the soldier point-blank in the forehead. The shot brought out 15 soldiers from the vehicles, all armed with automatic rifles at the ready. One of the soldiers on the inside of the gate moved quickly to unlock it. The body of the dead soldier was dragged out of the way, and the vehicles and soldiers stormed onto the base. They went right to the base commander's building. General Yi jumped out of his car before it was even stopped and ran towards the entrance. He was about to issue a 'search all the buildings' order when suddenly one of the enlisted men pointed to a car, recognizing the markings, and yelled, "That's General Hoing's car!"

General Yi spied the car and saw that it was indeed General Hoing's. "Search it, find him!" he yelled. Two soldiers rushed to the car and found it was locked. Without hesitation one of them smashed the driver's door window with the butt of his rifle. Berks silently but quickly attached the 10.5-inch barrel to his M4 assault rifle and switched the safety to 'semi.' After a half-minute search with powerful flashlights the North Korean soldiers moved to the trunk and tried the latch, but it didn't budge. "Shoot it!" someone ordered. One of the soldiers took a step back and aimed his rifle at the key hole. Berks could see what was about to happen and slid himself as far back as he could in the trunk, scrunching up into a ball and covered his head with his forearms. As one soldier leaned away, the other fired! The bullet came through the trunk, ricocheted downward off the front of Berks' armored vest just below his neck, nicked his arm, and went through the floor.

But it missed the lock.

Berks paid no attention to his wound, but he was sure the bullet penetrated the gas tank. He knew that a second shot could blow up the whole car. The worst of his fears was about to happen as the soldier took another half-step forward to take better aim. Suddenly someone yelled, "General, we found Hoing inside!" General Yi turned on his heels and ran inside ordering all the soldiers to follow him.

Berks let out a long, deep breath.

Once he was sure the soldiers were away from the car, Berks called Admiral Sears who conferenced in the Situation Room. Berks reported what happened. While describing the situation, he suddenly noticed something unusual about six of the soldiers waiting outside. Unlike the rest, they were dressed in winter camouflage uniforms. After closer examination he was shocked! "Admiral, there are six CHINESE commandos here. They must have come in with Yi."

"Are you sure?" came the question by an unrecognized voice; it was General Chaffee.

"Confirmed, Sir. Six Chinese commandos."

The President picked up his red phone. "Get me President Taos. Please."

Inside the building, General Yi's anger was almost out of control. As soon as he laid eyes on General Hoing, he yelled, "Arrest this traitor!" Three soldiers immediately seized Hoing, one tying his arms behind him.

General Yi slowly stepped toward General Hoing, taking one measured step at a time. He spit out the words, "You!" and flaring his nostrils wide open, "shall die like a dog." With exaggerated motions, Yi reached up, pulled Hoing's hat off and threw it to the floor. One by one he ripped the epaulets off General Hoing's shoulders, forcibly removing all insignia of his rank. Keeping his burning eyes on Hoing, he half-turned to one of the officers and ordered, "Assemble a firing squad."

An officer nervously chose seven men and led them outside. All Berks could see were the men marching out in single file. They were brought to a halt about 30 feet from the brick wall of the base commander's building. There they were ordered, "Left face, and dress right," putting the seven all in a line, arm's length to shoulder, facing the wall of the building. They were then ordered the equivalent of 'parade rest.'

Berks was mortified when he realized their purpose. He quickly reported his observations to Admiral Sears. Ideas flashed through Berks' head. He could explode the car and cause a diversion, but how could he take on all the heavily armed soldiers? He had to try. He prepared his fuses and released the latch of the trunk. His plan was to get to one of the trucks and get away with Hoing. Fortunately, he took a moment to report his plans to Admiral Sears.

Sears ordered him to do no such thing. "Just keep telling us what's going on. It's about to hit the fan and you can't stop it. Just protect yourself, now." The President, still on the phone, was thinking the same thing and covered half his face in worry. He thought to himself, 'Dammit, Lieutenant, your job is done; get out of there alive,' then asked himself 'but how?'

Just then, Tim handed him a phone, "President Taos, Sir."

Berks reported to Sears: "They're still inside. There's lots of yelling. It sounds like Yi is trying to question Hoing. I think they're going to execute the base commander too"; and he thought to himself, 'I'm a dead man.'

Yi was trying to question Hoing. He was certain Hoing had outside help to kill Pak and was demanding answers. He was getting none. He resorted to slapping and punching Hoing.

Outside, the Chinese commandos suddenly drew closer together. One of them motioned to the leader and handed him a phone. The leader took it and after just a few words, stowed the phone inside his coat and huddled his commandos.

Yi was getting nowhere and had reached the end of his patience. Looking hard at Hoing, he announced, "Time for you to die, traitor!" He ordered a hood over Hoing's head, but all the soldiers could find was an undershirt. Yi was beside himself with impatience. "Bring it, and get him outside."

They started hauling Hoing towards the door. He resisted with all his might, but it wasn't enough and he finally let his legs buckle. The soldiers struggled to keep him upright but it took all their strength. They finally got him to the door with his feet dragging behind him and his arms nearly broken. General Yi followed a few steps behind. The base commander was already outside, hog-tied with a rope around his arms and torso and gagged. The soldiers dragging General Hoing came down the three steps, then turned to bring him in front of the firing squad. Yi yelled at Hoing, "At least stand up like a man and die like a soldier!"

The officer in charge yelled the firing squad to attention. Snow flew from the ground as the soldiers snapped their heals together and yanked their rifles chest high, now awaiting the order to 'aim.' The soldiers with Hoing were half-way to the center of the wall when Yi stopped near the steps to watch. He was to give the order to fire himself.

Quietly the leader of the Chinese commandos approached General Yi. Almost no one had noticed he had drawn his pistol and was holding it flat and tight against his chest – finger on the trigger, safety switch off. His huge left hand covered his right hand and most of the pistol. When just two feet from Yi, the commando called his name. Yi turned to his right almost facing the commando and was about to demand the reason for the interruption.

The commando simply said, "Orders are orders, SIR." And with that he dropped his left hand and turned the pistol toward General Yi. Two shots rang out straight into Yi's chest, then a third quick shot penetrated his forehead. Yi's knees buckled and he collapsed to the ground on his back, mouth and eyes wide open. Yi's soldiers began to react, but the formed-up commandos dropped three of them before they could even level their rifles.

Berks leaped from the trunk and laid down a line of automatic fire at the feet of the firing squad! The officer drew his pistol, but without hesitation Berks fired a single shot to the head, dropping him to the ground.

The lead Chinese commando immediately took control. He ordered the firing squad to drop their weapons and put their hands over their heads; they complied. Berks and one of the Chinese commandos kept the firing squad under guard. The Chinese commando ordered the North Korean soldiers to release General Hoing. They hesitated, but a quick burst of automatic fire toward their feet made them do what they were told. While Hoing was being freed, the video man quickly untied his base commander.

When the Chinese commando was sure the situation was under control, he walked over to General Hoing who was still shaking but getting himself collected. "General Hoing, President Taos and President Grégoire send you their greetings and congratulations. We have been ordered to accompany you to Pyongyang and to keep you safe. Three helicopters are coming to transport us there. Come back inside, Sir, we will get you ready."

Two commandos walked with Hoing, gently supporting him up the stairs and through the door. Inside they were joined by the base commander and his trusted soldiers. One of them picked General Hoing's hat off the floor, brushed it with his arm and respectfully handed it to him. The General's shaking hand took the hat and clutched it on his chest.

The lead commando then went to Berks. Speaking in attempted English, he said, "Choo muss be Lewstenant Berk, U.S. Navy. Ches?"

Berks replied, "Yeah, that's me." The Chinese commando held out his fist for a fist bump, and Berks bumped it with a shy smile.

"Dey tell me you very brave man?"

Berks smiled wider and replied, "Not brave – crazy."

The commando chuckled. "I am Captain Li. I ordered to get Navy man home."

Through his smile and with a nodding head, Berks said, "Sounds right to me."

Li responded, "Very right. You blow up Pak. North Korea no safe place for you. U.S. helicopters come now to take you to ship."

EPILOGUE

It is four hours later, and the crowd in the Situation Room is larger now. Word has been received that General Hoing is safely in the April 25 House of Culture in Pyongyang, where he is meeting with members of the Political Bureau of the Central Committee of the Workers' Party of Korea. They are greatly relieved by the turn of events and gladly recognize General Hoing as North Korea's new leader. The assembly unanimously agreed with General Hoing's first order, ie: The arrest of Pak's half-sister, Pak Jin-Cha, and her uncle, Pak Chul-Moo. Their incarceration, or something more permanent, will put an end to the self-declared Pak dynasty of ruthless dictators.

General Hoing refused to accept the title of Chairman of the Workers' Party, but agreed to serve in that capacity until a proper election, as he promised, is held within six months.

It was also learned that it was General Hoing who had made sure the missile launched towards Tokyo was short of fuel, and had purposely given incorrect numbers to the programmers of the nuke.

Lieutenant Gene Berks is taking a shower on a U.S. submarine now steaming toward the *Ronald Reagan.* He is to be spirited immediately to Coronado Navy Amphibious Base in California, for a thorough debrief. Waiting on his cell phone is a text: 'Geno, Dad said the next time you're in D.C. stop by for a visit. Amélie.'

ABOUT THE AUTHOR

At 80 years old, I've read and reviewed many books and manuscripts. From when I picked up the first draft of Steve Trahan's *What's Your Hero's Name*, I was caught up in how he uses his broad span of knowledge to mesh it all together in producing a fresh, timely and unforgettable thriller.

The authors of today's bestselling fiction may write about Secret Service agents, but have they ever had to use their bodies to protect a high-level official? Steve Trahan is a retired Federal Agent who has protected a number of dignitaries, including President Gerald Ford, Pope John Paul II, and Princess Sonja, now Queen of Norway.

Other writers have described dead bodies in detail, but have they ever had to move one? Trahan has investigated dozens of suicide and homicide cases, removed victims' bodies, and attended numerous autopsies.

This author not only writes about intelligence agencies and secret agents but has considerable experience himself. He is a retired counterintelligence officer, and was the former Chief of Counterintelligence Operations in London, England, during the Cold War years of 1985 to 1988.

Many authors who write about politics have never run for any office; this one has – and is still involved in the leadership of his local and state party.

Indeed, Stephen A. Trahan served forty years in the service of his country, twenty in the U.S. Air Force Office of Special Investigations and another twenty as an Intelligence Officer with the Department of Homeland Security. He was also the former president of the Canadian-American Law Enforcement Association.

From digging up bodies to recruiting double agents to running alongside the Pope's limousine at the United Nations, the myriad of this author's experiences shine through in this remarkable story. This is his first novel but I suspect there will be more to come.

Oh, and yes, among his several hobbies is a particular love for snowmobiling, especially in snowy Quebec, something he's been doing since 1969.

— Donald Lefebvre